The writing of Elizabeth Berridge has been widely published and broadcast both in Britain and abroad. She has been well received by the critics on both sides of the Atlantic and in 1964 gained the Yorkshire Post Literary Award for *Across the Common* which was subsequently serialised by the BBC. Her other novels include *House of Defence*, which was translated into French, Portuguese and Spanish, *Be Clean, Be Tidy* and *Upon Several Occasions* also serialised by the BBC.

Her activities have included journalism, broadcasting, criticism and several television plays, in addition to a three year spell in publishing on both the editorial and publicity sides. Married with a grown up son and daughter, she divides her time between London and the country, which she says is the ideal way of getting the best of both worlds.

*Also by Elizabeth Berridge in Abacus:*

**ACROSS THE COMMON
SING ME WHO YOU ARE**

Elizabeth Berridge

# ROSE UNDER GLASS

First published in Great Britain by
William Heinemann Ltd, 1961
Published in Abacus by
Sphere Books Ltd 1985
30–32 Gray's Inn Road, London WC1X 8JL
Copyright © Elizabeth Berridge, 1961

Printed and bound in Great Britain by
Cox & Wyman Ltd, Reading

For Osyth Leeston, in friendship and gratitude

Extracts from this novel have appeared in the *Cornhill* and the *London Magazine*, and acknowledgments are made to the editors.

# Part One

WHAT AMAZED and affronted Penelope Hinton most about her husband's death was that the fortune-teller had been right. Persuaded to a small upstairs den off Oxford Street by a talkative and desperate friend one Saturday morning, she had been told that 'a sudden shock awaits you, dear,' and did she not believe in loved ones preceding her to the Other Side? If not, then she should prepare herself for what comfort the world could give, for she would need it.

Penelope had not mentioned this to Jamie, because she was ashamed of allowing herself to be dragged to such a place with its dubious certificates round the walls, and its signed, yellowing photographs of obscure musical comedy actresses ('I never make a move without consulting Yella') frozen into sauciness and swathed in feathers. How dared that woman with her dusty bang and pale eyes see so clearly the summer crowds streaming out of Lord's, the tucked evening paper under Jamie's arm, the nudging buses? It was a damnable intrusion into one's privacy, this stranger's peephole glimpse of future grief and loss. And anyway it seemed the woman's fault that Jamie had died so absurdly, putting an absent-minded foot in front of a lorry, the day's score still buzzing in his head, and the third day's play still to go. That last thought worried her long after the funeral was over: he would never know the result of the match. She had cut it out of the paper the following day, and noted that the promising young county player had made the century Jamie prophesied for him. But – and here was the nagging unquietness – perhaps he *did* know. Perhaps even now, peering across from that Other Side Yella had talked about so glibly and familiarly, he was preparing to follow the season's play, un-impeded by having to buy tickets, able to glide – a not-body – into the Members' Stand without the benefit of that hideous tie.

The autumn was terrible.

It was the first time that loneliness came to mean more to her than a word read, an emotion other than intellectually felt. She seemed to be the walking embodiment of it, the smell of it was sharp on her, and she developed an extra awareness. She could smell it on other people, like a secret illness, see the hollowness and fear behind walking, talking shapes, however clothed. A bare signal, an inarticulate call: *we are of the same blood, thou and I*. It frightened her nearly into madness. It pursued her on buses, into shops, into comfortable restaurants where women sat immaculate behind coffee or ice cream, down shabby streets where old women or limping men tramped the hours away, staring at workmen, or the cut-price goods in the sleazy win-dows. It dozed on park benches, feet on the gritty gravel. It was like a second layer to the London she had known all her life. Tall blocks of flats knew it, nurtured it, here it was locked behind walls, secured by doors; the muted scream of it doused by the radio or the whine of a lift. It was shut in behind the curtains of small houses in the suburbs; it hovered most mutely and fiercely in public places.

Of course she had friends. But they were friends she and Jamie had shared. 'We shall have to ask another man to make up the numbers if Penelope comes,' she imagined them saying as they wrote her their kind invitations. She had done the same herself in similar circumstances and she knew how difficult it was at the last moment to dredge up the odd bachelor or widower from a narrowing, ageing circle of acquaintances; one made fewer friends as one grew older. For this reason she had refused to stay with Sybil Matthews, who lived in Flintshire and could be regarded as her closest friend. Sybil was a widow like her-self (a word Penelope still dared not use even in the privacy of her own mind). But Sybil was gay and bouncy, full of innocent

4

flirtatious nonsense towards retired colonels and not averse to the furtive pinch in the churchyard after morning service. She even enjoyed the sherry-laden laughter of emancipated canons blowing jokes and pleasantries into her face at the safe and outwardly decorous get-togethers at hunt balls, agricultural shows and point-to-points, those immemorial playgrounds for the indulgence of the County's innocent seasonal lusts.

'Going to Sybil's is like visiting tipsy Trollope-land,' Jamie had once said, as they drove home after spending one hectic Easter in Sybil's comical Victorian house with its façade like a public baths, and veneered panels in the billiards-room. Her grandfather had built it and it suffered from too many afterthoughts as succeeding generations made more money and added bits here and there. The water-tower, for instance, had been such an after-thought, with its games-rooms for Sybil's twins; twins ran prolifically in the family. Logically, there should have been two water-towers, for the family had been conditioned to think in pairs. There were two tennis-courts, two summer-houses, two cars, two rowing boats: horses, pictures, jigsaw puzzles, guns, fishing rods, even books, everything was bought in duplicate, it was a family law.

Jamie had delighted in Sybil and her boys, and openly called the water-tower Matthews' Folly, waiting with ill-concealed impatience for it to fall down. But it had outlived him and now it was a poor joke.

'Give me time,' Penelope had written to all these kind, well-meaning people. 'Perhaps when spring comes . . .' What she wanted to be able to say was, 'When, if ever, I am a person again in my own right, I will be glad to see you. But it will have to be on different terms, for I will have changed – if I survive.' Such a statement was obviously too dramatic both for her to offer and for them to accept, so she was content to allow them their own interpretations of her neglect.

In the meantime she tried to learn how to live another person's life: the life of a woman alone, having to make her own decisions, form her own opinions, sleep by herself. Completely bound up with Jamie as she had been for twenty-five years, it

5

seemed absurd and pointless to do anything or go anywhere without him; she had always known what the poet meant by 'a singing rib within my dreaming side', and was now torn from that side, bare and cast away as a bone in a desert. The days lost their landmarks and only a spark of animal instinct drove her up from her bed, where on some black mornings she lay, a puppet in a puppet box, its master gone, unable to manipulate her own strings.

How did London cater for its drifting souls with time to fill in between noon and dinner-time? The very words 'dinner-time' became archaic even as they formed in her own mind. Yet she held on to them, aware that they were like the markings on a post, an ancient stone pointing the way in a wasteland. For to a person alone, what difference does it make what times one gets up, takes breakfast, or simply doesn't bother? Eat at midday or sleep the day away? Night could be turned to day and who would care, or even know? The terrible thing was that she could do anything now, anything at all; walk across the Alps, cycle to Samarkand, learn Judo or take a course in Russian . . . what did it matter? Luckily, at forty-four, civilized living had left its mark. She was not by nature rebellious and was not conscious of having missed anything in her life – on the contrary, it had been filled by one man and enriched and enlarged by mutual experience. Habit saved her in the early days and weeks, so that on most mornings she got up and dressed on waking, however early that might be; laid her breakfast, ate it; read the papers and her letters, and went out.

It was the going out that made her falter. She might have been in reality crossing a wilderness. So she planned her moves like a chess-player. To the British Museum one day, past the Roman heads, more alive in their chipped immortality than those who gazed indifferently at them, fresh in from the breezy Bloomsbury streets. To the Natural History Museum, a place to which one somehow never went unless one took a child, and into a lantern lecture on invertebrates at the dog hour of three in the afternoon; the thick voice exactly matching the grey screen where worms or centipedes wriggled in their disgusting

6

primitive blindness. Into numerous art galleries where new pictures hung so hopefully in their brazen shriek for attention.

But none of these expeditions could be shared, even in retrospect, with Jamie, so they became meaningless, even as time-killers. They related to nothing, so, terrifyingly, she felt nothing. Nothing revived her. Staring at the stone emperors, she thought, 'We are two stone people, face to face.' In the past she had loved the ceramics at the Victoria and Albert Museum, the tiny miracles of the jewelled watches and snuffboxes. Now they shone up at her dully, dead in their glass coffins. Neither did the compassion and depth of Rembrandt's paintings at the Wallace Collection revive her, although the spaciousness and cold elegance of the house itself eased her by enclosing her in its own mood of petrifaction.

She tried the parks. But Regent's Park was spoiled for her because she overlooked the opulent houses that faced on to its green acres; and it had always been a place for her and Jamie to walk in, whatever the season. But this year the smell of decay and the light blown smoke of the bonfires burning up the year's bounty, the distant sound of whistles as the keepers rounded up the stragglers at the 'All-Out' call, pursuing them on bicycles, the flushed faces of the lacrosse players over the tired yellow grass, merely depressd her. Her first real feeling since Jamie's death was one of savage joy as she stood watching the gardeners dig up the faded dahlias which had blazed since last August. Those dahlias had been planted on the last day of June, she and Jamie on one of their walks had watched them go in and word-lessly noted the beginning of the end of summer. That was still the trouble, that wordless understanding.

Everybody but Jamie needed words.

Penelope had always found communication difficult. Apart from a natural shyness, she possessed a precise and agonizingly honest mind, and it was sometimes impossible for her thoughts to filter through into words exact enough to please her. It was not until she met Jamie (on an Arms for Spain march in the mid-thirties, during which he had whisked her from under the rearing forelegs of a police horse guarding Downing Street) that she found someone who had instantly apprehended what she was trying to say – who flew as it were over the stumbling words and alighted at once on what was valid and true. She had perhaps been made lazy by this total comprehension, and over the years had gradually acquired a habit of reticence, content to let Jamie act as a kind of interpreter for her. It had not seemed worth while trying to reach other people anyway, for no one mattered except Jamie. They had, in effect, carried on a special kind of communication which excluded everyone else. Even the birth of their children had not interrupted this lifelong conversation; whilst politely enduring their children, they had not been touched by them, and now, with Jamie dead, Penelope still felt that she had nothing to say to her married daughters. Death she wanted to discuss with Jamie, no one else.

She continued to be enclosed in this hard shell of unspoken feelings and undelivered comment like a rose drowned horribly in an inverted glass globe, or a bird frozen to its singing branch, or a ghost in search of its identity; until one day, in the sharp spring weather, winter still nudging bitterly round corners, she met someone who broke through with no effort at all. And this unlikely person she met at a most unlikely place, which would seem to argue the existence of – if not God – at least a divine pattern and providence which, at that time, she was not able to accept. For by now she was dangerously reduced in body and spirit.

## 2

It HAD been a busy day at the launderette in Manor Road, but now, at nearly closing time, the flow of people was slackening. Soon the last-minute shoppers would be coming in for their bags; the spin-driers had nearly finished their ceaseless reverberations and, as a reminder to possible late-comers, the girl in the green nylon overall was rather ostentatiously opening the tops of the machines and taking out the soap-grids to clean them for the next day. Not too ostentatiously, however, for the owner was there.

Pye Rumpelow was on one of his weekly visits. He made a habit of visiting all three of his launderettes at least twice a week, to ensure efficiency of both machines and personnel. It was not easy to find women to run them who were both practical and courteous, and the part-time girls he had to employ as reliefs thought nothing of ruining customers' blankets or – as had happened here last week – of giving wrong advice on the treatment of stains. There was the unfortunate case of the cricket trousers. The girl had taken them from a customer, assuring him that she could deal with grass stains, left them soaking overnight in a too strong solution of bleach and the next morning they were in shreds. This kind of thing was, to Rumpelow, inexplicable and shoddy. Only these sort of idiocies made him lose his equanimity. This new girl seemed efficient enough, though. On impulse he went over and told her she could go early.

He had two reasons for this. The first was that he loved to sit and watch his dutiful machines that purred and pulsated in obedience to the red lights and switches; he almost longed for

9

them to go wrong, so that he could manipulate them with his deft hands, unscrewing tops and regulating the sudden mad gurgle that indicated an over-exuberance of suds. Leaning on his small table, with the plastic containers of powders and crystals in front of him, the bottle of bleach, the weighing machine at his right hand, he felt like a tribal elder, or even Buddha himself under the Bo-tree, listening to the women coming to the well, with their chatter and comfortable female noise. For hadn't this become in fact the equivalent of the village well, as the television set had replaced the hearth? 'Fire and water, the life-givers,' he mused. Water more than anything. During the year's long hot summer, reading of the drought in Australia, where for three years the heart of that great continent had been slowly burning to death, thinking of the sands of the Sahara, the painfully reclaimed lands of the Sinai Desert, he often suffered at the thought of all that water from his machines swept away down the drains. He often worked out that twenty-two thousand gallons were used in a week in one of his launderettes. Enough to make the desert blossom if you multiplied that figure by the total number of launderettes in London.

Pye Rumpelow had another reason for wishing to stay. For several weeks past he had noticed the same woman. This week she was at machine 9. Glancing down the check-sheets he saw that the girl obviously knew her, for her name was there. Mrs Hinton. She interested him, the thin abruptness of her shoulders, the elegant carriage of her neck and the fine abundant curling hair. Legs, finely turned, a typical English-woman's, nearing middle age. But there was about her an unnatural tension. She never read while her clothes were washing themselves, nor did she go next door for a cup of coffee, although there was an excellent coffee-bar there, which Pye also owned. She watched the revolutions through that little porthole as other people watched their television screens, as if the kaleidoscope of clothes and colour held some meaning she must discover. Unusual behaviour interested him, and he was a humane man. He felt strongly that she needed help.

She put in her second soap. Several customers came in bringing clothes to be serviced – young men who lived alone, older men, widowers perhaps, who would never sit through the whole business of feeding the machine with soap powder, watching the lights, and then spin-drying their clothes. They still felt this was women's territory, and handed over their soiled bundles of pants and pillow-slips, vests, pyjamas and shirts with impersonal, shut faces. He dealt with them all quickly and calmly. One or two of the women, finding the stillness of his face attractive, his very immobility comforting in the rush of their servantless days, wondered what he was thinking about.

Just then, his thoughts were not running to waste; behind the timeless attitude of the man at the receipt of custom – for thus had merchants squatted under driving rain and shattering sun for centuries – a busy, practical brain worked at speed. His thoughts had returned to the desert; now suppose he *could* pipe all that water, not into the city drains, but into some vast reservoir, where the suds could be neutralized in some way, to keep in time of drought . . . or even to feed a high, graceful fountain outside those great flats across the road, where the half-moon of rank grass still grew untended and absurdly fenced in.

An unusual bubbling noise suddenly brought his thoughts back to the present. Machine No. 9 seemed to be having a nervous breakdown. Boiling water and suds were streaming from the top in a white cascade. At once he dived for bucket and mop and cloth, went over to the machine and switched it off. Only then, when everything was under control, did he realize that the woman in front of the machine had not moved. Was she in some cataleptic fit? Only when he spoke to her did she seem to awaken from her abstraction, and her wide, very dark eyes stared at him in a kind of stupor.

She let him do what was necessary, then sat back. Pye set the controls again and took out a packet of cigarettes.

'Sorry,' he said, 'this sometimes happens at the end of a long day. Too many suds, I expect. Will you have a cigarette?'

After a bare moment of hesitation, Penelope Hinton smiled.

11

'Thank you,' she said. 'Was that my fault, perhaps?'

'I don't expect so. Even machines can be temperamental and become victims of some kind of fatigue.'

Almost defensively – but whether in self-defence or in defence of the machine he could not quite define as he lighted her cigarette – she said, 'It hasn't happened before.'

'I hope it hasn't upset you,' he said. He had at once noted the tone of voice; it was difficult, full of strain, as if the words had been dredged up from some far-off place. Apart from that, a cultured, soft voice; impossible to guess her origin. Deep. He liked that. He judged her to be in her early forties, allowing for some emotional strain. That suited him, he wasn't young himself. He noticed the time with some satisfaction and went to the door to turn the sign over to CLOSED. Soon they were alone. If she was aware of this she did not show it. Soon her things were done and in the drier. He busied around, finishing off what had to be done, and the woman came in to wash the floors. Only then did Mrs Hinton say, 'Oh – I'm sorry. I must have kept you over your proper time.'

He did not show his pique. 'I have no proper time, Mrs Hinton,' he said, with some dignity. 'Emergencies have to be dealt with.' Then he smiled.

It was the quality of that smile which made Penelope Hinton really aware of him for the first time. Only then did she notice that he wore a moustache and a small beard – but then so many men did these days. Then she saw that he was fair, but greying, and his eyes were those of a fisherman or a shepherd, blue-grey, serious, with a hint of far distances. The smile, which revealed strong white teeth, wonderfully emphasized the kindness of those eyes, and seemed the first warm and intimate thing that had happened to her since Jamie's death. Pye's plumpness, his lack of height, were eclipsed by that smile.

At once he noticed her pallor and could not guess what had caused it, but after a second's hesitation he said, 'You look as if the trouble with the machine has upset you. I'm going now. May I offer you a cup of coffee or tea next door? I am sure you will feel better then.'

12

She hesitated. For years decisions had been made for her, and habit alone nearly made her say yes. Then she remembered that this man was a stranger, and he had shifted the automatism of her day out of gear. But he looked grave enough, concerned enough, and she was grateful to anyone who could smile at a stranger with such direct sweetness. She began to feel a lessening of strain, and he added, gently, 'It's only next door. I do feel the whole thing is my fault. These machines have to be overhauled regularly, you see.'

'Well,' she said, picking up the laundry she had been folding and packing it neatly into first a polythene, then a special laundry bag. (Pye Rumpelow noticed the fine quality of the underthings, the excellent towels and pillow-slips.) Without allowing her to finish her sentence, he picked up the bag for her and led her out of the door. Adventures had always started strangely for him.

That day she did not stay long, and he learned very little about her; and when she went home he found himself thinking of the way she walked, the way she smoked a cigarette. She, too, sitting reading alone later that evening, wondered fleetingly whether he would be there again. That night she slept better.

Pye Rumpelow was, of course, there again. He found himself dropping into the Manor Road branch more often, and idly scanning the check-list to see whether he had missed her. One week he did, but only one. It became the usual thing for her to have coffee or tea with him next door when her laundry was finished, and the girl in charge earned a reproof from her employer for giving a knowing smirk as he hurriedly left one afternoon.

They talked desultorily, but she told him nothing about herself. He guessed she was either divorced or a widow, gaining this impression from her indefinable air of having once been a protected person, and now that protection, in some way he had not yet discovered, had been removed, leaving her vulnerable.

.     .     .     .     .

About a month later, Penelope sat opposite Pye at the low, inconvenient table of the coffee bar and felt a vague astonishment at herself. What was she doing, drinking coffee with a stranger every week, an odd, plump man shorter than herself, talking to him, being able to talk to him – feeling words draining out like pus from a wound?

They had been discussing art.

'But I've learned something,' she was saying, in her painful, dredged-up voice. 'I've learned, for instance, that pictures, and buildings, and carvings – oh, everything – have a dual existence. It's as if life itself is a duality. We're brought up with "me" and "you" and "me" and "it", and "either", "or". Then when you meet someone, and fall in . . .' she hesitated, 'fall in love, then these dualities queerly cease to exist. A picture is itself, to be appreciated and felt; the same with books, and – I'm being absurd –' she finished lamely.

'Not at all, it makes sense. Perfect sense. Please go on.'

'Well then,' she smiled, her long mouth crooked, as if twisted out of true, 'these things I've been driven to look at again, these pictures, and ceramics and things, I've found that they're themselves, but, apart from that, they're also what they mean to the person looking at them. But they've meant nothing to me, lately, nothing at all. Because I'm nothing, they give back a leaden echo – they throw my own numbness back at me . . .' She looked up at him nervously. 'I might just as well have been looking at a blank wall, blank, quite blank. Is it because one can't look at a thing without sharing it with someone else?'

Pye moved his empty cup to the left, got up, beckoned the waitress, who drifted over, waggling her small bottom in its long fawn jumper and giving him a tired look from her painted eyes.

'Not really,' he said. 'But one has to give something of oneself in order to get something back. For instance, you wouldn't take a dog to see a Giotto, now would you?' He paid, waited for Penelope to join him at the door. 'Come on, I'd like to show you something.'

He followed her out into the street, and looked about for a

taxi. 'A month ago I wouldn't have dared,' he thought, 'and she wouldn't have come.' He felt responsible for her, entrusted with her. A taxi drew up and he told the driver where to go. They drove clear of the traffic in Baker Street and were soon through small clear streets beyond Oxford Street and heading for the river, across squares where lights were flicking on in the tall beautiful houses, now embassies and offices, and at last catching up with the traffic again in Whitehall. By Big Ben he paid off the taxi.

'Now we'll walk,' he said. He did not attempt to take her arm, and they walked side by side over the bridge until he stopped.

'Now,' he said, again, when they were in the middle of the bridge. 'Look back, and along each side.'

Obediently she turned, leaned on the parapet and stared back at the Houses of Parliament. Lights pricked out, but the terrace was in darkness. Beyond, on the embankment, more lights, reflected in the water. The river flowed beneath them, its dark liquid smell rising. A police launch, winking a red rear lamp, moved mysteriously on the rising tide. Warehouses stood out against a tawny sky, grey, ragged clouds were transformed into tedded golden straw.

Penelope had always been short-sighted, and now the lights strung along the banks were blurred and ran together like their own reflections. It was a little like looking at the world through a bowl of water; outlines were soft, sometimes so much softened that they became something quite other than themselves. She had always been able to appreciate Seurat because his dots ran into space and light for her quite normally, whereas other keen-sighted people had to back away across the room to catch the shimmer of water, the translucence of sky. So now this river scene was for her doubly dusky, melting, and its magic made more mysterious as barges beat gruffly upriver, glooming like old worn-out bears hunted too hard.

Big Ben boomed out the hour.

'Remember that,' said Pye. 'Remember seven o'clock, and the date is today, April the something – I never remember exact dates – but it's not any time in the past, or the future. This is today, and a breeze is springing up.' He did not ask her whether she liked it, or what she thought about it. He merely offered her a cigarette as they leaned on the parapet, and cupped his hand round his efficient lighter so that her face was momently in the glow. He went on talking, and in the dusk she caught the deep, soft country inflections. 'This is something I always come to see when – well,' he shrugged, 'when I need to. You see, this is a private pleasure. And yet it's here for anyone who really cares to look at it – like the love of God. It's not bought by a corporation and locked away behind glass doors, on view from nine to four. What would you rather do, buy a book of Shelley's poems, or have his embalmed heart to look at?' He did not wait for her to reply and went on, nodding over to the Lambeth side of the river, 'I first came to London from over there. I suppose that's why this means so much to me. I didn't want to conquer London or anything like that. I just wanted to earn a place in it, so that I had the right to come on this bridge and look up and down the river, as a Londoner.' He paused again. 'See all those lights. And the reflections grow longer as you watch them in the water.'

'But you came from farther away than Lambeth, surely?'

Leaning there, drawing deeply on her cigarette, listening to that unhurried voice, Penelope's self-absorption thinned, and for the first time she felt curious about him; he interested her.

'Yes, my mother was Welsh, my father was a Cornishman. I was brought up in Cornwall, in a fishing village.'

Penelope spun her cigarette up in the air, so that it made a tiny firework for them to watch before it dropped with a scarcely heard hiss and was carried away on the current with the rising drift of odd things the river found in its journey.

'Let's walk,' she said.

As they went along the embankment, the long beaded curve of lights dipped ahead of them, and the slap of water against stone was mysterious at their side.

'Do you know Dickens's *Night Walks*?' she asked suddenly.
'No.'

16

She touched his arm lightly, apologetically, as if both asking and granting forgiveness for exposing what he might consider a flaw.

'It isn't important – it's only a fragment,' she said. 'But he writes that the lamps reflected in the river were the ghosts of drowned people – suicides; there they are below, holding their lamps up to the living. I always think of it when I walk along the embankment.'

'Do they hold up the lamps in reproach, or to warn the living not to join the underwater party?'

She laughed softly. 'I forget. It doesn't matter. I don't know why I have to think of how other people thought of things all the time. You're right, of course. It's quite enough really, to be pleased oneself.' She paused. 'It's good of you to let me share one of your private pleasures.'

After a silence, Pye said, 'Then will you dine with me? We'll go to Chelsea.'

He had a genius for finding taxis. Again they sat back while the lighted streets flowed past, and only once did Penelope have the merest niggle of guilt. Jamie wouldn't have liked it at all. He would have disapproved of another man taking her out. In deference to him, she pressed herself back in the corner far from her companion, although he merely sat quietly beside her, giving an occasional alert glance out to see that the driver was taking the easiest and quickest way.

She looked at him once, and smiled involuntarily as an idea struck her.

'I believe you were a taxi-driver yourself, once.'

'Yes, I was. I know all the tricks. Ah . . .' He leaned forward and rapped on the glass screen. 'Cut across here and down to your left, you'll miss the King Street rush.'

The man gave him a startled, hostile look, then did as he was told. 'It's tough, the test,' Pye said, leaning back. 'You've got to know London – well, like an insomniac knows the cracks on the ceiling, before they let you take a taxi on.'

'How long were you in it?'

'Oh, a couple of years. I'd made enough by then to buy a

bit of property, so I went in for some private slum clearance. That was before Hitler finished the job. We're here.'

He tipped the man generously, said something in an undertone that made him laugh and then came briskly back to find Penelope looking as if she wanted to run away.

'Not here?' he asked. She shook her head. 'Right.' He let out a piercing whistle, which brought the taxi back so fast that it nearly reversed into them. 'The Gioconda,' he said.

'I'm sorry,' said Penelope, as they found a table in a café two or three streets away. 'I know it's today, April the sixteenth – women always remember dates – but still.'

He gave her a brief smile, but said nothing. He was feeling his way cautiously with her. She seemed to him like a bird held precariously in the palm of the hand, or a mouse, frozen by fear. He dreaded the sudden leap, the scuttle to safety, which meant of course, far from him, the would-be spurned protector. He sat back, his hand over his eyes, as she regarded the menu. He was tired, drained. So much effort and control and deliberate giving out of warmth and calm reassurance had for the moment depleted him. He needed silence and a glass of wine to recover himself.

The wine did her good, too. Her cheeks became a little flushed, her eyes began to glow, and the tension of her face relaxed a little. Even her voice was less strained; her laugh would be low and deep, he thought, and suddenly longed to hear it.

'This is good of you,' she said suddenly. 'I'm afraid I'm not a very lively companion.' She added, as if to make amends, 'It must be strange to own that washing-machine place.'

'Not at all,' said Pye, amused by her effort to make social conversation. 'I own several "washing-machine" places. Like you, I rather baulk at the word launderette. It smacks a bit much of those bastardized French diminutives – isn't there a word pinarette? Sounds like a man in a frilly apron.'

At this small sally he was rewarded. Penelope laughed, and, as he had imagined, it was low and deep, but ended with a gasp, as if she tried to grab it back before it was fully out.

'It's odd, and a bit disgusting, really, but I can't help making money. I've opened a couple of coffee places right next door to my other launderettes, because why on earth must people be forced to look at out-of-date magazines while their laundry is being done? Or feel they must watch every convolution because of some Puritan conscience that tells them they ought to be doing it themselves?'

'It's certainly one of the better inventions of these last years,' said Penelope. 'Wash days used to be such terrible occasions. My mother used to have a woman in, she liked her things hand-washed, and the garden was full of sheets. I used to hate it, coming home from school. Then another little woman used to come and collect it in the evening and take it away for ironing.'

'My mother used to do it all herself,' said Pye. 'Perhaps that's why I started them. Cold meat and beetroot for supper, and the kitchen slippery and smelling of steam. Eat up your fish, it's getting cold.'

'Were you a large family?'

'Two brothers and a sister. But we haven't kept in touch. My father was a fisherman; it was a hard life, but a good one for a child. And you?'

She made a deprecatory gesture. 'Oh, I was an only child. Very ordinary childhood, London suburb and so on. I always thought it must be fun to have brothers and sisters.' She dismissed the past, said, 'But do you really feel so much for suffering womankind?'

She would not let him slip past her guard again. He seemed to her to be a shrewd man, determined that while a customer's clothes were being washed in his machines, the customer herself should drink his coffee and not waste his time or hers.

He looked back at her without smiling, countering her ironically raised eyebrow. She knew then that he had expected this snub and, like a doctor, had allowed for it, and she felt ashamed.

'I feel for everyone,' he said. 'Women particularly don't relax enough. I thought if they could drink a cup of coffee after the second light had come up – that gives them about twenty

19

minutes – then the fact that a machine had taken over that ghastly weekly chore would be really beneficial.'

'But most of us dash around doing the shopping in that twenty minutes,' Penelope replied. 'I suppose we think it an indulgence and a waste of time otherwise.'

'Time can be wasted or used. I suppose it's all in how you look at things.' He sat back while the waiter put chops and vegetables before them. 'But I hate waste, too. Waste of time or talent, waste of money, waste of emotions. It's the bug of the age – people mix up relaxation, which is necessary, with waste of time which to me is criminal.' He laughed suddenly. 'I suppose it's an obsession of mine really. Do you know in the war, I used to hoard paper bags, cardboard, newspapers, because I so resented the fact that all those millions of trees were cut down to provide the world with so much newsprint? Then I saw that this was stupid, for in a year I had filled a whole room with papers and cartons and so on, but they were still cutting down trees. So I sold the lot.' He shrugged deprecatingly. 'But I made a profit on that, too. Waste paper fetched a lot at that time.'

Penelope leaned across with wide eyes. 'Do you mean to tell me,' she demanded, 'that you are actually haunted – you feel guilty – about this extraordinary talent of yours for making money?'

He nodded.

'Eat your chop,' she said, suddenly solicitous. 'Now, you're letting your food get cold.'

She watched him as he ate, noting the mobility and humour of that face, compressed as it appeared beneath the high, broad forehead.

'But don't you see,' she said, after a while, 'this guilt of yours about money is just as Puritan as ours when we watch our clothes being washed without any effort? I think I know what you feel, because I find any form of self-indulgence – well, wicked, I suppose. For instance, I don't really know you, and yet here I am, having dinner with you.'

Unable to stop himself, for he had often wanted to ask her

directly, but had never dared, Pye glanced at her hands. She looked down at her wedding ring, then across to him. She shook her head.

'He's dead.'

She had not said the words aloud for months, and now to her horror found she could scarcely form them. With a muttered excuse she quickly rose and went away across the restaurant to the ladies' room. There she dashed quickly into one of the cubicles and cried bitterly.

When she came out, composed and powdered, he was ready to leave. He did not look at her as they stepped out into a street freshened by rain. The moon rode high in a cold sky, and by mutual consent they walked briskly along the King's Road and on to Sloane Square. Somewhere along Sloane Street Pye said, 'There's a place near here somewhere where we can have some coffee, if you would like that.'

'Yes, that would be nice, but let's walk a little further.' She did not want to sit facing him across a table again, although she was now quite in command of herself: more so, in fact, than she had been for some time. The words, said aloud to a stranger, became less her own private nightmare. She remembered, years ago, thinking how strange it was that there were so many married women about, and none of them looked as if they had passed through the cataclysm of love and passion that had dominated her first coming together with Jamie. She had not shown it herself. Now it came as a shock to realize that death (she could hear herself saying, as she had heard other people saying to her, *he's dead*) as well as love, was a universal concern, although of necessity privately experienced. It was something she faintly acknowledged, to realize that grief was not her unique portion, and yet it did not make her feel any less alone.

'We're nearly there.'

She had forgotten Pye, who trod patiently by her side, and she quickly apologized. 'I'm sorry,' she said, 'I'm afraid I get so sunk in myself these days I shall become an impossible old woman, twitching and talking to myself.'

'I really think you should have some coffee,' he said. 'And I think something else, too, if you'll forgive my interference.'

She glanced at him warily.

'I think you should move from wherever you are living, and find a small place which is yours and no one else's. Start living for today.'

'You mean I should remember the date is April the sixteenth . . . But my furniture is so huge, I'd never get it into a small flat.'

'Sell it then. Give it away. Have you any children?'

'Yes, three, but two are abroad. *Sell* it!'

They stopped under a street lamp, and for a moment the light filtered down through the new sharp green leaves of the plane tree that wreathed it. At once he thought, 'What a beautiful woman she must have been,' then, as the idea took hold, and something flickered across her face. 'But still is, or could be.' And as she saw his pale, used face, the deepset, intent and kindly eyes, she thought, 'How odd, he is no stranger, and he's right. He has said what needed to be said.'

'Of course,' she said aloud, 'you know that if I could face tomorrow, today would be no problem.'

They walked on, each sunk away from the other. The big cupboard could go, the double bed – yes, that, particularly – the enormous sideboard she had had from her mother. The dining table and the beautiful chairs; they were valuable, if she could bear to part with them.

He had stopped, was motioning her into a narrow corridor off the street, behind an open door. All at once she wanted to be alone to think about this new and revolutionary idea. She hesitated.

'Do you mind very much if I go straight home? I feel tired, I . . .'

'Of course not,' said Pye at once. 'I'll call a taxi.'

They sat in silence, each oppressed by the other, each feeling the need to separate and recover from the tentative confidences they had exchanged. Pye liked her for this, for he was feeling exhausted himself. He dropped her off at her flat, and they parted with conventional farewells.

Upstairs, she found there were two letters for her. One an invitation she would refuse, the other from Spencer Manley. This she took up with interest, settling down in a chair after she had taken off her coat, and turning on the lamp by her desk. The very act of settling into her own home was soothing; already she half-regretted the dinner, the sense of near-intimacy by the river and the peaceful green walk along Sloane Street. Now she could shut Pye out of her life again, for he wasn't really – Jamie wouldn't think so, nor would her daughter Sue – not really the sort of man she should dine with. And yet . . . Idly she opened Spencer's letter. She was fond of Spencer, nearly as fond of him as she had been of his mother, once her closest friend, and now dead. This letter, then, she read with a positive interest, and its contents were so extraordinary, coming as they did at this time, that she went to her desk, took out her writing paper and replied immediately.

Then she went to bed, after making herself some hot chocolate – for Pye had been right, she did need something – filled with the first stirrings of an excitement, a tentative feeling that tomorrow might after all be less difficult to face. Outside her window the mysterious spring was at work; leaves thrusting from dead wood, the scarce-heard rustle of blind, instinctive growth, painful, necessary.

# 3

SPENCER MANLEY was dealing savagely with the ground-elder in the vegetable garden when Penelope's letter arrived. He heard the creak of the postman's old bell as he rode up to the door on his bicycle, and turned his sweating face to shout to him to bring the letters over. But he saw even as he shouted that it was one of Dai's bad days; indeed the post was two hours late. It was no use complaining, for the afternoon delivery was unofficial anyhow, and only arrived because Dai lived with his parents in the cottage tacked on to the stables at the back of the house, and dropped the letters for the Manleys on his way home.

Now he threw some on to the seat inside the storm porch and shouted something unintelligible. He had his coffin look, Spencer noted; that meant he had been doing the Lord's work as he rode through the valley, slitting open the letters of known heathens and stuffing them full of Methodist tracts. His face, always full of a mad dedication, had grown embittered and wry with years of this thankless missionary work, and he had an unaccountable habit of cycling slowly up behind people as they walked along the lanes, his thin legs moving with stiff precision, and turning his head as he shot past them, calling out 'God is Love, remember that!' with venom and reproach.

Spencer straightened up and watched as Dai wheeled his bicycle away through the beech trees towards the stone arch that led from the garden to the stable yard. The Williams's cottage had, in the old days, when the stables were full of hunters, belonged to the groom. Luckily for the Manleys, this tradition of service to Glantmar had persisted, and as the services of a groom could scarcely be required for the one fat old pony they kept for their son, Mrs Williams helped Nika in the house instead.

'Bloody old fool,' Spencer muttered. 'God, what it is to live surrounded by madmen!' He threw an exasperated look around him as he came out of the vegetable garden, glad to be able to stop work, dismissing the hot smell of nettles that were encroaching on the spinach. The sky was too bland, it had that evening calm and luminosity he knew Nika had gone across the fields to savour alone – or rather, with Lewis. It was an absolutely quiet evening, even the throb of the milking machines had stopped. All around him the land sloped up, so that he could choose a series of mounting horizons. Woods topped the rise where he saw Nika walking, and where his son sat astride his pony, making her trot. Beyond rose the hills, nearly, but not quite mountains. Even at the back of the house, the land towards the farm rose slightly, so that the house and its grounds appeared to lie in the bottom of a bowl, secret, enclosed. The way to the village lay across flat fields, but was blocked by the group of beech trees that lay on either side of the short drive. To the south, behind him, rose the high wall of the vegetable garden, where he had always intended to replace the peach trees which had died the first winter they moved in.

He thrust his arms up and away from him in repudiation and made for his letters, as to an escape hatch.

From the hill Nika looked down at the house, and saw him. As she watched, frowning, while he sat on the porch seat and opened the first envelope, a sharp evening wind blew up and he was shut from her sight by a flurry of white cherry blossom, blowing like snow across the garden.

'Oh, do look, Lewis!' she called involuntarily across to where her son absently slapped his sandalled feet against the sides of the fat pony. But when she had at last captured his attention, the breeze had died down and the blossoms had settled on to the vivid spring grass.

'Did you see Dai, Mam?' Lewis shouted back.

Nika sighed. She had seen Dai, and the sight of him seemed to menace her. He tormented her son with tales of a fierce old God who hated the English and who lived in a stone and tin-roofed chapel over the hill, and he brought letters to her husband which threatened her very existence. Only a few weeks ago, while they were planting the first radishes and carrots, he had ridden up with a letter containing the news of Spencer's legacy. No one had expected Spencer's father to leave so much, and Spencer's share would be over three thousand pounds, which sounded a fortune to her. At once he had been aflame with plans to leave the bookshop he managed over at Oxoter, and get in touch with Stefan Brandt. Letters had been coming and going ever since – letters talking of London, of at last starting the publishing house they had dreamed of for five years. She suddenly felt desolate, and stood looking at the long, low house in the scoop of the valley as if this were the last time she would see it. It seemed to gather quietness around itself as the sun sank, it hoarded the last rays among the jumble of its chimneys and sent shafts of red light from its many panes. The wind sprang up again, the sky was losing its glow, it was getting cold; they must go in.

She started down the field after the pony and saw with pleasure that Lewis was much surer now, riding bareback as he was. He made the pony jump the ditch and then edged her through the sparse hedge that divided the garden from the field. Then he was up cantering through the beech trees where earlier thousands of snowdrops had thrust through the dead leaves and the light snow. As he approached the archway Spencer looked up irritably.

'Keep that pony away from the vegetable garden, Lewis! Is your mother coming?'

'Mam's coming now. I made Beauty jump the ditch, Da! She's been good today, so I'm giving her some sugar.' With this Lewis wheeled round and clattered over the cobbles to the yard where the kitchen windows looked over on to the stables and Dai Williams's cottage.

As he had expected, Mrs Williams was in the kitchen. She was getting ready to leave, having set the supper and left his tea ready. The pony came at once up to the window and huffed gently on it.

'That old beast!' she called out now in her complaining voice; her hat, which she never seemed to take off, scratched the other side of the pane. 'Now, Lewis, mind that beast's nose against my clean window! Drat it. . . .' But her thin mouth twisted into something of a smile and she had the sugar ready in her hand.

Lewis took it from her as she opened the window, and jumped off the pony's back. Teasing, he put the lumps in his pocket, so that Beauty had to nose softly all round him before he gave them to her.

'She deserves a treat, Mrs Williams,' he said. 'She jumped the ditch, and she hadn't any reins or saddle on. I think she's getting a bit thinner, don't you?'

'She's still a mite too full of wind, bach, that's her trouble. You've let her fill herself up with all that new grass, look at her blowing and puffing!'

At once Lewis put his arm round Beauty's neck. 'Mrs Williams, she's lovely!' he said reproachfully. 'She's beautiful, she's gorgeous. And I can't think why you won't let her come right inside the kitchen. She did once.'

Mrs Williams snorted and shut the window with a bang.

'And who went round after with a dustpan and brush? Not you, my fine boyo!'

Lewis led Beauty off, to comb and brush her in the little stable before letting her out in the field again, and round the front of the house Nika went slowly up to Spencer, where he sat re-reading a letter and smoking his pipe thoughtfully. He handed the letter to her without speaking.

As she read she felt her face redden, and her heart began to beat more quickly from fear, but all she said, as she handed the letter back, was, 'I didn't know you'd even written to Penelope. I simply can't believe she's willing to move out of her flat for us! She was always so happy there.'

'That seems to be the reason. As she says, she needs a new start. God! I can understand that.'

'All the same,' said Nika obstinately, 'it does seem odd. It's all she has left; she and Jamie loved that flat. And you'd think she'd feel nearer to him in it, with all their things.'

'Things!' Spencer pulled her ear in affectionate exasperation. 'You take root so quickly, darling. It's not going to be easy getting you away from here, but we must go. There's always a time to move, and this is it. I feel it in my solar plexus.'

Nika trembled violently. She bent down to where some primroses had come up of their own accord by the wooden portico. Whether it was her own intensity of mood or the angle of the slanting evening sun, they appeared twice as large as usual, holding an aura of light around their petals and leaves.

'Look, Nika. This isn't a new idea. You know perfectly well that Stefan and I have had this at the back of our minds for years. I'm not sticking in a bookshop at Oxoter all my life. I must get to London.'

Nika laughed shortly, then said in a dry voice, 'I wish it were like a pilgrimage to Mecca, so that you could come back here when it was all over. I don't want to go, you know that.' She touched the wall of the house. It was warm, and badly needed painting, for its whitewash had taken on a pale honey colour. It seemed to her suddenly that the house was listening, the light breeze carried their words from tree to tree, plant to plant, drifted them up to the attics, where clots of flies buzzed hopelessly against the imprisoning panes.

But in spite of this breeze, around the house itself everything was absolutely quiet. There was a momentary suspension of every activity: as if the birds had stopped in flight and the flies ceased their buzzing. At this time of the evening Nika was familiar with the summer hush, that seemed to settle like sediment in this hollowed-out valley, giving a heaviness to the meadows, the gardens, and especially to the house itself, so that sitting in the garden or walking through the rooms was like swimming through thick invisible seas. Now she knew what it was like to be a fly caught in amber. How did it get there? By enchantment, or by stupidity? She presumed the amber had once been fluid, but a moment later assumed she was wrong. The thing worried her.

'How does a fly get embalmed in amber?' she asked Spencer, who still stood thinking his quick, impatient thoughts and was already far from her. He did not bother to reply.

'I'll take a week off and go up to London,' he said, his voice taut with excitement. 'I'll see Stefan and stay with Penelope as she suggests, and we'll talk the whole thing over. She says she wants to move as soon as possible. That flat will be big enough for us, sure to be.'

'You'll have to give the Brisketts decent notice, won't you?' asked Nika, automatically passing all initiative over to him.

'We're due to renew the lease at the end of June,' said Spencer briskly. 'What a bit of luck! So that's when we'll move.'

The end of June, with the summer crowned by blossoms and greenery, the machinery of growth running at top gear, smoothly; hay harvest done, the corn still to come; beans and peas and strawberries and all the delicious things for which one battled through the dour winter and edgy spring. Nika stared at him, but habitual restraint kept her silent. She had given up trying to plead, to make him understand what all this meant to her, for he could not.

Abruptly, she went into the house. The large cool hall with the curving stairs waited for her, in silence and peace. Upstairs a child laughed in the bath, from the kitchen came the sound of Lewis's chatter, for he had, as usual, persuaded Mrs Williams to stop and talk to him whilst he ate his supper. These sounds were muted by passages and oak doors, but it seemed as if she could see through doors and flow into every part of the house without moving or even turning her head. At the same time she had a sudden incongruous image of the vegetable garden in its solid walls; Spencer had as usual left the spade and fork lying on the ground, and the twisting white roots of the ground-elder lay withering and exposed. Now he had torn them all up. With what savagery he had thrust them from the dark soil! A

29

plant had a relationship with the earth too deep for Spencer's taste.

She walked soberly upstairs, along the passage and into the nursery. The bathroom door was open, and a smell of powder and clean warm clothes came from it. The village girl who looked after Sally in the afternoons came out carrying the baby. They were both giggling. Nika buried her face in her daughter's soft neck. She smelt as new as good bread. At nearly three Sally could not really be called a baby, but at bedtime all children seemed to slough half their age. Even Lewis, assured eight-year-old as he was, looked small and vulnerable in the bath, losing the day's dust along with its vainglory and disappointments. Nettle-stings and gnat-bites stood out pink on the brown skin, and the white torso thrust him, in Nika's eyes, back to babyhood.

He came clattering up the stairs now and stood watching as Glynis settled Sally into her cot.

'She should have a proper bed,' he announced.

'It's almost a proper bed, darling, with the side let down. It's an enormous cot. She was lost in it a year ago. Shall I run your bath?'

'Yes, please.' Lewis hopped awkwardly from one foot to the other. 'But, Mam, you won't come in, will you? When I'm in, I mean. Daddy says it doesn't do.'

'Doesn't do? But . . . can you wash your back yourself, then? And your ears?'

'Oh, of course, Mam.' He went over to his sister and tickled her under the chin. 'I'll be quick, Sally, and if you're still awake, we'll have a story.'

Sally chuckled up at him, but her eyes were drowsy. 'The runaway tractor, that one,' she said.

Nika kissed her and went to run Lewis's bath. Everybody seemed to be taking a stand of their own, and she was the one who would have to fit in. It suddenly seemed unfair. Looking idly through the bathroom window she watched the rooks flying over the fields and realized again what such an uprooting would mean. London would be a cage to Lewis, and that view was hers for only three months more. In its place she would see, what? Chimneys, streets, houses, people, no sky. She had never seen Penelope's flat, in fact she had only visited London three times in her life and had hated it. Although they had only been eight years in this house, she felt as if she had spent centuries in it.

Restlessly she walked away, in and out of all the rooms. On the west side of the house the light of the setting sun still streamed thinly in through the upper windows. There were so many rooms that several of them were empty, and yet oddly enough these were the ones which seemed to teem with unseen life. The rats were no longer there behind the walls, for the rat-catcher had come and killed them all in their first year. Their runs had been seen when part of a wall had once been pulled down. In between the great slabs of stone and mortar and brick, twists of corn and hay and droppings had marked their runs, for one room over the old stables had once been a granary. The door still had a neat semicircle gnawed through it, so that before they had come to occupy the house the rats had run all over the house on their secret business. Not only rats: invisible things ticked in the rafters, spiders spun their furtive death-traps, bees made honey in the attics under the roof.

At the thought of the attics, she went through the little deal door with the coloured pictures of a long-dead King and Queen pinned to it, up a flight of old stairs, and here the stored heat struck at her. Up here were the mummified bats, old suitcases, the Victorian shell-house Lewis loved. The roof came down almost to the floor in one place, and she had to bend double to lift the window and let out buzzing clots of flies. Up here the very dust was alive, dancing in the long streaming rays of the dying day. Nika forced herself to tap on the wall of the sealed attic. Once they had meant to break down the wall and see what was inside. But she had always invented excuses and Spencer had lost interest. Up steps and down steps, each attic hotter than the last. The life of the house was drawn up here, it was potent, menacing, it bore down on her, making her heart beat quicker. She caught herself saying aloud, 'What do you want? Why?' Then, folded into and against the answer, she ran, sweating, down the unsafe wooden stairs that led to the kitchens.

As she appeared, dishevelled, through the seldom-used narrow door, Spencer turned with an exclamation. Her sudden appearance had frightened him.

'What on earth have you been doing? We've been calling you for ten minutes. Glynis has just gone and I've taken the meal into the dining-room.' He looked thoroughly put out, and this hid his fright. He saw she was trembling, but made no move to comfort her; she knew he hated her to run about in the attics.

They had just finished eating when the sound of a horse's thudding hooves came faintly across the fields. Spencer cocked his head.

'Hullo,' he said. 'That's Lesley. Are you expecting her?' Nika shook her head. 'Well, I'll get a bottle of wine. At least it keeps in a decent condition in the cellar.' He went off, his air of constraint much less marked.

As the hoofbeats came nearer Nika went out in time to see horse and rider rounding the trees and cantering up the drive. A youngish woman jumped off, waved, and led the horse round to the stables.

A moment later she ran into the house by the back door, came into the drawing-room, where Nika greeted her warmly.

'Spencer's gone to get some wine, you look as if you need it.'

Lesley flung herself on to the long sofa with a sigh. Her cheeks were flushed with the wind, and her black hair was blown into curls. At once, with a mannish gesture, she began to feel in her breeches pocket for a packet of cigarettes.

'It was such a marvellous evening for a ride, and Prince needed some exercise. Am I interrupting anything?'

Nika laughed. 'What on earth could you interrupt? In fact, you're a godsend. Spencer's talking of moving – can you do anything about it?'

Lesley looked at her. Her strong, weathered face changed, and she moved her supple body in disquiet, cupping workman-like hands round a match before she spoke. Her very attitude denied that hysteria had any part of life, and Nika felt comforted and impatient with herself; her pallor and her fluttering panic of an hour ago.

But Lesley said nothing until Spencer came into the room and began to pour out the wine.

'You're very quiet, you two,' he said, handing them their glasses, looking particularly at Lesley.

'Well, tell us something interesting, and then we needn't be,' she replied, looking full into his face. Their eyes met for a moment, then they looked away.

Spencer shrugged. 'The only news is this. We've the chance of a flat in London and I think it's too good an opportunity to miss.'

'Oh.'

The way she let the word escape, on a downbeat, halted Nika as she sipped her wine. It was, she realized afterwards, the unsuspected clue she had been waiting for, the last light touch on a gate which now swung open to reveal a new landscape. These moments of truth were so unremarked, so infinitely small; like applying one's eye to a pinprick in a piece of paper. She sat on with a sense of shock which would later permeate her mind and start off a relentless, constant revolution.

They were talking.

Lesley's voice was urgent, she was smoking rapidly, she turned at last to Nika. Spencer had his adamant face, which made his eyes paler than ever, tensed his cheek muscles to coldness, his easy charm was masked.

'But you can't want to leave the valley, Nika,' Lesley said violently. 'Spencer! Think what hell London is – you've always said you'd never get caught up in the rat race. You're mad. You'll lose all your money. How can you bear to leave . . . all this . . .' she gestured round the long room, the garden outside, its long shadows fingering the house, the call of a night bird. Spencer went to the window, his tall thin body turned away from them. Violently he drew the curtains, to shut out the night. Without a word Nika went to light the two Aladdin lamps, one standing, one swinging from a beam.

As she nursed the flames into incandescence she heard Lesley's voice again, steeled into calm. As she turned it was easy to say, 'If Spencer wants to go to London, then of course we'll have to go. I shall miss the garden, and you, Lesley. Lewis will hate it, of course, poor little boy. He loves this house.'

'And I hate it,' Spencer said, turning. 'But that doesn't seem to matter to either of you.' He looked at Nika for the first time since he had come into the room. 'What did you say, Nika?'

'I said we'd have to go, if you wanted it. I know you and Stefan have planned this publishing idea for years. I think perhaps the legacy, and now the flat – well, are both signs . . .'

They burst out laughing, and she sat down stiffly as Spencer came and put an arm round her.

'Signs, portents – you're like a witch!'

'But a lion hasn't whelped in the streets of Oxoter,' said Lesley dryly. She had recovered her usual practical calm. 'I must say I'd have expected Nika to fight you over this, Spencer. This house is the only thing she's ever cared about.'

'Thank you,' said Spencer, almost inaudibly.

Nika smiled. At this moment the only thing she cared about was to make Lesley realize that Spencer was going away. She did not like herself for this, but the memory of that small dying 'oh' still lay in her mind, expanding like the secret invocation om to fill the world. For this she would sacrifice the house.

'Shall I make some coffee?' she asked, getting up. But Spencer stopped her.

'No, I will,' he said. He felt a need to escape from both of them, they were pressing too closely on him. 'What's that? Someone's coming downstairs.'

He was at the door when Lesley said lazily, 'Don't bother to go and see, Spencer. You know there'll be nothing there.'

He turned in nervous rage. 'Christ, don't talk like that! It's probably the boy. Nika didn't say good-night to him.'

But there was no one there. Spencer steeled himself to walk up the stairs and along the passage through the nursery to Lewis's room. Both children were asleep. But Lewis turned in a hated, familiar dream, clenching his fists and calling out; fighting, obstinate, afraid. Gently Spencer turned him on his side, picked up a small, white fur bear Nika had made for him when he was a baby and which he still took to bed with him, and put it in his hands. 'You're too old for toys in bed, son,' he said, 'but here's Mr Pog. Now you won't dream any more.'

As if in obedience, Lewis sighed, clasped the bear, settled down.

'God,' said Spencer to himself as he made his way to the kitchen, lighting lamps as he did so – he hated the living darkness that gathered in corners and corridors – 'it's time to go. I wonder if Nika ever suspected anything. I was a fool.'

Making the coffee, he wondered what they were talking about. Would he ever understand women? Did he want to? What exhausting wells of emotion they were; they reached out for you like mermaids, always from their own element, never yours: they dragged you down to their own liquid depths until you choked and gasped for air and had to fling them off in self-defence.

In the drawing-room Lesley was talking. Her shock had turned to bitterness; she wanted to wound.

'The country life is too big for some people,' she said, lighting another cigarette, her head turned away from Nika. 'You're all right, you always lived in it. But it's too much for Spencer. He hasn't the necessary self-discipline. He feels oppressed by the changelessness which is really constant change; clouds, seasons, ploughing, reaping . . .'

'No, he doesn't feel for the land and the kind of rhythms it exacts,' Nika agreed quietly. 'You're quite right. He goes at the garden in a kind of rage. He can't accept the slowness, the toughness of its cycle. He just can't tune into it. He likes a faster pace, he likes people. Because they react to him. Here, he has to react to the inanimate and it maddens him.'

'You understand him better than I thought,' said Lesley, in a tired voice. She seemed to droop in her chair. 'You are stronger than I thought.'

'Yes,' said Nika, 'I am strong. Here.'

The thing lay between them, unspeakable.

At last Lesley said, 'What kind of person is this Stefan he wants to go in with?'

'That's a long story. Stefan was one of those Jewish orphans the Red Cross brought over in the war. He was adopted by a Welsh couple over at Llanvyrnwy where I was brought up, and my father took a great interest in him – he was a brilliant boy. But he hated the place and ran away when he was sixteen and got himself a job in publishing. That was ten years ago. But he's always longed to start up on his own.'

'Not quite on his own,' said Spencer, coming in with the coffee. 'With me.'

# 4

STEFAN BRANDT sat in his little room high up in one of the narrow streets off Covent Garden and re-read Spencer's letter. It was midnight, for the water-cart had just passed, and outside the first lorries were arriving, and their noise relaxed him. It was like the beginning of another day, and so it was for the market people. He loved this midnight to dawn activity in the heart of the sleeping city, it put him one ahead of the rest of the world. Living here, Stefan felt he was able to stretch the day to the full twenty-four hours; he needed little sleep, and liked noise around him, it helped him to think, especially noise connected with work, for other people's work fascinated him. He liked the shouts and the grinding gears, sounds which rose so clearly at night, with a quality of their own that daytime noises never possessed. The feverish shifting of sacks and crates into the great maw of the market to him was more romantic than the singing of the spheres, a phenomenon in which he had never been quite able to believe. This was the world turning, and he turned with it.

It had not always been so. Marooned on a hill farm in Wales in early childhood, nothing had turned for him there but the wide skies, casting their cloud shadows on the pitted, sheep-bitten mountains that rose smoothly all around. A larger, lowering silence had surrounded him then, accentuated by the thin call of curlews, the bleat of sheep, the cluck of hens, the clatter of pails and the earthy animal noises of pigs and cows. Hughes had been his name then, for he had been legally adopted. Hughes, indeed! Viennese by birth, and Welsh by adoption. The first thing he had done when he was twenty-one was to reclaim his own name, assert that at least one Brandt still lived to challenge the world that had destroyed the rest of his family. He had worn out his gratitude long ago among those infertile hills to which he had always been a stateless stranger.

Stefan's childhood had been a constant source of irritation to him, luxury-loving as he was by temperament and heredity. He had never responded to the brisk, uncomprehending affection of his adopted mother and father. He had brief memories of laughter and music in a small room that opened on to a busy, noisy street, a room that smelt of rich food and scent, but a room spiced with the sudden acrid stench of fear and sudden silences as heavy boots tramped by outside. He remembered a small fat dark man, his father, playing a violin, a stone crashing through the window and the music stopping on a high note; he remembered the tinkle of glass forever mixed with the tiny clash of his mother's bracelets as she snatched him from his chair. The rest he refused to think about.

Mrs Hughes had never seemed to him to be a woman at all, with her scoured bony face and her eyes the colour of rain. She had won him over in the first place by giving him an orange, which he had never eaten before, as fruit at that time was forbidden to Jews in Vienna. Fruit he had from Mrs Hughes, and eggs and chocolate, and there were no soldiers to be dodged in the village street, only staring children. He had become used to these things, and when the shock of his transplantation had worn off, he accepted them until one day he had asked when he was going home. He had learned English quickly, and thought at first that Mrs Hughes had not understood, so he repeated the question. At last she had said carefully, her face against the flank of the cow she was milking, 'This is your home, Stevie. I am your mother now. You are my son.'

He had stared at her in horror; at the old stable, patched with corrugated iron, at the cow, which now raised its tail and flopped its disgusting pancake all over the stall. He had screamed and said what Mrs Hughes had told Sybil Matthews later were unforgivable things, unless one remembered that they had come from a child. In German and in English he had repudiated her, with her man's boots and the sack over her shoulders, and her labourer's hands. He had sobbed in horror against the cold winds and the porridge and the home-baked bread.

'I suppose it isn't enough for the poor child to survive, Mrs Matthews,' she had said later, with dignity and pity. 'We are poor, but he has nothing. But this he cannot know.'

Her husband took it differently. He had never wanted to adopt a foreigner in the first place, he said. And if Mrs Matthews hadn't been in the Red Cross and in charge of the adoptions, his wife wouldn't have thought of it. As it was, he added ferociously, she needn't think he was leaving the farm to him. The boy was like a changeling with his snivelling ways and puny build. Often Mr Hughes would watch him as he went trotting and crying with cold, plunging through the frozen mud in the rubber boots bought out of the egg-money, following Mrs Hughes as she strode across the fields to mend hurdles or round up the cattle. He would turn aside and spit viciously, cursing the ill-luck of his wife's barrenness.

When Stefan was sixteen he ran away. The farm was pledged to a big raw-boned cousin, Mr Hughes's brother's second son, and one of his earliest tormentors. 'Jew!' the boy would call to him from behind hedges, as he kicked his way slowly to school. 'Poor old wandering Jew! Who crucified Jesus?'

To which Stefan had quickly learned to reply, dodging the stone that followed, 'We did – and we've been crucified ever since.'

He made his way to London partly on foot, partly by lorry, which had landed him in Covent Garden. He spent his first night wandering about the market, given apples, buns and cups of tea by the market men in return for helping them with the crates. The next day he went to a public library and read the list of jobs advertised outside. There was one asking for an office boy at a publishing house, offering a small wage but good prospects. Stefan took his best suit out of the paper bag in which he had carefully packed it, changed, went along and was taken on.

When he was twenty Mrs Hughes died, and, as a last despairing gesture towards the boy with whom she had failed so disastrously, left him three hundred pounds. This she had put together over the years penny by penny, from her egg-money, the cakes she sold, the jam she was famous for in the village. Stefan had cried bitterly when he heard about it. For the first time in his life he knew what it was to feel guilty towards someone else. Previously he had taken the world's guilt towards him for granted, now he began dimly to see that it did not only take jackboots to create victims. He made the journey back to the village to visit her grave and make his private peace with her cold body under the withered wreaths in the extended churchyard that was as yet nothing but a field. As a further act of contrition he called on Sybil Matthews, and there he met Nika again, with Spencer. It was at that meeting the idea of a publishing house had been born. Spencer's last words had been, 'Keep in touch, anyway.'

The two had kept in touch now for five years. Spencer had been drawn to the quick-thinking, stimulating Viennese like a flower bending to the sun, and Spencer was the first Englishman Stefan had ever felt easy with. He responded to Spencer's quiet fanaticism, understood his determination to get out of the bookshop in Oxoter, a job he had only taken when he married Nika, so that they could live near her mother, who was then dying of cancer. Spencer was content to drift for a certain time, he did not believe in making efforts, putting plans into execution. Life lapped him around like water; he flowed easily with it, until the current changed.

The current had changed when Spencer's father died. Tomorrow he would be up in London, they could talk. Stefan sat on in his room until the crescendo of the market began to slow down. Yes, Spencer was the right man to go into this with him, of that he was sure. There was a certain rigidity of purpose about him; he would be content to keep to his own side of the business, which would be the selling side, and his experience of the book trade was invaluable. He was a tidy man, which Stefan was not, an unsentimental man, slow-thinking, perhaps, but with a gift for accurate detail. Stefan had also noted that people found him charming; that would be useful, one needed a front, and he saw himself working away at schemes whilst Spencer played for time and established the sort of relationship with authors and agents and booksellers for which he had neither the time nor the patience – he was honest enough to admit – the talent or the necessary background. In England, he had been quick to note, there was still this distrust of the volatile foreigner; the old-established firms liked to deal with one of their own kind. Only one doubt troubled him. Was Spencer shrewd enough? It was a cut-throat game.

The next day Spencer put his head out of the window of the train as the smoky back gardens heralded the approach to London, and drew great breaths of the smutty, choking air that blew full in his face. He was full of a scarcely liberated excitement that had begun at Banbury. By the time the blackened bubble of Paddington Station had been reached he could scarcely wait for the train to stop before he seized his suitcase and leaped out. It was a dull day, but to him Praed Street, the spilling over of the cheap leather goods on the grey pavements, the piles of greengrocery, the newspaper-sellers, the great red buses roaring by, intoxicated him. With an emotion near love he read the scrawled items of news on the stands: 'Princess Margaret surprise', 'Another woman strangled, Killer sought in Soho'. With a naïveté that surprised him he bought the early evening editions of all the papers and sought for the promised surprise item. Failing to find it, he read about the Soho murder, taking a back seat on top of a No. 27 bus. He was smiling as he walked up to Penelope Hinton's flat in Regent's Park; London had greeted him in a properly dramatic manner.

Sitting having tea with Penelope sobered him. He had been prepared for a feeling of embarrassment, for he had not seen her since Jamie's death, and the flat seemed different to him. It appeared larger, as if it had expanded away from its solitary

41

occupant; Penelope appeared to walk through the rooms more like a visitor than a woman in her own home. But she put him at his ease, there was no hint of the emotion he had dreaded. She was thinner, but composed, and there was a careful air about her, as if she was guarding a small flame that might at any moment blow out. But the flame was there, it had not been entirely extinguished. He found himself admiring her composure.

'You see, Spencer, I would prefer to move. I don't need all this furniture, all these rooms. You would find it perfectly comfortable for the family. The children could have the two rooms upstairs; they're rather hot in the summer, though, with the flat roof. Oh, and you'd have to fasten a gate on the steps up to the roof. There's no garden, that's a drawback, but of course the park is so near. . . .' She led him round, showing him things, telling him of the pieces of furniture she could either sell or leave for him.

'But how does Nika feel about it? She loves that old house of yours, and she's country-bred. It might be a little strange to her.'

Spencer frowned. He found himself unable to discuss Nika with anyone, not because he was so close to her, but because lately he had found himself completely unable to understand her. The longer he lived with her, the more of a mystery she became. It was a shock to him, all the same, to realize that even as he said, 'Oh, she'll settle down; and it will be easier for the children's schooling', he did not care greatly whether or not she wanted to make the move. He knew she did not, of course, but that seemed to him quite incidental, and her objections, mostly wordless, childish and petty. The rigidity which Stefan had sensed in him had become all the more marked since the news of his legacy had made him realize that his ambition to go in with Stefan was on the point of being realized.

Penelope watched him quietly, then she asked, 'This publishing idea you mentioned in the letter, is it sound? I couldn't understand whether you had definitely found a job or not.'

Spencer lit his pipe, walked away to the window, a habit of

his when women asked awkward questions. He had made the same gesture of repudiation when he had told Lesley that their sporadic affair must end. Why did women constantly ask questions? When they were not asking you about yourself, they were telling you the answers; mostly wrong, because subjective. He longed for the evening, for Stefan's objectivity.

Then, remembering that Penelope was his hostess, and that she had known him all his life, he tried politely to tell her about Stefan and their plans. She interrupted him with dismay:

'But Spencer! Stefan Brandt! Sybil told me about him, I remember. He was wretchedly ungrateful to the Hughes, and, after all, they did their best for him. Sybil was terribly put out.'

At this he laughed outright.

'Come now, Penelope, be fair! You know Sybil as well as I do. She's always put out if things don't work out exactly as she planned! You'll like Stefan – he's immensely talented – but there's a certain amount of surface glitter you'll have to discount. He's not after my money, if that's what's worrying you. After all, he's sinking everything of his own as well. Look, sometimes you have to make a leap, you just know it. It's the only thing to do.' He walked restlessly up and down, gazing at one of Jamie's abstracts propped on a shelf; all greys and yellows, with a bold scarlet blob to balance the composition. He prevented himself from remarking on it. Lamely he said, 'I've got a hunch, that's all.'

'All right. I know it's not really my business.'

She had seen him looking at the painting. It was one she was trying to like, although it meant little to her. Every week she put up a different picture, trying to decide which she could live with. 'But Spencer, do remember you have two children. Shouldn't you invest something for them? Buy insurance or something? God knows what I should have done if Jamie hadn't thought . . . if there hadn't been something to fall back on.'

With the swift impatience of the young, Spencer said, 'Oh, we've years to think of that,' and was at once appalled by his words, as he watched her composure crumbling. They seemed

43

to stand on different sides of the world; what was an echo to him, like news of an earthquake in Tokio, heard over the radio, to her was urgent and immediate. She had, after all, endured the earthquake.

He left to meet Stefan soon after, and Penelope sat and thought about him. Basically he had not changed since he was a boy. Physically frail, thin-faced, attenuated, red-haired, with the greenish eyes that went with such colouring, he had always looked as if he were edging from the cover of some thick, protective forest, ready to run if anyone trod too hard on a dry twig. Actually, of course, he was very tough indeed, with a hard core of egoism that had nearly wrecked at least two young women before he finally married Nika. She had watched him veering automatically towards mature, warm women; watched him, too, retreating swiftly when their warmth threatened to overcome him, terrified at the protective instincts he had aroused. 'He hugs his private wound,' Jamie had once said, 'but he isn't quite sure what it is.' His parents had found him 'difficult', she remembered, as parents commonly do when they cannot accurately estimate their children's reactions. Irritability had bubbled constantly below the surface, as if some mental garment pricked and chafed like a hated woollen vest. As a boy he had bitterly resented any encroachment on his privacy and yet at the same time longed for it, courted it avidly. He played many secret games, but always let his family know of their existence, although they were not to share in them.

Penelope sighed sharply. Well, his parents would not know of this new adventure. He had not said a word about his father's death, and neither had she, apart from a letter written directly the news had come. Evidently it was not to be spoken of. She got up to clear away the tea things, and the sight of the two cups gave her a pang of pleasure and pain. It was strange to have someone else in the flat, someone to adjust to. At least it drove off for a little longer the introspection and selfishness of a solitary middle-age. As she carried the tray through to the kitchen the telephone rang, and it was Pye Rumpelow.

He had been out of town for a week or so, and hearing his voice over the telephone was reassuring. Coming after the oddly unsettling conversation with Spencer, the calm positivity of Pye's personality made him all the more welcome. He seemed to her to be an old friend; someone of her own cast of mind, her own generation. Surprisingly, she heard herself ask him to dinner the next evening, ostensibly to meet Spencer.

Through the haze of smoke, across the empty bottles in Stefan's flat, Spencer stretched his long legs and was happy.

'But we still haven't got the capital, Stefan,' he was saying. 'We've got to live as well. You're not married, lucky blighter.'

Stefan brushed this aside. 'How much notice will you have to give Brunton's? I suppose you won't mind leaving them?'

'No. Good God, why should I? A month's notice will be good enough, when we're absolutely certain when we can start up here. How about you?'

'I've learned all I can at Newcome's. They're not likely to pay me any more, either. And it's a closed circuit so far as directorships are concerned. No, I've told you I want to get out and be independent, and that's it. Now I must look around – with a bit of luck I might find a small publishing house and buy it. Then you can come up and we'll really start to build.'

'Can't we start from scratch?'

Stefan shrugged. 'Could do. Might have to. Three thousand is more than some of the most successful publishers started with – but today it's a fleabite.' He leaned forward, his black eyes gleaming behind his spectacles, drained his glass and tapped Spencer hard in the chest. 'What's really wanted is flair, boy. I know I've got that. And you've got the selling experience. Flair is what counts. It's that extra sense, that flutter in the belly, the something that clicks. Why waste it making money for other people? Jump in up to the neck, that's what I say.'

He looked very Jewish as he sat there, all shrewdness and

pleasure; confidence and enthusiasm flowed from him in an energizing stream, and Spencer was filled with an excited respect and affection. 'Of course,' Stefan went on, 'we could lose everything in six months. That's why we really should have at least one more person investing in us. I've got a thousand to put in: saved like mad over the years. At the moment you'd better not risk more than two – after all, you've a family to think of. The only other people I can think of who'd put money in would want a say in the publishing and quite frankly, Spencer, I don't want anyone else in with a veto. It never works. It's got to be our show.' He got up restlessly. 'Don't you know anyone with money to spare – invest, rather – but who wouldn't want to interfere?'

Spencer shook his head. He was suddenly dashed. If Stefan lost confidence, then where were they?

But Stefan went on eagerly, 'Damn it, we're worth taking a chance on. You've had a decent education, you know the selling side. I've come up the hard way. It's an irresistible combination. What about your friend the widow? Hinton was a well-known painter – surely he left her some money?'

Spencer stared at him. 'Penelope? Stefan, really! I don't expect Jamie made all that much, and she's got to live on it for the rest of her life – she's not old. For heaven's sake, man, we can't batten on widows and –'

'Orphans?' Stefan's black eyes sparkled. 'She's a widow, I'm an orphan . . . go on, ask her to have lunch with us!'

'Damn it, Stefan, I can't do that. She was my mother's closest friend.'

'Then ask me to dinner. Can't do any harm. Come on, boy. We only need another thousand, that'll get us through the first year. She'll double her money. It'll give her something to think about.'

They looked at each other, Stefan with a mischievous glint in his eyes, Spencer with a certain shocked reserve.

'You're outrageous. But I don't see why you shouldn't come to dinner. I'll ring her now.'

He did so, and when he returned shook his head reprovingly.

He was more deeply affected by Stefan's light-hearted ruthlessness than he had expected, and his voice was reluctant as he said, 'She says come tomorrow evening. Apparently she's asked someone else, too, so it'll be a small party. I think she's curious about you. Bad boy makes good and all that. Probably wants to report on you to Sybil Matthews.'

They joined hands in a solemn dance, then Spencer drew back and said, 'For God's sake don't wear that awful tie with that – that suit. Haven't you anything quieter?'

'I shall dress according to the part. Respectable English publisher; quiet, tasteful, and oh-so-knowledgeable. No *küss die Hand*?'

'No *küss die Hand*. And now I must go. Tomorrow at seven-thirty. No clowning. And no talk about money.'


Stefan's entry the following evening, at a few minutes after half-past seven, was spoilt by Pye Rumpelow, who arrived on the doorstep at the same time. They made an odd pair, Penelope thought, as she greeted them as they came into the drawing-room. Stefan, small, dark, smooth, wearing his least drastic Italian suit and plain grey tie, and bearing with an air of modest pretension a huge bunch of carnations; and Pye, round and fair, shrugged for the occasion into a fairly decent dark suit. He looked thinner, she thought. How dark clothes reduced a man! Yet it was Pye who made the impact, standing quite still, saying nothing, his eyes smiling. There was a controlled power about him; beside him Stefan looked twice as volatile and somehow frail, like a piece of fluff blown from a stocky dandelion. As she thought of this, Penelope's mouth curved into a smile of pure pleasure, and the two guests caught her expression and relaxed. The evening then began to roll forward to the sort of effortless success no one had foreseen.

It was an excellent meal: Penelope had, as a gesture towards Spencer's guest, provided Wiener Schnitzel, followed by a lemon whip, which she knew to be Pye's favourite. Spencer had brought in some wine. It was not until they were settled in their chairs with coffee and brandy that Stefan said innocently, 'And when are you moving up here, Spencer?'

'Oh,' said Spencer, falling into the trap, his conscience lulled by food and the brandy he was slowly turning in his glass. 'That depends on when we really get going, doesn't it?'

This interested Pye, who raised an enquiring eyebrow. 'Penelope said you managed a bookshop. Are you opening in London, then?'

'Well, not actually. Stefan and I are thinking of going into publishing together. I've come into a small legacy and he has a little, so –'

'Publishing!' Pye sat up. 'Is there money to be made there?'

'Apart from horse-racing, it's the quickest way of losing it I know,' Stefan interrupted, as Spencer opened his mouth to speak and shot a scandalized look at him.

Pye leant forward, turning a small cigar between his fingers. 'Ah,' he said, with interest. 'Can you guarantee me that?'

Stefan looked foxy. 'Of course. Take the two Rathbones. They started with ten thousand a couple of years ago. Nice little office, and not a bad list they bought from old Martin Burns when he was sent to jail for obscenity. You'd think it was a gift, wouldn't you? No. They managed to lose the whole lot, went bankrupt in eighteen months. Look at last week's *Bookseller*: Baines and Baines have had to sell out to Dunton's. Jericho and Swanstead, too, they've come in under the Halstead umbrella –'

'Baines and Baines sold out at a very nice price,' Spencer interrupted, in his turn. 'Isn't that shocker Cyril going to retire on it? Who'd have thought he'd have got thirty thousand for that list!'

'He wouldn't have got half that if it hadn't been for the quiet line in pornography he's been peddling for the last couple of years. And he won't retire. He's busy buying property while London's skyline's changing. He's got a stake in that new Beano building going up near Green Park.'

Pye was sitting forward; now he laughed with pleasure. Penelope, looking at him with trepidation, thought she had never heard anything quite so joyful from him before. He laughed with his whole body, as he had first smiled at her with his whole being. She could see that he was excited by Stefan's words and guessed what his next words would be.

'How much have you two got to start with?'

Stefan took a deep breath and started to explain. At just the right moment he broke off and sat back, and as if to a cue Spencer spoke.

'Don't tell me, Rumpelow, you *want* to lose money?' he exclaimed.

Already he was warming to this man, looking at him with unreserved friendship.

'Not exactly, no. But it's a question of siphoning off profits. I have a phobia about paying excess tax, and that's what I'll be doing shortly. You see, everyone must come to the village well, that's the secret. One gets bored with easy money. Anyway, money should be put to work, don't you agree?'

Stefan, in particular, couldn't agree more. He had sat enchanted all through dinner while Rumpelow gave them brief details of his various interests. The idea of putting coffee-bars next to his launderettes had particularly impressed him. It was simple; it showed the same kind of flair, although in another field, that he felt he possessed himself, and from that moment he had given up the idea of getting Penelope's money and had concentrated on Pye instead. The man obviously progressed by a series of well-timed hops. Hop, one idea; hop, another. And they all linked up, they all added up to money. Lovely streams of money that could make presses start, print the name of Brandt a thousand times on book jackets, title pages, writing paper, labels, postcards. Thousands of people would handle books with his name on the spine. The enchantment of creating this name, setting machinery in motion, himself the motivating force, intoxicated him.

Penelope was watching him with an air of disquiet. She saw him as a dynamo of disruptive energy. He had swept Spencer into his humming circle of plans and ambitions; could he succeed with Pye too? Pye saw her expression, was moved by it;

49

he had come to know the smallest change in her face, and now he leaned across and spoke quietly to her.

'I shall go into everything very carefully, my dear Penelope,' he said. 'But you must admit that it would be a welcome diversion from launderettes and coffee-bars.'

'But we could sell our books in your coffee-bars,' said Stefan. 'On the Continent we have racks of papers about for customers to read while they sit and drink. Why not over here? Why not infiltrate books into coffee-bars, eh? eh?'

'They wouldn't buy books as well as coffee,' said Spencer positively. 'And they'd shy off if they thought they were expected to. No, that's impossible. It's hard enough to get people to buy books at all.'

'They'd settle down all day with one cup of coffee and read all the papers while they were about it – and probably steal the books as well,' said Rumpelow. 'No. The people with too much time to spare aren't usually the ones with money to spend. You must watch your psychology, young man.'

Stefan subsided. Pye watched him in silence, then laughed.

'What a little eaglet you are!' he exclaimed. 'Don't try to carry off too many fat lambs before your talons are stronger.'

Spencer said, 'But really, Rumpelow, do you think this might interest you? We're eager to start, and –'

'I suggest you get some plans on paper first and then come and have lunch with me and we'll discuss the whole idea again. I want to sleep on the idea, and perhaps carry out a little private research. Penelope, it's getting late. Don't let these two keep you up and tire you. Thank you for a wonderful meal and a most entertaining evening.'

Stefan rose, slightly diminished, but the warmth of Pye's handshake disarmed him.

'You and Spencer have a night-cap,' said Penelope. 'I shall go to bed when I've seen Pye out.'

In the hall Pye said, 'You've decided, then, to leave this flat?'

She nodded. 'Spencer is very eager to take it over when his plans are settled.'

'Then we must find one for you. I know just what you want, I think. Don't allow yourself to be hurried, but don't waste any time. I shall telephone you in a day or two.'

'Pye,' she said. He turned and looked at her. 'Please don't do anything rash – that publishing idea. I don't know about that young man at all –'

'Rather me than you,' he said cryptically. 'I only do things I enjoy. If I have any rules, I suppose that's one of them. So don't worry.' He pressed her hand and was gone.

'What a remarkable man,' said Spencer, when she returned. 'He looks as if he's come straight down from Mount Olympus.'

Penelope stared. 'What do you mean?'

'Zeus. The questing Zeus. That extraordinary head, and those eyes.'

Stefan laughed. 'But Zeus created problems. Let's hope Mr Rumpelow can solve ours. Good-night, Mrs Hinton. Thank you so much. I do hope we shall meet again.'

'I'm sure we shall,' said Penelope. Then, feeling her words lacked warmth, she added with a smile, 'And I do hope all your wonderful plans come to something. You must tell me if I can help in any way.'

Stefan looked at her shrewdly, about to speak, but Spencer hauled him off. 'Look out, Penelope! He's starting ticking over again. You'll get the job of unpaid office cleaner if you're not careful. Now do go home, Stefan, there's a good chap.'

IT IS ARGUABLE that opportunities come up, all the time, for every one of us; seen briefly, in most instances, like the flick of a silken scarf round a corner, uncatchable, tantalizing, gone before grasped. Was it the one thing, the one person, who could change our lives?

Stefan had always been peculiarly aware of this, and in the weeks that followed his visit to Penelope's flat something happened to him that he was instantly able to recognize and grasp. Had it happened to another man, at another time of his life, or even a year ago, it would have passed him by unregarded. This recognition was not entirely a rational matter; it was signalled by a subdued excitement that gave him an uncomfortable feeling of breathlessness for a moment before his head took charge. He had had this when, as a boy of sixteen, he stood outside the offices of Blundell and Pickering, applying for the job of office boy.

It happened at a publicity party given by his present firm to launch a new series of travel books. Taking time off after the usual exchange of greetings, the carefully dropped items of publicity information to the right people, he stood in a corner to think about his next move. Then Bonny Chalmers was led up to him by a man called Middleton, a paperback publisher he knew well and whose flair he had at once perceived. The name Bonny Chalmers meant nothing to him, neither, immediately, did the name of Mary Fay, breathed into his ear by Ernest Middleton before he went off to intercept a famous author trying to back his way out of the party and catch his train home.

Bonny Chalmers was a big woman. She was built on a noble

scale, and some people saw in her a touch of the Indian. Indeed, she gave the impression of being partly American, in her expansiveness, and the slight accent that edged her gay and booming voice. Her deep bosom, instead of being confined by any sort of support, hung as comfortingly free and low as nature had made it, and swung enticingly above a soft stomach, which was also barely confined. All the same, her figure, if large, was not unwieldy, for she carried herself with a certain free and upright dignity one associated with progressive aunts in the 'twenties.

It was inevitable that Stefan should find her irresistible. She must have been a dozen or more years older than he, but if he even noted this fact, it was unimportant. He could not take his eyes off her breasts, which were always in subtle movement beneath the shining stuff of her dress. He was prepared for her voice before she spoke, and it matched her rich body in its enticing boldness. A beautiful, well-painted face topped this bounty, somewhat bizarrely set off by black hair highlighted by a central bronze streak. This hair had been the reason for Ernest Middleton leading her over to Stefan, although he did not learn this until much later. On the other side of the room she had been talking to two desiccated women reviewers, the kind who looked as if they were always turning over in their minds clever phrases to discomfort authors and gain applause for their own tiny wit. One of these had been foolish enough to try and score off Bonny by asking her which was the natural colour of her hair.

'You won't believe me, whatever I say,' Bonny had boomed back, smiling, 'and you're certainly not going to check with my pubic hair; so live in doubt, darling. It's the only state of mind that leads to creativity.' She had no reason to fear either of these women, because her books were in any case too lowbrow for them to review, and her sales too large for them to be able to harm her. All the same, Ernest Middleton, a nervous man, had blushed and at once made an excuse to lead her as far away from them as possible, and had chosen Stefan as a refuge.

53

At once they began to talk, and it was then the breathless feeling seized hold of Stefan. It was not only that her whole personality attracted him violently, it was two facts that came out before the party thinned. One was that she wrote, under the name of Mary Fay, the sort of romances that sold twenty thousand a year, not counting paperback sales, was worried that this vein might be drying up and in fact had written two historical romances which her publisher did not want to do, and which she was anxious to bring out under her own name. The other was that her publisher was the old firm of Oliver Prentice. No one suspected it was on the rocks, but Bonny told him this in all innocence. She also told him that the old man was dying and that when his son took over he wanted at once to sell the business and get out. He had always wanted to settle in New Zealand.

'God knows why, except that he looks a bit like a sheep himself, poor darling,' said Bonny, waving her cigarette-holder vaguely to a corner of the room. 'There he is, over there. I'm supposed to dine with him afterwards, but he's so deathly dull, and not at all interested in my books, although they've kept the firm on its feet for ages. I only really put up with him because of the old man, who's an absolute poppet.'

Stefan followed her gesture. A tall, damp young man with bolting eyes was watching them. Signing for Bonny to wait, he went over first to one of the young blonde women who were as prolific at these parties as blades of corn in July and led her over to David Prentice. He introduced them with enthusiasm, saying that the blonde was a poet, wasn't she? and he believed that Prentice wrote poetry as well as publishing, didn't he? Then he mentioned casually that if Prentice would like him to take Bonny Chalmers home, he would; they lived in the same direction. Prentice was at once revivified.

'Oh, do, thank you so much,' he stammered. 'She, she terrifies me. It's the old man she really likes, not me at all, but I have to – she's one of our most important authors –'

'Ah well,' said Stefan kindly. 'If you're quite sure . . .'

But David Prentice was already leaning eagerly towards the

54

young woman, and later, when he and Bonny left, the two of them were still close together.

Over dinner Stefan found himself telling Bonny a great deal about himself, which he had never intended. It was a great relief, as if his frantic ambitions were dropping into a great pool of quietness, for she sat back, watched him, and listened. It was as if some hunger of which he had not been aware had risen sharply in her presence. He found himself forgetting the urgency of an introduction to Oliver Prentice, of making a bid for her books, of doing something about the firm before the old man died and the vultures came in to buy it up.

So when she said, a complete non-sequitur, over coffee, 'You'll need a great deal more than five thousand to buy young Prentice out,' he frowned for a moment, as if this were an intrusive thought, and did not reply, looking at her hands to distinguish which, if any, were the significant rings. She reached across the table and patted his hand, noticing this.

'I've been married twice,' she said. 'But both my husbands have passed over.'

He stared at her, entirely without comprehension.

'I see you don't believe in survival. Never mind. Or perhaps you are shocked at my outliving them both?'

Stefan recovered himself. 'Not at all,' he said. 'They were lucky to have had you even for a short time, my dear.' Unexpectedly Bonny blushed.

'Oh, I don't think I wore them out,' she said anxiously, 'although my second was never a really virile man, of course.'

'How divinely innocent you are, I adore you!' exclaimed Stefan. His hand trembled as he swept off his expensive spectacles and gazed hotly at her. He knew the value of this gesture to a woman like Bonny. She, out of a well of sentiment, was no fool. She had a perceptive insight that confused her enemies and sold her books. She would know, as she looked into his dark, unprotected eyes, noted his thick, childish lashes, that this gesture was not made lightly. The first line of his defences was disarmingly down. He gave himself to her, figuratively speaking, and her reaction was immediate.

'We'll talk it all over at my flat,' she said.


Stefan now began the happiest period of his life. He emerged each morning from Bonny's bed like a mole from its burrow. Indeed, the nights themselves were like explorations underground. The sexual act, for him, instead of a nervous, necessitous and precarious pleasure, brief and searing, became a deep descent into the dark, a healing return to a security he had thought he would never know again. As he held Bonny in his fierce, punishing grip, driving them both to the point of fulfilment, a sudden image would sometimes impress itself before his closed eyes. A child, desperate for its mother, crying out and clinging with fear. Then a dark shape blotting it out, and love rising to meet its need.

His interest in dirty jokes vanished, and some of his friends said, not without envy, that the mystique of sex had got hold of him. But he was too absorbed, too astonished at being so happy, to bother about their teasing. He called Bonny 'the big woman', an unconscious echo of his Welsh childhood. For in scattered communities where surnames were so often held in common, people developed an instinct for the truly individual, and earned nicknames that stuck to them longer than their patronyms. So, in this larger, but perhaps equally cohesive circle, everyone knew who Stefan meant when he said that the big woman was due to bring out two real winners next year.

He had found out that Bonny's books were like her: expansive, garrulous, and abounding in happy endings. Her heroes were well-bred if pecunious, and always with a backlog of curious knowledge to draw on that ultimately discomfited their rivals in love or in business or in war. Once a reviewer referred to her as 'a kitchen Buchan', which made her go into helpless laughter once Stefan had explained what it meant. She modelled her heroines on women like Lady Hester Stanhope, always slightly eccentric, riding up to modern oil-wells on white chargers and astonishing sheikhs with their horse-jumping ability. Judo kept them pure for the much-delayed arrival of the maligned, penniless Foreign Office type.

These romances, full of verve and action, satisfied her own bounding love of romantic adventure. She wrote each one in six weeks, going to the smallest of the Channel Islands to do so, and saying that contemplating so much sea and so little land and so few people made her able to populate her own mind, turning the sea into a desert and the island into an oasis. She was lucky enough to have travelled extensively as a young woman, having had a father who spent his life actually following in the footsteps of as many of his heroes as his length of life and the position of his finances allowed. These heroes included General Gordon, which of course led them to Khartoum; Hannibal, a hair-raising journey across the Alps, her father sulky because he had been firmly discouraged about taking an elephant; and Stevenson, solely on account of *Treasure Island*, which led them first to Scotland and the small room where the book had been conceived, then on to the South Sea island where he had died. Bonny's father had died there, too, and she told Stefan that his death had been caused by a heart attack brought on by too much rapture. He had been tormented by inarticulateness, and she had had to compensate, feel and express as it were, for two people.

'That's why I talk so much, I suppose,' she said. 'But you should have seen his poor eyes bulge with feeling when he touched a small boy who was a grandson of one of Stevenson's servants.'

Since her father's death she had travelled to India with her first husband, who had died suddenly of snake-bite, and had lived for a time in Italy with her second, who was killed in the war. Now, she told him, she rarely went abroad, unless she could live there for any length of time.

'I hate holidays, darling,' she would say. 'Two or three weeks – it's absurd. There's something *infra dig* about those sort of excursions. Some people need them, of course, like letting the cat out at night, or is it the dog? But one should be free to come and go as one pleases. Holidays! Those dreadful people, two weeks in a year off the lead, it's demoralizing. One's whole life should flow to such a natural rhythm that such things become extinct.'

This unexpected arrogance had shocked Stefan, and yet in a sense it matched his own. He had no time for mediocrities or for a mediocre way of life, but had already begun to school his intolerance, realizing that it made people dislike him. Knowing Bonny was like biting through a sweetmeat with unsuspected rock-like pieces of nut embedded in it. And she meant what she said; her statements were never made for effect, however outrageous they appeared.

'Yes,' she would say, after one particularly arrogant outburst, 'I know. There's no such person as the average, normal man. But why the hell then do so many fascinating individuals dress up in that dull skin? Why be trapped behind a bank counter, or a shop counter, or a desk? Why read my sort of books for escape from their own intolerable dullness? Let us –' and here she threw her arms out wide –'let us all be nomads!' And while Stefan was convulsed with laughter at her extravagance, she went on soberly to say that when these feelings became too strong, she at once flew off to Guernsey and there took boat for Herm, for it was time to write another book or she would lose all her friends, as well as her income.

Yes, knowing Bonny, thought Stefan, after the first dizzy two weeks, was also like dipping into a treasure chest, sinking one's arm in up to the shoulder and finding silks and embroideries, golden cups, sapphires, rubies, ivory back-scratchers, jars of preserved ginger, curious wigs, unguents, small books of outlandish knowledge. Knowing Bonny, making love to Bonny, almost completely absorbed him.

Almost, but not quite. From time to time during these weeks he dashed off letters to Spencer saying that he was on the verge of something. What it was he could not say, indeed he did not know himself, but something would come up. In Bonny's magic he believed implicitly.

# 6

AFTER SPENCER'S return to Wales, life at Glantamar became uneasy. Nika, instead of waking out of nightmare into the day's sanity, faced nightmare every time she opened her eyes to the muted sunlight of early morning. These mornings had never seemed to her so lambent, never so beguiling in their clarity and promise. For it was a hot June, one of those sudden spells of blue skies and constant sun and warm breezes that drew up all the scents of the earth and grasses and flowers as the heat of an oven matures and disperses the smell of a rich cake.

Conscious of time passing, a time that could never be recovered, she got up early, so early that as she walked through the garden gate the Friesians in the surrounding fields seemed to be standing knee-deep in milk. They looked patchier than ever, like poor negatives, standing there in the dawning, mist-filled June fields like the beginning of creation. And how clean, purer than water, this sharp, unbreathed air! It flowed over and through her in currents from the long blue mountains that bulked towards the west. She went rapidly through the dew, and felt like a walking statue in the absolute quiet; and as cold, as unrelated to anything living, absolutely non-participant. It was too early on these mornings even for the distant clatter of milking machines to break into the silence that lay behind the scattered chorus of bird-song, the raucous crowing of a sudden cock, the sharp yelp of fox or dog away in the next valley. Once she watched the sun come up like a bubble over the distant mountains. Within the thin skin of the bubble, yellow glowed like silk; it was as if someone were blowing colour into it. Then the bubble burst and the colour spread rapidly over great tracts of pale blue sky until it was undoubtedly day, and she was no longer alone. The first morning of the world must have been like this – and so, she remembered, had been that first waking morning when they came to the house. Full of purity and promise, a challenge. Now it was nearly the last morning and that challenge had not been met. It was wrong for her mind to be so knotted with problems when the country lay open and generous around her. It was like spitting in the face of God.

Starting for home to get the breakfast and awaken the rest of the family, Nika found herself trembling with rage. Far from joy at the prospect of a new beginning, she felt increasing fear. A nagging sense of failure in the things that mattered, made worse by Spencer's utter inability to understand what this failure was, to accept that there had been any failure at all, made her silent. She spoke little, and then only to the children. Between Spencer and herself there was an uneasy truce. He had got his own way, and tried not to glory in it. Often he started to speak of his plans, of how sorry old Brunton was that he was going, then he would stop, light his pipe and go upstairs to sort out his books and papers, ready for the move. He lived in a vacuum, his thoughts speeding ahead to London, wondering whether Stefan was really trying hard enough, longing for letters, a telegram that would summon them to London.

The vicar's wife telephoned her about a week after Spencer's return.

'It's about the fête, Mrs Manley, it's nearly on us again, how time flies! Could you look after the needlework stall as usual? And I do hope you've something of your own. How's the patchwork quilt going on?'

Nika held the telephone, listening to the efficient, chatty voice, unable for a moment to speak.

'Hullo? Are you there?'

'Yes, I'm here. Oh, Mrs Peters, I'm so sorry. But we're – we're moving, you see –'

'Moving!' She could hear the sharp intake of breath. 'Moving! This is sudden, isn't it? When are you going? Where are you moving to?'

'We shall be gone before the fête, I think. We're going to London. My husband's business takes him there.' Her voice was painful.

'London!'

Nika might have said Tibet, Mrs Peters sounded so shocked. 'London! And you never said a word at the meeting the other day. But we shall miss you terribly.'

'How astonishing,' thought Nika dully. 'She sounds quite upset, and I never thought she really liked me. Shall we be missed, then?'

'No,' she said, 'it wasn't decided then. But I tell you what. I'll finish the quilt and bring it along to you before –'

'My dear, what an uprooting! And Lewis will be badly missed in the choir, such a beautiful voice . . .'

'Yes. I must go, the meat's at the back door, and . . .'

'All right. I'll come and see you and you must tell me all about it. I don't know what the vicar will say. Well . . .'

The meat was not at the back door. Nika sat down on the stairs, feeling dry and weak. The house was empty, Lewis at school, Sally out with Glynis. It had been said, and now everyone would know. The cutting of threads had begun. She must think of what to do with everything: with Lewis's pony, with the vegetables and flowers springing up in profusion, the pieces of furniture too big to take to London, the oil lamps they would no longer need . . .

'Oh God, what shall I do?'

If only they could leave, secretly, at night, running like cowards from the reproachful house, the amazed valley, the living things in the garden. Tell no one, let no one know where they were going. Then their letters would merely have the address crossed out and the two words 'Gone away' scribbled over it in pencil. Gone away, like foxes. Never mind where to, never mind why. There would be no empty rooms to walk through, no villagers to face, no startled questions. For people stayed in this valley. It took wars or floods to uproot them from their homes, there was a tradition of staying put. The old families – like her own – stayed, and their children stayed, whether they lived in great houses or clung to the hillsides in damp cottages. She felt ashamed that a way of life should be changed, a family torn up, for the sake of a dream, a business, for the sake of money.

'Oh, be fair,' she told herself, as she went slowly upstairs to fetch the patchwork quilt. She'd better get on with it, she'd never finish it in London, and there were all those pieces of stuff to use up. She was Spencer's wife, wasn't she? Then why didn't she follow him unquestioningly? A man had his own life, his own dreams to fulfil. She started to open the chest where the quilt was stored and stayed looking at the materials inside with a kind of horror. What had happened to her and Spencer? Surely it should be enough to be with him, helping him, sharing this ambition of his if she loved him. And, if she loved him, then leaving this house should mean nothing, nothing at all.

But, going downstairs again, the quilt over her arm, the pillow-case stuffed with pieces of material slung over her shoulder, that *if* came up again to hit her. Slipping her hand over the polished bannister rail, the quietness of the house around her, she was filled with terror at the thought of leaving this refuge. Ten years with Spencer, eight of them in this house. There had, of course, been Lesley; but oddly that betrayal did not touch her feeling for him. It had begun, must have done, when she was away having Sally. Or even in the months before, when she was big with child. And that was over now.

She settled in the little breakfast-room. The sun was high so that the sharp shadow of the damson tree fell across the floor where she had spread out the quilt. The squares of brilliant colour, solid in the clear light of afternoon, lay all around her, muting the delicate velvets and watered silks she was using as contrasts. She began to work with neurotic haste, trying one colour against another, until her mood quietened and her hands slowed to less obsessive, nervous movements. This grading, contrasting and careful sizing had the power to absorb and soothe her as did few other things.

As she worked she found herself thinking intensely about

Spencer, with troubled tenderness. Asserting his own self-sufficiency, he yet wanted the relief of offering it up to some-one else, someone who could not exist outside his own imagina-tion: the beloved, the essential, the wholly beautiful, the human yet non-human woman, who would know and understand him without making use of that knowledge to hurt and humiliate. A woman who would appear and disappear at will. He caught echoes of this perfect being in other people's poetry, other people's books. Occasionally he met someone who possessed one or more of the qualities he most desired, most feared. To her he would expound his eager theories of personal relation-ships, seeing himself at last utterly fulfilled: the lover and the beloved, the wholly devoured and the devourer.

Nika knew that up to the time of meeting her, each one of his youthful, frustrating affairs had started as unexpectedly and as suddenly as a journey on a mat down one of those spiralling descents from a tower at a fair. His own emotion, so hopeful, so eager, so warm, propelled the mat with dizzying force. Then, as his own impetus failed, exhausted, the mat slowed down, steadied to a stop, tipping him off at the bottom, empty, bruised, a little hardened, a little more disillusioned, a little less sure. He would kick it aside, saying that he had never really intended making the descent at all, the experience had been an ill-considered whim, of no importance. Like a puzzled, spoilt child, he had at all costs to save face, and it was this that made him cruel, and added to his wayward attraction.

Squatting on her heels, pinning the squares on to the black-out material she had saved from her mother's wartime curtains, she asked herself what he had seen in her. Why had he turned to her, married her? As she wondered about this, the blackness of the material behind the vivid squares gave her a perverse pleasure. Shadow behind sunlight, the smile like a golden helm over a darkened, hidden face. She had become aware, in these last months, of the value of a dappled, protective colouring. Did one ever really know another person, or was the most one could do to try to understand, to make allowances, and hope for the same indulgence back? Gradually she stopped thinking, even

63

caring. The sun emboldened the bright colours beneath her, and she worked on, absorbed, like a monk illuminating manuscripts in the safety of his cell, until steps and shouts outside in the garden told her that the children were home. It was time for tea.

Lewis burst into the room behind her and came up curiously to see what she was doing. His feet kicked into the pile of sorted squares, and at once she spun round in a rage. For, careless about so many things herself, Nika could not bear a wanton disarrangement of her work.

'Sorry, Mam,' he said rapidly, giving her a sweaty kiss. 'There's going to be Cubs in the village. Mrs Jones's sister, the fat one with the dogs, she's going to form a pack, she says. And then we can go and camp on Lone Tree Hill. All the boys are joining. I can, can't I?' His mother said nothing. And as if to strike against this silence of hers, a silence that heralded disappointment, he repeated, urgently, on a rising note, 'Can't I, Mam?'

## 7

WHEN PYE met Stefan again he was at once struck by the change in him. His nervous ebullience, which was almost cockiness, had sobered into a relaxed confidence. His face looked less avid, more open. As they had their first drinks, Stefan said, 'I thought you'd be wondering why I didn't ring before. But I wanted to be able to have something more – well – concrete to discuss while we had lunch.' He lit a cigarette and added, 'That is, of course, if you still feel the same. Spencer thought we'd rushed you a bit that evening.'

'I'm never rushed,' said Pye, smiling. 'I'm still interested. But first of all, tell me what's happened to you? Have you found your publishing house? I hear from Penelope Hinton that Manley is all set to move into her flat when she's found the other one, so I've been looking around for her.'

Stefan remembered to ask how Penelope Hinton was, and nodded without really hearing the reply. He was unable to pretend much interest in a person whom he had decided was not now really important to his schemes.

'Let's eat,' he said. When they had ordered, he looked at the wine the waiter brought and waited until it was poured out. He lifted his glass and said seriously, 'We can't drink to it yet, but I feel it's on its way.' Then he went on with a rush, 'Don't misunderstand me, Rumpelow. I'll tell you all about it. The point is, you mustn't think . . .' All at once he was on edge with anxiety, and launched into an account of the meeting with Bonny with a subdued excitement that astonished Pye. Had he been mistaken? He had summed Stefan up as a young man with a particularly incisive mind, not over-scrupulous, and of a driving ambition that went beyond mere enthusiasm. When Stefan had finished, he said, after a pause, 'You don't want me to think that you are having this affair just to get Prentice *père's* publishing house when he dies, or even to buy the option of Miss Chalmers's books?'

Stefan flushed. He had not specifically said that he was having an affair and the brutal frankness of the words diminished the small cloud of glory he walked in. Pye looked at him reflectively. He preferred people to be at a disadvantage, one was so much better able to sum them up. It interested him that Stefan should be sensitive on this point, and also that he should possess in addition a quite unexpected emotional honesty of motive.

'Look, Brandt,' he said. 'It's certainly important for you to meet the old man. If Miss Chalmers is his mainstay, it looks as if you might make an offer for the firm – or for her books. Without her books the firm will be worth very much less. I presume you've been finding out as much as you can about their position?'

Stefan nodded. At ease with facts, he at once attacked his steak with enthusiasm, quoted figures, explained the significance of Prentice's back-list, the firm's valuable connections – now largely neglected – with the States and the Scandinavian countries.

'If we could put in an offer now,' he said, 'we might pull it off – but it's a long chance. But it would be a far better investment for us to buy a concern that's going – even half-going; there are some books in that back-list that brought me out in a sweat, they're begging to be reprinted. The authors are so old they're on their way back.' He leaned towards Pye, his face damp with emotion. 'There are things in that back-list,' he repeated, then was silent. 'And,' he went on with awe, after a pause, 'they don't appear to owe anyone anything. No bad debts.'

Pye nodded. 'That's something, certainly. But how much would they want? The big firms will be after them any time now, surely, and if Miss Chalmers told you all this, she might have told a great many other people as well.'

The horror of this prospect, together with its frightful reason-

66

ableness and his own blindness, was suddenly too much for Stefan. Gulping down the rest of his steak, he sprang to his feet.

'I must telephone,' he said. 'Excuse me.'

The telephone was just off the small bar outside the dining-room. As he dialled Bonny's number he prayed that she might not be out at lunch. He could have sobbed for joy when he heard her voice. Scarcely announcing himself, he croaked at her:

'Have you told anyone else about Prentice selling out?'

'Why, no, I don't think so. I think David wanted the news kept from his father, or he'd disinherit him or something. The old man is most eager for the firm to be kept in the family. I can't think why I told you. Now wasn't that an odd thing? Unless of course it was destiny, and –'

'That's what it was. It was indeed, my big beauty. Now, will you telephone David Prentice and invite yourself to tea this afternoon? Then pick me up here as soon as you can and take me with you – don't tell him I'm coming. I'm at Mario's. I love you.'

Cheese and coffee were on the table when he got back, and Pye was spearing gorgonzola on to a tiny biscuit. He looked up with a grin that at once transformed him into a satyr.

'You look very breathless,' he said.

'I am, indeed I am,' replied Stefan. 'But I should have thought of checking up before. Listen. I have a beautiful idea.'

'Well,' said Pye, at the end of it. 'That's sound psychology, if not sound ethics. We can put down ten thousand. But that's a flea-bite, as you know. They'll expect five times that. Still, it's up to you. I'll back you, and any other help I can give –'

'Don't go!' cried Stefan, as Pye rose. 'Let's have some cognac.' It was in vain that Pye protested he never drank brandy in the middle of the day. Wildly Stefan grasped a waiter and ordered three cognacs. 'Bonny should be here any minute. You must meet her.'

They talked desultorily until they heard a deep voice greeting Mario with familiarity.

'Have you managed to replace your chef?' she was asking. 'I haven't dared dine here until I had the chance to find out. I'm not interested in the kind of food temporary cooks fob one off with.'

Bonny came up to their table, with Mario trotting beside her. He appealed to Stefan. 'Mr Brandt, was not the steak well cooked, just right?'

'Mr Brandt ate far too quickly to give any considered opinion, but I found mine excellent,' said Pye, rising to his feet. He had not been in this restaurant before, but knew now that if he came again he would be well looked after. He made a mental note to bring Penelope here. Then he looked at Bonny and found her pleasing. She topped him by half a head, and today she wore a kind of red sombrero with her black suit, and a brilliant silk scarf that deliberately clashed with her bronze-streaked hair. The outfit gave her the look of an outrageous cowboy of Indian extraction. Pye saw at once the absolute fascination she must have for Stefan; through her he could realize the kind of opulence and panache that had to be kept strictly in check in himself. Here she stood, contradicting the dourness of Stefan's Welsh childhood, blotting out the gauntness of poor Mrs Hughes, protecting him from the beating rain of the hills, the poverty of the farm. Bonny was for him a return to a life he had never known, only sensed, through his parentage. Pye felt an enormous warmth towards them both, and as they sat in the emptying room, drinking coffee and more cognac, he knew that this was the right thing to do, even though he would probably not lose money. In fact, he might even make some more.

At last he rose, said, 'It's time for your tea-party. Good luck.'

'Can we drop you anywhere?' asked Bonny as they stood looking for a taxi.

'No, thanks. I'd better walk, or I'll drop off to sleep.' He did not say that he intended to go straight to Penelope's flat, on the off-chance that she was in. These two burned and revolved like catherine wheels, and now he felt he needed Penelope's coolness and the quietness that surrounded her like an aura. Even her melancholy was at this moment a refuge.

'I like that man,' said Bonny, settling into a taxi. 'He's a good man. How odd you should say he feels guilty about money. But that's a sign. He's lucky for you, Stefan. Now, let me handle David, we don't want to frighten him out of his wits, poor lamb.'

The publishing firm of Oliver Prentice was in a quiet and still unfashionable square near Queen's Gate. At the back of the large old house ran a mews, noisy with the clatter of a printing press, tradesmen's vans, and smelling unaccountably of fish. The founder of the firm, David Prentice's grandfather, the first Oliver Prentice, had once kept his carriages there, until he had bought up a small printing press and installed that instead when horses and carriages went out and the mechanical era came in. Oliver Prentice, his son, had gradually bought up the entire mews which now housed the press, trade and dispatch departments. It was a small, dying empire. They went in through the pillared front door. There was a shabby elegance about the hallway, which the partitioned-off reception office did little to reduce. A thin, elderly woman wound a handle attached to the house telephone and called thinly into a tube. After a time of listening she put it down and came out to them.

'Mr David is with his father,' she said severely. 'Mr Prentice senior does not often come to the office, and must not be over-tired. However, he will see you. Please follow me.'

She looked like a housekeeper as she led the way up shallow, beautiful stairs, covered with faded carpet, the walls lined with portraits of men and women whose faces seemed familiar. Stefan stopped at one without comment and smiled. It was the first Prentice. High, broad forehead, sharp-nosed, enormous eyes, probably myopic. A beard covered what had probably been a microscopic chin. It echoed David, but a David without weakness.

'Dead,' said the housekeeper figure sharply, turning, and with a touch of jealousy. 'They're all dead on this wall,' and did not allow him to stop again until she trod softly across a corridor to a large oak door, opened it, and said, 'Will you kindly wait in here?'

The room they had been shown into was of parlour dimensions. It was domestic and comfortable, oddly dwarfed by an Adam fireplace and made majestic by a high carved ceiling. More pictures, signed caricatures, books in old bookcases, oak chairs, a rosewood table with a bowl of sweet peas, the firm's catalogues of current and forthcoming books, the trade papers.

'They've divided this room,' said Bonny. 'The proportions are spoilt.'

'It's too nineteenth-century for words,' replied Stefan. He could sense that the whole quietly decaying house, the superior receptionist, despised him. It made him feel temporary, and he didn't like it. And now his plan was spoilt because the old man would be there, as if he had come up to protect his son, Stefan thought wryly. Still, he'd wanted to meet him. You never knew. . . .

'It's no use, Stefan,' Bonny was saying, looking less positive than usual.' 'I can't intimidate David with his father here. I wouldn't upset the old man for the world. He's dying.'

'That's why we must be quick.' Stefan moved impatiently to the table, contemptuously riffled through the catalogue listing books for the spring and summer and threw it down. 'I only want a promise of first offer. I know it's a long chance. Now remember, a little gentle blackmail about changing your writing name and letting poor Mary Fay disappear from the scene completely; a hint of the option clause not being renewed, the suggestion of a word to his father . . .'

'Stefan, you are either joking, or else you're behaving like a monster. Which is it?'

Stefan did not like the way she was looking at him, so at once he gave a laugh that was half a snigger; he almost never laughed aloud, for the sort of things that really amused him were too bitter and too wryly slanted.

'I'm merely telling you how to get your historical novels published, my dear. The turn of the screw. But in any case, if the old man is here, the whole thing's a waste of time.'

At this moment David Prentice came in. He was easy in a worn sports jacket and old flannels and once again Stefan felt an interloper. David's very shabbiness and nervous courtesy made his own dark, too well-cut suit, even his own personality, immediately unacceptable.

'Father's come up unexpectedly, Bonny,' said David Prentice now, greeting them distractedly, and concealing his surprise at seeing Stefan. 'He'll be simply delighted to see you. But don't over-excite him. Miss Frost is livid, simply livid.'

'Don't be frightened of Miss Frost,' said Bonny, like a comforting nurse. 'You know she adores him, and it's natural for her to disapprove of everyone your father knows.'

'Well, she doesn't adore me,' said David miserably. 'You're lucky not to be in publishing, Brandt. Running the staff alone is murder. Women are terrifying . . .' He smiled apologetically across to Bonny and valiantly tried to mend his sentence.

'You don't have to pretend that you're not afraid of me, David. I know you are, and it's partly my fault,' said Bonny. 'Well, are we going to see your father or not?'

The door opened, as if her words had been a cue, and a very tall old man came in. He was completely bald and wore a hearing aid, so that the black box over his ear looked like some kind of growth. He seemed to fill the room with an evanescence of fading power and physical strength. He stood well over six feet tall; the shreds of fat that had once been heavy jowls looked grotesque, disfiguring the lower part of his face and thickening the powerful neck. Here was the ruin of a bully, thought Stefan, a power machine run down, a man who belonged to the industrial revolution with a quirkish passion for literature. He was entirely unlike the mild, yet shrewd intellectual whose portrait harrowed the visitor on the stairway. And yet more than anyone else he had been responsible for educating the masses, making available in pamphlet form the potted philosophies of rationalist thinkers and reformers, a great supporter of the Fabians until their ideas had taken root. Then the abrupt

71

change in the early thirties, which had nearly wrecked the firm; his pro-Fascism which had prevented the knighthood he had been so nearly offered for services to literature.

Here was a man who had to swim against the current at whatever cost, and who, now that his early ideas had all been adopted, suddenly had no further interest in them. He had switched to an earlier period, his father's period, perhaps for self-protection. Stefan felt briefly sorry for David, dwarfed and puzzled by this irrational giant of a father. Now, coming across the room to meet them, Oliver Prentice looked like a tree struck by lightning.

He came straight over to Bonny and took her hands, kissed them. As he straightened up he seemed younger.

'You do me good,' he said, in an unexpectedly gentle voice. 'Bonny, my dear, you always did me good. Why don't I see you more often?' He turned to Stefan and said, 'Young man, isn't she a beauty? They don't make women like Bonny today. Who are you?'

David introduced them, and there was a slight pause. Luckily, at this moment, tea was brought in. A bright-looking, fair young girl who looked familiar to Stefan carried the tray. As she set out the teacups, he realized that it was the same girl whom he had in desperation chosen at random for David Prentice at the party. She smiled at him, winked. David caught his eye and coloured.

When she had gone out, shutting the door quietly behind her, Oliver Prentice said, 'Pretty enough, but they're all mass-produced today. Like those dreadful paperbacks.'

'Father, please don't start about paperbacks again, you'll only excite yourself.' David seemed on edge. He could not guess why Bonny had come, nor why she should have brought Stefan with her. Surely Stefan's firm was not interested in her books? They were after all rubbish, not the kind of thing Newcome's had on their list.

'Paperbacks are the only things I can allow myself to be excited by, David. And as mine is probably the only small, still voice left to condemn their horrible vulgarity I can see no reason why I should forfeit the privilege of saying what I think about them.' The old man turned to Stefan, suddenly alert.

'So you're Brandt, Newcome's publicity man, eh?' His eyes had the saurian trick of suddenly veiling themselves, as if a second thin skin flicked suddenly across. 'Decent firm, Newcome's,' he went on. 'You've some interesting books on your list. You like publishing?'

'*Like* it!' Stefan laughed and said no more. He found it difficult to explain his passion to strangers, and before David Prentice's lacklustre droop found himself impotent to say more. Bonny came vigorously to his rescue.

'Now, Oliver, this is a young man who thinks of little else, he –'

As she talked on with enthusiasm Oliver Prentice watched Stefan intently. His smile was a mere flick of the long thin mouth, but it signalled complicity. He had recognized a fellow-fanatic, and then remembered something, interrupting Bonny to ask, 'Are you the fellow responsible for getting Piludin's memoirs?'

Stefan was astonished, then wondered why. Of course Prentice would know all about that, as he would know about everything else that went on in the publishing world. Stefan's sudden decision to fly to the Argentine to interview the last Polish general and sign him up with Newcome's had made news at the time, but that was two years ago, and he never dwelt on his triumphs.

'Yes,' he said.

'Then I know about you,' said the old man, nodding. 'Now, David, why don't you take Bonny into the office and discuss whatever it is she wants to talk over with you – you're in charge now, you know.' He gave this last sentence a sarcastic overtone, and gestured dismissal, then he added sharply as they rose, 'But those historical books of yours aren't any good, Bonny; you can't browbeat us into taking them, you know.'

'Someone else will, I suppose,' said Bonny calmly. 'I want to look over my contracts, anyway. I particularly want to check on the option clause.'

With that she swept out of the room, barely giving the badly frightened David a chance to open the door.

When they had gone, the old man shook his head. This action gave him an air of senility, especially when he chuckled at the same time, 'Wonderful woman that,' with a suggestion of nostalgic lechery. 'But she can't write, never could. Got her thumb on the public pulse with those romances of hers. Historical books! They'd never sell.'

Very quietly, almost hoping that the deaf-aid would miss his words, Stefan said, 'I don't agree, sir. I've read them, and I think, with pruning, they'd be a great success. Not under the name of Mary Fay, of course, but in her own.'

'So you want to buy her from me, is that it?'

'No. I'm not here on official business. I just came along with Bonny after lunch. I understood she wanted to see your son about something.'

Oliver Prentice rolled his large head back and almost laughed. 'You don't fool me, young man. I'm an anachronism, I know, but once I was very like you.' He tried to pour himself some more tea, but his hand trembled and he gestured impatiently for Stefan to do it for him. When the cup was ready, he took out two ampoules from a small gold snuffbox and shook them into the palm of his hand, threw them to the back of his mouth and swallowed them down with tea. Then he leaned back and shut his eyes. After a few moments his voice was stronger as he spoke.

'I expect Bonny told you I can't last more than three months. Well, that's true. I've carried too much weight all my life. Fatty heart. She's worried about her future. David will carry on for me, but he doesn't like Bonny's books. He thinks he's a highbrow – wants to throw out all the people who've built up this business. What do you think about that, eh?'

'I think it would be a mistake, sir. It would upset the balance of your list.'

'Oh, would it? And what do you know about my list, eh?' He paused and they looked at each other. 'Don't tell me. You know all about it. You know as well as I do that there are only two good books there. Now you tell me which two they are.'

'The Benvenuto Cellini you're doing with Schirach's of New York and Ira Solentov's short stories. You just beat us to them, you know.'

The old man chuckled maliciously.

'Shall I tell you how? Gallacher, the literary agent, is one of my oldest friends. He knew Solentov slightly, and by a stroke of luck he was on the Queen Mary at the same time, on one of his visits to the States. Over one or two nightcaps he persuaded Solentov to let him handle his work. There's a great deal of luck in publishing, my boy, as well as flair.' He stared at Stefan with interest. 'Odd you should pick on short stories. Everyone knows they're poison to the bookshops. But these will sell, they're worth fifty bad novels. But they'll take some promotion. You're right about Cellini, of course.'

'Your fiction's patchy,' said Stefan, flicking through the forthcoming list, frowning. 'What one really looks to you for nowadays are belles lettres.'

'Belles lettres! They're finished.' Prentice spoke so violently and with such fire and pain that Stefan was startled. 'No one has the stature today. No one has the time to write essays that illumine, or letters that live; where are the great conversationalists now there are no dinner tables? To produce a Boswell there must be a Johnson; a small flea needs a large dog. Where are your true eccentrics, your dedicated explorers? These tomfool expeditions after Yeti are laughable; we're a nation of Loch Ness monster watchers, sky-watchers, bird-watchers, safari-goers, with cameras instead of the seeing eye. The world's diminished so that we are diminished with it. There are no ideals that can't be contained in a short leader, no thinker whose ideas can't be cut to size by the popular press and the antics of the professional entertainers in that idiot box. Would Darwin have made a feast-day for fools? Would Byron have written jingles?' He sank into a dream, as if ranging in thought before the portraits of the men whose letters and manuscripts lay locked away in drawers, and whose work his father had published. Then he sat up and said, with an amused grunt, 'The only man I can think of who

75

might have enjoyed life today even more than when he was alive was Tom Moore. That rascal was a great entertainer . . . oh, and Dickens, born for television, the old mountebank . . .'

There was a knock on the door and Miss Frost came in.

'Excuse me, sir,' she said, 'but your car is here. I hope you're not overtired.' She did not glance at Stefan, but he sensed her disapproval.

'Thank you, Miss Frost. Will you call my son and Miss Chalmers, please? They're in the office.' Then he turned to Stefan and said, 'Come to dinner one evening.'

As Bonny came into the room Stefan could see that she had been disturbed in the middle of battle. There seemed even less of David than usual.

'Can I give you a lift?' asked Oliver Prentice as the chauffeur tucked him into the car. Bonny shook her head.

'Thank you, no, Oliver. I have a call to make quite near. Bless you and take care of yourself.'

The car drove away, the street was empty, and the doors of Oliver Prentice Ltd were closed behind them.


But Stefan never dined with Oliver Prentice, for two days later the old man was dead. He read the obituaries with Bonny over the breakfast table, but she seemed preoccupied. She had never told him exactly what had happened when she was in the office with David, but she did not seem surprised when Stefan told her that evening that David Prentice telephoned him at Newcome's to ask whether they could meet.

They met the day after the funeral at one of Oliver Prentice's clubs. The heavy leather furniture seemed to hold the ghost of the old man, so that their greetings were subdued and oddly furtive. David came to the point quickly.

'Bonny told me you wanted to go into publishing on your own,' he said. 'My father liked you when he met you that day. He said – oh, a lot of things about you before he died.' His mouth twisted, as if he did not want to remember them. 'What I want to know is whether you'd like to come in with me, as a director, of course. Halstead's want to buy us up, and it's tempting. But if you'd join me, I wouldn't sell.'

Stefan drew a deep breath. The room seemed to recede into endless distances; he sat very still. Halstead's had been cornering shaky publishing houses over so many years, so quietly, that it seemed strange there were any left outside the umbrella. He could guess roughly what they would offer. His sort of money would be a piggy-bank contribution. Also, what about Spencer? And was it what he really wanted? Wouldn't the dead weight of a dying empire be stifling? On the other hand . . .

'Look, Prentice,' he said. 'Tell me honestly. Do you really want to stay on in publishing? It's a kind of drug, really, and it's either your kind or it isn't.'

David looked away.

'I've always hated it,' he said. 'What I really want is to go out to New Zealand. My mother came from there, you know; her people were farmers. Anyway, I never meant to get trapped in it, and I wouldn't if my brother hadn't been killed in the war. He was much older than I – and very like my father. But the old man insisted, and, oh well, I just drifted into it, I suppose.' He looked round him nervously. Spirals of cigar smoke rose from one or two chairs near the windows, their occupants hidden. Newspapers rustled in corners. A waiter passed with glasses on a tray, noiselessly. 'I want to marry and go in for sheep-farming, I've always wanted that. Then in my spare time I could start a small literary magazine. It wouldn't matter if it didn't pay.'

Stefan choked back a laugh. Sheep-farming and a small literary magazine seemed wildly incongruous companions; no wonder old Oliver Prentice had been impatient with his son. Then he suddenly remembered something, something he had unaccountably forgotten in the excitement of the greater chase, and cursed himself for not thinking of it before.

'Prentice,' he said urgently, 'what about the Corunna Press? Isn't that your own show?'

Young Prentice gestured feebly, then nodded. 'Oh, that! Yes. The old man bought it for me. He clinched the deal just before his illness. It was a sop to the rumours, you see. People were beginning to see we were shaky, and buying up another firm, however small . . . and of course,' he added loyally, 'he wanted to give me a niche of my own, I suppose. Decent of him. I've hardly done a thing about it, though. We were going to make it a vehicle for really avant-garde books, a sort of prestige branch of the firm, you know.' He turned away bitterly. 'He never thought I was any good, so he thought I could lose money quietly in a corner, while he –'

'How much do you want for it?'

'The Corunna Press? You're not serious?'

Stefan began to talk, and at the end of half an hour David Prentice had been hypnotized into selling him the Corunna Press for fifteen hundred pounds, the price to include, in addition to its own paltry back-list and battered office equipment, a free choice of half a dozen out-of-print titles from the Prentice back-list, to be transferred at once to the Corunna Press. This was legal, but only just, and David demurred at first, saying that Halstead's would expect the list to be intact when they took over. Because now, if Stefan definitely wouldn't come in with him, he would sell.

With a pang of envy Stefan asked how much they had offered, and when the sum of eighty thousand was mentioned, he felt again as he had done on the stairs of the Prentice building, with Miss Frost going ahead of him, and all the portraits of dead authors pacing him. 'One day,' he swore to himself, 'one day I'll have that kind of money and maybe even buy up Halstead's.'

'Look,' he said, 'I'm not trying to take the Mary Fay books away from Prentice's, David. And that's one of the things Halstead's are after, together with the printing press and the building and the rest. They won't notice a few O/P titles tossed in as makeweight. After all, the Corunna Press is nothing but poetry and the odd difficult novel – and, oh, those weird cookery books full of devastatingly funny misprints.'

'You've not really looked into it, Stefan,' said David, with a quiet grin. 'You don't have to haggle. I've accepted your price. But the Corunna Press also controls all rights in old Gaylord's stuff, that was why I wanted it in the beginning.' A brief gleam of his father's shrewdness showed for a moment in his long face, and he added, savouring Stefan's startled look, 'He has a certain standing now, since he's just been given the Beckwith Prize for Poetry. Anyway, let's get back to the office and I'll show you his new collection. The manuscript came in last week.' As they stood on the pavement, sniffing the warm open air of the streets with relief, he added, 'And Bonny isn't likely to renew the option clause in her contract with us. I reckon you'll have her, too, next year.'

Now the burden was in process of being shifted from his shoulders, David seemed to expand. His hangdog air lifted from him, and his air of self-deprecation became shy charm now that he was at last changing the course of action he had been frightened into for so long. A half-terrified guilt bubbled across his mind as they waited to cross the road. He had buried his father yesterday, and today – But he felt an overwhelming sense of gratitude towards Stefan for refusing to come in with him; it was only in obedience to his father's memory and to Bonny's threats of what she would do if he did not make the offer that he had done so at all. Brandt was not his kind of man; he could never have worked with him. He felt a fleeting pang for the Corunna Press and its miscellany of obscure poets. All the same, there was something else. He turned to Stefan as they set off briskly along the Mall and said, 'Oh, you know that girl you introduced me to when you rescued me from Bonny that time? Well, her name's Dorothy, and we're going to be married.'

'Splendid,' said Stefan automatically. He had not heard a word. He walked rapidly, his head bursting. They would buy a house in Covent Garden, if it could be managed, and he would live on the top floor, just as he did now, only they would own the whole thing. At fifteen hundred it was a bargain. The Corunna Press. It had a certain ring about it, and it would grow. It might seem as if he had gone to an auction to buy a Dresden bowl and come away with a mixed lot of cracked china, but he had known all along that one was fantasy and the other reality. In life cracked china was the reality, and he had to come to terms with it. It was what one did with the cracked china that mattered.

He patted David's arm.

'Will you wait here a moment?' he said. 'I want to send a telegram.'

# 8

SEVERAL WEEKS later, Penelope stood in her flat watching the man from the local auction rooms denigrate her furniture. Pye had kept his word and had found her a small mews house – or flat, rather, since the rooms were all over a vast two-car garage. At first Penelope had thought that the rent would be too much, until she realized that the sum she was asked included the garage below, which she could let. Having to watch these financial details was new to her, and curiously invigorating, for she had never handled large sums before, merely drawing her housekeeping money from the bank each week. It was satisfying to find that she was, if not as capable as Jamie in ordering money matters, at least adequate.

The three rooms were not large, nor were they very high, and so most of her furniture would have to be sold or given away before she moved in. There had been a hurried correspondence with Nika, who had advised her to move it all out, as they, too, had far too much to bring up from Wales. In writing this, Nika had hoped that Penelope would not be hurt, but it had occurred to her that it would be less painful to see one's flat full of other people's furniture than to come suddenly upon a familiar desk or table that belonged to a past time. She knew the power of possessions well enough, and it had taken her a long time to understand and accept the fact that Penelope was willing to give up her home, even though, as Spencer had told her on his return from London, 'she rattled about inside it like a dried nut in a shell'.

So now Penelope watched as Mr Turnbull, paunchy and knowing, with craftsman's hands and watered-down eyes, looked up from his grubby little book and said, 'You won't get much for this lot, missis. Frank's my name and frank's my nature. You ask me and I'll tell you.'

'Oh no, please God, not a character! I don't think I can bear it,' thought Penelope, turning from the window with a tight little smile. 'I know they're very old-fashioned, but they're well made,' she said. 'The sofa, for instance, and the chairs, they're all newly sprung.'

Mr Turnbull did not reply at once, but pressed his hand briefly on the tarnished brocade. 'People like foam-rubber now, it's all foam rubber these days. Foam rubber and veneer, that's what they want, and that's what they'll pay for.' He shrugged and went on round the room, humming thinly. After a while he added, 'And covers you can zip on and off.'

Penelope said anxiously, 'Oh – not that little round table, and not the chest. My daughter wants that chest.'

'Take out all the best bits and you might as well keep the lot for what you'll get for 'em,' said Mr Turnbull, suddenly becoming a man with a grudge. 'Anyway, there's worm in the table and that chest's got a broken hinge. Sentimental value, shall we say?'

His intimate leer was perhaps only imagined, for he had an old scar at the corner of his mouth, which lodged a small fleck of saliva. This gave his face a cynical twist out of all proportion to his blunt features, and he evidently used it to intimidate his customers, for whom he possessed a scarcely hidden scorn. Nothing, Mr Turnbull had found in his long life of buying and selling, was ever quite what it appeared. Even eminent persons, the nobility among them, were guilty of offering him worm-eaten cabinets and fake china.

Penelope followed him from room to room, wishing she could turn him out. He made her feel sick, and her humiliation increased as he became even less impressed, the more of her things he saw. All these had either been left her by her mother, or collected haphazardly during her wholly satisfying, unsettled married life. That dome-shaped black leather trunk, for instance, where the children had kept their dressing-up clothes, and which was now full of Jamie's canvases and paints and brushes, had been picked up in Scotland for four shillings. The auctioneer had made a gruesome joke about bodies in trunks, she remembered, as he knocked it down to them, for at the time there was a wave of such murders. The pretty mahogany dining table and the matching chairs which she had polished every Saturday morning throughout her childhood. The matching sideboard with the little gilt handles like sheaves of wheat: in one of the cupboards her father had kept the whisky which had in the end destroyed him.

It was right they should go. The past had too much power, it imprisoned, it weighed her down, it made her unable to function in the present. These things possessed her more than she did them. But as Mr Turnbull made his grubby notes she found herself wanting to protect her furniture from him, stop him making them less than they were, prevent them from becoming shabby to themselves. With a conscious sense of absurdity she found herself mutely appealing to cupboards and chairs and tables as they stood guardian over worn patches of carpet, 'Go on, use your power over him, not me. I'm not part of you any longer. I refuse to be. I dare not be. I don't want to sit on chairs worn to the shape of the body I once loved – I won't look at children's ruined stools and bedside tables. I want all the past's trampled footsteps to be washed away like the sea over busy sand.'

'Well, that'll be the lot, missis.'

Once again they stood in the drawing-room; her life, dented, worn and not liable to fetch much, already transferred to the little black book, now snapped tight with a thick rubber band.

After seeing Mr Turnbull off the premises, a nicely insulting phrase to be savoured in revenge, Penelope shut the door behind him and went slowly back upstairs. Was there anything longer than a hot still June afternoon? Surrounded as she was by the things she had betrayed, time seemed to hover, then halt. She had a definite sense of Jamie in the room, by the window where they had often stood watching the slow sails of the boats on the lake, the drift of children along the passage to the park.

'No,' she said aloud. 'No, I simply can't bear it. Don't you see, I have to go. I'm cut in half here. Jamie –' Absurdly, she found herself backing out of the room, grabbing a coat from the hall, almost running from the flat. Her heart was pounding as she sped downstairs and into the hot street where the glare hit her full in the face.

She recovered herself as she walked along the narrow passage between old walls and cringing, broken shrubs into the park. She refused to look back and up at her drawing-room window. Why? Was someone standing there watching her cowardly retreat? It was all so impossible, so mad. She was far too stable to imagine such things – after all, hadn't Jamie himself often said, 'The dead to their graves, the living to their dinner'? And he, of all people, would not want to frighten her. If she were to let go, then he must, too. She told herself that it was in her own mind that the backwash of twenty-five years did not settle all at once; it was she who was obstinately, hopelessly holding on to Jamie, conjuring him up, so that he could reproach her for trying to dismiss him.

She had sunk down on to a seat under the spreading shade of a giant willow, and as her mind churned with these questions her eyes took in the solidity of the squabby ducks on the flat, bright, pewter-coloured water. She had always thought of herself as solid as one of those ducks. Jamie's friends had always thought so. She could almost hear their voices now, as they sharpened their neuroses on her calm, saying, 'Of course, Penelope is so marvellously equable, she doesn't suffer.' And she had smiled and gone to make more coffee. For they were right – or at least they had been. Until now she had never suffered or felt lost. She had spent her life making a comfortable and secure background for Jamie while he fulfilled his role as dreamer, creator of pictures and murals, talker. She had looked and listened.

God, how she had listened! Wherever they lived, Jamie's friends had come for week-ends, to talk in the garden, in the kitchen, in the nursery. She was called in when they shaved, for solitude, she had noticed, was something they shunned, and having her around was not quite that, but the next best thing to talking to themselves. They did not have to be witty at these times, and yet they tried out remarks on her which she would recognize at a party afterwards, much polished, better delivered. Penelope was safe, they recognized, because she appeared to have no malice in her, because she didn't attempt to cap their jokes; and because she listened quietly they thought her wise and tolerant, perhaps a little stupid. But they liked the image of themselves she reflected back, and so they fell, indulgently, half in love with her.

She got up from the bench and walked along by the lake until she came to the Clarence Gate exit. There she crossed the road and turned down the street with the garages and the mews flats above them. With a sense of shock she wondered how she was going to squeeze herself into something of that size. Then she was behind the station and across Marylebone Road and walking fast towards the little cinema. Why? Why, on such a lovely afternoon, a cinema? 'It's cooler inside,' a poster told her. Looking up, she knew why she had come. It was a repeat of Garbo in *Camille*. She had seen the announcement from the bus yesterday, and how could she resist that long profile, that far from – and yet quite – perfect face? Years ago she had missed *Camille*. Always, when it was on, something had happened to prevent her from seeing it. Other films she had seen, with that elusive, vulnerable face, the long, sensitive mouth that on any other woman would be ugly, redeemed by eyes as deep as Circe's and a brow pure as Adonis'. For that is what Garbo was, both male and female, that was both her poison and her divine appeal.

The film started; Garbo in her carriage, her lap heaped with camellias. The story, old as the world itself, unfolded. Robert Taylor, young, wooden, took fire from his Marguerite; the paste jewels sparkled from her reflected brilliance. The voice, ah, the voice . . . Penelope was soon, as always, in tears. Even Garbo's laughter was more melancholy than anyone else's despair. In that voice hope flared up like a flight of dawn birds, only to fall, inevitably, like them, to the levelling guns.

When the lights went up, she saw to her horror that she was the only person in her row weeping. People looked at her with amusement. On her way out a young girl in tight blue jeans said with a shrug to her companion, 'But it just isn't tragic any more. When you think of the awful things happening in the world all the time, how can you cry at a thing like that?'

That, thought Penelope, as she recovered herself to mount a bus to Putney, was the way the world went. Didn't young people read their Donne? *Any man's death diminishes me, because I am involved in mankind.* One man's death, or the deaths of a thousand men. One could not increase the flow of tears, for the terror and mystery were the same. And if there were no terror, or pity, no basic flinching, then the deaths of a thousand men meant nothing. If you multiplied a billion by nothing, the answer was still nothing. Perhaps the young rejected the small personal tragedy because they were still shaken and dazed by the piled-up corpses at Belsen and Auschwitz; for them the oily smoke of charnel houses still blackened the sky, darkened the future and blunted their pity.

She went on thinking about this as the bus neared Putney and the road where her daughter Sue lived in a small new house, expecting her to tea. She was late and felt guilty about it, a state which her daughter's anxious face, when she opened the door, did nothing to quell.

'You're late, Mother,' said Sue, as Penelope knew she would. 'I've had the kettle on and off three times.'

'Oh dear, I'm so sorry, darling! I'm afraid I slipped into the Classic to see *Camille*. It's coming off tomorrow.'

Sue shook her head at her. Stockily built, broad-faced, her expression, at any rate when she was with her mother, was usually one of indulgent exasperation. She accepted her mother's whims, but did not understand nor approve of them.

'You're a romantic, Mother, that's the trouble with you. And you're emotional. The two add up to a good cry in the dark, with a wonderful feeling of release afterwards.' She looked at her mother closely. 'Do take your coat off. For heaven's sake, a coat today! Wouldn't you like a wash? When you come down tea will be ready. I can see you've been having a wonderful time.'

When she heard the tea trolley being wheeled into the drawing-room, Penelope came downstairs. She felt refreshed and cool after her wash and quite able to deal with her daughter's most irritating remarks. It was just as well, for Sue looked up from pouring the tea as she came into the room and said, with a half-laugh, 'Of course, you always cried at the cinema. I used to dread the lights going up when I was a child.'

'How unnatural you were,' sighed Penelope, sinking into a deep chair by the open French window. As she noted the roses, the carnations, the neat profusion of her capable daughter's garden, she added silently, 'And still are.' Aloud she said, 'Nothing interested you except the news.'

'I felt the news was the real world. I felt it threatened me, even then, so I had to take particular notice of it. That town crier swinging his bell! I used to dream about him.'

'You never told me,' said Penelope, taking the cup Sue now offered her, and choosing a thin cucumber sandwich.

Sue looked at her oddly for a moment, then away. 'No,' she said. Then she rushed on, 'The films we saw were never real to me. Love and death – well, how could they touch a child? And *Camille*! Dick and I saw that last year, and really, Mother, it's pure ham. Dumas knew that as he wrote it. He pulled out all the stops. Surely it was as vulgar in his day as –'

'What rubbish! What *is* the nature of tragedy, then?'

Sue looked at her, astonished. Tragedy did not belong here in Putney. She stood in the sun, outlined by it, blocking it from Penelope, solid, with her thick dark hair almost vibrating in the strong light. Like this, she bore a strong resemblance to Jamie. Irritation at her mother's sudden question, and a remembered anger at the vague liberalism both her parents had believed in and practised even more vaguely, made her hostile.

'I think it's an indulgence to regard coughing to death smothered by camellias a tragedy,' she said briskly.

87

Penelope was at once reminded of the girl's remark outside the cinema. 'It just isn't tragic any more,' she had said. 'When you think of all the awful things happening in the world . . .'

'When you think of all the awful things happening in the world at this moment,' Sue was saying, moving to her chair, 'that kind of drama is as dated and as obscenely funny as the bustle.'

'I wonder why you all think this way,' Penelope murmured. 'I was wondering on the bus whether it's because your generation has seen so much slaughter; millions of people horribly humiliated and tortured before their deaths and all for the sake of one mad ideology.'

'Oh no,' said Sue at once. 'That was your generation, not mine. Ours is the Bomb, and the slaughter ahead. That's what worries me. Dick and I went on the Aldermaston march this year. It was quite an experience.'

'Your father and I took part in every demonstration to stop Fascism spreading over Europe, but it wasn't any use. So I'm driven back to the individual, the personal tragedy: that, after all, is the core of life – and death. I've thought a great deal about death lately. Whatever it is to the one who dies – and we can't know that – the sense of personal loss isn't assuaged by knowing about "all the awful things" that are going on in the world. . . .'

She glanced across to where her daughter sat, expecting a rebuttal, but was amazed to see her suddenly flinch, as if she had been touched on a raw nerve. Sue said, with violence, 'How can you grieve for someone you've never known? I suppose you think I've been heartless about Father's death, but we children only really saw him as a stranger. No – I must say it – because I'm going to have a child myself and I'm damned if I'll treat it the way you treated us. Father behaved to you as if you were the only other *real* person in the house, and you behaved the same way with him. Friends used to say what a devoted couple you were. They never realized what it was like to be the children of such a devoted couple!' She turned her back on her mother,

88

and looked blindly into the summer garden. Through her numb sense of shock Penelope realized that this was what Sue had been wanting to say for years; she noticed her hand was shaking and the tea spilling into the saucer. Quietly she put her cup down and waited.

'The walls were thin in that funny little house we took one summer by the sea in Sussex, do you remember? Jane and I could hear you talking after we'd gone up to bed, and Father said in that exasperated voice he always seemed to use when he talked about us, "Let's get rid of the children and go off by ourselves for a bit, darling." Then you said something we couldn't hear, and he got annoyed and said, "Oh, for God's sake! What does it matter if they're unhappy for a couple of weeks? They'll soon forget it, and appreciate us all the more when we get back. Do we always have to carry them around in our pockets?" And Jane cried, but then she went off to sleep and I tried to go on reading *Hiawatha* – and I wrote a bit of my own at the end of the book, with that dum-di-dum rhythm.' Sue spoke the words as if in a dream:

> 'Through the forest my dear mother
> Walked and walked and gave her children
> To the Cyclops, nothing caring.
> Eat them up and stew their entrails
> In a stewpot. Father says so.
> Father says it doesn't matter.
> Then they'll love him all the better.'

In the silence that followed Penelope said in a flat voice, 'That's why you tore the page out. I remember that copy, it was bound in calf. I hated books being mutilated.' She put an arm round her daughter's shoulders. 'Drink your tea, dear. And I'd like another cup. Naturally you're in a nervous state now.' She tried to smile. 'Perhaps when your child is grown up you'll be confronted by a slice of his childhood he's elected to remember. Think of all the nice things that happened – your father used to say I put myself out too much for you . . . all those expeditions to the sea, with Jane dragging behind so that we almost missed the bus home! The pantomime . . .'

'*Aladdin* was fun,' said Sue, blowing her nose.

For a moment Penelope could have slapped her.

'The Playdells took you to that.'

'Oh yes, of course! He bought us huge ice-creams in the interval and I dropped mine down someone's back. He laughed like mad.'

'He was always a vulgar man,' said Penelope, with displeasure.

Sue grimaced, then poured out more tea. She looked composed, and at the same time reckless, as if she must seize a chance that might never come again.

'Don't be absurd, Mother. You know as well as I do that he was terribly good to us. We adored him. We felt safe with him. That enormous red face. He was *with* you somehow, he really *saw* you when he looked at you.'

Penelope felt she had had enough. She was about to change the subject and ask about her prospective grandchild when Sue spoke again, almost dreamily, and not looking at her:

'It was such a change to be with people who really liked having us around. I honestly don't know what we'd have done otherwise. After all, children aren't animated dolls, to be lugged around and arranged on chairs. It was so strange, we never felt part of *either* of you. Father was always painting and you always seemed to be talking to his friends so that they wouldn't disturb him, or having to hurry over whatever you were doing with us, in order to get back to him. Then when you were alone together and we were out of the way, your voices seemed to change; almost as if you two were the only members of a secret society.' She laughed shortly. 'I don't feel I shall be like that with Dick when our child is born.'

'No,' replied Penelope, 'I don't expect you will.' She felt very tired – what with Mr Turnbull, then Garbo, and now Sue – and guilt had replaced the first outraged shock of her daughter's outburst. 'Your father and I had a very rare relationship. I'm sorry if it tended to exclude you, that was selfish of us.'

Sue said, with sudden warmth and pity, 'It was selfish of him. Because now you're quite alone.' At the naked look on her mother's face she drew a sharp breath, aware that she had been cruel. And yet with that awareness was a tiny sense of triumph at having – at last – penetrated the shell of someone loved, someone who had for years been rejecting her.

# 9

June continued to be hot, and the dusk brought no appreciable coolness. From his bedroom window at Glantamar Lewis Manley watched the trees shift together, moving in close around the house, their leaves forming a dense protective shield against the coming of darkness. An owl hooted twice from the empty barn. Across from the circular garden, beyond the yew hedge that guarded his retreat (so private that Lewis called it 'Mr Pog's house', not daring to give it his own name for fear it would then have being and come to harm) his pony ate the sweet summer grass for the last time in her own field and huffed through her dowager's nostrils at the dancing gnats; beyond all these familiar things rose the fairy hill, encircled by Betsy's Lane, which led, a haunted path, to a haunted pool, widdershins to the next village.

Keeping his eyes on the pine-topped hill, the small boy made a sign of his own invention. He pressed his two thumbs into a straight line and above them his fingers formed the apex of a triangle. So he thought of himself, his sister and God. This sign kept safe the child asleep and sweat-damp in her cot beyond the open door that connected the two rooms. Once, at midsummer, he had seen a sign from God strike down from the hill, so he knew it was in answer to his own. Mad Dai the postman had told him so, although his father had said it was only summer lightning or a falling star. He believed nothing his father told him, because no one else gave such uncomfortable answers. Mad Dai knew everything, though. He knew whom God had touched, and who lay outside His mercy. A terrible thing was that both Lewis's mother and father lay outside this mercy because they went to church only three times a year and let him play cricket on Sunday. But God had touched him and his sister, and the touch hadn't worn off yet because they were too small to sin, and in time Dai had promised to take them both over the fairy hill to chapel, where true men and women worshipped and made proper stern prayers with lots of feeling and cries to the Lord, Who liked such things and understood the Welsh. In church, Dai said, the old organ drowned the singing – and a good thing too in a way, for everyone knew the English had no voices because they had no souls to sing with. Sad it was, poor dabs. Sad, too, Dai said, his great pale eyes loking down at him over the slung sack of letters, sad for the boy bach to be half English – that way you were nothing at all, like a good rice pudding spoilt with water added, or good flour baked in a shop to a pappy town loaf.

At this memory Lewis made his sign fiercely until his thumbs ached, and stared at the hill.

'Why am I only half Welsh, Mam?' he had once asked.

'Because I am Welsh, but your father is English,' Nika had replied.

'So the baby is half and half, too?'

'Of course. You're both lucky. You're a nice mixture.'

A nice mixture! Wandering off to Mr Pog's house, he had carefully collected three jam-jars, two small, one large. Then he meticulously filled one jar with water and the other with mud. Then he had tipped them both into the third to see what happened. This was half and half. He stirred busily with a stick. This was the nice mixture, then; you couldn't tell which was mud and which was water. Dai was wrong. Smiling, he idly rolled over on to his stomach to watch two ants feinting with a pine needle, urging it towards a crevice in the roots of the great weathered yew tree. Only when they had succeeded did he roll back again to taste his triumph over Dai.

He stared. What had happened? The nice mixture had gone. The water was very clear and the mud very thick at the bottom. So that was half and half. Glaring at the black mud he realized that here was his father letting him down again. He had no

93

right to be English and to take them all away, especially now that the Cubs were going to camp, and he'd miss it. He supposed that London acted like a magnet to the English blood in his body. Dai had said that no one with one drop of Welsh blood could keep away from Wales, for there were magnets in such blood that drew you back to the mountains, whatever.

Now, remembering that, he shut his eyes, tightly and made a wish, the same one he had made last week, dropping his penny down St Garmon's well. But he'd rather trust fairies than saints any day, so he turned his eyes up towards the hill and said in a fierce whisper, 'Turn us all into stones, King Pendragon, and let the yew tree hide the house forever, but please, please, if the furniture van comes tomorrow to take all our things to London, let me come back one day.'

The air was full of the milky dusk of summer, not the solid rough dark of remembered winters, and as Lewis moved to pull his head from the open window something seemed to shimmer down from the sky over the far hill. It was as if someone had quickly shaken out a light yellow ribbon. King Pendragon had given his sign.


Half a mile away a car moved along a lane. A woman's deep voice said, 'Hullo, summer lightning! Steady, the bridge is round this bend past the farm.'

'If we don't come to it soon, I'll begin to think the place is bewitched,' a man's voice answered from the darkness of the driving seat. His companion laughed softly, as if to show that she was in agreement but wanted to say nothing more. Farther on, over the old wooden bridge, grey-green trees stood gappily on either side of the long winding and badly worn carriage track. Attracted by the headlamps, the white face of a cow thrust between the trees and stayed there, suspended, moonily chewing. To their left came the snicker of a pony. A sliced lemon moon rode summer high above the dark mass of the house ahead. There were no clouds. The car lights cut a swathe through the soft darkness as they bounced slowly over ruts, scratched past squat thorn trees crouching at the last wide curve.

Lesley opened the gate and stayed to heave the iron bar back into position as the car went on feeling its way along the drive. The overgrown bushes cast a dense shadow and something scraped against the bumper. At once the driver stopped the car and got out to investigate. Flashing about with a torch pulled from his pocket he lit up a stone sundial, grainy and rough with age, then called Lesley. When she joined him he was slowly tracing the letters that ran spirally around it, from the top of the stem to the bottom.

'Have you damaged it?'

'No. We've run off the drive. I couldn't see it, anyway. I say, this is fascinating. . . .' His fingers traced the letters as his torch picked them out, one by one. The date first, 1710. ' "Haste, Traveller," ' he read out slowly, ' "Haste, Traveller, the sun is low" . . . Damn! Lesley, haul aside those weeds, they're choking the next word.' He crawled round on the dewy grass, scraping moss from the deeply incised letters, intent. ' "He shall return, but" . . .' then he emerged from the other side, triumphant, '. . . "but never thou." ' He looked up at her, in the darkness she could tell that he was smiling. 'I say, I like that. I've never seen that on a sundial before.'

'It's certainly a change from "I count only the sunny hours" and all that sort of thing,' said Lesley indulgently. 'Do get up, Jory, the grass is wet. Strange, I've never noticed that sundial before.'

'You're not as inquisitive as I am,' he said. 'Come on, let's get up to the house.' Under his breath he added, ' "He shall return, but never thou. . . ." ' Aloud he muttered, 'It's a bit doom-laden, isn't it?' and carefully eased the car back on to the drive. Turning a slow bend they drew up at last on the paved square before the wooden storm portico. Apart from this protuberance the house presented a flat, tranced face to them as they stopped and the fussy noise of the engine died away. At once the silence flowed in again and Lesley drew a swift breath at the closeness of the trees, the sudden sharp smell of crushed camomile. She did not see a small figure draw quickly back from a window set above the porch.

'You'll love them,' she said uneasily.

Her companion was delving in the back of the car, there was a clink of bottles. 'Help me out with these,' he said. 'It doesn't matter whether I love them or not. People are the same everywhere, the drink's the only thing that varies. And this time I've brought my own.'

The paucity of the man hit Lesley like a cold draught, and she at once regretted her perverse, vain whim of bringing him. But it was too late for regrets, for the door was at this moment thrown open, and the strengthening moonlight streamed in and outlined the woman standing there, her thick reddish-brown hair worn loose about her shoulders, eyes startled in a reserved and unwelcoming face. So a priestess might have appeared, disturbed at her last rites, and Lesley scarcely recognized Nika in this role. As if to make a bridge between them, she called out at once, but kept her voice low as if to waken nothing in the absolute silence.

'Jory called on me unexpectedly, Nika darling. He insisted on being allowed to come and help pack up books. I've told you all about him, haven't I?'

Nika sent a long, disbelieving look across to the dark figure who was still scrabbling about among the clinking bottles.

'Oh, hullo, Lesley,' she said. 'Yes, of course. Actually I expect the men will do all that tomorrow. But how nice of you – yes, do come in and cheer us up on our last night.' Her voice grew warmer as she spoke, it hastened on as if she needed to hear her own words spoken before she could believe them. 'Anyway, there are some books I wanted to look out for you – and I'm sure Spencer has put aside some records you liked.'

She ushered them into the hall and then threw open a door on the right. Instantly lamplight streamed out and made the hall even higher and more shadowed. She began to talk again, as if they were very late guests at a party which had taken all her energy and could only be endured by determined froth. Dazed, Lesley and the unknown Jory were drawn into this queer illusion, learning that Spencer was in his study bundling up papers and so on, he must have heard them arrive and would be out in a moment. Oh, they'd brought drinks, how lovely, *what* a marvellous thought, she'd find some glasses if they weren't all packed. . . .

The long drawing-room with its wavy oak floor and its ground-length windows was lighted by the two Aladdin lamps and an additional hurricane lamp hooked on to a beam. Although the next day it would be empty, Nika had crowded all the vases and containers she could find full of flowers: roses and lupins, pansies and pinks and marigolds. There were great bowls of buttercups and vetch and rosebay willowherb, and trailing garlands of travellers' joy. A brass can held spreading sheaves of grasses and green branches. The enormous French sofa stood where it always had been, cutting the room in half: it gave Lesley, for private reasons, a guilty qualm.

'Everything looks so solid, so immovable. I simply can't believe they'll be in a strange house, hundreds of miles away, this time tomorrow,' she murmured to Jory, who was staring round with his usual undisguised curiosity, his thin eyelids blinking rapidly over small black eyes like the shutters of an immensely efficient, split-second camera. He at once noted the odd effect of the massed flowers, their scents filled the air. The peppery smell of lupins balanced the sentimental wedding scent of the eglantine, while cloves blended with the sweet heaviness of roses. Above all it breathed the fresh neutrality of grasses and boughs. Something hidden very deep under the cheap salesman's veneer stirred in response and made him uneasy and excited. So had the first Druids decked their altars: he found himself looking for oak branches, and found them. But what tetchy god was Nika placating?

Seeing Jory so enrapt, Lesley quickly stepped across the room and left it by the second door, which led to the passage near the kitchens. She wanted to find out whether the rest of the house was as undisturbed as the drawing-room. But here, in the first of the big, stone-flagged kitchens, signs of change lay everywhere. Cupboards had been unsystematically cleared, witnesses to the panic of an abandoned ship, or a burglary, with the indiscriminate blind grabbing interrupted by the sound of the owner's key in the lock. Dirty linings to drawers, a box full of half-finished sauces, tins, oddments of dried herbs, mouse-nibbled. Behind a cupboard, half-pulled from the wall, were scattered mouse-droppings and an old letter, evidences of Mrs Williams's slack ways and Nika's sleep-walking attitude to her house. This troubled Lesley, for she kept her own small cottage in perfect order; an uncared-for room affected her like a rumpled bed at noon. Over most houses cleanliness, order and polish lay like a protective skin; here that skin was missing, and rawness was the result. Seeing Nika rummaging through a half-cleared cupboard, Lesley thought that the occupants of such a house were raw too, as raw and defenceless as disorder could make them. But she said nothing, only wiped the glasses as Nika found them and put them on a black japanned tray with a crystal jug of water. As she carried the tray out and along the passage, she said simply, 'You have some lovely things, Nika. I hope they won't get damaged tomorrow.'

Nika understood the unspoken meaning. Yes, she should take more care; she had some lovely things, that was true. But they were just things. On impulse she pressed Lesley's arm and said, 'Why don't you come up with us tomorrow and see they don't come to any harm? I can't think how on earth we'll get them all in; the flat's a mousehole compared to this house.'

She could have jammed the words back even as they formed, even as Lesley's face took on a luminous quality of pleasure. Unable to stop herself she went on, 'It would be a change for you, and a huge help to us. Besides, you're the only one of our friends Spencer doesn't hate to have about.'

'I should have been a flagellant,' she told herself coldly, as she held the door open with an anticipatory smile. Spencer was standing by the window, dwarfed by and trying to disregard the beech branches, talking to Jory in his usual easy and charming manner. For a moment she hated his sense of occasion: indeed, although he was unaware of it, the occasion had this time passed him by and left him a blind outsider. He did not like Jory at all, she could see that. As Lesley went straight up to him, no doubt to tell him of his wife's invitation, Nika, aware of her own bad manners, quietly poured herself a long glass of sherry and left the room without a word.

She stood in the stone-floored passage with relief, and shut her eyes. As she relaxed, she became gradually aware of a disembodied tension, nothing at all to do with the complications she had just created by her hateful, rash invitation. The house itself seemed to be giving out shudders of protest, as if too many pieces of heavy furniture, beds, sideboards, chests, had been pushed over its sagging oak floors, its enduring tiles, for too many years. Sighing and whimpering in its sleep, as restless as the small boy upstairs who beat with the same pulse, the house creaked and stirred. It was no new thing, this curious silent pull, only the troubled tension was unfamiliar. She knew the current moved, as insistent and unremarked as an undertone, past many shut doors, up the perfect curve of the moonbleached stairs, along dark passages, and up that final flight of all, into the five hollow attics. Up there was the extreme dryness of old age, the smell of stale lavender and wrinkled apples, of life in retreat: silence and dust. Cobwebbed moonlight, pale and furtive and insubstantial, poured thinly into four of the attics. And at that moment Lewis, who knew these attics better than his parents, walked alone in the fifth, the sealed-off one, in a dream. He was afraid and joyfully hugging his fear, for it was innocent. Behind the wall the unknown room: the walls melted, there hung a skeleton, his own. There he was, forever immured. In a dream-shout he cried, 'I'm here! It's me, in the hidden attic!' But the searchers passed by, walking stealthily outside the walls, up and down, hollowly, acting out the dream of the house. The white moonlight on his face roused him, he started up in bed wide awake, but it was a dream he was never to forget, a dream that took his heart away and hid it in the attic high above the fields and rooms and grown-ups and kept it safely sealed, mummified like the bats, until the time was right for him to come and claim it back.

Downstairs his mother shivered. Some fibre of her own being

99

had been touched as Lewis sweated out his dream. Now she moved along the dark corridor to the children's playroom, and was astonished at the whiteness and strength of the summer night flooding in as she opened the door. The curtains had been taken down and the windows had a bare and shabby look. So had the abandoned toys and tattered books that lay about the floor, cruelly illuminated. Dolls all but torn to pieces lay in a broken wheelbarrow. For the last time Nika knew what it was like to leave this house, and the agony cut so deep that she bent double as if seized with a stitch. She gulped her sherry and reached blindly up on the shelves above the fireplace for matches. For a moment she stopped to drain the glass and was immediately light-headed, for she had eaten nothing all day. She set fire to the mess of papers and cardboard that lay in the grate; then, as if to kill the pain she felt by adding to it, she took up armfuls of books and threw them on, with legless rag dolls, cut-outs she had laboured over on rainy afternoons with her son – the beginnings of a puppet theatre, made out of cereal packets – dolls' furniture conjured from acorns and conkers, with pin legs and woven wool backs to the tiny wobbly chairs. Violence matched the violence done earlier to these small toys; she was possessed by the need to tear and rend; the strange unease of the house seemed to gather intensity, as if this was what it demanded. To her the fire became terrifying, became the destructiveness of Inquisition, and further back into time than that – a great sacrificial consuming. Consume, consummatum est. A doll's face met her tipsy gaze, one she had stitched and painted herself; it writhed free of the flames, blue eyes starting, curls charring before it collapsed into the yellow triumphant roar.

Nika gave a shout of pain. Unlike her son's dream-shout, it was heard. Lying awake after his startling dream, heart pounding, Lewis heard it, but it came to him like a physical pain, a summons to action rather than a sound. He flung back the sheet and quietly left the room, treating the moonlit patches of floor like puddles, either tiptoeing through or carefully skirting them. Unerringly he turned down the corridor at the bottom of the stairs, led by the crackle of paper and the acrid smell of smoke. For a moment he stood amazed in the doorway of the playroom, his great dark eyes seeing his mother wildly poking the fire with the broken handle of his green wheelbarrow.

'You children break and destroy everything you're given! I can't take all this rubbish with us –'

Her guilty, angry words belied her expression. The boy thought he had never seen anything in the world so sad as his mother's face then. It was too sad even to make him cry. Then something exploded inside the doll writhing in the flames. Some small unexpected burst of air eddied round the stuffing and he cried out in a voice that echoed all loss, all fear, 'Where's Mr Pog?'

At this, Nika at once came to herself. She knelt down and clasped her arms around his waist. In her ordinary, gentle voice she said, 'He's upstairs, of course. Isn't he in bed with you?'

'No! He was too hot, he said he'd sleep on the floor. I forgot him. I thought –'

'Darling! I would never, never come into your room and take anything of yours! And, anyway, Mr Pog is one of the family.' She bunched up her hand and rubbed it against his stiff cheek, trying to make him smile, but even speech was difficult for her. To his added horror, for the first time in his life he saw his mother cry. She let the tears roll down her cheeks as she knelt, and then wiped her face on his pyjama jacket. This was horrible: also her breath smelt queer and sharp. She said unsteadily, 'Look, bach, you can see I've only burnt the things you put aside yourself. You said they were broken. Oh, as if I'd come creeping in and –'

'You've left a bit of the theatre,' said Lewis coldly, and started to gather up the fragments of scenery and cardboard characters that still littered the floor – Robin Hood, Little John, part of the greenwood tree. Methodically he collected them and threw them on to the fire, watching his mother sharply as he did so. Silently they finished off the pile, and he pounced on a toy trumpet he had won at last year's village fête, blew into it experimentally and tucked it away in his pocket.

'I'll keep this for Sally.'

'Let me take you up to bed,' said Nika at last, and bent to lift him. At once he said, 'You're not coming back in here again, are you? It's all finished now.'

She shook her head, then carried him up the stairs, murmuring words that didn't make sense even to her, in her adult world where words meant not one thing, but several at once.

'You see, one can't stay in the same place all one's life. The time comes to move on and some things have to be left behind -- you go into a new house and somehow new things get added on to you and there's no room for the old ones. You know how a caterpillar sheds its old skin, oh, lots of times . . .' She opened the bedroom door awkwardly, with a push of her elbow, for he was heavy, and she was not in the habit of carrying him. Half-listening, he noted tiredly that she trod right through the moonlit puddles as if she didn't know they were there. She didn't know everything.

As she straightened the wrinkled and kicked-about bedclothes, she breathed comfort gently over him. 'All the same, Lewis, it doesn't stop you remembering.'

Scarcely looking at her, he twisted away and scrabbled under the bed, bringing up his small white bear, with its eyes sewn crookedly. Nika had made it for him long ago; at once he hid it under the clothes, smiled at his mother and was suddenly asleep. As the smile faded a disappointed crossness pouted his lips, as if a doubt he could not communicate had entered his mind. Sighing, she went through into the next room where her fat daughter lay in untroubled oblivion, one podgy, acquisitive hand clutching a mauled rabbit. She was wet. Nika changed her nightdress, spread a fresh undersheet, and powdered her hot little body before laying her down again. She was really too old to wet the bed, but these things would have to be taken care of when they moved, not now. Her tension relaxed as she worked swiftly, dexterously; always, looking at her daughter's full Etruscan mouth, she felt a corresponding surge of gaiety and indulgence. Sally was the happiest of them all. She adjusted the curtains, so that the moon should not harm her with its seeking fingers, and softly left the room.

As she went slowly, heavily downstairs, letting her hand slip along the baluster rail, the moonlight contoured her head with a shining, reddish mist. To Jory, waiting for her in the hall, a full glass in each hand, it looked as if she were crowned with living fire.

'I've been looking for you,' he said. He did not add that his curiosity had already taken him into the empty playroom, with its dying pyre.

For a moment she did not remember who he was; then, her mind still caught up with her children, she saw a link which led her to the name Jory. (Odd for a Welshman, that name.) His mouth was the grown-up version of the baby one in the cot; here in the dim light of the hall, it was tilted up, boldly curved, full of dark sensuality and easy laughter. Soft-moving, small, dark – what did he do? A traveller in something or other, used to the queer things people did? His *forte* – or so Lesley had once told her – was understanding women. No doubt it was the transitoriness of their relationship that made it so successful, for Lesley's cottage was a half-way call for him between Barmouth and Chester. Nika supposed he might have the magic of the medieval pedlar about him, springing up suddenly with gifts and knowing the value of a quick and mysterious disappearance. Here he was now with a gift, and, descending the last stair, she gratefully took the proffered glass.

'They're looking out records. Come on.'

Insinuating a small, deft hand under her elbow he led her across the hall. From the direction of the drawing-room came the beat of a blues and the chatter of drums. It was impossible to dance to it, but Jory took the opportunity of sliding his arm round her waist and fitting some eccentric steps of his own. He caught up a small lamp and holding it high above his head, his glass in the other hand, he somehow manœuvred Nika across the floor. Laughing a little, she opened the door for him and they swept through to the smell of flowers.

Lesley was lying full length on the rug in front of the empty fireplace sorting records, Spencer beside her, crouching, his hand on her nape, and they were silent. To Nika's raw apprehension they seemed enclosed in a private cocoon of effortless intimacy. Lesley looked up.

'Heavens, what a ritual couple you are, with that lamp and the votive glass. Jory, must you play at being the light of the world? Do put it down and give me some Dubonnet, well-laced, please.'

Spencer said nothing, scarcely glancing at his wife. He seemed absolutely locked away, methodically dusting and setting aside records. Then he uncoiled himself and went to the old portable gramophone, wound it and put on another blues. 'Early Ellington,' he said briefly and went back to crouch on the rug beside Lesley. Her dark eyes drank him in as greedily as her mouth took the Dubonnet. Almost at once, a deep negro voice breathed out:

> 'Saddest tale that ever was told
> On land and sea
> Was the tale they told
> When they told the truth on me.'

At once the deep pained cry of the saxophone took over and a marvellously melancholy keening filled the room. It was as if some distilled, cynical sorrow had been exactly translated into music. Nika tilted her glass and let a few drops of wine fall to the floor. Jory caught her eye and clasped her again, surely, and without permission. They moved round the room in the same nerveless embrace. Over his shoulder Nika saw Spencer just as close to Lesley, although they had made no perceptible move towards each other, enmeshed in their own listening silence. She knew they were caught, all four of them, caught and held tranced in some ritual demanded of them before they could abandon the house for ever.

Jory manœuvred her through the door and again they danced in the hall. Their footsteps made little noise, only a quiet shuffling, and when the record died with the repeated melancholy fall of words, they still moved in the same compulsive fashion. An old waltz followed and their feet automatically conformed to the new rhythm; Jory's mouth moved, soft as a moth, on to hers, and in a kiss that was not a kiss but a completion of this purely trance-like fusing, they swung round and round as one person. It was as if at last the moving currents Nika had sensed had swept into them, for together they moved in and out of rooms dumb with moonlight, frozen in disorder. From time to time the music stopped and then started again, with sometimes a violin, sometimes a saxophone, sometimes a voice to act as the leading thread through the maze in which they found themselves. Their steps quickened or slowed, as, like swans in a death dance, they whirled compulsively on.

At last, exhausted, they reached the stairs again, and collapsed separately, softly, on to the third one up, where the wide curve began and the wall supported their backs comfortably. The music stopped and Jory lit two cigarettes, handed one to Nika. He felt altogether unlike himself, and yet this did not make him uneasy. There was no sexual challenge in the young woman who fitted so flexibly into the corner of the stairs beside him. He felt curious about her, anxious for her well-being.

'Have you been happy here? Lesley's talked a lot about you both; odd she never thought to bring me over before.'

Nika laughed lazily. She still felt light-headed, floating.

'I expect she told you Spencer and I were slowly devouring one another, like a snake its tail. She thinks the country is too big for us – and she's right, of course. It demands the sort of discipline we're not able to accept. At least, Spencer isn't, and he's come to the end of struggling against it.'

'I asked whether you'd been happy,' Jory reminded her. 'But you make it sound as if not. Funny, I don't associate you with a failure of that sort. I should have thought, whatever else you may not be able to do –' he was remembering Lesley's impatient dismissal of Nika as a housewife '– you'd have made a success of living.'

'That's nice of you.' Nika pressed his hand briefly, and asked him to bring over an ugly vase that stood with several brass candlesticks on a small table near the stairs. 'We'll use this as an ash-tray, I don't want to start a fire.' They were talking in whispers, as if listeners were near, and she repeated his words as if they must be exactly defined. 'Happiness. It's a curious word, isn't it? I've always wondered exactly what it means. I know that I've had an extraordinary sense of being fully alive here, but in another world almost. Like airmen who fly right above the clouds and exist in that timeless bright space with all normal contacts suspended. God-like. Elated. Free. Divers get it when they go down too deep . . . what's it called?'

'L'ivresse des grandes profondeurs. It's nitrogen poisoning really. A kind of drunken ecstasy with no hangover.'

'But a kind of concentrated happiness, surely!' After a pause she went on thoughtfully, 'Lewis – our son – he's been happy. Oh, too much so! Nothing will ever come up to it again for him – he's more the child of this house than our child. He flows with it. It's watched and listened and shared with him, even more than it has us. What's that?'

'Only a fox barking. Quite near too. What beautiful hair you have.'

She stared solemnly at him, pushing her hand up and through the flung silky mass, pulling it around her face like a small animal hunching itself into its furry shoulders. It occurred to Jory that she was more aware of her hair than any other woman he had met. Was it because it was the only arresting thing about her – her one claim to an unusual beauty? The extreme loveliness of it, the colour, quantity and texture denied her any other pretensions. It threw into sharp relief the earnest set of her pale features and when she scraped it back, as she did now, he saw with appreciation one other perfection, the long sweep of her jaw-line which ended under a delicately set ear. It seemed an act of homage to bend his lips to it. But she drew away automatically, as if nothing could be allowed to interrupt her introspective questioning. He half-listened to her soft voice, and through it heard the muted music from behind the closed door of the drawing-room, the creaking of old wood, and once more the sharp yelp of a fox. It was very near, something must have frightened it. The full tide of moonlight poured down the stairs from a window set somewhere high above them, but still they were deep in shadow.

'We've been living someone else's dream for eight years,' she was saying, and Jory understood this dream. He had the sudden feeling that he too was caught up, possessed, as if something was whispering, 'You are mine and if you remember nothing else you will remember this night – but for no reason of your own, no conquest.' This was a night that had no beginning – he could scarcely remember driving here – and no end. The dawn would never come. Uneasily he half-remembered the words on the sundial, tried to quote them to her, but could only bring out, raggedly, ' "Haste, Traveller, the sun is low" . . .'

Nika whispered, bending sideways to him, ' "He shall return, but never thou". So you found it then, how odd. It's such an unequivocal statement. *Never thou*. And yet in an odd way we'll always be here, like the others before us. The next people who come will have us listening and watching and sharing . . .' She stirred and said sharply, 'Jory, I'm afraid.'

'What of?'

She made a helpless gesture with her hands, then with an effort said, 'There's something else to be done.'

Remembering the votive flowers, the leaping fire in the play-room, the spilling of the wine, he said out of his own dark Welsh past, 'But what?'

'I don't know. There was a day last summer, you see. From early dawn it was like today. The sun poured down and we took our lunch up on the hill above the house. It was so drowsy and hot – somehow expectant. The boy thought he'd see fairies, that kind of a day. All the normal sounds drifted up to us, lovely un-urgent country noises, harvesting, milking, and a sort of ex-hausted bird-song, but no birds in sight. And all the time there was the house below, drinking in the heat after that awful winter. From where we sat we could see the windows flashing out messages, warning us not to be away too long –'

Jory stirred with a soft grunt of indulgent laughter.

'Very fanciful.'

'Yes, I suppose so. But in the evening the awful thing happened. We went down the hill rather groggily, a bit drunk with the sun, and old Mr Williams met us and said that young Gwyllim was dead. He was the youngest son of the farmer who rents the land from us. He'd been working in the heat and then drank some ice-cold water from the pump round by the stables and dropped down dead.'

'I thought that was an old wives' tale.'

'It is, and they're right. He was lying in the straw in the barn. He was only fifteen.'

'But that could happen anywhere, at any time. I don't see . . .'

'No,' said Nika in a tired, idle voice. 'Why should you? It's just that the place is full of hidden violence. All those old Border battles, treachery and murder. The land's steeped in it. Summer visitors come and say how marvellous it is, but they don't know that in the worst winters farmers shoot their stock rather than watch them starve, and inconvenient new-born babies are still smothered in outside privies and old women up in the hills are worn out with work and go in deadly fear of their husbands . . .'

'For God's sake! You speak as if there were a special curse on this valley! You forget that I'm Welsh too. These things happen all over the place.' Violently he said, 'The trouble with you is that you're beginning to act up to the Romantic Celt label stuck on us by the English.'

Nika stretched her arms out wide. 'Oh, I'm tired out, but let's dance again. Never mind, Jory, it doesn't concern us any more. But that is what Spencer is really running away from – and do you know, I can't blame him.' At this discovery she was silent. Then she chuckled and said, 'London will soon knock the celt off the gingerbread.'

Jory stood up and pulled her to her feet. Restively, to hide a sense of disturbance, he said, 'They're very quiet in there.'

'Aren't they? But do you mind? I don't. They're lost, like us, but they don't know why. Let them have their lovely emotional last evening. Lesley will tell Spencer that she couldn't bear to come with us to London, it wouldn't be fair to me, and Spencer will give her a pile of records they've been playing all the evening, especially that one that goes, *Saddest tale on land and sea, dum, dum, dum, the truth on me.* What is the truth on Lesley, I wonder, and does it really matter?'

Nika threw back her head and laughed with such fierce gaiety that Jory dropped his arms and stood, hypnotized. At that moment the rusty jangling of the doorbell cut through some New Orleans jazz that had started up, and before they could move Spencer opened the drawing-room door and stood there, looking at them. He was flushed, like a child startled from sleep. Nika went across the hall and threw open the front door as if to welcome the disaster she feared.

The old man who stood there was very tall, his shadow cut sharp as a knife across the floor. Although they were blinded by the moon which now stood directly above the house, they could sense the exaltation on his face. Like a prophet he held up his right hand, and from it dangled the body of a young vixen. Blood dripped from its delicate snout on to the patterned stones of the storm porch. It was obvious that life had only recently been battered out of it.

'The missus said I was to come and show her to you right away,' he said. 'It's late, but we could hear you was still up. It's this fox that's been bothering us –'

'Yes, a long time,' murmured Nika. 'But, oh, Mr Williams, she's beautiful! What a shame. How did you catch her?'

'In my trap by the hen run. She's that cunning. I wonder you didn't hear her yelpin' and cryin'. Caught by the fore-leg she was and I nearly let her stay there, but I thought she'd gnaw herself free by morning. I had to belt her over the head.' He looked at the crushed skull fondly. 'Proper little madam, an't she?'

'What about her mate?'

'Gittins got him last week. We're well rid of 'em. Aye, the Lord's good, as our Dai says. "Take us the little foxes," he says to me. "It's the Lord's word." ' He threw back his head in soundless and toothless laughter.

Spencer was staring at him with disgust.

'I'd offer you a drink on it, Mr Williams, if I didn't know you spurned the fruit of the vineyard for whose sake you destroy the little foxes.'

Surprised and abashed by the English heathen's familiarity with the scriptures, Mr Williams opened his mouth and shut it silently. Nika came to his rescue.

'Well, tell your wife I understand, and we're both very pleased. Do believe that. We'll see you in the morning before we go.'

Mr Williams looked at the sky. 'Dawn won't be long, missus. I'll to my bed, then. The missus don't give me no peace till I brought this to you. Turr'ble excited, she was, indeed. No harm, we heard you round the back.' He gave Spencer an indignant, unsure nod. 'Good-night then, both,' he said, and went off, cradling the dead vixen like a child over his arm. As the moonlight caught the reddish-silver sheen of its body, Jory noticed the same glints in Nika's hair. Above them, wakened by the noise, a child's face peered from an upper window. Lewis saw the dead fox and gave a loud cry.

'I'll go up,' said Spencer. 'For God's sake make us some coffee, Nika. And can't we run to sandwiches or something? I'm starving.'

He ran upstairs two at a time, and into Lewis's bedroom.

'Dai said his da would catch the fox,' said Lewis as his father came into the room. 'Was it the vixen?'

'Yes, it was.' Spencer sat on his son's bed and for want of something to do punched the pillow into shape.

'But I saw her with her cubs yesterday, up in the hills. What will happen to them?'

'If they're old enough, they'll live, son. If not, they'll die. How old do you think they were?'

Lewis suddenly rolled his head from side to side as tears spurted down his cheeks and were shaken into his ears.

'Too little, they're too little!' he sobbed out.

Spencer reached out and held him to his side. 'Take us the little foxes,' he thought savagely. Life in the country was all destruction, death in the country was truer. He longed for morning to come. A last dawn in this cursedly lovely house which had brought him no happiness, this hated valley which spurned him and which he could never understand. Within hours the great furniture van would lumber slowly up, and by this time tomorrow they would all be in the anonymity of London. Life in the centre of the machine, the only safe place to be. The shouting hoardings, the acrid smoke of Paddington station. Busy streets and people who spoke his own language. No time to think, except among accepted grooves and among men and women worn smooth by friction against each other, not hard and knobbly, full of cruelty and conscience and Old Testament damnation. He longed for Stefan's pure drive and sureness, Rumpelow's smiling confidence and serenity.

The boy lay quiet against him. For the first time he recognized the truth in his father's uncomfortable answers. He dared one more question.

'Shall we ever come back?'

'You might,' said Spencer. 'Yes, I think perhaps you will, Lewis. But not me. Ever.'

Downstairs the ashes grew cold in the playroom grate. The moon began to fade and an uneasy dawn wind blew through the kitchen window where the two women stood silently making sandwiches. Jory watched the coffee. The night's mood had broken, and with the first light the tension dispersed. Jory said, as Nika brushed past him, '*Heddwch?*' and she nodded. Yes, at last it was peace.

There was nothing left to say, nothing more to feel, and when, much later, the four of them hovered before the open door, saying good-bye, after packing piles of records and books into the back of the car, the same uneasy reserve that had marked the unexpected arrival now put its seal on the departure. At last the car drew out of the garden for the last time, its noise wavering back over the fields, and Nika and Spencer went up to bed.

Separately, silently, they undressed, washed, lay beneath the light covers, and Nika felt ,just before she drifted into sleep,

111

that if she were to go downstairs again she would hear the gramophone playing and see two shadowy figures revolving, dancing, now absorbed forever into the living tissue of the house. This then was her gift to it. What kind of people would come after them, she wondered.

'Spencer,' she called softly into the grey light, 'London will be all right for us?'

He sighed, groped for her hand. 'London will be splendid,' he said.

# Part Two

IT WAS the newest New Year Penelope had ever entered. Soon after Christmas, on returning from a visit to Sybil Matthews, she found she had become a grandmother. This hard, unavoidable physical and emotional fact affected her in various ways. She at once felt twenty years older, and yet, seeing her daughter sitting up in bed, feeding the baby with immense concentration, she was able to reach back through grandmotherhood to motherhood itself.

'Is Dick pleased to have a boy?' she asked.

'He didn't mind which it was.' Sue touched her son's small downy head. 'We're going to have four anyway. They're bound to be a mixed bunch.' Her voice was full of simple pride and certainty, as if she and Dick had a firm hold on their future, and could regulate the flow of life at will. Penelope could not help feeling a prick of irritation. She felt intuitively that with each new child Sue would be putting her own unsatisfactory childhood one more step behind her. There seemed to Penelope to be the tiniest air of reproach in everything her daughter said; this of course may have been her own guilty imagination, but she had become wary. Sue's outburst of the previous summer still lay between them, its emotional impact thinned by time.

'Have you found someone to help you?' she asked. 'Don't you think a girl living in would be a good idea? A baby takes up a lot of time.' Almost idly she reached out for the book Sue had been reading. It was by Dr Spock. She smiled and flicked over the pages. 'How I wish he had been able to help me when you children were born,' she said. 'How sensible he is! But did you see that article last Sunday about displaced fathers? I do hope, Sue, you won't let Dick feel left out.'

Sue took the book away from her mother, as if to relieve a child of a dangerous toy.

'I'm looking after the baby myself, Mother. I'll have a woman in to take care of the house. As for Dick – well, he's an adult, isn't he? He's properly adjusted to life by now, or he ought to be. This child has only me to look to. I am all he knows.'

Later, travelling back to her mews flat, Penelope could not dismiss the picture of her daughter sitting up there in bed, in that aseptic ward, looking so young, jealously holding her child to her. It seemed so long since she had done the same thing, and yet, then, all her joy in her first child had been centred in showing him to Jamie. She had not planned any of her children; the thought of such a thing was repellent to her. They had arrived, inconveniently sometimes, and she had coped with them. She supposed – although it did not appear to apply to her – that people were right when they said that children fulfilled a deep biological need, provided a double affirmation of identity. It had been enough for her and Jamie to make love, which they did frequently, passionately and with impulsive enjoyment.

She got off the bus at Victoria and walked the few streets that led to the mews. It was odd, walking here, knowing that she was on her way home. Odd to put a key in the door beside the black-and-white garage, enter the narrow hallway to mount the straight stairs to the three rooms at the top. When she had first moved in she felt as if she were playing some childhood game, buying new furniture, fitting it in as if preparing a doll's house for someone else. Getting it ready the previous winter had taken the edge off her self-absorption; it had been – almost – fun to choose a modern studio couch for the sitting-room, new chairs, match up materials for curtains and carpets, re-furnish her bedroom. What had been difficult was when it was finished and the light-coloured cupboards and tables and chairs stood about instead of her heavy inherited pieces. Now she must start to live with them. Living alone, she had discovered, created a new set of tensions. Every action and reaction had to flow from her, like a current travelling out along a piece of wire and back again. There was no circuit. Nothing happened unless she set it in motion. There was no one to say, 'Let's have some coffee, I'll make it.' Or, 'Shall we listen to *Firebird*?' If she wanted coffee she made it herself, if she wanted to hear *Firebird* she had to look it out and put it on the record player. Then she had to listen to it alone, and know that, when it finished, it would stay on the turntable until she took it off. Life alone was a series of exhausting decisions, necessary efforts to create a pattern in which she could exist.

Pye, having lived alone for a good many years, had come to terms with this; he knew all about it, and by self-discipline had rid himself of this particular tension, as well as many others. He had anticipated Penelope's difficulty when the flat was finished, and for Christmas had given her a small Siamese kitten. As she opened the door now, she heard the high-pitched call of welcome as Mishti-San ran down the stairs to her, tail erect, sapphire eyes gleaming with pleasure and reproach. As she bent down to stroke the little cat, it gathered its body together and leapt on to her shoulder, biting her ear gently and purring.

Upstairs, as soon as her coat was off, she went into the kitchen and began to cut up rabbit for the kitten, which stood by her side now, nipping her ankles in anticipatory greed. The kettle on for tea, Penelope watched the creamy body and crouched head with a certain tender pleasure. Having the cat to look after curtailed her freedom and she was glad of this. The sound of Mishti-San's cry in the early morning, waiting to be let out – for it hated to use the sandbox in the kitchen – had several times lifted Penelope out of one of her threatened, nameless depressions, black and vengeful, which drove her about the bleak countryside of the mind where all was loneliness, unkindness and loss.

Now she lighted a fire, and settled by it to read *Nightmare Abbey* again while she drank her tea. As the evening darkened she rose to draw the curtains and noted with pleasure the soft light from the lamp outside. Later in the year it would shine through the leaves of the lime tree that grew up near-by through a crack in the cobbles. It was the only tree in the mews, and Pye had commented on her luck in having it there. At the time she had scarcely noticed it, and now it reminded her that he would be calling in later on. With her daughter still on the edge of her mind, she wondered why she had never mentioned him to Sue or, for that reason, to any of her old friends. Of course, Nika and Spencer accepted him. But like this new flat, the new furniture, he was part of a life she was slowly building up around herself, a life somehow tinged with guilt, for it excluded Jamie, and it excluded also part of her old self.

Feeling guilty was not new to Penelope, although living with Jamie had to a great degree blunted its probe. It had its roots, she supposed, in an awareness of inadequacy, and Sue's attitude had reawakened it in force, and today, although she tried to suppress it, she found herself guilty about her children. Roger, her son, had gone out to Kenya in his teens, and seemed happy enough farming; he did not write many letters to her. Jane was in America, just married to a painter. Of all the children, Jane was most like Jamie; thin, eager and quite relentless. Would they have scattered so much if they had been happy at home? She was still brooding over this when she heard Pye's three sharp rings on the bell.

He came in with the damp chill of evening blowing behind him, a bottle under his arm.

'Oh dear,' she exclaimed in a flurry, 'we'll have to have omelettes, do you mind? I haven't started to cook yet.'

He looked at her intently, noting her nervousness, her distraction, with a sudden spurting irritation.

'I don't in the least mind,' he said, putting the bottle on the sideboard. 'What I do mind, though, is your hangdog welcome. No one is coming up the stairs with a whip and a bell.'

This intuitive remark confused her. She smiled quickly and said, 'I'm sorry, Pye. Do take off your coat and come to the fire.'

As he did both the things she bade him, his annoyance faded.

Her ready compliance was that of a good child, justly scolded. 'Now you can offer me a glass of sherry and relax,' he said. 'We can eat later. What's the matter?' He held out a hand to the little cat, who at once ran to him and patted it with her paws, standing up on her hind legs as she did so. He played with her as he went on, 'Let me guess. You've been to see your daughter? How is she? Well, of course. Delighted with her baby, which she intends to bring up in accordance with the latest theories. Right?' He set the purring kitten on the floor again.

'You're impossible,' said Penelope. 'Thank you so much for the sherry. Will you open it?' Against her will she was smiling.

'Here's to doom and retribution,' said Pye, pouring a glass and handing it to her. 'Can't you learn to like yourself just a little?'

She thought about this, then shook her head. As she looked across at Pye he suddenly ceased to be the very symbol of her unearned, unwanted and undeserved so-called freedom. Mishti-San now jumped on to his lap and settled into the warm arc of his thighs, kneading gently with her paws. A loud, extroverted purr vibrated through the room as she settled, like a sea-washed pebble, staring at Penelope with half-shut eyes.

'Shall you breed from her?' asked Pye, stroking the creamy back with firm, gentle hand.

'It's so extraordinary to be a grandmother,' said Penelope, as if in some way this question were related. 'I? No, I shan't breed from her. I did breed them once, you know, but that was in the country. It would be impossible in a flat. Have you ever heard a Siamese queen calling? It's an unearthly noise, no, that's quite wrong – it's *too* earthy. It's absolutely primeval, persistent as nature, the first female thing howling for the male to complete it.'

Pye smiled. Her words told him a great deal more than she supposed. Her attitude to sex, for one thing, which he had already guessed to be idealistic, fastidious, and yet passionate. For another, her honesty, which was one of the things that had held him after his initial attraction to her. People who took trouble to choose words with precision were likely to be correspondingly discriminating in personal relationships. This special kind of emotional honesty was rare in a woman; before meeting Penelope, he had been convinced that it had no part in the feminine make-up.

As she went into the kitchen to prepare a meal, he sat on in front of the fire, nursing the cat. Women he had always attracted easily, simply because he had the trick of appearing to be utterly absorbed by them – which indeed he was. He regarded them with an intensely subjective interest, and the idea of starting up his launderettes and coffee-bars might well have been the unconscious outcome of this absorption. He listened avidly to their heated, emotional interchanges on the tops of buses and in front of the machines in his launderettes, and loved them for the drama and intrigue they dredged from lives which, outside their own family circles, would appear to be dreary in the extreme. Women were the core of life, men existed merely on their bounty. His personal relationship with them had, however, been less fortunate; one marriage had ended in disaster, and this had been followed by a series of uneasy and unsatisfactory affairs which would have reduced him to cynicism had his warm, outflowing nature allowed it. Over the last few years, if he desired a woman, he had preferred to buy her rather than pay exhausting court to the tenuous and boring personality that so often lay behind a fascinating face and body. The innocent vanity of these women touched him, for he respected all vulnerability. It had therefore been a relief to enter the cool, civilized atmosphere that surrounded Penelope. Her marriage seemed to him an enviable thing, although he doubted its perfection.

As he sat there he realized that she was not trying to carry on a shouted conversation between the two rooms; she did not attempt to overwhelm him with her femininity: she let him rest. For this he was infinitely grateful, for friendship of this undemanding kind was something new to him. He wondered sometimes how she regarded him. As a source of comfort? A filler-in for her dead husband? But whenever he found himself analyzing their relationship thus far, he always checked his thoughts sharply.

A coal fell from the fire and he bent to retrieve it, holding the little cat closer as he did so. At once a buried childhood memory surfaced abruptly, as the smell of onions and mushrooms drifted to him from the kitchen. Cat. Fire. But it was a very fat, barrel-shaped tortoiseshell cat he saw, at ease on a multi-coloured rug of some kind, the sort made from scraps of odd materials, old lisle stockings and cut-up underclothes. And the fire was different, too, a grate, a black one, with an oven by the side and a kettle swinging on a hook. His aunt's kitchen, with the long flabby green sawdust-filled sausage that lay along the bottom of the back door to keep out the fine sea-mist. Now why should that picture suddenly obtrude in this clean modern room, himself sunk in an expensive crimson armchair and a very different woman cooking for him?

'It's raining,' said Penelope, coming quietly in. 'Everything's ready. Do come.'

So that was it. The fugitive rain he had heard on the window, the coal from the fire, the sense of security. Do come.

As they ate in the room that was half kitchen, half dining-room, Pye asked, 'Why is it extraordinary to be a grandmother? How does it feel?' He was adept now at picking up her thrown-away remarks. Also, because he lived vicariously, he was curious about this state from which he, as a man, was barred.

She considered. 'I feel – well, put in my place. Tidied up. Perhaps I should start to knit or something. Pull out wise saws. It makes me think of old age.'

'You've a great deal to do before you can take refuge in that bolt-hole. Life isn't a series of attitudes.'

'Who's pulling out wise saws now?'

'All right, I am. This is a delicious omelette. You're an excellent cook. But then, so am I.'

She rose from the table to make coffee, and put fruit salad and cream in front of him. She said, with her back turned, 'I don't fear old age. I suppose you're right, it is a kind of bolt-hole; back to the simplicity of childhood and all that; an abdication of rights.'

He interrupted with mild astonishment:

'Abdication! My grandmother didn't think like that. She was an old tartar. She ran a small fleet of fishing boats, and had hands like snarled-up rope.'

Before she could stop herself this absurdity, Penelope said, 'And blue eyes like yours.'

He nodded. 'Yes, I do take after her. She hated to be beaten.'

'Tell me about her.'

She set coffee on the table between them, poured it out, then settled her elbows comfortably and bent her head to listen.

'She had to bring up my father single-handed. Her husband was lost at sea when he was a young man. It's a very ordinary story, really. She had to make a living for her children and she did. She was as tough as an old boot, and oddly enough, to me she was always the same age. Or rather ageless. Big and grey-haired and striding about in men's sea-boots, cursing.' He looked at Penelope with amusement. 'Do you see yourself as that kind of grandmother?'

'No, I was opting for lavender and antimacassars. But you've destroyed the illusion.'

He offered her a cigarette, took one, lighted them both. Mishti-San patted his knee, but for once he took no notice.

'She didn't see herself as anything, Penelope. She just was. That's what you've got to be. Yourself. Not as a woman in middle age, or old age or anything else. Just a woman. Letting go of one life and making another.' As he spoke he privately wondered whether women ever learned to let go of anything or anyone.

Penelope bent down and lifted the kitten on to her lap.

'It's easy to say. If I were a religious woman . . . or if I had a fishing boat . . .' She smiled and shrugged. 'Youth's all right. Old age is all right! It's the years in between that can go so wrong. Don't you find that middle age is like adolescence? One is unreasonably depressed, elated, too emotional or not enough so, restless . . .' She sighed. 'No, you're not like that.'

'No, I'm not. But as you know, I hate waste. And it's wasteful to think like that. It's like letting a lettuce run to seed.'

She gave a short laugh.

'Have you tasted one? It's very bitter.'

'Exactly. No, your trouble is that you've been over-protected, so that now you're too vulnerable; a skin short. May I talk of your marriage?'

He noticed her defensive withdrawal, but she nodded.

'Well, do you know the habits of the great pied hornbill? It walls up its mate during the incubation period, and feeds her through a hole. Then, when the young are hatched, he chips away at the dried mud and lets her out –'

'Oh,' said Penelope, like a child. 'But suppose –'

'Yes, suppose he was killed. What would the mother do then, poor thing? I hope she'd fight like hell to get out of that damned cell.'

Penelope got up, spilling the kitten off her lap. It sat and washed its hindquarters indignantly as she went across into the other room. From between the door-jambs, holding to them, she said, 'Cell! You make me feel like the prisoner of Chillon, pacing round his pillar. Won't you ever accept that Jamie and I had a wonderfully integrated and full life together? If I feel like a cripple without him that's my affair.'

'But you don't! At least, you're beginning not to. And you feel full of guilt because you don't. That's what's been making you ill.' He rose from the table and led her over to the big crimson chair and made her sit down. Then he sank on to the floor cross-legged, pretending not to see her tears. He spoke urgently, knowing that what he intended to say might expel him forever.

'No one should make themselves indispensable to another person, my dear, it's a sign of inadequacy. One must build people up so that they can face themselves and the world alone. After all, we're all naked under our shirts, as Forster once reminded us. Then, again, what about "love, the beloved republic, which feeds on freedom and lives"? Jamie needed you to feed on. You were his freedom and it was all right, because he looked outward anyway. You might have thought that he was yours, but you were wrong. You ran to Jamie as an animal runs to its burrow – as now you'd like to run to old age, to hide. But it won't do, Penelope! You can't negate life. You've got to come out of the burrow and see the world as it is, deal with it on its own terms. I'm here to help, to support, but not to absorb. You've got to grow up.'

As he watched, she turned her head away, took up the kitten from the floor and hugged it.

With a sense of loss he said, 'Shall I go?' And when she nodded he went slowly down the stairs and out of the door into the rain, forgetting his coat. Oblivious to the increasing downpour he walked all the way home, thinking of that upper room over the grey cavern of the garage, the silent woman by the fire, with the kitten held tightly, tightly, up against her neck.

## II

Durinc the next two weeks Penelope did not communicate with Pye at all, nor he with her, although they both sat down on several occasions and wrote letters which they immediately tore up. They each stared at the telephone. Penelope even dialled his number, then put the receiver down as the calling tone echoed in the room she had never visited. It was, after all, for her to write, she knew that. He only wanted an indication. His words could not be forgotten, nor perhaps forgiven: indeed, she went to sleep thinking about them with a sense of outrage, rebutting them with arguments that renewed themselves first thing in the morning as she opened her eyes to the light.

After her first resentment of what she considered to be an indirect criticism of Jamie, as well as of her own attitude, she began to think about their life together as she had never before dared to do. For some odd reason she remembered the fortune-teller and the rage she had felt then at the probing finger put on her privacy, that complete little world that had excluded everyone else. Yet she was forced to admit that she had not been the whole of Jamie's world; apart from what he gave his friends, he had put a great deal of himself into his pictures, yet these had always seemed an extension of their own relationship and she had never resented them. Pye was right: Jamie had looked outward, towards the world, whereas she had looked only towards him. But what else could a non-creative person do?

One evening she took out all his pictures – or rather all she had kept with her, for storage was difficult in this small place – spread them on the floor, propped them up on the chairs and against the walls.

The effect was extraordinary. It was like walking back into the life that had ended on that summer day nearly two years ago: the views of Calais, of Bruges, of Wales, of Ireland; scenes in the Vosges mountains; quick, nervous sketches of the London docks; still-lifes; portraits, especially that one of herself at a window, his favourite, her head half-turned to look over the small harbour – where was it? – somewhere in Sussex. That had been before his abstract period, before people started collecting his work, commissioning murals; before life became easier and money no longer a problem.

She spent a long time looking at them; noting their excellences, their weaknesses, wondering what she had been doing while he painted them. Probably shopping for food, looking after the children, waiting for him. She had spent a long time waiting, she remembered, with a faint smile. Probably that was why she liked the portrait so much: the very poise of the head was listening, waiting, passive.

She sat a long time in the middle of all these canvases. What was she waiting for now? She picked up the portrait and tried it out on various walls; previously she had thought it pretentious to have oneself put up for every casual visitor to see and comment on. Now she felt differently. She went into the combined kitchen-dining-room, which was long and L-shaped, tried the portrait on a wall there and stood on a chair to see the effect. Casual people would not wander in here. In its pale frame it blended at once with the washed yellow walls, it did not obtrude. It could not be seen from the living-room, and the wall she chose faced the window over the mews; in an odd way it, too, let in light and air. After she had hung it she looked at it for a long time; she had been a young woman then, and as she had turned from the window at last to smile at Jamie he had come across and kissed her. Then she had run down to rescue one of the children from an upturned boat on the beach below.

She returned to the living-room and saw Mishti-San sitting on one of the canvases, part of the kaleidoscope of places and people which vibrated around it. Lifting the kitten off gently she went over to the round mirror on the wall and looked deeply into it. Age had touched her face, draining it, deepening the eyes; yet it was still the same – essentially – as that of the expectant young woman in the portrait. Once again Jamie had put on her a benediction of timelessness, so that age had no meaning, no importance, unless it were an added beauty of depth. Wherever he was, if he was anywhere, part of him surely remained with her and in her, whatever she did, wherever she went. But she could no longer be content to see herself through his eyes. That quizzing glass was gone, she was forced now to seek her own identity.

As she collected the canvases, an idea struck her and she went at once to the telephone. Some time ago a young director of an art gallery had asked her whether she would consider a retrospective exhibition of Jamie's work, and she had refused. At that time she had been unable to look at any of his pictures, certainly not go through them, sort them out.

Julius Bergdorf was in. He was delighted she had changed her mind. Early work? He would, he said, come round and see her and they would discuss things. The exhibition could not be until April at the earliest, as works would have to be collected from all over the country. Why didn't he see her more often? She made some rejoinder and rang off, arranging for him to come one afternoon the following week.

Then she put the pictures away, and in a calm frame of mind wrote and posted a short note to Pye.

The following day, at about tea-time, two dozen daffodils and a dozen tulips arrived by messenger. Inside was a card, which said, in Pye's neat, small hand:

'It is the mind that maketh good or ill. The elements of pain and pleasure are everywhere. The degree of happiness that any circumstances or objects confer on us depends on the mental disposition with which we approach them.' I was infinitely grateful for your note. You will know these lines, for you were reading the book the other evening. Let's meet soon.

Pye.

The next afternoon she went to see Nika, who at once exclaimed as she opened the door, 'Penelope, you look wonderful! So much better. What's happened?'

Penelope, somewhat embarrassed, countered by saying, 'Oh, it's one of my good days! How are you?' and thinking how pale Nika looked, as if her heavy weight of rich hair were draining the life from the face below it.

They settled in what had once been Penelope's drawing-room, now become a much lived in living-room, the centre of family life. It had accommodated itself to the change remarkably well, Penelope thought. It seemed smaller, warmer, more domestic. A large, old-fashioned sewing-machine was on a broad oak table by the window, the sofa and chairs were covered with a serviceable, faded chintz, pulled about by small fingers, obviously climbed over by children. Spencer had put up shelves, which were crowded with books and periodicals. One of Jamie's pictures, a large one of Hampstead Heath, full of the grey-green mystery of early morning, was over by the fireplace.

Nika sat down and picked up a pair of Lewis's trousers which she had been mending.

'How am I?' she repeated, poking the fire. 'Well, I exist, that's all. I expect it's this cold weather.' She looked across at Penelope and said, 'One of the compensations of coming to London has been getting to know you better. I feel I can talk to you.'

Penelope was glad. She had become increasingly fond of Nika over the past months, and felt towards her as she might towards a beloved younger sister. They had spent a good deal of time together the previous summer and autumn, each helping the other with the moving out of and into new homes. Nothing brought women closer, she reflected, than these kind of practical activities. So she was able to say now, with concern, 'Then you can tell me what's really the matter.'

Nika said at once, as if she had been awaiting the opportunity, 'I feel exploited.'

The word dropped into silence. It was a strange word, an ugly one, one that Penelope had never connected with marriage, for that was evidently in Nika's mind.

'Unless one measures what one gives, how can exploitation come into it?'

Nika flushed and looked up with hostility. 'You were so lucky in your marriage, Penelope. I wonder if you've ever realized how much. But then you're exceptional. You've never measured emotion, have you? But you might be happier now if you had.'

Penelope stared at her, then dropped her eyes. This was the third time a verdict had been passed on her, she could no longer take it. Sharply she said, 'One doesn't put love, or any other emotion, into a separate banking account – like a pension to draw on in one's old age! If you do, it's like the gold coins in the fairy story, you open your purse and find it full of withered leaves.'

'I'm sorry.' Nika let the trousers fall to the floor from her lap. 'I didn't really intend that as criticism. Perhaps I'm envious. But now Spencer's got us all up here, I feel he doesn't really need me at all. And I was always so strong, at least I thought so. But now I need him, and he simply isn't there.' She looked round the room, frowning. 'Even when he does come home – which isn't often – he's completely withdrawn. He's like a djinn released from a bottle. He's full of a new, sizzling energy, dashing off to Covent Garden early in the morning, sometimes staying there until midnight. He brings manuscripts and proofs home at week-ends and sits at that table without a word, drinking cup after cup of black coffee. Then he has to go all over the country, seeing people. He doesn't seem to know that we exist, the children and me. . . . Oh, the awful thing is, that I *know* I'm being a fool.'

'It's all right. Say it. But now listen to me. Spencer's only doing all this for you. He's got to make a go of it, after all. He's taken a big risk. He's got to make this transplantation successful. Surely you can see that – it's you and the children he's thinking of.'

As she spoke she knew this wasn't so, and Nika knew it too, for she gave a harsh laugh and shook her head.

'The children!' she said. 'What future he sees for them I don't know. I'm sorry to go on like this, Penelope, but if I don't tell someone I'll burst! You didn't realize that we had to find a school for Lewis when we came up. I only had a couple of months to do it – you know how difficult these things are. Naturally I thought some little private school – there'd be lots in London. Then Spencer said we couldn't afford anything like that. It would cost too much. Those offices they've managed to get, they had to pay a lot for them – and of course there are endless expenses to be met until something starts coming in. He said all this and then he had to drag in politics as another excuse. Politics, ethics, as if he cares a tuppenny damn about them! He says that as we're Left we ought to support the government schools and send our children there. You know how he lashes out at all those Labour M.P.s who preach socialism and send their children to public schools. Well, he's taken up this attitude about it and says our children must be guinea pigs. He says that Lewis should get a scholarship to a grammar school when he's eleven. That's in two years' time.'

Penelope did not fully understand. Nika's voice had risen to a pitch of scarcely controlled hysteria. All this talk of schools was beyond her. Her own children had gone to small private schools first, then boarding schools. There had never been any doubt or trouble about it.

'Nika, what kind of school is Lewis at now, then?'

'He's at what you would call in your day the "tin school" or "council school". You wouldn't have dreamed of sending your children there – you scarcely knew they existed, did you?'

Penelope shook her head. She had never thought about it. Like winkles at Southend, day-trips with funny-hats, brawling outside murky public houses, council schools were outside her experience.

Nervously she said, 'Isn't education supposed to be much

better all round now? I mean, opportunities –'

'Listen,' said Nika impatiently, 'I had to go to some Education Authority or other. Spencer hadn't time. There was a dreadful man there with egg on his tie and dandruff on his collar. He sneered at me and said Longhill School was very good, all sorts of people sent their children there. He dared me to say it wasn't good enough for mine by his very look. He said that if the child was bright he could take his eleven-plus and go on to a local grammar school. If he failed, there were new secondary schools being built. He seemed to think I was lucky and talked about opportunities in education. I felt awful, like some pauper out of Dickens. . . .' She sat down, her hands shaking. After a moment she looked at the clock and said with a small cold smile, 'Come and see for yourself, if you'd like to. It will be an education. We'll go and meet him. I'll get Sally ready, she likes a walk before tea.'

Deeply disturbed, Penelope put on her hat and coat and waited while Nika dressed Sally, who had been asleep. Together they carried the pushchair down the stairs and went out into the sharp, grey January afternoon. As they walked towards the church, the greyness seemed to intensify, silently closing about them as if the sky were being lowered. Up a street and along by a low brick wall that bordered a playground set in grass and flower-beds, tombstones along each side. Nika nodded to it and said shortly, 'This is called "the burial", where they play. On fine afternoons Sally likes to go on the swings.'

'Swings, swings,' chanted Sally from her chair, waving her chubby hands in the air.

'Not today, darling, it's too cold.'

Past a vast crater where half a street seemed to be demolished, and earthy pits scattered with bricks and shattered stone masonry lay in humps under the cold sky. At once Sally began to chant again, and Penelope, who was feeling tired, had to ask what she was saying.

Nika repeated the child's words flatly.

'She's telling you that this is "the debris". That's what the children call it. They prefer it to the burial.'

131

'Why on earth the burial? What a strange name. It looked like a playground to me.'

'It's where the victims of the plague were buried, and of course it's part of the church grounds. I don't know when it stopped being a cemetery. I think the children get some relish out of it, anyway. But I have to drag Lewis away from the debris, he loves it.'

As they passed the bomb-site, several big boys rushed down the slope off the pavement and began hurling bricks at random, calling in wild, hoarse voices.

'I suppose they can work off their surplus energy in these places,' said Penelope uncertainly. She wished she hadn't come; the expedition had taken a macabre turn: burial, debris, and wild children darting like rats in a charnel house. Her heart sank still more as they rounded a corner and came up against a very high, blackened wall, over which surged a confused noise like maddened breakers over a promenade in a high wind.

There were two tall, grey arched entrances, and over one was written, in deeply incised, high letters: BOYS. Over the other, a good way along the road, was the inscription: GIRLS AND INFANTS. Nika stopped by the boys' entrance. They stood looking in at the grey asphalt that stretched to the walls of the school, a wide area, unbroken except for red-brick lavatories with brass taps and bowls with metal cups chained to the outside walls. Iron railings protected worn stone steps that led to the school building. Down these steps swarmed boys of all ages and sizes. Women stood near, with shopping bags, and boys ran all around them, like silver fish, making for the lavatories or the brass taps, or merely for the gate, through which they flew like released prisoners. There was fever in the air, fever to get away from stone and brass and asphalt and red brick and from the close smell of one another in stuffy, cold classrooms. So they scattered like sharp-voiced birds at a gunshot.

Lewis came running down the steps, his satchel over his shoulder. He was alone. As he hesitated at the bottom of the steps a red-haired boy collided with him and sent him sprawling. At once a woman shouted, 'Mind there now, Sid, or I'll do fer yer!' She clumped on broken plimsolls across the yard and cuffed the boy. Lewis had seen them and now came over at a shamefaced trot. Scarcely nodding to Penelope, he said in a fierce mutter, 'I told you not to come and meet me, Mam!'

'Say good afternoon to Mrs Hinton, Lewis,' said Nika coldly.

'Afternoon,' Lewis mumbled.

Penelope at once smiled and gave him sixpence. 'Why don't you buy some sweets?' she said, to cover Nika's nervy disapproval.

At once he ran off to join the scrambling, shouting crowd of children round the entrance to a small paper shop, where gobstoppers and liquorice laces and brightly-coloured packets of sherbet were displayed beyond the forest of grubby waving fingers.

'Don't push, skinny!'

'I'm not, don't push me then, old slob face!'

'You owe me a penny, Billy Turton. Give it 'ere or I'll smash yer!'

'Smash 'oo? Like to see yer try.'

'Ow, my toe.'

' 'Ere's Taffy then. Wodjer want, Taff? Stolen any beef lately?'

Lewis, his face scarlet, rejoined them at last. He had bought a bag of toffees and now he unwrapped one, his head bent, and gave it to Sally. The woman with the plimsolls passed them and smiled. Her ginger-haired son stuck his tongue out at Lewis from behind her back.

'What a duck,' she said, poking Sally with one finger. 'You sending 'er to the infants next year? Lewis can bring 'er, can't you, dearie?'

Lewis shook his head. 'She's too young,' he said.

Penelope caught in his voice the beginning of the London whine, which juxtaposed oddly with his Welsh intonation. The flattened vowels disguised his natural lilt and emphasized a certain barbarity of tone.

They walked on. When they were past the burial, Lewis asked in quite a different voice whether he could push Sally, and

Penelope suddenly realized that what she had just heard was the voice he used deliberately at school, for protective colouring. At once she began to understand a little how Nika felt. As he went ahead with the pram, Nika said, exhaustedly, 'You'll think I'm just a snob. I know I shouldn't mind, and that lots of people send their children to schools like these, and that it's the only way to get a full and working democracy in this country . . .'

'You're quoting Spencer.'

'Yes, I know. And theoretically he's right. If I say it often enough I'll begin to believe it. I'm with him when he says he hates the old school tie business and the exclusive brand of man-child the public schools turn out and the horrible class barriers we're stuck with. But that's even worse now than it was before, because it's a new kind of snobbery that's creeping in – a money snobbery. But in practice I can't go through with it. Spencer's all right. He never had to go to a school like this – he's never even been to see this one. I don't like the teachers and they don't like me, although for Lewis's sake I've crawled to them. He's not doing well, because he's out of his depth. The village school was different; there were only a few children, taken at their own pace. Mr Jones always said he was a bright boy, but he isn't here –'

'Nika, what were you going to do with him if you'd stayed on at Glantamar?'

Nika's voice grew warm. 'He was all set to try for a place in a cathedral school. They take them at nine. He had a very real chance of a scholarship there, the vicar said. Lewis has a very true, pure voice.'

'Well?'

'That was all forgotten in the move. Now he'll have to take his chance. Penelope, it's so difficult for a country-bred child, and Spencer just doesn't want to bother, he doesn't *want* to be told that he's thrown him to the lions.' At Penelope's protesting gesture, she went on at once, 'Look, there are over forty children in each class and the tempo and noise upsets him. He doesn't sleep. Then there are the awful parents. I don't mind that old slut who just spoke to us. She's kind enough. Anyway, she's real. What I can't bear are what I call the borderline parents.' She paused to collect her thoughts asnd then continued, 'It's a question of values. And their sense of values is so hideously wrong that I feel I can't go on exposing Lewis to them. Look. He went to tea with a boy once or twice and came home asking why we didn't have a car or a television, or why we didn't go abroad for our holidays. They're all grocers or jam manufacturers and second-hand car dealers . . . all climbing up as fast as they can. Half of them are only using the primary schools to save money for public schools later on, if they've got to pay. When they can see their precious children stuffed into famous blazers they'll sit back and work harder than ever and wait for the right accent to pour out of their babes' mouths and annihilate them. But what the voice says doesn't matter, so long as it's pitched in the right accent. What's inside the head doesn't matter, so long as it's covered by the right cap. God, sometimes I think everyone's going mad!'

To her own horror Nika found she was walking along sobbing. Her tears were hidden by the dusk, which had settled thickly about them, illuminated only by the soft street lamps – safe until next year from the blue gallows-fruit the council had planned. This pain of Nika's was so seldom expressed that relieving it, even through incoherence, was painful.

'So this is what our Leftist ideas of the thirties have led to,' Penelope was thinking, as she paced quietly along at Nika's side. 'All those ideals, all those speeches! Equal opportunity. How short-sighted we were!' Would Jamie have insisted on his children sharing in the 'equal opportunities' of today? How much easier life had been when the classes were distinct, and one class could campaign for another less happily endowed without any fear of participation! This absorption of the so-called privileged classes into the State system was the real revolution. It was like a doorway, jammed with people trying to get out fighting with others determined to get in. Selfishly she was glad to be out of such a battle.

Lewis was waiting for them at the door. He had taken Sally

out of her pram and was sitting on the steps with her, under the lamplight. The two children were singing together, Sally carefully repeating the words as he sang very slowly:

> 'Rownl'n rhodio mynwent Eglwys
> ABC
> Trewais fy nhroed wrth fedd f'anwylyd
> FGI
> Cwympo' i lawr . . .'

Lewis stopped as they came up, and Nika said, 'Oh, that's a sad song, Lewis. Can't you teach Sally something a little more cheerful?'

'She can have a cheerful one in her bath, can't you, Sally? Anyway, she doesn't know what it means. Do you, old pumpkin-pie?'

'What does it mean?' asked Penelope. She had been moved by his voice as much as by the unknown words spiralling clearly up out of the uncertain evening.

'Oh, it's a nonsense rhyme,' said Nika, putting her key in the door.

'It means, walking to church, ABC, with feet among the graves, FGI. And weeping, falling down with weeping, LMNOPQ, and so on. We often sing it. It's a very nice jolly song, I think. I'll play it for you after tea.' Lewis said all this with a certain challenge in his voice, and Penelope looked at him in astonishment, blaming herself for not having taken as much interest in him as she should. She saw now that he was certainly thinner. He had none of the well-fed confidence she associated with the average schoolboy. He seemed to have lost his engaging frankness of manner, which had struck her when she first met him. Instead, there was this challenge, a sharp wariness about his eyes as if he were on the look-out for a surprise attack. His expression had opened out as he told her the meaning of the lullaby, but soon closed in again defensively, as if to protect the song from her.

As Penelope helped Nika up the stairs with the pram, Lewis

carefully led his sister up, saying something to her in a low whisper which made her laugh. She suddenly shared Nika's fear. Suppose he didn't get a scholarship – even if he did – how could he endure two more years on that asphalt island? What of the feverish pace, the cramming, the one-sided emphasis on 'brains'? Was all this going to help him develop into a balanced and happy human being? She thought of Sue's child, her own grandson, but could feel no active anxiety for him. Sue would have it all worked out somehow. But who could help Nika over this problem? There was only one person who might influence Spencer, and that was Pye Rumpelow. At once she felt lighter in spirit; it would also give her an excuse to telephone him.

## 12

SPENCER WAS not too pleased when the telephone rang at the office some days later. He and Stefan were deeply involved in lists of figures, costing several sheet deals for American books, and quibbling in a tired way – for they had been working since early morning – over how much they should allow for publicity.

'We can't advertise, it does no good anyway,' Stefan was saying, as the bell shrilled through the half-empty offices. 'Advertisements don't sell books, so don't think they do, Spencer. Damn. Who's that, I wonder?'

'Hullo, Corunna Press,' said Spencer, trying to keep the irritation out of his voice. Stefan infuriated him over these issues. He had been trying to prove for the last half-hour that small, cleverly placed advertisements for technical books would bring in a good many orders. It was a matter of missing the nationals and trying the small specialist trade magazines. 'Hullo,' he said again, 'Corunna Press here.' The words 'Corunna Press' still gave him a thrill, and took the edge off his annoyance.

'Rumpelow here. That you, Manley? I'd like a word with you if you're not too busy.'

'I am busy. Hellishly busy. But I'll meet you for a drink. Is it important?'

'Yes. Nika seems to think so. So does Penelope. If you like I'll come round. I'm near-by.'

Spencer looked at his watch. Nearly seven. He supposed he'd have to eat some time; there'd been no time for lunch.

'Look, Rumpelow, can you pick up some hamburgers or something? Then we can eat as we talk.' A little ashamed at his ungraciousness, he added, 'Do come, it's time you saw how things were shaping.'

'Right, I'll bring some beer. Be with you in half an hour.'

'Coming in to keep an eye on his investment, eh?' said Stefan sharply, steadying a pile of papers, his spectacles shooting off daggers of light where the tilted lamp on his desk caught them.

'Not really. He wants to talk about something. Sounds as if the women have put him up to it. Ah, what the hell. Look, we'd better tidy up a bit.'

They started to file letters away in one of the second-hand metal cabinets. This was a battered remnant of the brief Prentice ownership of the press, and several of the letters had worn off the cardboard slips. Spencer inked these in carefully on a postcard, cut it into strips and sellotaped them into place. Stefan swept all the American costing sheets into a vast drawer of his desk and slammed it shut.

'Once we're running properly we'll get a girl in to do this. Then a carpet and a bookcase. These shelves look tatty.'

'I'm not happy about those awful books of poems we're committed to,' said Spencer slowly. 'Can't we postpone them? The list looks pretty dicky. The only real sellers are Bonny's historical novels and the vintage car series.'

'Don't forget Maxim Gaylord. And the reprint of the potty parsons. That'll go like mad. People adore reading about the clergy smuggling brandy and racing the wreckers to the rocks.'

'I hope you're right.'

'I know I'm right. Next to literary mandarins in their underpants there's nothing like a hunting parson to ravish the reviewers and lure the libraries. And the poetry list isn't all that bad. Some of the little fish might grow into big ones.'

Spencer shrugged. Most of these thin collections seemed to him, with his experience in a bookshop behind him, to be born remainders. But he had argued enough with Stefan for one day.

'I'm putting all the manuscripts under consideration on this shelf, with the teapot on top. That'll keep them safe, and we can't forget them as we'll want the teapot tomorrow.'

'What we need,' said Stefan dreamily, 'is a scoop. Someone's memoirs. *Heads of the Famous: Hair I have Dressed,* by Mr Bobby-pin of television fame. Glossy jacket, big toothy smile, and Lady What's-her-name all done up in curlers. Before and after. We sell serial rights to the *Sunday Snooper* for fifteen hundred, then bring it out in hardback. Sell ten thousand straight off at a guinea a copy. Then one of the paperback boys will buy the rights for five hundred – no, seven-fifty. With a bit of luck Stinky might do it in the States. Then we can afford a secretary, a bookcase, and a carpet. Wall-to-wall.'

The bell pealed from below, and Spencer jumped up from where he was riffling through a pile of books, checking torn jackets.

'Can't think what he wants,' he muttered, half to himself. 'Shall I take him straight up to the flat?'

'Bring him in here first. Let him see in what austerity we work.'

Minutes later Pye Rumpelow came firmly into the office. He had some interesting-looking striped paper bags in his hands, and several bottles thrust under his arm. He looked round and smiled.

There were two desks in the fair-sized room, and Stefan sat at the larger one, with the worn leather top. Obviously the days it had seen in its youth had been good ones and it lent Stefan a certain solidity as he sat behind it, although he had littered it with wire filing baskets, ash-trays, gaudy American books and an old box of pens. These, together with his typewriter and the telephone, gave him a busy, driven air. One wall of the office was covered with shelves, a lucky fitment they had inherited. Over by the window a plainer desk with a typewriter on it, in the corner by the fireplace a gas ring, and on the mantelshelf cups and saucers and a carton of sugar. Piles of books stood on the floor, unbound sheets in tough rubber bands, cardboard boxes full of invoices, galley proofs. Pinned on the wall above Spencer's desk was a large map of the British Isles, with flags stuck in the various countries, as if a war were in progress.

Pye went over to this, and his attention was caught by a notice pinned beside it. Pye loved notices. More than once he had got off a bus in order to read one.

MEMO RE BLURBS (he read)

Clichés will not be used: i.e., villages will not nestle, nor will peace be hallowed. We will not presume to tell reviewers that our authors' work is colourful, nor that the writing is perceptive, nor that their characterization is shrewd. We will not presume to compare them to Dostoevsky, Shakespeare, nor even Dickens. We leave comparisons and clichés to reviewers, who abound in them. It is recommendation enough that these authors are published under our imprint.

Blurbs are at all times to be informative, crisp, lucid, and, if possible, witty. Then STOP. Quotes of previous work, if laudatory, to be on the back flap. If damning and laudatory, juxtapose in the interests of controversy. Hints at odd and interesting sexual divergences pull if subtly done, implying that to a progressive and liberal-minded reader such things are a part of life. Assume the reader wears no mental dog-collar. Those who do will adjust it more firmly, those who do not will bark in open defiance, feeling supported and flattered.

Rumpelow read this through carefully and shook his head. 'What supreme arrogance!' he said.

'Not at all,' said Stefan. 'In time it *will* be prestige for people to come in under our imprint. You wait and see.'

Rumpelow wandered about the room, looking particularly at the mantelpiece, which seemed to him to be Adam. This fact, together with Stefan's confident words, made him look at the two young men with renewed respect. He even began to believe in the Corunna Press, and this investment of his. He had been impressed with Stefan's speed at getting what he wanted. This house, for instance. Who but Stefan could have persuaded his landlord to sell it to him, so that he hadn't even needed to move? It was the only house in the street, sandwiched between tall warehouses, and the landlord had complained of the noise at night. This had been enough for Stefan to work on, and in the end the old man had come to accept as his own idea retirement to the comparative peace of Penge, where citizens kept decent hours, lullabied by the Epilogue on television rather than the shouts of Covent Garden porters. All the same, he had been shrewd enough to ask a stiffish price, and the mortgage was heavy. Pye had seen the two good-sized stockrooms on the ground floor, and now he opened the door next to Spencer's desk and peered in.

'Nice room here for a dwarf,' he said.

During the six months they had been dealing with the exhausting business of the change-over – attending to all the details of shifting and checking stock, vetting agreements, interviewing printers, paper-suppliers, block-makers, authors, trying to clear up the delicate business of overseas representation (for this had been done automatically by Oliver Prentice Ltd, which had also taken over the distribution, and this had now of course stopped), in addition to putting through books to launch the new company – Pye had kept away. He realized that he could be of no help at this preliminary stage, and believed one should recognize one's limitations: any other attitude led to a waste of effort. He had also been busy with his own concerns, staff had given him a great deal of trouble, and he had been content to see Stefan and Spencer for an occasional lunch or dinner. His father had died in the previous autumn and he had decided to keep the cottage he had bought for him. This was on the coast by the Helford river, and he had an idea he might like to have it for holidays.

He had welcomed Penelope's telephone call about Spencer's son, since it gave him an excuse to see how things were shaping. He loved paying unexpected calls on his friends, and had learned many curious things in this way, and many a good business deal had come out of it. He was an adept at pulling aside masks. What better way than to come up quietly from behind and give a quick and gentle twitch? He told himself he liked to know people, and how better than to catch them in the bath or in dirty house clothes, the remains of a meal on the table? None of them, he found, played the gentleman at home. Penelope, alone among his women friends was an honourable exception. He had never caught her looking slapdash or untidy: he had come to the conclusion that her private face was much the same as her public one, and this added to his growing esteem and attachment even though it daunted him. Many a time, when an acquaintance had tried to play him for a fool or a philistine, he had been able to exercise a pleasant sense of power, putting out his hands to pull down the whole pretentious house of bricks. Then, at once, out of basic kindliness and a sense of shame at the ease with which people could be stripped bare, he would be horrified at this public crumbling of defences, and to repair the damage would offer money, another drink, a meal, noting with melancholy satisfaction the façade gradually build up again like a film run backwards in slow motion.

'Perhaps you'd like to see the book-list,' said Stefan, who had been watching him with suppressed amusement for some minutes. 'We've had to change the layout, of course, and the printer. Poor old David was hopeless. It's late for spring, but –' The telephone bell shrilled again, and with a grimace he picked it up with one hand, thrusting a lemon and magenta striped booklet across the desk with the other. 'Hullo. Corunna Press. Yes, Brandt speaking. Who's that? Who did you say?' He whipped off his spectacles and blinked, naked, down at his papers. A look of such incredulity crossed his face that the other two turned their heads to him and frankly listened. 'Yes, of course I remember you, Miss Frost. Oh? Mm, mm. Well, we're only starting, you know. We're not very grand. I see. Mm. Well, I'll have to consult my partners, but . . . yes. By all means. Tomorrow then. Shall we say eleven o'clock?'

He put the receiver down, replaced his spectacles and lay across the desk, barking with laughter. He flung out a hand to the smaller office and said, 'Rumpelow, I think we've found the dwarf.'

He walked across and flung open the door, frowning and biting his lips. It was a small room with a large window. He looked at the wooden desk, the hard chair, the two wide shelves and the dirty grey walls.

'Who on earth was that? What do you mean?' Spencer asked. Stefan started to explain, then shrugged it away. 'Oh, come upstairs, I'll switch the telephone through to my flat. We can't stand about while miracles happen. And Rumpelow's come with food. I'm starving. Bring the list with you.'

He switched the light off on his desk and the office grew gloomy and cavernous and untidily empty. 'Yes,' he went on, half to himself, 'we'll simply have to paint that office.' Then he ushered the other two through the door and locked it behind him with a large key.

Upstairs the contrast hit them at once. It was a relief to see Stefan's comfortable chairs, to be once more in ordered domestic surroundings.

'In here,' said Stefan, and Pye followed him into a small, clean kitchen, and started to unpack the parcels he had brought: French bread, several portions of cold chicken, a Gruyère cheese, some cheesecake. He put the beer in the refrigerator.

'I suppose you have butter?' he said. 'I'm afraid I forgot it.'

'Marvellous!' exclaimed Spencer greedily. 'And to think I didn't really want to answer the telephone. By the way, what's the trouble, Rumpelow? Anything serious?'

'Depends how you look at it,' said Pye, busying himself with the food. His movements were deliberate, careful; he handled plates and forks as Stefan passed them to him in such a way as to enhance their value, so that the operation made the hastily assembled meal into a banquet. 'It's about your boy – oh, nothing's happened to him. But maybe we can talk about that later. Brandt is longing to tell us all about his mysterious caller, and judging his moment.'

He was right, for Stefan waited until they were sitting at the table with laden plates in front of them and long cold glasses of beer close at hand before he said, 'Do you remember my telling you about Miss Frost, Spencer?'

Spencer frowned. 'Miss Frost? Miss Frost? Good God, not that frightful ogre on guard at Prentice's?'

144

Stefan nodded.

'The same. Well, now Halstead's have taken over they've given her the sack, poor old girl, after thirty years. No pension, or so I gather. She didn't actually say. But she wondered how we were getting on with Mr David's firm, and whether we needed any help.' He ignored Spencer's gasp of dismay. 'I thinks she wants to guard us – anyway, she's coming in to-morrow to talk about it.'

'Tell me a little more about this phenomenon,' said Pye, as Stefan attacked his food with abandon, and then launched into a full-scale description.

'You sound as if you'd known her for years, instead of for only several minutes,' Pye commented.

'Several charged minutes,' amended Stefan. 'But it's this quality of loyalty that interests me. She's obviously eager to transfer all that feeling for old man Prentice to us, through the medium of Mr David's baby, which we have now adopted. In this way she keeps in touch. Funny, though, I thought she hated me. She's the type of Englishwoman who instinctively loathes Jews.'

'Ah, but Oliver Prentice might have said something. From what I gather, he liked you well enough. And don't forget, jobs aren't easy to get at her age. How old is she? Fiftyish?'

Stefan gestured to indicate that it might be more or less.

'She's bound to know a good deal about publishing,' said Spencer slowly. 'If she can type and keep accounts it would be worth considering. The point is, will she run us?'

'If she tries to, she's out,' said Stefan, in a hard tone.

Pye glanced at him with interest. That hardness was new. He was beginning to get the feel of the reins, that young man. Also, Pye noticed, he had taken the decision without consulting Spencer, and Pye wondered briefly how long these two dissimilar young men would run in harness.

'I'm rather at sea in your business,' he said now. 'It's different from getting a row of machines in motion and letting them work for you. After all, clothes have to be washed, and food eaten. Financial empires have been founded on those two simple hypotheses. But do books have to be read? They may be a need, but do people really think of them as a necessity?'

'We must make them a necessity,' said Spencer eagerly. 'After all, a man must do something after his basic needs are met.'

'He can always make love,' Stefan put in, his mouth full. 'Or go to bed with an improving book. Which would you rather do?'

Spencer flushed. 'Oh, for God's sake be serious. Rumpelow asked a perfectly reasonable question, and if we don't consider it we're out of business.' He turned his back on Stefan and went on talking to Rumpelow, 'Of course publishing is trickier than running launderettes or coffee-bars, but the basic principle is the same: the public must be persuaded to buy what you offer –'

'If you say "food for the mind",' Stefan interrupted, tearing a chicken leg apart, 'I'll scream. Boloney. Of course we're just as much in the market-place as you, Rumpelow. Publishing to-day isn't a question of a shining knight riding against the dragon Ignorance, as it was in old Prentice's time. People's eyes are open already – all the hard work's been done. They've got the television and cinema to improve their beastly minds; they've also got books. Millions of 'em. Thousands too many. And they've got the theatre. But do they want to think great thoughts or see great plays? No. Hazlitt said that men are at home in the grovelling, the disagreeable and the little, and only by an effort do their minds soar to the grand and the lofty. Well, we've got to cater for both. But it's the little grovelling minds that are going to keep us fed and clothed, because there are more of them. Only when we can afford it' – he winked ironically at Spencer – 'can we contribute something grand and lofty.'

Pye sat back, vaguely troubled. There was some tension be-tween them he didn't quite like. Then he put it down to the long hours they worked together; they were tired out, needed some diversion.

'Well, let's have a look at your list,' he said. 'Not that I'm a judge of literature.'

'You won't find much there,' said Spencer dryly. 'Have some more beer.' He refilled the glasses and prowled about restively, ending up by leaning out of the window, as if to dissociate himself from the others. A moment later they heard him whistling to someone below.

'Bonny's on her way up,' he said, turning.

'She's very welcome, now that my basic needs are met,' Stefan grinned, deliberately baiting.

'In that case we'd better go. Coming, Rumpelow?'

Rumpelow hadn't heard. He was industriously looking through the book-list.

'I like this one,' he said, 'this one about parsons. It's got pictures, too. I think parsons' lives were fascinating in the eighteenth and nineteenth centuries. Do what you like after Sunday service; hunt, write poetry, go hawking, dine with the gentry . . .' He did not see Stefan throw a triumphant glance in Spencer's direction, and went on, 'Good heavens, that old chap! Maxim Gaylord! Where did you find him? Is his stuff any good?'

Before anyone could reply the door opened and Bonny came in, muffled in a fur coat. She filled the room at once with warmth and good humour. She was bareheaded and her eyes shone.

Stefan went towards her, helped her off with her coat, and kissed her hand, keeping it in his.

'Beer or coffee?' he asked.

'Coffee, please, Stefan. I've brought some rum.' She settled on the divan and kicked off her shoes. 'Those stairs! How nice to see you all together. Are you being terribly serious?'

'Stefan won't let us be,' said Spencer in a lighter tone. He went over and sat on the divan, began to stroke Bonny's bare feet. 'He's in his tradesman mood. Quite maddening. Anyway, Rumpelow and I are just off, we've got something to discuss.'

'Oh,' exclaimed Bonny at once, 'do discuss it here! And we'll have lashings of black coffee with rum. I can't be left alone with Stefan in that mood, it's too depressing. He'll start to bully me about my books, and I won't have that. I've had a tiring day.' Her eyes took in the crowded table. 'You've been eating well. Anything left?'

Stefan came in from the kitchen with a tray of coffee and brought her over a piece of cheesecake. His mood had changed abruptly and he struck Spencer across the shoulder lightly, shaking his head at him affectionately.

'I still want to know how you got old Gaylord,' said Pye.

'David Prentice got him,' said Spencer. 'Why? Do you know him?'

Rumpelow laughed. 'I met him once,' he said.

'Go on, do tell us,' interrupted Bonny, before he could say any more. 'Gorgeous cheesecake. I can't make it like this. And don't be mean with the rum, Stefan. Lollop it in – that's right.'

They sat sipping their coffee, and Pye began to talk.

'I met him just after the war, when I was driving a taxi. I was cruising slowly over Chelsea Bridge late one night when I saw this chap wandering towards me with his hands in his pockets. He looked pretty old to me and pretty dirty, and I took him for a tramp. When he hailed me I nearly didn't pull up. He hadn't shaved for a week, but when he gave me the address and hopped in I realized he was an educated man.'

'Ah,' murmured Stefan mockingly. 'What power lies in an accent!'

'Anyway,' Pye went on, 'he talked to me all the way and seemed to be quoting yards of poetry. Homer, he said it was, and I couldn't contradict him – never did Classics at school. Then we got to where he wanted to go and he told me to wait. It was somewhere behind Victoria Station. He came back after a few minutes and said the people were out. Then he gave me another address. This time they were in – this was off Baker Street. But a man opened a window and began shouting as soon as he saw who it was, and told him to go away or he'd call the police. It was pretty late by this time, nearly three, so I asked him what he was after – did he want a bed? "Of course," he said. "What d'you think?" So I took him back with me and he talked the rest of the night. Told me he was a poet and down on his luck. Stayed a week. Then he went off and I got a postcard from him from Rome. That was over ten years ago. But I've never forgotten his name. Or him. Odd, isn't it? I've never heard a man talk better.'

'He was a frightful old scrounger in his early days,' said Stefan. 'But now anyone who ever bought him a pint or lent him ten bob will be around. Didn't you know he's been given the Beckwith Prize for Poetry? Haven't you read any of his poetry?'

Pye shook his head. 'I'm a philistine,' he said. 'I seem to have a blind eye for poetry. Never seem to see it in bookshops, never notice it reviewed. I've trained my eye to slip over what I used to consider to be the inessentials.'

'How honest you are!' exclaimed Bonny. 'Will you read him now?'

Pye shrugged. 'I might, if I've time, and as I've an interest in the Corunna Press. Who'd have thought that one day I'd be one third of his publisher?'

'Did he ever pay you?'

'What for? The taxi? Yes, in fact he did. He was a very honest man. That was his last pound.' Pye got to his feet and stretched. 'Come on, Manley, time we were off.'


With his back to the wall, a tall glass in his hand, looking across the crowded saloon bar of a small pub off King Street, Spencer said at last, 'You were very mysterious up in Stefan's room. What's up?'

As usual, Pye came straight to the point. 'Nothing drastic,' he said. 'But I thought you might prefer not to discuss it in front of the others. Penelope seemed to think that Nika is extremely upset and worried about young Lewis . . .' He caught Spencer's instant frown and withdrawal and went on, gently and with warmth, 'Look, I know it's none of my business – classic opening for butting in – but do you really have to send your son to that school when you know he isn't happy there?'

Spencer made an impatient gesture. 'He won't be happy anywhere away from Wales and that confounded house,' he said stiffly. 'As for the school, I know it isn't ideal, but all I can think about now is the fact that I've sunk almost every penny I possess into a publishing house. And it's chancy. It's all right for Stefan, he isn't married, but . . .' He drained his glass and shouldered up to the bar, returning a moment or two later with two more beers. 'I've four people to keep, Rumpelow.'

They drank in silence, Spencer trying to fight down a growing feeling of being got at, trapped.

At last Pye said, 'I don't think if Stefan had a son he would sacrifice the boy like this.'

'Sacrifice!' Spencer spat the word out angrily. 'What an absurd thing to say! Lewis is having the same kind of education as thousands of other boys in this country. Nika knows how I feel. If these boys aren't being sacrificed, how can he be?'

'I had that sort of education,' said Pye, without rancour, 'and I know how hard it is when you're not with your own kind. My mother was a middle-class woman, I suppose, but my father was a Cornish fisherman. I was in between the two all the time. Lewis isn't as tough as I was. He's like you, Manley, and certain things could break him.'

'Like me? He's his mother's boy!' Spencer looked across at Pye in amazement, then smiled faintly. 'Like me? D'you think so?'

'I do. He is essentially your son. He clings to his mother because he's a child, and because she's there all the time, and because he identifies her with his Welsh childhood. Ideally, for all of you, he should be sent away to school somewhere in the country, then he could find a balance.'

'Oddly enough, I'd thought of that. Although, mind you, I don't altogether like boarding schools at his age.' Spencer looked more warmly at Pye, his exhaustion, his irritation, subsiding under the other's quiet power. Days spent alone with Stefan had drained him of more than his initiative. When he spoke again the edge was off his voice. 'We had hoped to get him into a choir school – he loves music, and he has a very true voice. But somehow, with the move and everything, I didn't do any more about it.'

Pye looked into his glass, and Spencer felt absurdly guilty, and for once without self-justification.

'Is it too late?'

'No. But it will be soon. They interview them at nine, you see. I sent off all the forms before we moved. Now you come to mention it, I think he should go some time this month, but I thought he was settled, so – Oh, I know Nika's upset. She's had a difficult time – but then so have I.'

'You look as if you need a break,' said Pye. 'I know all about the tension of opposites and so on, but life will be much easier when you're out on the road more. At the moment you spend more time with Stefan than with your wife; and that's death to a workable partnership.'

Spencer laughed. It astonished and touched him that Pye should understand so immediately, without sitting in judgment. He said eagerly, 'Actually, Lewis stands a decent chance of a scholarship. What really worries me is what will happen when his voice breaks. It might happen before he's fourteen, and if I can't afford the fees, then what shall I do? He'll be out, then . . . although I know they do all they can for the boys.'

Pye looked at him in astonishment.

'Good God, man, that's years ahead! You'll be on your feet by then. Surely you have that much belief in yourself?'

'Maybe. But I'm only one third of the Corunna Press, and what I want doesn't always seem to be put into operation. But never mind that now. At the moment I'm working sixteen hours a day for nothing, and that doesn't give one a feeling of security. I'd expected it, but –' He shrugged.

'I like your boy,' said Pye slowly. 'If I'd had a son I'd have imagined him to be very like Lewis.'

'Were you ever married?' asked Spencer. It had never occurred to him to ask this question before; he hated probing into people's lives just as much as he resented them probing into his.

151

'Oh yes,' said Pye. 'A long time ago. It broke up. For years I thought my wife wasn't able to have children and was sorry for her. Then I found out – never mind how, it's an old story – that she'd got rid of three. Three! Without telling me. It was something of a shock.'

Spencer stared at him, at last shaken out of his self-absorption, appalled. Pye smiled wryly. 'Well, that's probably why I'm so interested in your youngster. Drink up. Will you have another?'

'No, thanks. I'd better get home, or Nika won't like that either.'

They walked in silence to the Underground.

'Look,' said Pye, 'I don't want to interfere. But if you're busy, let me take this over. I mean I can take him to the school for the interview or whatever's necessary. And of course, if –'

Spencer laid a hand on his arm. 'No, thanks,' he said. 'No money. I'll have a talk with Nika. Believe me, I'll call on you if I'm so damned busy I can't get away from the office. But you've put enough in the Corunna Press . . . and, no offence, but he is my son.'

They shook hands and Spencer ran down the steps to buy a ticket. 'He is my son,' he thought, 'and it's taken another man to make me realize it. Poor devil, the things women can do to men. I suppose,' he told himself wryly, as he stepped on to the train, 'it takes men like me to even things out.'


'What a curious man Spencer is,' Bonny was saying to Stefan at that moment. 'He has the kind of eyes the Aztecs had. He's always wondering what you're trying to do to him, and resenting it in advance. He lives in corners.'

Stefan lay at the other end of the divan, his shoes off, his feet resting in Bonny's lap, where she lay like a seal washed up on a sunny beach, completely relaxed.

'Oh, Spencer's all right,' he said, laughing. 'I'm not trying to do anything to him – except make him into a publisher the hard way. He wants all his medals pinned on before he's got a decent uniform to pin them to.'

Bonny reached for the round box of Turkish delight that lay on the floor by her side, and forked a piece into his mouth, then took one for herself. 'I wonder whether he was an Aztec in a previous incarnation,' she asked lazily. 'But you don't believe in reincarnation, do you, darling?'

'I do not,' said Stefan, his mouth full.

'What a pity. I'm convinced we were lovers in another life. Otherwise why should we be together now?'

'I suppose you were the Queen of Sheba and I was your devoted slave?'

'Something like that. Stefan, I think I've got a book for you.'

He alerted. 'By you?'

She shook her head, licked her fingers. 'No, by a man I met at one of my development circles. He's a spiritualist,' she added, seeing Stefan's look of incomprehension. He sat up abruptly, swinging his legs on to the floor.

'Please, Bonny, no. We're doing a lot of tripe – but tripe that sells. I couldn't bear to publish the meanderings of Big Chief Red Feather given to sundry gullible ladies gathered in a darkened room in a back street of Sidcup.'

She was not annoyed.

'It's nothing like that. In fact, I forgive you your ignorance. It could be rather remarkable. Why not a series of *I Was There* titles? Historical events as seen by an ordinary looker-on? This man says he was at the crucifixion. I've read a bit of it and it's good. You do feel he was there.'

'But what about *The Robe*? Wasn't that the same sort of thing?'

'It's quite different. And what's so extraordinary is that this man has done no research at all, and yet his descriptions of Jerusalem seem completely authentic. He's a bus-driver.'

Stefan groaned.

'He writes at night and in the morning there it all is, pages of it. And he doesn't know what it's about until he reads it. His sister types it out for him.'

'Does she know what it's about, or is she a clippie without visions?'

Bonny suddenly looked cross. 'Now, Stefan, you're being stupid. You don't know anything about these things, so don't jeer.'

He gave a tremendous yawn, which broke from him without check.

'Darling Bonny, let's go to bed. Please.'

She rose with a certain decisive dignity. 'You go, by all means. You look very tired. I must get home, it's late. Will you read the manuscript? It's only twenty thousand words at the moment. It won't take you long.'

'I'll read anything if you'll stay. I'll even say I believe that you were once the Queen of Sheba. Please stay, Bonny.'

But she had already swathed her scarf round her head, and now she handed Stefan her coat for him to slip over her shoulders. She let him kiss her, long and tenderly, then she drew away.

'I'll drop it in tomorrow,' she said.

Stefan went downstairs with her, profoundly disturbed. As he sought for a taxi he realized that this might be an ultimatum, and fear and resentment began to spurt, like tiny bush fires, into life. He had the presence of mind, as he shut the door on her when a taxi was at last found, to murmur that he was sorry. Might they dine together the next evening? He was rewarded by her usual warm smile and a nod of assent.

## 13

The spring strengthened, and March brought unexpectedly mild weather, with warm nights that smelt tantalizingly of summer. On one of these nights Nika and Spencer sat in Stefan's upstairs room sunk in a torpor of well-fed tiredness. Nika had said, for the second time, that they really ought to be going, for it was past midnight, but Spencer had not moved. He lay on the floor, carefully sticking in press cuttings, gloating over the good ones, cursing the bad.

'The children will be asleep, don't worry,' he said lazily. 'Mrs Piggott will have seen to them before she goes to bed, and she's only in the flat below, don't forget. She'll leave the door open. You know, Stefan, I never thought the old boy's poems would haul in so many good notices.'

'They're selling, too. No one will dare to say he hasn't read them,' said Stefan. 'Good thing we tied up with that recording company; the E.P. has given the book a push.'

'All the same, I wonder he didn't object to the rest of the list. We must get some more good stuff. Really good stuff, Stefan.'

'It'll come, don't worry. Bonny's got some good notices, too. That'll shake her.'

'What a pity she couldn't come tonight, you cooked such a splendid dinner,' said Nika.

Stefan frowned. 'Well, I know now that a good materialisation séance at Bristol is more important to her than a decent meal with us. And that, for Bonny, is something. Still, I wouldn't swop my soufflé tonight for the ghost of Hamlet's dad.'

'Did this chap Stan drive her down?' asked Spencer, teasing.

'No. He's driving his bus. And as long as he keeps to that route, it's all right by me. What did you think of his crucifixion stuff, Nika?'

'Horribly readable. You can smell the sweat and corruption. I can see it as a serial in one of the lesser Sundays.'

Stefan nodded gloomily. 'We'll clean up on it. That's what depresses me. The big woman's so jubilant, it's obscene. Damned fellow came to the office the other day, scared the pants off Miss Frost. Looked like one of Cocteau's outriders from *Orphée*. Enormous, about eight foot tall, all in black leather and a helmet with a kind of Mercury plume on it. Beastly. When he's not sitting on his backside in a bus, he's on that motor-bike. Like a special messenger from hell, delivering copy.'

The bell shrilled through the flat. A moment afterwards there came a shout from the street. Stefan looked out of the window, threw down some keys and, turning back, said, 'It's Pye. I've told him to come up.'

A few minutes later Pye walked in, looking battered, although he was tidily dressed in a decent suit, and as plump as ever. He wore an unusual expression for him, one of harassed puzzlement, and his habitual calm had evidently been shaken.

'Sit down, old boy, we've been celebrating our first successes,' said Stefan. 'How was your party?'

'Awful,' said Pye wearily. 'I don't know why I go to them. What an odd lot of people one collects. Do I change or do they? Do they move on or do I? Anyway, it's no good. Perhaps I'm getting too old for parties.'

'Oh come, Pye, you weren't in the mood, that's all,' said Nika. 'Wasn't Penelope with you?'

'No, she didn't want to come. And thank God she didn't.' He shook his head as Stefan gestured to the array of bottles on the side table.

'Well? Something happened. Are you going to tell us or not?' Spencer shut the press-cuttings book and rose to his feet, to throw himself into an armchair. He selected a cigar from a box – one of the extravagances he and Stefan occasionally allowed themselves – and the room began to fill with its moneyed aroma. Pye shifted restlessly, then burst out as if he could no longer contain the words.

'You know,' he said, 'it was one of the worst moments of my life. There was this man, with the party roaring round him, the women with their teeth gleaming and eyes shining, and the men gently sweating and trying to impress anyone near enough to hear – although that was almost impossible, you know how all those trivial conversations build up into a noise like the Severn bore, sweeping right through the room –'

'For God's sake, man, we've all been to parties. What happened?'

They were all looking at Pye curiously, and he returned their look, but as if they were extensions of his own bewilderment.

'Well,' he went on after a pause, 'there was this man, and he was pretty drunk. He stood looking around, desperately, I thought. I was feeling pretty desperate myself, after shouting pleasantries into cardboard faces for a couple of hours. He stood quite still – he was a big man, with an oddly small head and that transparent skin of the very fair, and I could see the blood fairly coursing through a vein above his eye – and suddenly he lifted up his chin and gave a great shout. "I need a friend!" he shouted. Then again, "I need a friend!" The room stilled. It was extraordinary. Everyone looked at him, then away. Someone shouted, "Mind my bike!" There was a sort of scattered titter. People moved away. Someone called across, "We all need a friend, old chap!" And a tipsy woman started to sing, "There's a Friend abo-ove, who has my loo-ve . . ."'

'Here,' said Stefan, 'get this whisky down. You need it.'

'This man,' Pye went on, holding the glass in his hand, 'I saw he was going to burst into tears. For some reason I couldn't let that happen. Because the crowd there – or most of them – really thought he'd taken over some sort of new catch-phrase they'd be hearing soon on the telly. I wanted to get him out before they realized that he'd broken the most important convention of all; showing emotion and a real need in public. That thin skin on which we all skate, you know? So I took him by the arm and began to lead him out and we looked at one another. He was pretty glazed by that time, and when he got to the door he turned back and said it again, but differently. He sort of threw it helplessly into all those pink faces, spiky with laughter.' Pye was silent, drank his whisky at speed.

'What did you say to him?' asked Nika.

'I didn't get a chance to say anything.' Pye's blue eyes suddenly blazed with laughter. 'When I got him outside at last he lowered his face into mine and said, "I don't want a friend with a beard, blast you!" and knocked me down. When I got up he'd gone.'

'Poor swine,' said Stefan.

'I knew you'd still be up, so I came straight here.'

Through the open windows the noise of the first lorries arriving in the market seemed very loud. They lurched past where, earlier, queues had stood outside the Opera House. Spencer went over to one window, looking down, calculating how easy it would be to spit on to the orange-coloured netting sacks that bulged with cabbages and carrots and onions. It was too easy, for they passed crawling in bottom gear as the drivers manœuvred skilfully down the narrow street. Nika tenderly examined Pye's face for damage, parting the fine, close greyish beard with long fingers.

'There's no mark, Pye,' she said. 'But you ought to have some coffee. May I make some, Stefan? I know where you keep everything.' She hesitated as Stefan nodded, and with her hand on the door leading to the kitchen, said, 'I know how you feel. I passed a man a week or two ago standing in the street, pressed up against the window of an empty shop. He wasn't selling anything, just looking into people's faces as they passed. He seemed to be holding something out, so I looked. It was a torn cigarette packet, and scrawled on it was, *Please help me, folks.* I gave him half a crown and went on. Now I shop in another direction.'

'You didn't tell me this,' said Spencer.

'No,' she said, turning the handle and going into the kitchen. 'I felt too sick.'

The men glanced at one another. Stefan said, 'Poor Nika. She and Pye really care about people. But then, everywhere, all the time, someone is screaming for help. I feel sick every time I have to go into a public lavatory: all those desperate, obsessive graffiti.'

Spencer gave a short laugh. He was still wondering why Nika had not told him of this before if it had upset her. She used to tell him everything. 'I wonder what this chap did after he left you?' he murmured. 'Of course, Pye, you asked for it.'

'Of course. But Stefan's right. I do care about people. Can one care too much?' Pye walked restlessly up and down. He stopped to look at a painting on the wall, listened to the confused shouts from the streets. 'You're certainly in contact with life here, Stefan. You can't bear to lose it even at night, can you?'

Stefan lifted his hands in surrender. 'I love it,' he said. 'I wouldn't live anywhere else. It's another London surging up when the daytime one dies. It's a kind of rebirth every midnight.'

'It's contact, not communication.'

'I can communicate all right, if that's what's bothering you. I can put on a sweater and flannels and walk right down there in among them and drink tea and they talk to me. Don't forget, they were the first friends I had when I came to London. Maybe it's because I'm obviously a Jew. A lot of us work in the market.'

'That's nothing to do with it, sucker,' said Spencer. 'I bet I could do the same.'

Pye shook his head. 'Your voice is all wrong,' he said. 'But that isn't what I meant. I can't help thinking of that poor devil. Everyone has so much in common today that real communication is almost non-existent. Eye might meet eye across a crowded bus, and for one second there's communication – but it can't be followed up. You can't hold a moment like that in the hand, just as you can't hold happiness. We talk an awful lot, but we only really communicate for moments at a time – and we here are the lucky ones, I suppose.'

Nika walked into the silence that followed his words and began to pour coffee.

'How noisy the lorries are tonight, Stefan,' she remarked; 'I don't know how you sleep through it.'

'I need very little sleep. Anyway, there's a room at the back, it's quieter.'

Pye started to speak as if he had never finished his sentence. He stirred his coffee thoughtfully, settling back in his chair. 'Yes, we're lucky. We're holding out, just. You know what I mean. People react to a common reactor – television, cartoon strips, traffic jams, vulgar advertisements, gossip columns, the Royal Family – and they're losing the power of reacting to each other. We've been losing it, in fact, since the beginning of the nineteenth century. So that a man can stand in the middle of a room, surrounded by people he presumably knows, or thinks he does, and can shout aloud in agony, "I need a friend!" and when someone tries to get through, he punches him in the face.'

'But we must learn to accept aloneness,' said Stefan impatiently. 'Your man was a fool to expect any response to his shout. He didn't really expect it – or even want it – that's why he punched you. You had encroached. Now a whisper would have been different.'

'A man doesn't always want to whisper.'

Stefan gestured. 'We must accept aloneness,' he said again. 'It's the only way we can learn about ourselves, and that means about God, Who is after all nothing more than a contorted reflection of ourselves.'

Spencer smiled and settled back indulgently, but only Nika exclaimed at what was to her mere blasphemous bantering, and Stefan, delighted at her reaction, at once turned to Pye.

'Well, Pye, there's your man standing out in the middle of this dreary party, shouting out of his black loneliness and inability to communicate. Of course, he might just be drunk and lusting for all that tempting man-or-woman-flesh standing around. But you're a romantic, you see him as God, and so will I for the sake of an argument. All right –' he ignored Pye's gesture of protest –'who is he but God? God Who created colour and light and mad-looking vegetation among all those cooling rocks, and pricked out the stars with his thumb and set the sun and moon in place? Then he looked around in horror at the loneliness of it all. "I need a friend," he whispered to himself – yes, he'd whisper that. So on the fifth day he created life.'

At once Spencer began to conduct, and sang the appropriate bars from Haydn's *Creation*, 'And God created great whales,' then waved him to go on.

'And apart from the whales,' pursued Stefan, with a slight bow, 'out came everything that crept and hopped and flapped. Out they came from the grey mud, from that first great watery womb, instinctive. Down flew birds, crying like curlews in astonishment at being there at all. But they can't speak to Him, so He's no better off. They can't smile at Him with love. So on the sixth day he cried aloud among all the bird and animal noises and the roar of the waters and the humming of the stars, "I need a friend!" So he made a mammoth effort and created man in His own image. That was poor old Adam, His first big let-down. For Adam is too like God Himself to be able to love Him and anyway he's too innocent to know what God is or what love is. God can't live with him – he can't claim him as Friend (note the capital F) because Adam is scared stiff.'

'Come now, Stefan, how can he be scared stiff if he's in a state of innocence? If he can't know love, he can't know fear. Innocence is a pure state.'

Stefan waved the objection aside. 'Who wouldn't be scared of his creator? I say he couldn't smile at God with love, which is what God wanted.' He tried to meet Nika's eye, but she merely filled his cup and wandered over to the window. She was held like an unwilling child to a frightening story. Spencer now lay stretched out in the shadows; Pye lighted another cigarette. No one spoke.

'Poor old Adam,' sighed Stefan, enjoying himself. 'He can't respond to this tremendous light that pours over him and burns him up, because he doesn't know how to. Anyway, he feels inferior. Inequality has been created. And there's something missing in this lush garden God has made for His favourite. Being

God, He's sexless because He has no need to reproduce – Adam must do that for Him. He's fooled by His own laws of nature which have taken over from Him the second He hatched them, and made Him for all time the one great Outsider. So there they both are, in what we call Paradise, sitting back to back and swotting flies and boring each other silly. Sometimes God nips round in between the trees trying to catch Adam out, and surprise a smile of pure love and joy on his face. But all He sees are those poor dab's white eyeballs starting with terror.

'Everything's spawning, reproducing, flowering and falling and dying and being reborn. And maybe this is harder to accept than the act of creating the universe – because it is harder to live with the results of one's actions than to make that first act. So only God is changeless for infinity. Then He looks at Adam while he's asleep and realizes that He's projected His own loneliness on to him, the incomplete man there, lolling under a tree, the man with a burden. So out of pity He takes a rib out of Adam's side – He's probably run out of raw material, at the rate He's been creating – and makes woman. This is to break man's intolerable loneliness and complete the life cycle.'

Nika made a sudden violent movement. 'As an afterthought, the very last thing to be created!' she exclaimed bitterly.

'An afterthought, yes,' said Stefan, winking at the others. 'But being created last gives woman the right to the last word – which she's had ever since. Because Adam doesn't look at God any more after that, not even in terror. From the moment he wakes up and finds that gift beside him, his eyes are veiled from God. Instead he looks at Eve and smiles at her with love. Because here's a love he instinctively understands and can use.'

Pye interrupted him lazily.

'You've forgotten the handicap. The Big Fella played fair when He knew He was one up on Adam in the little matter of good and evil.'

Stefan looked blank, then his voice sprang out again. 'Do you call putting the Tree there playing fair? Telling Adam in effect that the flowers are not for him to pick? Making sure it was the first temptation? Testing His own product?'

162

'He had every right to, and He gave Adam an even chance. There was the choice between knowing the woman and knowing God. Adam chose the woman, mortality and suffering. He was the first sinner.'

'And in revenge,' Spencer put in, 'God cut them both off from the Tree of Life.'

'That's what I said,' murmured Pye. 'Adam chose mortality.'

'He didn't think of anything other than the apple Eve held out. And as if he could resist such a challenge even without the serpent!' Nika burst out. 'How you do complicate things! Adam never thought at all. He was used to Eve giving him things. They weren't to know it was an aphrodisiac.'

There was a shout of laughter.

'Well, that's certainly a new interpretation! You could start a splendid heresy with that idea,' said Stefan. 'So you think Adam was amply compensated, Nika? With God decently veiled from him and Eve still in the first flush of her delicious nakedness and dawning sensuality, and no other man to lust after her. Yes, that must have been bliss at first. I should say they were chased from that garden singing.'

'I wouldn't say they sang for long, with all that God threatened: sweat and sorrow and fear and subjection. Don't forget that Adam had once known God in all His purity and beauty. His was the first *Angst*.'

Spencer stretched and got up. 'We must go, it's past three,' he said. 'The allegory's entertaining if not convincing, Stefan. But think,' he added suddenly, at the door, 'what different creatures we would all have been if God hadn't turned those two out of Eden! *He* sowed the first niggles of doubt and guilt and jealousy and divine retribution, not the serpent. Think of it, flawing His own creation.'

' "For I thy God am a jealous God" – that's the core of our western tragedy. The hubris, the nemesis, the tortures, the terrible implacability. Oh, I know I like to think of myself as a victim,' said Stefan, his voice tired and flat, 'but I'm no more a victim than any of you.'

Pye gave him his warm, embracing smile. 'Well, then, Stefan, if you realize that, your intimate, inside story of lovers expelled from Eden has some point.'

They walked downstairs, Stefan switching on lights as they did so, passing the darkened, silent offices on the second floor, the packing rooms on the first, and so into the street, lighted and alive with movement.

Spencer stood looking around him with pleasure: there was a cool, bruised smell. Then, taking Nika's arm, he nodded good-night and walked her away, his head still alight with the resentment Stefan's fantasy had called up: indignant at the problems that had descended upon mankind, upon himself, because the first man had not been allowed to possess the first woman without guilt. God's problem – and Adam's – was his own.

A moment later Pye left Stefan standing on the step, biting his knuckles in concentration. He stood there long after Pye had disappeared along the street, then at last went in and closed the door. Inside story of lovers expelled from Eden. Maybe Pye had something there: a de Mille epic with all the trappings and the false, rotten heart of heresy. Still, treated as myth . . . Sighing, he ascended to his high room, to spin more dreams before the day began.

# 14

PYE WALKED briskly, instinctively avoiding the angled, parked lorries and busy brooms which cleared away crushed cabbage leaves, squashed tomatoes, packing straw, all the debris spilled from boxes and crates. On the long covered pavement fronting the cobbles three men practised golf shots with sticks and a few Spanish onions. The sound of iron wheels on stone rumbled from inside the market, innocent tumbrils. Under the false, pillared front of St Paul's church men drank coffee at a stall. The atmosphere was curiously rural, and he thought how fitting it was that Inigo Jones should have called his church the finest barn in Europe! As he turned into King Street a man called to him from the open front of a shop where he was stacking carrots and onions on one side and apples and oranges on the other, and threw him an apple. Smiling his thanks, Pye caught it and walked on, munching.

Then he was suddenly looking into an empty shop that might have been a snack bar by day. There, in the emptiness at the back, an old man stood, slicing bread with a machine, utterly absorbed. The light bulb swung above, striking desultory gleams from his bald head. The concentration of that solitary figure brought back the memory of another, temporarily forgotten. In the silence Pye seemed to hear again that desperate appeal – for it had been an appeal, whether the man was drunk or not.

*I need a friend*

And whether he was drunk or not was incidental. Drunkenness merely unlocked doors of the mind to reveal many an incongruous prisoner bemused by his temporary freedom. Pye could not bear other people's loneliness, yet his own sense of aloneness was necessary to him, and voluntary. It was a quiet cell into which he withdrew to replenish his strength. He stopped, realizing that he had come too far, and had missed his favourite short cut through to St Martin's Lane. He retraced his steps and turned down into a narrow cut opposite tall tenements and made his way with relief along the paved lane past bow-fronted houses that had belonged to the London Pepys knew when he was making those furtive entries in his diary. It was absolutely quiet here; this was where he would like to live, at the centre where there was no noise or movement and where he could think.

*I need a friend.*

It bothered him that he had not been able to meet this need; failure was new to him and, like any unfamiliar sensation, unsettling. People did not often resent him because he never, he thought, interfered without cause, but maybe this time his own warmth had been too much, an intrusion, as Spencer had perceived. But what drove a man to shout out such a thing? Had he betrayed each of his former friends because of a peculiar, sadistic pleasure in first achieving intimacy, then crumpling it like paper and tossing it away? Did his own need, too barely exposed, burn friendship out? Or was he one of those unfortunates who were quite unaware of some element in themselves which repelled intimacy and blighted emotional response? After all, the ability to form satisfying personal relationships did not lie with everyone. It was part instinct, part luck, part hard work, endless unselfish giving. Hope. Loyalty.

*I need a friend*

But what was a friend? Both confessor and confessee, the screens down. Was such absolute mutual trust, effortless communication and understanding, the Greek ideal, possible only in adolescence, and only between young men or young women, rarely between man and woman? Was it recognizable only at that poised moment when the clear childhood stream met the

166

rushing fouled river of adulthood, with its half knowledge, its prejudices, its lies and evasions? Pye shook his head. Too easy, too generalized. It could happen at any time, to anyone; that was why life was worth living. But one became wary with age, unwilling to risk one's vulnerability, fearing to offer the fragile cup of one's own distilled essence, and warier still of accepting another's. There could be no return to the childhood pacts sworn in the deep secrecy of attics or woods, thumbs cut on penknife blades, the mingling of blood. A brother to share your fear and your loneliness and your delight. Another you walking about, an extension of yourself. In Tahiti friends exchanged names, each actually taking over the personality of the other, becoming the other. Nothing could be closer than that merging.

Pye passed the stilled fountains of Trafalgar Square, walking diagonally across to Whitehall, the impressive bulk of the National Gallery behind him. Through the Arch lay St James's Park, the ducks quiet, the grass recovering from the assault of many feet, the water cool and secretive. He had always responded to the self-containedness of the London lakes. But then, at this time, all London was mysterious and magical, for the violated country seemed to stir under its stones and behind its buildings; each plane tree an outpost awaiting its opportunity to take over.

A taxi, late or early, passed him at a cruising pace and he saluted the driver, feeling that they alone owned the city. For the birds, who would awaken at dawn, very soon now, had not yet put in their first piping claim. A man emerged from a sewer near Scotland Yard and then vanished.

*I need a friend*

Friends were like ships signalling, like these sleepless traffic lights; the warning, the beckoning, the stop. One had to read them accurately or invite a punch on the jaw. The desolate seas, like these streets, would be featureless without them. What port are you bound for? What have you seen to the nor'-nor'-east? Mermaids or typhoons or the white back of Moby Dick? Friends were extra eyes, extra limbs. . . . He was very tired and a fragment swam through his head, 'Lamps for my gloom, hands guiding where I stumble.' But the poet meant the deathless dead, their tried words would never wound, nor betray, nor forsake.

He leant on the bridge at Westminster and remembered Penelope. Here had been his first real contact with her. Here she had talked about the lights. The reflections, she had said, were really other lights held up from the river bottom by the ghosts of suicides. Suicide. He looked deep into the noncommittal water, his mind flinching away from the one thought that had lain there like a silent watcher all night long, only rising now with the sun into full sight. He knew now what the man had done after he had knocked him down. Knew beyond reason and beyond any logical doubt.

That cry, that repudiation. After the failure of the private whisper, the public shout. Then at what point in a man's or a woman's life did communication with other people become impossible? When did a hand held out in friendship become a weapon? No one called out like that until he was past being able to give or receive in friendship or love. Was that perhaps the final loneliness? Was it at that precise moment the trap closed forever?

He shivered as Big Ben struck five-thirty, and the birds took over London. The first traffic had been stirring for some time before he moved away. A policeman strolled by, gave him a sharp glance before deciding to nod civilly.

'Lovely morning, sir,' he said.

It was really far too early, but Penelope's mews flat lay behind Victoria towards Pimlico. He could be there in a quarter of an hour. He could not, for some reason, face his neutral room. He started to walk quickly, compulsively, shaken out of his usual serenity by a bubbling panic. He had never in his life measured his own need and he was too tired to do more than acknowledge it now. As he went briskly along his legs moved automatically, like a man at the end of a long journey, and he caught himself wondering just how much love came into friendship – and how was friendship different from love? But he was too sleepy, too unwilling, and altogether unable to answer his own question.

Penelope Hinton awoke with the fear of birds beating about her head. She sat up in the first bleached emptiness of dawn, expecting the bed to be on a precarious platform cantilevered into space. A low rumbling some way far below emphasized this feeling of suspension. Cautiously she looked about her. The birds had gone, then. The twittering and the clap of wings and the soft collapse of her walls, that had gone, too; the dream was merged into the dawn sounds of an awakening city and the first underground trains. But the sense of oppressiveness and strangeness persisted. The window was in the wrong place; someone had pushed the ceiling down to a preposterous, claustrophobic level. Buildings seemed to crowd about her. She could not sense the park.

Just as her heart began to beat unpleasantly fast she saw the red-shaded lampshade by her bed. Beneath it lay her reading spectacles and the empty cup of the night before. The kitten's warm body stirred beside her, clawing gently into her arm. She lay back, looking round this room as if it were entirely strange to her. It was odd to think that she would never again wake up in the shared bedroom in the flat near the park. Another thing was odd, too. This was the first time she had awakened for months without instantly thinking of Jamie, seeing his face dissolve as her eyes opened. The dream of the birds had chased him away, and for some reason this filled her with panic. Closing her eyes again, she heard the rustle of their wings once more as they came in flocks, bearing greyish-green leaves in their beaks, perking bright looks at her. In they hopped over the window-sill and it was comical at first to see them rubbing the leaves over the walls and ceilings. Comical until the walls and ceilings began to melt where they had been touched and a fretwork of holes appeared. The dry rustle of their wings and beaks increased as more and more birds, some tiny, some the size of crows, and all colours, flew in and out of the holes, bearing away lumps of plaster, bringing more leaves to hasten the destruction. Then as if at a signal they all rose up, hovering above her, their eyes crowding like black stars, wings beating, claws drawn back, and they burst up and through the collapsing room. Exposed, she trembled in a bed left like a forgotten piece of furniture in a bombed house.

'God! I must get up and make some tea,' she said aloud. 'I'll take one of those sedatives tonight. I shouldn't still need them. I'm better now. It's absurd.'

She thought she had done with pills to replace the comfort of a shoulder and a murmured word when a nightmare swept down. Impatiently she pulled on her Chinese dressing-gown and went through into the kitchen to put the kettle on. At once she shuddered. There on the window-sill were two pigeons, looking in at her and cooing in expectation of bread. She ran to the window in a nervous, shaking rage, flung it open and shooed them away. As they flew off in loud flapping outrage she seemed to hear a whistle from below. Then she pulled the window towards her and was fastening it when once again the whistle sounded. It was followed by a low call.

'Impossible,' she told herself, but looked out to prove the impossibility.

Down below stood Pye Rumpelow. They stared at one another without a word. Then he said, 'Don't be alarmed. I've come from Stefan's. Nika and Spencer were there and we've been talking half the night and I've walked about the rest. I've been thinking about –' he paused –'friendship.'

Penelope's face relaxed. 'It would be an act of just that to ask you up for a cup of tea. I'm making one now. I'll come down.'

A few moments later he stood in the little kitchen beside her, leaning heavily with both hands on the table. 'You look extremely elegant for this hour of the morning. Couldn't you sleep?'

She shook her head. 'I always seem to wake abominably early these light mornings. Anyway, the kitten wants to go out.' As if she had heard, Mishti-San came and stood beside them, her pink and white mouth opening in a yawn, stretching her long clumsy paws and elongating her creamy body into ludicrous thinness.

Penelope ran down and opened the door for the kitten, then came back as the kettle whistled, and made tea. She carried a tray through into the sitting-room and Pye stretched out on the divan by the window and looked down on the tree outside. She brought him over a cup and said, 'You were right. I was lucky to have that tree.' Then she looked closer and said, 'Pye, you're exhausted. You simply must sleep.'

'I've a man to see at twelve,' he said, drank half his tea, handed her the cup and let his head slip back on to the cushions. He was at once asleep.

Penelope could not believe it. Only babies and the very old dropped off so immediately. She brought some light woven blankets, pink and yellow – her latest extravagance – from her own room and put them over him. Her hand hovered above his face, the broad brow, but his eyelids did not twitch, nor did his expression change, unless exhaustion gave him more than his customary pallor and thinned the plump cheeks. She sat down and watched him as she drank her tea. It was new for her to care for him and it gave her an immediate sense of security. She was unaccountably touched and curious at the chance that had brought him here, at the intimacy of sitting by a sleeping man. He did not look vulnerable, nor clenched into torpor, he had not retreated into insensibility; he had merely retreated into some inner world, there was about him now the calmness and certainty of a monk. Looking down at him, she wondered why and when he had first grown his beard: to defeat a barber's rash, hide a weak chin? No, this beard of his was an essential part of the man. It gave each feature added significance and alertness, emphasizing his startling smile by breaking up the planes and surfaces of his cheeks. In fact, it was abominably right. It had an Elizabethan swagger, yet lay close to his skin, well disciplined, comforting. This was a face that quickened into kindness and instant understanding; this firm, full mouth accepted life and dealt with it. Having him there switched the day from what she had feared it was going to be into one of pleasure and ease.

She left him sleeping and had her bath. Then she half-dressed and lay on her bed and tried to read, but fell asleep in the middle of a sentence, the book dropping open on to her chest. Much later the noise of a motor-bicycle starting up along the mews awoke her with a start. It was nine o'clock.

At once she got up, dressed, went into the other room, remembering her visitor. He was still asleep, so she prepared breakfast – coffee, toast – fetched the milk and papers. Then suddenly he was awake, sitting up refreshed, not puzzled, asking the time.

'You've plenty of time,' said Penelope, laughing. 'It's half-past nine. Will you have breakfast now, or would you like a bath first?'

'Ah, that's one of the social differences between us, Penelope. I bath at night, like the working classes – and not every night, either. I'll just wash.'

When he came back she said, 'What an extraordinary remark. It must be because it's so early. Shall I fry you some bacon and egg? I don't have kidneys in a silver dish, I'm afraid,' she added, teasing.

'Now that's disappointing. I used to adore those descriptions of country-house breakfasts: ten different dishes on the sideboard, everything from cold beef to kippers. Porridge and egg I always got if I was lucky.'

'Well, so did I. Children were never indulged. And that wasn't my background anyway, as you know perfectly well. What curious ideas you have! Look, do let me cook you egg and bacon. It smells so good for one thing, and I'm never tempted to cook it for myself.'

'Cook it now, then, and we'll have it together,' said Pye. 'I'm sorry I went off to sleep like that. It's a habit I cultivated in the war. Useful, but scarcely polite.'

He heard her laughing as the bacon began to frizzle and smell, and followed her into the kitchen. She had already set the table and as he went over to see whether anything more was needed, he caught himself looking at the portrait on the wall. It was not the first time he had seen it there, and as always he longed for the young Penelope to turn away from the window and smile at him. Unable to stop himself, he looked across the kitchen at the other Penelope, and at that moment she turned, smiled, and held out two plates of bacon and eggs. As he took them from her he stared at her with such surprise and pain that she exclaimed, 'Pye, what's the matter?'

He shook his head. 'It's nothing.'

They sat down in silence and began to eat.

'Well,' said Pye with an effort, 'isn't it usual to tell your dreams at breakfast?'

Penelope shrugged. She felt oddly ill at ease.

'One has usually forgotten them by then.'

'You haven't,' said Pye. He was recovering his self-control, and smiled to coax her. 'I should guess that you were woken by one, and, according to the old saying, you can't break it until you tell it. So tell it.'

She told him about it, gaining confidence as she went on, forgetting his passing look of pain. As she spoke, the birds lost their power, the walls and the roof were whole again. She was clothed and protected, given back to herself. He made no comment when she had finished, merely shook his head at her.

She said, looking down at Mishti-San greedily lapping milk, 'That's why cats are so much better to live with than people. They don't lie awake in the night and weep for their sins, or frighten you with nightmares.'

'No,' replied Pye. He seemed to find it difficult to talk this morning. 'They have the supreme art of living in the present. Lucky creatures.'

As they smoked over their coffee, Penelope asked how he had enjoyed his party, and why he had ended up at Stefan's.

'Oh,' said Pye, reviving. 'It was dreadful. You were quite right not to come. I called on Stefan pretty late because something was bothering me and we began to talk about God and ended up as usual with the flesh and the devil. By the way, have you a newspaper?'

173

She handed him both of them and he looked through them thoroughly, scrutinizing the stop press. Nothing. Of course, it would be in the evening edition, if at all. Bodies were sometimes washed into hidden places, caught on debris, trapped by the tide. He rose to go.

'If you take any more night walks,' said Penelope, 'you must call in again for breakfast. It has been nice.'

'Better still if you come with me. We ought to make the most of this mild weather. Let's have dinner very soon – a late one – and then just stroll about. Stefan's right, you know. London's a different city at night.' At the door he turned. 'And thanks, Penelope. I needed a friend just then.'

'Who doesn't at some time or other?' she replied, smiling gravely at him as she closed the door.

'Damn,' he thought, in a kind of anguish and fear as he walked swiftly away, his heels striking the cobbles. 'I shouldn't have gone to her.' It was as if that smile had been waiting for him all these years. Why couldn't he keep away? Who was he to fall in love at forty-five? It was a shock even greater than last night's punch on the jaw, the revelation by the river. He cursed the fragile dividing line between love and friendship, over which he had stepped so easily, so unintentionally.

'This evening,' he told himself, 'I am going to get very drunk indeed.'

## 15

LEWIS HALF-WOKE to that same morning, a sound like sea washing over pebbles in his sleep-stopped ears. A sound like rooks cawing and hustling as they gathered in the dusk. A sound like a controlled wind blowing through dry branches. Beech, because he remembered whole sheltered groves of them even in spring with the brown remembrance of winter kept intact among the green bustling of new life.

This was a dawn sound. He stumbled out of bed and across to the window.

His room overlooked the narrow passage that led to the park and gave him back a green echo of his lost time. Then, staring along the greening cone of the path, he saw at the far end men in khaki on khaki-coloured horses. In that neutral light colours became less than themselves – like discoloured pictures in old albums. Piebald, roan or grey, to Lewis the horses were khaki too. He watched them, a long line of them, it seemed, passing along the outer circle of the park, each framed briefly between the trees. Then he listened as the sound of their hooves on the road died away. The compact secrecy of that long line filled him with joy. Horses. His mother was right then. You never knew what was going on in London.

It did not occur to him to follow them. That would be a revolutionary act, and action was impossible to him since the violent uprooting of the previous summer. Now, although he did not fully realize it, passivity had become security. No longer able to flow with life like a river between safe banks of habit and routine, Lewis had slowed down, dulled to a backwater.

Thought then, instead of movement, instead of the bold rush in pursuit of the horses. *Watch the wall, my darling, while the gentlemen ride by.*

Climbing back into bed, he thought over his discovery. It worried him that he had taken so long to recognize that light and rapid stepping. Shutting his eyes, he held the image of Lesley's horse in front of him. A roan, with a high arch to the neck. Why Lesley's horse, and not his own pony? The answer came at once. It was the sound. Of course, the sound that belonged to that time when the house and the garden in the hills had belonged to him. At night, when she rode over to see his mother and father, he had always known when she was coming. Far off on the main road, across the silence of wood and meadow, he had heard – could hear now – the sharp clopping of Panda. He smiled to himself at having remembered the name. Sometimes it was Panda, sometimes it was Prince. The noise would lessen as the rider turned into the long lane, soft with mud and cow-droppings, that led past the very old Colonel's house, with its windows open summer and winter. (In the snow they were still open, and the old man had once told his mother that he took a couple of wine bottles to bed with him, filled with hot water, as a concession to his eighty years.) Along the lane then, until it led past the farm. Mr Humphreys had a haystack opposite his house, for easy cutting. Wrinkling up his nose under the bedclothes, Lewis at once smelt the sweet hay, as the farmer cut it like one of his wife's fat fruit cakes. That had been one January, a warm and blue day. But he mustn't lose track of Panda. There she was, going strongly over the hard surface of the lane; here her hooves rang out strong and sharp. Then a pause. Lesley was getting off to open the gate. Then the hollow sound as she urged the horse over the wooden bridge that crossed the narrow stream that bounded the Glantamar land. Now she was on the long stony drive that crossed the big field where Mr Humphreys's geldings were allowed to graze with Beauty. A stone rung as it was kicked aside; the trotting became louder and yet muffled in the soft bits of the drive. His father always meant to fill in the ruts, but never had. Then she was at the iron gate that led into the garden. Pause, a clear call, and the ground shook as Panda wheeled triumphantly into sight. . . .

Sighing, he turned over on to his side. These early morning sounds from outside, they were like the first far-off skirmishes of an invading army, the muted stealthy preparations for attack. Away across the park came the sudden bark of a sea-lion, the truncated roar of lion or tiger awaking from dreams of freedom to iron bars and concrete floors and the composite stare of the crowd. Nearer, on the lake, the ducks stirred with loud quacks. Lewis conjured up the picture of those blunt gentle beaks pulled out of the warmth of their wings, their necks straightening out to greet the pearly sheen of the captive water. The light strengthened. The sound of birds outside his window, the sharp twitter of sparrows, the coo of pigeons, brought the unavoidable day nearer. The enemy was closing in. Shutting his eyes against the light, he heard sounds from the street. The first buses rumbled past, a lorry revved up, speeding along the road that led to the heart of London, perhaps following the great yellow and grey signboard that had excited him so much when he first came from Wales. He had caught at them like a prisoner being carried away from his own camp, noting all the signs along the road, so that he would be able to find his way back: a curious tree, a white hump of a house, a factory chimney that spelt the Midlands, the spreading smoke and sprawl of low houses that was Birmingham. Then, the signposts. He loved rolling the words 'To the North' on his tongue. One day he would, by following these instructions, stride out and away from London, to the north. It had a cold sound, it hinted of sinister things, like the splinter of ice in Kay's heart.

A rough voice sang a sudden snatch of song down in the mews below. The workmen had arrived. They had arrived with the spring, throwing down scaffolding which clattered tinnily on to the cobbles outside like a badly played scale. They were painting the outside of the house, and sometimes from their perilous swinging platforms they would bend down to peer in at him and grin. Just then, someone pulled the bedclothes away and scrambled into bed beside him.

It was Sally. Still warm from sleep, she crept beside him and patted his face. At once he was comforted. Dear fat Sally, the day held only pleasure for her. She loved it. She loved people, even the ones along the Terrace. She loved to chatter all day long. And now she wanted to be amused, and demanded a story. He groaned in mock dismay to make her more eager. His thoughts were still hazy with the horses and the dawn and the pictures he had flicked through in his mind like old postcards, so that he would never forget anything at all about Glantamar.

'Lewis, tell me about the van again – those children in the van.'

'But I told you that last week, Sally. You tell it to me.' He knew she wouldn't; the part of story-teller always fell to him. Sally was a born listener. When she grew up she would be the sort of reader writers hope for. She yearned for a story, and even at three years old was a creative listener, so that the story-teller went to great lengths to surpass himself. She listened with the grave attention that did not allow her to interrupt, except in the interests of the story.

Knowing that he would soon begin, she now settled herself comfortably against his shoulder and waited.

'Well, it was a summer's day in a place a long way from here. A place you had to go through big black towns and over great rivers to reach, then you were over fields, and . . .'

'Bang, there you were in the mountains.' Sally could not resist this, and her brother nodded, blowing her fine hair out into a fan over her face. 'Yes, bang you were in the mountains. Well, in that beautiful place was a big house, and in the big house lived a family like ours. They were a happy family until one day the father said, "I feel I am buried alive among all these mountains, and this house has too many rooms. We shall go to a big city where I shall have many friends and I shall make a lot of money." So one day when the boy was at school, sitting by the window at his desk watching Mr Jones the schoolmaster putting Welsh verbs on the blackboard a shadow fell over his exercise book. It was the shadow of the great big green furniture van, the biggest anyone had ever seen in the village. All the boys got up to look at it as it went by. And it made a dreadful noise, changing gears to get up the hill. Mr Jones rapped on the board with his long pointer and shouted out, "Boys! Back to your places, please. That van has nothing to do with us. . . ." ' Lewis could not go on, and to encourage him Sally said softly, 'But it had to do with the boy by the window. It was the van come to take his home away inside it. Oh, Lewis, poor boy!'

Lewis steadied his voice, blinked, and went on, 'Anyway, the boys all looked at the one by the window and Mr Jones said to him, "Lewis Manley, what is this word on the board? Stand up, please, when you answer." And the boy stood up and said in a clear voice, because he felt a bit queer, "Cofio, sir. To remember." Then he sat down. Then Mr Jones took off his spectacles and smiled at him, and said, "Good boy. That is what we want you to do. To remember us, and to remember the Welsh, for you have a fine voice for the Welsh singing. Now we will all stand up and sing the Welsh anthem for Lewis, who is leaving us this afternoon." And they all stood up and sang.'

There was such a long silence that Sally said at last, 'What happened then?'

She knew perfectly well, for only a week or two ago Lewis had been able to add a happy ending for her. To him this ending only became real as he told it to her; even now he scarcely believed it. But his face cleared as he went on, 'Well, they all got to London, and lived in a place which hadn't got a garden, except one everyone else shared, and this garden had two horrible ogres, called gardeners, who burnt all the leaves before Guy Fawkes day, to stop the children having a bonfire . . .'

'But they *did* have a bonfire!'

'Yes. They made one of old boxes and things, but it wasn't half as big as the one they had in Wales. That one was as high as a house and the sparks flew right up to the moon. Nothing's any good here. And the boy went to school in a place like a great prison, or a castle kept by a giant, and people shouted at him all the time and twisted his arm, and corridors and class-rooms smelt of cabbages and dirty feet. . . .'

Sally suppressed a giggle, and Lewis pinched her. Her mouth opened, but she decided after all not to cry, or it would spoil the nice end of the story. She didn't want to be left with cabbages and dirty feet until the next morning.

'So he hated this place and planned to run away when he was older. But then, one day, his father came and said, "No school for you today, son. We're going down to the country today. Not Wales, but Oxfordshire, and we're going to see about a new school, a choir school where you'll do a lot of singing and live there in term time. If you sing well and do a few sums and talk to the headmaster, and if you like him and he likes you, you might be able to go there. But this isn't a promise, mind, it's a try. So do your best." So they took a train and got to another city. But a nice one, and the school was more like a church, all grey stones and lots of green grass and great stained glass windows, like the church in the village. And the boy sang, and did as he was told, and it was easy. The headmaster looked like our vicar, with a kind of black cloak on. Then they came home. And a few weeks later his father came up with a funny smile on his face and showed him a letter and said, "Well done, Lewis, you've won a scholarship. You'll be going to St Magnus's as a choirboy as well as a schoolboy." So everything was all right.'

'Everything was all right,' sighed Sally, as Nika came in with her orange juice.

'Lewis, it's time to get up or you'll be late for school. It's going to be a lovely day, so Sally and I will meet you and have tea in the park, if it's warm enough.'

Lewis threw back the clothes and said grumpily, 'No, thank you. You and Sally have tea in the park. I don't like it.'

Nika looked disappointed and her voice was sharp.

'Don't be absurd, Lewis. If you don't want us to come to the school gates we'll wait for you by the fence that runs along by the zoo and where we can see the animals over the top.'

'I'd rather come straight home, thank you,' said Lewis. His

obstinate voice was cold, and his mother sighed sharply as she went out of the room. Sally asked curiously why he didn't want a lovely picnic.

'Because of the people. Because of the hundreds of silly people! It isn't our park, stupid. It's everyone's, and I hate their silly faces.' He stuck his tongue out at her and ran down to the bathroom.

In the tiny kitchen that looked over the mews Nika stood cooking the breakfast. Although she had been doing this every morning for nearly a year now, she still had the strong feeling that this was an interlude, and not entirely real. Perhaps it was the size of the place, she thought. Being so high up and not being able to walk out at ground level into your own garden. She missed the garden most of all. The house she had nearly exorcised; its memory existed as a secret, in some inviolable place in her mind. Back in the autumn she had thought about it continuously, seeing the heavy tracks the cattle would make in the dew, the soft mists caught up in the spiders' webs in the blackberry bushes, the wet brussels sprouts she used to cut for lunch, shaking them to make a rainbow for Lewis.

It still seemed odd to buy vegetables, and not feed the waste to pigs; odd to buy fruit for jam, to have milk delivered instead of fetching it in cans across the soaking, sunny fields. . . . She shook herself out of nostalgia. It was spring. It was London, and soon she would be able to see the red and blue and white sails of the boats on the lake; the crocuses had been wonderful, but the snowdrops had been poor things compared to those which flourished wild at Glantamar. . . . The toast was burning. As she removed the charred pieces she heard the workmen outside, calling to Sally.

She was tired this morning, and no wonder, after that late night at Stefan's. What rubbish men talked! And yet how revealing it was. She had never before seen Pye and Stefan in such an unhindered light. She had always suspected that Stefan never saw people as people, but merely as a means to some end or other: last night, the human problem that had upset Pye so badly had merely become for Stefan an allegorical exercise.

Grudgingly she had to admit that the argument, if you could call it one, had been well spun, but this made her distrust him more than ever. He whirled his ideas in the air like so many tough, gossamer-thin lariats, lassooing whom he wanted. A bright-eyed spider. Whereas Pye . . . she would always be grateful to him for persuading Spencer to retrieve that slip of paper about St Magnus's. Another fortnight and the chance would have been lost. She wondered what he had said to Spencer that evening, but had not liked to ask. Things had gone a little better between them since then.

Hearing Lewis and Spencer coming upstairs, she at once bundled the rest of the breakfast things on to the trolley and pushed it into the dining-room.

Spencer looked quite fresh. He was actually joking with Lewis as he opened his letters.

'One from Sybil,' he said. 'She says she'd love to have the children for Easter if they'd like to go. What a glutton for punishment that good woman is. Let's see, you break up next week, don't you, Lewis? Then you've one more term to go.'

Lewis rolled his eyes and nodded. Sally pointed at him, shrieking with laughter. 'That's Beauty! That's Beauty!' she shouted.

'It beats me,' said Spencer, half joking, 'Lewis still thinks more about that blessed fat pony eating its head off in Sybil's fields than of going to a new school. I don't know why we bothered, Nika.'

Lewis shot his father a grave look. 'It'd be boasting if I was pleased out loud,' he said. 'Boys aren't supposed to boast about getting scholarships. They keep quiet or people sit on their heads.'

Spencer was startled into silence, but Nika asked who had told him that.

'That boy down the Terrace,' he said, 'the boy in the pink and black blazer. He sat on my head, anyway, because I went to a State school. It'll be nice to go away.'

'I'll write to Sybil today,' exclaimed Nika, furiously wondering which family the boy in the pink and black blazer belonged to. 'How sweet of her. I'll take them down, Spencer, and stay overnight. You'll be all right, will you?'

'Yes, fine.' He finished his coffee, ruffled Lewis's hair, made a face at Sally and was gone. 'Home early tonight, I hope,' he said from the stairs.

As she tidied the room, made beds, and then dressed Sally for her walk, Nika wondered whether Spencer really would be home early. He had meant it when he said it, she knew that. But she also knew that the impulse might well be lost in the mêlée of the day. And he would still expect her to be there, waiting. She knew she was taking up an unreasonable attitude again, but she was deadly tired of waiting. Sometimes she wondered just what she was waiting for. How would he feel if for once she wasn't there?

'Oh, sweet heaven, how I would love to get away,' she thought, savagely pushing the pram, bump by bump, down the long stairs. 'How I would love to leave them all, just for a little while, and go right away.'

## 16

THEY had chosen to eat Chinese food that evening; the light in the restaurant made everything golden, but subdued, like the light of a brilliant dying sunset. They had not talked much over the meal, although they enjoyed it, and their silence was, as usual, companionable.

Penelope looked at Pye, thinking how many times she had sat looking across tables at him, and what a distance there was between them. And was suddenly tired of this physical distance and of never being touched. At that moment, as if in direct response to her thought, Pye reached out a hand, took hers. The bottle of wine stood between them, and their coffee cooled. A yellow panel glimmered behind him, and Penelope withdrew her eyes from the flowing lines of the mandarin etched on it, who regarded a flower in his hand with the same bland look of the waiter who had recently filled their glasses. It seemed only civil to leave her hand in Pye's, and in all civility she did so, giving him a smile that was made tender by her extreme tiredness and tension. He leaned his head against the wall and looked along it towards her shadowed face.

'You are very beautiful and you are also – this evening – completely yourself,' he said quietly. 'I'm afraid, Penelope, that I must admit I am in love with you.'

As if he knew she would pull her hand away in instinctive reaction he at once held it tighter, and she found herself looking at that hand. Firm, square, full of a dry pulsing warmth that penetrated not only her hand but her whole body. The almost forgotten sensation it caused made her tremble, and her body hollowed with desire. She unclasped her fingers and pulled her hands on to her lap, and in a childish panic said in a strained voice, 'That's impossible. We must finish our wine and I must go home.'

Pye looked at her gravely, a flicker of animation in his eyes. 'That sounded rather abrupt and rude. Unlike you.'

Perhaps it was the tumult her body was in that made her raise her eyes to his with the ghost of coquetry. 'If you only realized it, Pye, it's a great compliment. I can't bear you to say those things to me. I have to get away.'

'Let's have some more coffee first. That's cold.'

He beckoned a waiter, and more coffee was brought almost at once. He offered her a cigarette and lighted it.

'But, Pye,' she said, 'you're still looking for something I found a long time ago. You can only find it once.'

'You're quite wrong,' said Pye. 'I stopped looking a long time ago. That's why I think I've found it now. You only know what you've been looking for when you find it.' He watched the smoke from his cigarette thoughtfully. 'When one is young there's this fury . . . this hunger . . . of wanting another human being to *know* you, understand you, think as you think. It's all egoism. Know and be known; that's the quickest way of being destroyed. At least, that's what I found.'

Her hand still lay on the table; he took it again gently, and she left it in his.

'It wasn't that way with me,' she said, in a whisper.

'I know. You were lucky. So neither of us needs that kind of relationship any longer. There are other kinds, less urgent, but just as necessary. You can't jump into the river in the same place twice.'

She found herself repeating his words. They had a sanity and a logic which steadied her, reduced the shock of hearing him say, 'I am in love with you.'

'You see, I do love you, he was saying. 'I've thought about it a great deal, and I know it's true.'

Seeing her cup empty, he pushed back his chair, and at once a waiter hovered. Her coat was brought, and as they left together each of the five waiters bowed and said good-night, their five mandarin faces broken up into broad smiles.

'They're pleased to see us go, poor things. They want to close up,' said Penelope, adding in amazement, 'It's nearly midnight.'

The restaurant was empty, and she had not noticed it. All the evening people must have been coming and going, but she had not been aware of them.

'I don't think they were smiling because of that,' said Pye. 'What a child you are!' He motioned a taxi towards them with his usual ease and gave her address.

They sat apart. Penelope was in a state of profound emotional shock, and was grateful that he made no attempt at swift back-of-taxi embrace, with its ugly lurching ungracefulness. The journey was completed in silence, and she still said nothing when they drew up outside the mews and the driver looked round to ask whether he could drive out the other end.

'You can drop us here,' said Pye. 'We'll walk.'

The normal business of getting out and walking over the cobbled stones to her own front door was so difficult for Penelope that she had to hold Pye's arm. 'But this is extra-ordinary,' she told herself, 'this is how a butterfly must feel when it's breaking out of the chrysalis: this awful sickness and fluttering and fear at being suddenly aware of life outside, and knowing there are walls around you, hard gummy walls you have made yourself and must now tear down. I shall faint if we don't get indoors quickly. I simply can't stand up any longer.' As Pye opened the door with the key she handed to him, the last thing she saw was the lamplight shining through the new green leaves of the lime tree up against the wall.

Upstairs. Pye must have carried her, for she opened her eyes to see his face on a level with hers; she lay on the divan. He was holding out a glass of brandy. She took it, shaking her head at him. 'I didn't invite you up,' she said, with a faint smile.

'It's a hard thing to be reborn,' he said. 'Who was it said that the true birth of man takes a long time?'

'Dear Pye,' said Penelope, 'have you a brandy for yourself? You simply can't kneel there being profound, I won't allow it.'

'I don't need brandy now,' said Pye.

His body was warm, and his gentleness stilled the twitching nerves of her own limbs that had lain untouched for so long. Lying alone had been an unrealized torture to her, and only when he kissed her did she have a long moment of terrible sadness and guilt. But Jamie had been thin, his hands long and delicate, his bones light. Pye's hands were warm and positive. They seemed to radiate healing currents and awake desire and life where before bone and muscle and flesh had been mere necessities for walking and functioning and covering with clothes. Pye's limbs lay heavily on her own, and yet the resilience of his firm-fleshed body was reassuring. In the acute moment of the act, the melting away of physical awareness merged with such a mental lightness and release that Penelope thought she was floating. Instead, she was crying bitterly. The long agony was over.

She awoke to find herself covered by one of the brilliant Shetland blankets from her bed. There was a smell of coffee, and a small lamp glowed by the electric fire.

'You look nineteen,' said Pye, coming in from the kitchen. He, too, had flung a coloured blanket around himself, and tied it with her dressing-gown cord. He looked rather like a tubby Indian chief and she burst out laughing.

'Oh, I'm so glad I'm not, and you're not! I think it's such a terribly tentative age, and prickly, and . . . well, if I were, I should have been in tears –' She stopped abruptly and blushed.

'There are different kinds of tears. And innocence isn't purely physical. I've made some coffee, and now we'll both drink brandy.' He radiated a deep cheerfulness, and was ready to talk. 'You're very brave, Penelope. I really thought you'd run away. You looked so frightened in the restaurant.'

She stretched lazily, with abandon, and the blanket slipped to reveal her breast. At once she pulled the blanket up, holding it while she drank her coffee. Pye moved to her side, pulled it away, to cup and kiss the breast.

'You should be proud of your body,' he said. 'You're a beauti-

187

ful woman, but you really are most unversed in the arts of love. Haven't you heard of the excellent immodesty that should exist between lovers?'

He was teasing her, and he looked dangerously attractive; he was young and completely carefree, compact and self-assured; his eyes, in the light of the lamp, gleamed bluer than Mishti-San's. Reminded of the kitten, Penelope called her.

'She's asleep on your bed,' said Pye. 'I saw her when I went in for the blankets. How inconsequential you are! Oh, Penelope, I do love you.'

He sat on the floor by the divan, his head on her lap. He was waiting for her words, hoping, but not asking. Instead of speaking, she bent to kiss him, then drew away and smiled.

'Yes, for the moment it's enough for you to smile at me. I can read what I like into it, can't I?' He jumped up and began to dress. 'Penelope, darling, please stay liberated – completely liberated – for your own sake first, then for mine.'

He kissed her and left.


The reaction was terrible. It started before dawn.

She had been dreaming about Jamie, and as he bent towards her his face shifted and dissolved like a shaken jelly and became Pye's face, gazing down on her with the intense anxiety she had come to associate with the final act of love, before his eyes closed and his face drifted away somewhere to the right, and she sat up, trembling. Now the tension of the past two years had been dissipated and her body no longer troubled her, the words Pye had murmured came back to her with sickening force, and it seemed outrageous that any man other than Jamie should say them to her, for they meant nothing, nothing at all. What she could not bring herself to think about were the words she had murmured back.

All at once she was overcome by nausea, and half rolled off the divan, the blanket still round her, one hand clapped over her bruised mouth. She got to the bathroom just in time and was horribly, shudderingly sick, kneeling there on the cold black and white tiles, her head bowed as if in propitiatory prayer.

When she had recovered, she turned on her bath, and then began to clear up the flat, hastily washing the brandy glasses and cups, shaking the cushions, replacing the blankets on her bed, thoughtlessly disturbing the kitten as she did so; destroying evidence. As she stood in the kitchen she saw the blank space on the wall where her portrait had hung. 'Thank God all the pictures were collected,' she said aloud. 'Thank God it wasn't there.'

She sank into a deep, hot bath, scrubbing every inch of her body as if she had been in the mud of a rugger scrum, and as she stepped out refused to acknowledge that she felt extremely well. She examined herself carefully in the long wall glass and then turned away sharply. This had been her first action after she and Jamie had become lovers, as if she expected her body to change, sprout a tail or wings.

Back in the bedroom she packed a suitcase, looked out the kitten's carrying-basket and then had what Pye called one of her hot breakfasts, a cigarette and a cup of coffee. Then she telephoned for a cab and sent a wire to Sybil. The cab arrived before nine, just as the telephone bell began to ring. It was still ringing as she ran down the stairs and slammed the door behind her.


'But, my dear, leave everything now and go to Greece! You're mad!'

'I may very well become so, Sybil, if I don't go away. Look, there's this cruise all round the Greek islands, with a load of professors on board to lecture all about them.'

Sybil made a face of comic dismay.

'How horrible! Why not a gentle trip to Madeira and lie in the sun without all that culture?'

'Because I must keep my mind active. Anyway, I've always wanted to go to Greece. I couldn't bear to lie in the sun with

all those dreadful people. I don't want people, Sybil, I want
*things.* Old things –'

'They'll certainly be old,' Sybil burst out, with one of her
loud laughs.

'For Christ's sake can't you leave sex out of it for a change?'
This, she realized too late, was a give-away. Penelope almost
never swore. She saw a flicker of curiosity in Sybil's eyes, and
rushed on to cover her mistake: 'I can't stand London, Sybil.
Suddenly it's too much for me. I can't explain, but I must get
away, think things out. You'd be a kind of protection for me,
that's why I'm asking you to come. I want to absorb facts until
I burst with them. Don't you realize that I know nothing, absolutely nothing about anything?'

Sybil stared at her, shrewdly assessing this unaccustomed
nervous excitement, then sobered. But she let an offended
expression dwell on her face until she was sure Penelope had
noticed it.

'I don't really think it's my idea of a holiday, darling,' she
said at last. 'And it's madly expensive. Why not ask Nika to go
with you? I'm having the children for Easter, anyway. They
can stay on.'

Penelope looked at her in awe. For once Sybil had said
exactly the right thing.

'Of course! What a wonderful idea, Sybil! She'd adore it,
poor child. I can pay for her, too, if any of Jamie's pictures sell
at this exhibition. If not, Spencer can always pay me back bit
by bit. You'll take good care of Mishti-San? Watch out for
rabbit-traps?'

'Look, Penelope,' said Sybil firmly. 'Ring Nika now. No,
tackle Spencer first, as a matter of form. Men like to be
consulted.'


'Then you'd like to go?'

Spencer had for once come home early, and was already re-
gretting it. His meal was not ready, and Nika was having a
difficult time with Sally, who had started a cold and kept

screaming that she couldn't breathe through her nose. Lewis was in one of his mad moods, standing on his head just inside the bathroom, with his feet against the door, so that when Spencer went in – one of the disadvantages of the flat was that the lavatory and bathroom were together – he knocked him over. More roaring.

'I'd like to what?' shouted Nika above the din.

'Don't shout!' Spencer yelled back up the stairs. 'We'll discuss it later.'

At last the flat settled into quietness. The burnt macaroni cheese had been eaten, the baked apples and custard dispatched, and they sat by the fire with their coffee.

'I couldn't believe it when you rang,' said Nika. 'Now do explain.'

'Well, Penelope has suddenly got this idea of going to Greece, and she wants you to go with her. She's staying with Sybil and rang me from there. If I'll see to the retrospective exhibition of Jamie's that Bergdorf's putting on, and if we manage to sell any of the pictures, she'll pay all your expenses. If none of them sells, we can pay her back bit by bit. Seems a decent enough offer to me. I'll be surprised if half the pictures don't sell. His reputation has bounded up. The dealers are looking for his early stuff.'

'Greece,' said Nika dreamily. 'What utter bliss. I feel guilty about you, though. Will you manage all right on your own?'

'Oh, I'll only sleep here. Probably eat with Stefan most of the time. He and Bonny are getting together again now he's taken on her protégé. She cooks marvellously.'

Remembering the burnt macaroni, Nika flushed.

'I wonder if it's because Penelope wants to avoid the exhibition. It's not like her to make such a sudden decision otherwise.'

He shrugged.

'Anyway, you'll go. You're not looking too well. You seem so tensed up these days.' He added, toying glumly with her fingers, 'I suppose you're still missing Wales.'

'I try not to think about it. I really do. It must be some lack of inner harmony or something. Pye said once a person should be able to adapt to almost any place if one had that.'

'Pye's panacea! He should market it.' Spencer dropped her hand and frowned. It seemed to him that for a long time they had been ranged one on either side of a field of magnetic force that kept them apart. If only it could be switched off, this tension might disappear. Getting away from each other might do it.

Nika was looking dreamily into the fire. 'When I close my eyes sometimes I can feel – oh, how can I explain? – that absolute silence, the extraordinary peace of Glantamar.'

'Glantamar! It almost finished me.' Spencer flung off his chair in sudden rage. 'When I think of that house! The hostility of it! I wonder, since you're supposed to be so sensitive, that you didn't feel its horrible menace. Sometimes at dusk I used to feel as if an invisible clammy winding sheet was being wrapped around me.' He was sweating without being hot. 'It wanted to add us to its other ghosts.'

Nika was still gazing deeply into the fire. She felt relaxed and calm. Then the house seemed to build up before her eyes, and yet behind them. She was walking up the stairs, passing an old woman with something odd about her eyes. Each was a different colour. As she noted this, the woman nodded as if she knew her well. Then the stairs faded, the house crumbled into a piece of glowing coal and there was Spencer, sweating with indignation and fear, staring down at her.

She looked up at him unsmilingly. 'We're part of its ghosts already,' she said.


'I'm glad Penelope isn't going alone,' said Pye, when he heard the news from Spencer the following week. In his new disordered state of mind he could imagine the hazards: attractive dons – were dons attractive? He knew nothing about them, but supposed they had a dry, cool charm that would suit the classicism of Greece. Absurdly, he was filled with hatred for all men bred within cloisters, with their tittering pedanticisms, for he saw at once that Penelope would divine in them a guarantee of sexual neutrality and would therefore be at ease. He could imagine her listening to them, giving them the whole of her attention, watching their faces with the intensity of the short-sighted person. Anyway, he told himself with growing rage, their interest in women was probably merely academic. They'd be too busy procuring small boys in Athens. Bloody pederasts.

'Why on earth she should take it into her head to go off to Greece beats me,' said Spencer. 'Didn't she tell you she was going?'

'No,' said Pye. His tone did not invite questions. He should have guessed something like this would happen, though. There had been no reply when he rang, and he had kept on ringing the whole morning. All through that day he had thought about her, and now, a week later, he still did so, seeing her wrapped in that coloured blanket on the divan; the soft hair on her neck, the delicate eyelids closed, heavy with satisfaction, the slight shoulders and small, still full breasts, the vulnerable droop of her wrists. With helpless, loving rage he had put down the receiver at last, feeling responsible, feeling that something unaccountable had happened. When he had called round in the evening, there were no lights showing, no reply to his ring. She had run away from him again, leaving him for the first time lonely, filled with desolation and the fear that if he lost her now he was condemned for the rest of his life to the dreary niche he had always occupied with women. The only thing he could do was to write to her, and the only hope he had was that he would say the right thing.

Penelope found Pye's letter on her return from Wales. She did not open it, tucked it away instead in her handbag behind her cheque-book. She had deliberately given herself only a few days in London before the start of the cruise, so that she could truly say she was too busy to see him. By taking this course she was aware of her own immaturity, her own cowardice, and aware, too, that she was giving him pain. But going into her own place again, she was overwhelmed by a sense of amazement, of affront even, of disbelief. She had not expected, on the verge of middle age, such passion and such abandon. She had supposed she had simmered down in obedience to her children's unspoken desires – for as they grew up surely their parents should grow old? To accept that fact now seemed to her – although they would never know of it – a belated apology, a twisted way of making amends for the exclusive and excluding love she and Jamie had shared. A punishment, too, for her friendship with Pye, which had flared so spontaneously and dangerously into something more.

Wandering round the three small rooms, still in her outdoor clothes, she was overcome by fear and a sense of utter loneliness. For by allowing Pye to make love to her, and, she had to admit, by loving him back with joy and release, had she not put that life with Jamie completely into the past? It was an irrevocable action, the curtain ringing down on the second act of a play while the set was changed. With this idea in her mind Penelope felt the emptiness of that set. She suddenly missed her old furniture, each piece with its aura of enduring safety. Everything was gone from her past life, and she hated the new low, spiritless things with which she had been prompted to replace them. This flat was exactly like a stage, with the scene set for a seduction, rain outside and the insidious creeping of old age in the corners. All at once she felt utterly unable to fulfil any rôle whatever when the curtain went up.

'I wish I were dead,' she said aloud to the empty room. But how? Gas? Sleeping tablets? They seemed a sordid means to a doubtful end. They would underline her failure; more important, such a negative gesture would reflect on Jamie, and, she was amazed to discover herself thinking with pain, also on Pye, who had courage and who hated waste.

The door-bell rang, and at once she ran to the window in a kind of panic. With relief she saw it was Nika and went down to let her in.

'I had to come,' said Nika. 'I knew you'd be back today. Isn't it exciting? I wanted to ask you about clothes and things. . . .' Then she noticed Penelope's pallor, and exclaimed, 'Are you all right? Let me make you a cup of tea, you look exhausted.'

'I'm all right. I'm a bit tired, that's all. I suppose it's the journey. I was just wondering what to take with me. How lucky you came, Nika.'


A few days later, they stood at the carriage window, talking to Spencer, who had come to see them off, when Penelope caught sight of Pye hurriedly weaving his way up the platform, with various parcels in his arms.

'He's thinner,' she thought at once, and her whole body contracted inside her clothes.

He came up to the window, having recognized Spencer, and looked at Penelope. She gave him her hand.

'I'm sorry, Pye,' she said.

'Please write, Penelope. Here are some chocolates and fruit – oh, and a book for the journey. Good-bye, Nika, have a good trip. Good-bye now . . .'

As the train steamed out, the two figures on the platform grew smaller until they were entirely engulfed in black smoke. It was then, as she settled back in her seat, that Penelope remembered the letter in her handbag. She had still not opened it.

## 17

Venice.

My dear Pye [wrote Penelope],

I was greatly touched by your letter, and by your understanding, which I am careful not to take for granted. You are
of course right in many of the things you say, but this journey
is, for me, not essentially a flight from reality – I hope it will
be rather a flight towards a new *kind* of reality. It is after all
the first positive step I have taken on my own since Jamie's
death. Yet I feel I'm travelling for all the wrong reasons and
the whole thing is still so unreal as to make me bad company
for Nika, who is struck dumb by Venice (where we have 'the
whole morning', as they say in the itinerary notes, in which to
see it for ourselves! This sort of thing, I feel, will be the snag
of this trip). For instance, to Nika, this keyhole glimpse of
Venice means bells, fountains, marble angels, little bridges,
stalls of flowers, their scent overlaying the smell of standing
water, whereas I, on my third visit, take all these lovely things
for granted, and glower ungratefully at the four horses on top
of St Mark's, which are frozen into what is – for me, anyway –
an impossible attitude. I thought only camels moved with their
two left legs forward and their two right legs back? Wasn't the
first moving film ever made shown to prove how a horse moved
its legs. But what a stupid quibble this is, after all!

As we progress towards ruins – and what a marvellous choice
of yours, the Rose Macaulay book, so very many thanks – it's a
blessing to see the buildings here still standing up, although
of course the *palazzi* are crumbling quietly and elegantly away,
the water eating into their foundations so invisibly and in-

sidiously that one day it will not surprise me to hear that palace after palace has dissolved without fuss into the dark smelly water of the canals (so like the water in the Regent's Park lake), like children's sand-castles. I suppose that's what Cocteau meant by his 'half-woman, half-fish, rotting away among the Adriatic marshes'! Perhaps it's a mistake to visit any city after so many poets have written about it.

It's nearly noon – we're waiting for it to strike, in fact, and crowds are filling the Square. We're sitting eating ice-cream after eluding one of our party, an earnest woman who wears her British cardigan and strap camera like heraldic badges. Ah, there it goes now, and the negro figures on either side of the famous clock each strike the bell. True to tradition the pigeons fly up, clouding the air with their wings. How stupid they must be! Unless they are bribed to put on this spectacular alarm flight every day. Anyway, it's all very effective; moving, too, in an obvious sort of way.

Nika is going off to look around the small shops; I do hope she won't come back laden with glass and beads or we shall be sadly over-burdened too early on. I shall post this before we are rounded up again to nose out through the Adriatic into the Ionian Sea. Olympia, with its echoes of the Games, is our next objective. The thought of Greece begins to seep into me, I am excited. Greece promises milk and honey – and yet I dread the drop of poison that could spoil the whole lovely cup.

Yours affectionately,<br>Penelope.

Rereading this letter, sealing it, posting it, Penelope frowned over the pompous opening sentences, the querulous tone. But it was too late to rewrite it now. 'Anyway,' she thought, having put it all down, 'I feel better.' Which was selfish, but true.

Penelope's letter reached Pye as he was leaving the house. A cold swirling wind edged its way down the street as he fingered the thin envelope with its foreign stamp, looked at her curiously dominant handwriting. The women Pye had known before had never been the kind who wrote letters. Holding this one from Penelope, he was overwhelmed by an emotion entirely new to him and his hand shook as he opened the envelope.

On the bus he sat behind a woman whose hair smelt strong and coarse, like the wet coat of an old sheep-dog. If she had been a dog it would not have offended him so much. Nor would it if her hair had not been the same colour as Penelope's. Also, Penelope smelt delicious, and he had a sensitive nose. Frowning, he read the letter through three times, searching so assiduously between the lines for hidden meanings that he could at first make no sense of the actual words. Then he steadied and his habitual control took over. Naturally she had said nothing, she was an intensely shy woman. But all the same, he was disappointed. Unaccustomed to writing letters himself, he had taken a great deal of trouble over writing to her. He had written three drafts before sending the final letter, and had expected – what? – some immediate, warm response. He read the end again. *Yours affectionately.* Was she his? And he wanted more than affection.

Disturbed by the mood of her letter, he was unaccountably irritable at the launderette he visited first that morning. It was the one in Manor Road, where he had first met her, and he could scarcely bear to look at No. 9 machine, imagining her dark head and strained face, the overflowing suds to which she had been so oblivious. Things went wrong all the morning. A pair of blankets was missing from the drying-room, there was a squabble over a ticket, a woman complained about a service charge: her laundry had been spread over three machines instead of two and she was voluble about the two extra sheets she could have brought over if she had known this. 'It's a waste of money,' she said. 'After all, I almost live here. I come in twice a week. I bring all my things here – you know me.' Her high monotone screwed Pye's nerves into dangerous tightness. He handed her bundles over and said with quiet ferocity, 'Then I suggest you live somewhere else, madam.'

The part-time girl, resting from an uncertain acting career, giggled at this. At once Pye turned to her and said, in the same voice, 'And you were thoughtless and foolish if you know this customer as well as you should. You can collect your week's money at the end of the afternoon.'

At noon he was on the telephone, trying to get a replacement. The clock in St Mark's Square striking twelve, the pigeons flying up, Penelope sitting in the sun writing to him, were jumbled together in his mind with the torrent of excuses and counter-suggestions from the various staff-bureaus he was telephoning. One girl could only come in the mornings, her child was at nursery-school. Another could come in the afternoons, but must leave at five-thirty sharp because she had to get home to cook her husband's supper. . . . Women, he decided, would drive him mad.

By the time he reached home again, having given himself a good dinner, he was in a better frame of mind. He read her letter again, and this time was able to smile. She had at least written, that meant she was thinking about him, letting him share her secret trepidations. It was like letting him see her tired, without make-up, defences down. Cheered, he began to regret her flight less, for an exchange of letters could – surely – increase their intimacy, for one wrote what could not always be said. Already he sensed an ease, a certain dry humour which was not always apparent in her conversation. What she needed now, he told himself, was a climate of intimacy without its obligations. This, then, was what he would try to establish for her.

As he began his letter he felt as he had done the first time he took her to dinner: the bird held precariously in the hand, the nervous animal that must not be frightened away.

Forget love [he wrote]. I am aware that you cannot allow yourself to be in love with me. Can you therefore think of me as a new occupation perhaps, instead of taking up bridge or good works? If it interests you, explore the idea of me as a new country, as you are discovering Greece. (It will at least be a solitary exploration, unaccompanied by women wearing heraldic badges.) I can't offer you rocky islands and temples to Apollo, or wine-dark seas, only the rocks and gales of a wind-swept childhood; suppers of herrings and shivering salty dawns bringing in the boats, youths and men with blistered blue hands. My mother's determined reading by oil-lamp, mixing the Mabinogion with *A Child's History of England*, so that my head spun. It was her fierce Welsh blood that drove the bony adolescent out of the fishing port and into the new gimcrack towns 'to better himself'.

'I don't often think about myself; but if I did, it would be as an amalgam of the old and the new – my scanty upbringing, my inheritance of the cardinal virtues, my hatred of failure and corresponding need of success, security, and the feeling that behind all this a greater pattern moves. An acknowledgement of something else – something ancient – a belief, I suppose, in the holiness of all living things, so that instead of offering gifts on an altar to an unknown god one offers instead – in thanks-giving – what one can to one's fellows. You see, I don't want to intrude on your life with Jamie.

He had to write the name that threatened his happiness, but the effort made him lay down his pen. This name had to be written, conjured with, accepted, just as he would have to go to see Jamie's pictures in order to fill in the blanks of Penelope's life. These things done, he would no longer be the outsider, the usurper, for he would have absorbed into his very life-blood the occasions, the emotions, which had made Penelope what she was at the point of time when he had met her.

So forget love [he wrote]. I may have intruded at the be-ginning, but it's fairly obvious to me now that what you had with Jamie you still have together. But I do know he shouldn't resent me – wherever he is, and to you he is a living presence – he would know you needed someone else to care for you. I care. I –

But he couldn't go on. Tomorrow he would look at the letter again, decide whether or not to rewrite it, whether or not to post it.

S.S. Helena<br>(At sea)

Spencer darling,

I'm keeping a journal to show you when I get home. It's all so terribly exciting. Venice was marvellous, but how I wish you had been with me! We could have taken a *vaporetto* and gone swishing down the Grand Canal to the Lido, where it was hot enough to bathe and not crowded. Penelope seemed unmoved, and sat and wrote to Pye in St Mark's Square. I hope the children have got the postcards I sent and that Sybil will tell Lewis all about the Bridge of Sighs.

We share a cabin on B deck. It's very comfortable, and the food is goodish. This is a small ship, Greek of course, about three hundred people and no classes, which is a good thing. We don't dress for dinner, and afterwards there's dancing or lectures. I've felt too tired to dance, so have taken copious notes. The lecturers seem nice enough, especially Professor Deacon, who is apparently a friend of Maxim Gaylord and was interested to know that you had published his poems.

I won't bore you now with details of Olympia. We drove there yesterday, right through the mountains. Imagine a thousand years of the Games, tied up as they were then with the religious ceremonies, and yet now it's a wilderness, scattered with stumps of temples. Zeus overthrown and all that shouting and clamour gone.

The Peloponnese has been written about so much, yet it still seems unreduced, if you see what I mean, because here I begin to feel the essential toughness of Greece, its spirit twangs back at you like a harpstring. There isn't the softness that has spoilt the south of England, for instance. It is all so magnificently uncosy, like North Wales but without the chill.

I may add to this later on. So now I'll just send off the postcard of the Hermes of Praxiteles. I saw the marble at Olympia. Isn't it magnificent?

I do hope you're not feeling too deserted, alone in the flat, and that you are eating well, and enjoying Bonny's cooking! I comfort myself that you would hate going everywhere in droves, darling. And you wouldn't like the deadness of museums. I can detach myself quite easily and merely extract what I want. Soon we shall be sailing through the dark, it is infinitely mysterious, the liquid stir of the dark water beneath us and the dark air melting into an unknown sky all around and above us and the great moon . . . No, you wouldn't like most of the energetic day-business, but oh, I do wish you were here to share the nights with me! Odd to think that it is Tuesday tomorrow, Tuesday in the Aegean Sea, not Tuesday in London.

My love, as always,
Nika.

Nika's letters were gay, excited, full of pleasure and regret, as if the farther away she moved from Spencer the easier she found it to communicate with him. The deadly field of magnetic force that thrust them apart when they were together switched off when, as now, she idled through blue seas in company with people who were strangers and expected nothing from her. So she wrote about everything that happened, how she felt, what she did, how she missed him. The tension of his presence removed, she longed for him to share her pleasure, forgetting that her pleasures were not his. Away from him, she saw him as an entirely different personality, he became to her untroubled mind almost benign, humorous, understanding; he and the children moved as if on a screen. She saw them with the happy tolerance of one looking back on holiday snapshots; forgetting the tantrum that had preceded the smiling group, the bitter argument over whether or not to bathe. In retrospect, even wasp stings can be amusing.

Spencer replied only shortly to these long letters. He was not jealous of the people she mentioned. He read them tolerantly, with some amusement, thinking what a child she was, half wishing that he too could throw himself open so freshly and innocently to experience. Occasionally, as he laid the sheets aside, a fleeting guilt possessed him. Such small things pleased her, she asked so little, really, and yet he could not make her happy! If he were honest he had to admit that he did not try very hard. Instead, here he was, hoarding his emotions and reactions like a woman, or like a squirrel his nuts, going over them one by one when the cold threatened and he was alone. That vital interior life gave him no time, left him no energy to extend himself to other people, even to Nika – especially to Nika. Sometimes he wondered whether, like a tree entirely devoured by white ants, yet outwardly untouched, normal, he would not some day crash to the ground.

Something of this he must have hinted to Bulfont, fingering her last letter. He felt badly talking about her at all, especially to old Bulfont, a publisher's reader and celebrity-memoir ghost, who knew every cynical trick of what he called 'the compensatio.i-dream market'. They had been drinking steadily since noon, and now it was nearly closing time. They peered gravely at each other over their glasses.

'Ah,' said Bulfont, bringing out one of his stolen phrases, 'alcohol preserves everything except secrets, dear boy. The wife's in Greece, is she? Let me know if you want a bit of fun one evening. My wife's one of those intense women, too. One of the best, mind you, but intense. Gets a man down.'

Spencer nodded. All his repressed resentment against Nika flared up. There she was in Greece, probably sitting in some temple or other, smiling up at the sun through the ruined pillars, imagining herself in touch with the old gods, while he suffered the sharp winds of an English April and the tarnished talk of a man like Bulfont.

He said, in astonished self-pity, 'I'd like a silly woman, a really silly woman – but pretty, so that I didn't have to listen, only look.'

Bulfont nodded into his half-empty glass. 'Gets a man down,' he repeated. 'Can't live on that intense level, I'm too busy. Do you know,' he went on, looking up sharply, belligerently, into

Spencer's face, 'when she brings me a cup of tea in the mornings she offers it to me as if it were – well, a gift from the gods. That's what. A gift from the gods. Imagine that! A cup of tea! It's her age, of course. And we've no children. She's only got me.'

Spencer looked at him with disgust, at the ruined, whisky-veined face. He did not know whether he hated Bulfont or himself more. He seemed to see Nika clearly, suddenly, Nika with a glass of wine, her fingers cradled round the rim, offering it to him with a kiss. For a moment he understood what betrayal was.

Some time later he left the pub. Walked until he felt sober, was again desolate. Empty, dead, lost. On impulse he went into the nearest toy-shop and chose presents for the children: a miniature American taxi for Lewis, a doll with its bathroom set all complete in a box for Sally. The woman behind the counter smiled at him as he picked them out; he always looked lost in shops and traded shamelessly on it, hesitating as he paid.

'Are you posting them, sir?' she asked. 'Shall I wrap them extra strongly for you?'

He gave her the grateful, shy smile which had saved him hours of tiresome work ever since he was a boy.

'That would be kind,' he said, knowing that to her it was a pleasure, yet bored to receive such eager service. As he went out he found himself longing for a woman who would kick him hard; quarrel, shout, fight, get furiously angry, call his bluff. He looked at the parcel swinging from his finger. He'd take the presents down himself – catch the 4.10 and stay a couple of days, Sybil wouldn't mind. He could stop off at Shrewsbury, go on to Chester, call on bookshops there. It'd be useful. And he could also call on Lesley, of whose hostility he could be reasonably certain.


'Is it possible,' Penelope wrote, 'to come to Greece and remain unchanged?' 'Quite impossible,' she thought, laying down her pen and looking through the port-hole at the dark blue sea, the golden coast of the Peloponnese away to the west. How could one take up life again after this kind of baptism? Habit could never be resumed, for life never remained in quite the same place if you once laid it down. She looked at the thin pages of Pye's letter; his small, compact, very black writing seemed to bring his physical presence into the cabin. She caught herself imagining that hand travelling over the paper, some of its warmth came through the muted words.

In a queer way [she wrote] what you started, Greece is carrying on. Here there is something painful and unavoidable in the very clarity of the air. The sun strikes sparks from the sea as we cruise between these delicious islands, strikes sparks from the piled white houses, magnifies the details of the statues (so that even I can see them without my glasses); the honey-coloured columns of ruined temples stripe the ground with black shadows; the dark green of the pines emphasizes the silver of the olive groves – here it is all contrast and balance. And the delicious smell of thyme drifts across the water. The people, when we meet them, smile at us. There is a beauty of line, a spareness, a painter would love to catch. Here there is no room for sentimentality; the very awareness of the great stretching heroic and aggressive past forces one to live in the present, and from there to step to the future. Tombs, temples, frescoes, fragments, make me aware of a past I could very well get lost in, so that my own individual, immediate past begins to wither into insignificance. You will understand these things, my dear Pye. One cannot jump from autumn to spring: winter is a necessary transition, otherwise the organism couldn't stand it!

Tomorrow we land on Delos. Nika seems strangely excited and in love with it all. She is indefatigable, and looks extremely overtired. I find it almost too much myself and the excursions exhausting. There are too many of us. Think of it, pilgrimages, either coach-borne or on foot, of culture-hungry, middle-aged women, following lecturers who are packed to the eyelids with facts and scholastic poses: all in love with Greece for their own reasons – as I am, of course. But oh how I long for some brief privacy! Middle age seems to be the time – judging from this trip anyway – that people nowadays can afford to travel. So many women, some with sons, some with friends, a few with husbands. And all thinking that age should make a common bond. It seems a strange time of life to launch oneself upon Greece, and yet perhaps it is the only time when one has leisure and money enough to do it in comfort. . . .


At this moment Pye sat writing to Penelope, although he had not heard from her for several days. In his small, neat, bare room, not much larger than the cabin in which Penelope sat awaiting the summons to dinner – for he was a frugal and tidy man who did not take up much space – he had been thinking about her so intently that it seemed as if he were really in communication with her. He had found that he could write to her most easily if he imagined he was talking to her in the dark, for thoughts flowed freely then. But what could he say? She knew about his early years in London, he had touched only briefly on his painful marriage, its coldness and deception; he found he could not send echoes of those years over to Greece, they would flutter dully on to her table like the leaves of an old calendar, to spoil her pleasure. Only the previous evening he had seen a film in which lovers walked away from each other along wet streets, and all life seemed to him at this moment a walking away, away from commitments, away from untenable emotions, away from possible hurt. He felt tired and middle-aged and used-up. Almost angrily he began to write again. He would say exactly how he felt.


. . . One never stops growing or suffering or learning [he wrote]. One changes direction once, twice, a hundred times – or never. Like fluid lava (have you seen any yet, or have I got the wrong country?), lava that was once hot, pulsing and full of its own black and nervous dynamism, pushing and nosing its way like an eager, violent puppy through stones, over valleys, villages, over any life – insect, animal, human – that lies in its infinitely various path. That puppy is grown to a monster with a thousand heads before its wildness cools, becomes immovable: it has become forever violence embalmed together with its victims, in that closest embrace of all: the pursuer with the pursued, the torturer with his victim, the liar with the deceived, the innocent with the vicious; all have become one truth, melted and fused to the bone, absolutely translated. Absolutely selfless, the true, the longed-for annihilation.

But I don't want, like lava, to flow over and absorb you. I no longer want to merge. I don't court annihilation, my own or anyone else's. I've always existed on my own terms and always will. I require a certain amount of solitude. I have always thought that a man and a woman should be strong enough in themselves to cast separate shadows. . . .

He threw down his pen in self-disgust. He was a fool. Who did he think he was deceiving? If Penelope were here now, here in this room, he would see to it that they cast no separate shadows and there would be an end to talk. He turned up his radio to an unbearable pitch and flung himself on his bed. Perhaps Stefan had been near the truth with his absurd allegory that evening. Adam had indeed paid dearly for his choice. And yet Pye could not bring himself to curse God.

Stefan sat alone in his redecorated office. From behind Miss Frost's closed door came the efficient, comforting, unremitting clack of a typewriter. White walls, grey shelves, red-seated chairs, even red linoleum. New metal cabinets. Everything was under control. The telephone rang and was immediately answered. Stefan bit his nails, took the call when Miss Frost put it through. She insisted on this, never allowed him to answer the telephone directly. Her reason had a finality that expressed itself in all she did. 'It doesn't do, Mr Brandt.' Many things, Stefan had learned, didn't do, and now he crouched at his desk, feeling hungry. It didn't do, he had been told, after Miss Frost had been with him for less than a fortnight, to fry sausages or drink beer in the office in case someone called. He might drink tea or coffee, that was all. Even sandwiches were frowned on. He should go up to his own flat, or else out, for a meal, a change of scene, or exercise.

One of his daydreams was to catch Miss Frost at her own lunch, but this he had never succeeded in doing. Once or twice, at about twelve-thirty, he had sprung towards her door, having heard a dry mouse-nibble of biscuits from inside. But as he flung the door open, there she was, impeccable in her white blouse, mouth and chin crumbless, pale eyes reproachful at his omission to knock, leafing through invoices.

Miss Frost was a marvel, he had to admit it. In some obscure way he wanted to win her approval, which would carry with it the approval of those heavy portraits up the stairs of the old Prentice building, of the old man himself. Once or twice he thought he caught her looking at him in an odd way, as if they were conspirators. Sometimes, but very rarely, he got her to talk about Oliver Prentice, who was, of course, God. He guessed there had been 'words' between her and the new manager put in by Halstead's; things had changed for the worse since the take-over: everything was streamlined, new, vulgar. But she could never be coerced to say much, she kept her distance much as a good upper servant of the old school. He found himself depending on her, even though he would never admit it, and made jokes about 'the old girl' to Spencer and Bonny. When she was at her most tiresome – and she had very definite off-days, when she was full of umbrage and obscure outrage – he merely had to remind himself of her one eccentricity to make allowances. But even this eccentricity she raised to the level of ritual.

At six o'clock each evening she made herself a cup of tea and smoked a small cigar, always the same brand, ten to a tin box. After lighting this she would toss the match into her waste-paper basket, lean back and close her eyes. On two occasions at least she had set fire to the waste-paper basket and Stefan and Spencer had rushed in in response to her tiny, ladylike shriek. Now she had a metal one, so the risk of fire was diminished.

'Suppose someone should call?' Stefan had asked, innocently, before he had learned that she was never in the wrong.

'No one will call, Mr Brandt! The office closes at six o'clock.'

It was nearing six now, and still Bonny hadn't telephoned. He buzzed through, asking Miss Frost to try her number. She rang back in a few moments to say there was no reply. Stefan felt deflated: Spencer was still out of town, Bonny up to God knows what. How did they expect him to run the whole show alone?

'Miss Frost,' he said, through his extension, 'will you ring up that girl from the *Trade Gazette*? MacPherson or something like that. Publicity. I think I should ask her to dinner, she's a useful contact.'

Cheered at this idea, for the girl was attractive and intelligent and had obviously liked him, he at once started to go through a few current headaches. There was this sheet deal with Moray's of New York. They were trying to charge him two dollars ten per copy, including royalty, f.o.b. their warehouse, and for a re-order of 250! Before, the price had been one dollar ninety-five. The challenge of a haggle over price revived him. As long as he could set balls rolling, he was all right. Spencer was too soft for this sort of thing. Only he could deal with it. At a pinch he could do everything himself. He didn't need anyone.

He was about to buzz for Miss Frost to come in and take a stinker to Moray's when his call came through. Yes, Miss Macpherson would be delighted to dine with him. Where should she meet him? He named a small, discreet but inexpensive restaurant, was business-like and brief. As he made to call Miss Frost a second time the subtle aroma of her cigar penetrated the big office. It was no use. It was six o'clock. He would have to write the letter himself.

## 18

Nika had so far managed to keep her morning sickness a secret from Penelope. But today, as the ship lay anchored off Delos, the first passengers already climbing down into the caique, she felt she could scarcely endure the journey in the small, bobbing boat, although the sea, as usual, was calm.

'Are you all right, Nika?' asked Penelope, as they stood by the rail. 'This holiday doesn't seem to be doing you any good. You look so pale.'

Nika looked at her guardedly. 'Do I? Oh, I shall be all right. I was trying to keep my journal up to date after you went to sleep last night. I'll be quite an expert on Greece at this rate. Do you want to know all about Apollo's birth, for instance?'

Penelope looked thoughtfully across towards the island. It was bare in the morning light, bare and craggy, with Mount Kynthos rising high from shrubby rocks. Then she said quietly:

' "Shall I tell how Leto, resting on Mount Kynthos, gave thee birth . . ." Oh how does it go on? "Alone in sea-girt Delos . . . something, something . . . the dark blue billow drove." No, it's no use, I've forgotten it.'

'Well, what is it?' asked Nika, intrigued and puzzled and not a little amused.

'It's part of the Homeric hymn to Apollo. I learned it – oh, years ago. I never thought I'd actually be here. There are so many gods, aren't there? And they each have their own place, although they've never seemed quite real to me.'

'You might have made Apollo real if you'd remembered

enough to declaim in his temple,' said Nika, laughing. 'Oh dear, here's the boat back again.'

The journey across was not bad at all, but she kept her face away from Penelope's anxious eyes. They stepped out on to the flat beach and walked up past the Roman ruins, the excavated streets and shops, and once or twice Nika stopped to run her hand over a curved stone jar that once, long, long ago, had held grain against the winter. When they were well on their way Penelope stopped and pointed to the left.

'Nika, do look! They're just like Siamese cats stretching in the sun.' It seemed absurd to wonder at that moment whether her own little cat was missing her, but she did, as she gazed in pleasure on the long line of honey-coloured lions ranged one behind the other along the coast. Who had put them there, what they were guarding, who had carved them, why they had not been overthrown when the island was sacked two thousand years ago – all these things remained a mystery.

The rest of the party passed them as they looked at the lions, yellow, sinuous, silent; guarding, like all great cats, some ineffable secret. At last they moved on slowly, just keeping sight of the energetic, stumpy figure of the lecturer who would talk to them at Apollo's temple. It was hot and there was no shade. As they made their way up the hillside, Nika stopped here and there to identify some small flower which looked like a kind of rock-rose. She debated whether to take a root or two home with her, but it seemed unfair to pillage Greece still more.

Half-way up the hillside was a small rock temple, roughly carved, 'the oldest known temple in Greece,' the lecturer was saying. One or two of their party were taking photographs; others were scattered down the hill photographing a small palm tree. The lecturer was explaining that it was a tree like this, at just about that very spot, where Leto had stood, grasping the trunk after her nine days' labour, at last giving birth to her twins, Apollo and Artemis, while Poseidon raised the waves like a dome over the island and anchored it to the depths of the sea with four pillars.

'In this way Hera's prophecy was fulfilled,' he was saying. 'She had said that Leto would only give birth in a place where the sun's rays never penetrated.' He tried to lighten his talk with a joke. 'Leto was different from the other women Hera was so jealous of, because she had actually been married to Zeus. And it was Ortygia, a woman who had resisted his overtures, and who had been turned first into a quail and then a floating island for her virtue, who gave Leto sanctuary, after Hera had chased her all over Attica and Thrace and Euboea. Ladies sometimes stick together, you see.' He smiled as his audience was swept by faint giggles, and went on, 'But like a woman, Ortygia exacted her price. She made Leto promise that Apollo would build a temple on the top of Mount Kynthos, and then she changed the name of her island to Delos, the Brilliant.' He raised his stick and pointed up the hill. 'There's nothing left of it now, but – as an understatement – the view from the top is rewarding.' He led the way up and the stragglers followed him.

Nika and Penelope sat down by the grotto. Above them the songs of invisible larks spiralled down from the blue sky.

'So this is where "Apollo leapt into the light and all the goddesses cried out with joy",' Penelope murmured, quoting again from her ragbag memory. Then she saw Nika's face and said, with concern, 'Nika, you're not at all well. Do tell me what's the matter.'

'This seems a good place to tell you,' said Nika faintly. 'I'm going to have a child, Penelope.'

Penelope instinctively looked round. Here? Then she laid her hand on Nika's wrist. 'Have you told Spencer?' 'What stupid questions one asks in a crisis,' she thought. But a sense of shock was all that registered. As Nika shook her head, Penelope felt acute fear take complete charge of her body, fear, and disappointment. Suppose something happened on the trip? Nika looked dreadful. As if guessing her thoughts, Nika said, 'Please don't say I shouldn't have come. I had to. I wanted to get away. I'm usually very well when I'm pregnant. I had the mad idea that the child would be some great Classical scholar, absorbing all this through me. . . .'

Ashamed of her panic, Penelope said warmly, 'He might well

be, my dear. But shouldn't you see the ship's doctor, just in case? And you'll have to cut out all this walking, and rest. Are you glad?'

'I don't know. I don't know how Spencer will take it. I daren't tell him before we left; he'd worry about money and regret letting Lewis go to the choir school.' She did not add that she also dreaded Spencer's attitude to her pregnancies. Whether he feared for his own security or hers she had never been able to understand. She knew they had never quite recovered the happiness of that marvellous first year of their marriage, when they had rested so easily in each other, miraculously cradled. Now she wondered whether he would find someone else when she grew unwieldy, as he had once found Lesley.

'Let's walk down,' she said. 'Penelope, I'm sorry. I'll try not to spoil this trip for you. Maybe I shouldn't have come, anyway, I should have told you before.'

'What nonsense!' said Penelope briskly. 'It isn't an illness! You won't spoil anything, Nika, I couldn't have come alone. I shall just have to look after you, that's all. And I shall enjoy doing it.'

They went down in silence, Penelope watching each jarred footfall over the stony slope, full of fear, full of self-reproach. She had grown selfish, that was another of the traps middle age set for you.

Down on the flat ground, in the full sun, they wandered in the Roman city, listening to the chorus of frogs in the marble pool.

'Odd, isn't it,' Nika commented, 'how the baths and plumbing – and the frogs – have survived while the temples have crumbled?'

They looked desultorily at the mosaic floors, which reminded Penelope of Pompeii, where she and Jamie had gone many years before, but they were glad when they could leave the lumber of the past and return to the ship.

Nika ate no lunch, and while she lay on her bed Penelope had a word with the doctor. He was cheerful when he left.

'Rest up for a few days. Better give Delphi a miss, though.

Pity. Take it easy in Athens, you can stay there a couple of days, anyway.'

For the rest of the day Nika stayed in their cabin, and she and Penelope had dinner there. She seemed much better, her colour returned. Later on Professor Deacon looked in and had coffee with them. He was an immensely tall man, with thick-lensed glasses and a head of springing white hair that made him look like some sort of crested bird. He gave Penelope the feeling of knowing so much that his knowledge could only be let out in dribbles, like a blocked fountain. At his lectures the fountain played freely: he was by far the most interesting of the dons aboard.

'I wonder why your parents gave you the name of Nika,' he said, as he sipped his coffee. 'Do you know that *Nike*, spelt with an e, is the Greek word for victory? There are temples and statues everywhere to Athene-Nike. There's a little one by the Parthenon, and of course when the Parthenon was new it was dominated by a magnificently garish Winged Victory, all gleaming gold, overlooking the Saronic Gulf. . . .' He broke off, and gave an apologetic laugh. 'Sorry, I'm lecturing. But you might like to know that the Athenians clipped the wings of their Victories, to prevent them from taking flight. When you see the Parthenon you'll know why, oddly enough. It's so light! Seeing it by moonlight, as I've done so often, I'd never be surprised if it soared up and away.' He nursed his coffee cup in his big hand. 'I'm being foolish. You must let me take you to the little temple of your namesake when we get to Athens.'

The next day Nika felt better. She insisted on getting up and joining in the visit to Aegina. The very sight of the mountainous island excited her. With Penelope she sat in the shade of the branched-over roof of a modern *taverna* within sight of the sea and drank a glass of the local wine, cool and resinous. All around them surged the people from the boat, armed with sticks and notebooks, ready for the assault on the pine woods,

Aphaea's temple and the steep reaches of Oros, highest peak in the Saronic Gulf, where once the altar to Zeus had stood, and where now only earth terraces gave evidence of a pre-historic town.

'Are you going to the top?' asked a pleasant, sturdy woman of Penelope's age as they set off. She was accompanied by her son, a thin, intensely serious youth of eighteen.

'I'll see how I feel when we reach the first temple,' said Penelope. 'I must say it's shadier walking in these woods than it was scrambling over the rocks yesterday.'

'Are you better, Mrs Manley? What a pity you missed Poros. It was just like an iced cake,' said Mrs Barlow. 'I expect the heat knocked you up.' She did not notice her son's quick snicker at these words, and if Nika heard, she did not understand why he thought them funny.

'I'm fine now, thanks,' said Nika, hoping that no one on board would guess what had been wrong, since it was too early for anything to be obvious.

They had left the old port and the town behind, and were walking steadily upwards, through pine woods. From time to time they paused, to take breath and make sure of their direction.

'No wonder Pericles called this the eyesore of Piraeus,' said the boy, Douglas, somewhat smugly. He waited for questions. Obediently his mother said, 'Oh, what a strange thing to say, dear. I think it's perfectly lovely.'

He gave a pleased snort, of mixed derision and pride in knowing all the answers. Classics was his subject, he was going up to Oxford in October. Unable to resist a captive audience of three, he gave a quick sketch of fifth-century Athens and the part Aegina had played in the see-saw balance of power between the League and the greedy Athenians. Nika only heard snatches as she climbed.

'You see,' Douglas was saying, 'Aegina had a larger fleet than Athens. Pericles saw it as a threat. It was too close. In the end Leokrates starved the people into surrender.'

Was there no end to violence? Nika thought wearily.

215

'Pericles was a marvellous man,' Douglas was saying enthusiastically, panting as he was from the climb. 'A bit Churchillian, I've always thought. It comes out in his funeral oration.' He began to quote, ' "For the whole earth is the sepulchre of famous men. . . ." '

'I'd rather read Pindar,' murmured Penelope. 'Much good fine words did for all those dead soldiers.'

In case she had sounded too flattening, she gave Douglas a quick smile and said, 'You remember the eighth Pythian ode better than I do, I expect. It's lovely, isn't it? A sort of swan-song of the old, golden Greece.'

Douglas frowned, then recovered himself.

'Of course,' he exclaimed. 'Didn't he write it in honour of a boy who came from here? A wrestler . . . I can't remember it, though.' He was still put out at having his quotation interrupted, and he was mouthing it silently when Nika called out sharply.

'Oh,' she cried. 'Oh, Penelope, do look!'

Suddenly, before and above them, in a clearing, was the most beautiful temple she had yet seen. Like all the others, it was in ruins, there was no roof supported by the Doric columns, which rose, slim and golden, against the massed green of the trees and the deep blue of the sky. She ran up to the flat platform and sank down between two of the pillars. Here, too, was a glittering view of the sea and the mainland.

'Let's rest here and have a cigarette,' said Penelope. 'The others must be miles ahead.'

They sat in silence and smoked. Above them the sun burned down as it had throughout centuries of war and peace. It was absolutely quiet, a lost place.

'Who was Aphaea?' asked Nika softly, as if she might disturb the goddess.

'Oh, she wasn't anything much,' Douglas said casually. He was wandering round in between the pillars, letting his hand flap on the weathered stone. 'Twenty-two,' he counted. 'She was supposed to be the goddess of the woods, the moon and the underworld. There used to be some sculptures here, but

216

they've been taken to Munich. Mother, hadn't we better get up to the top? It's quite a way.'

Mrs Barlow rose with a sigh, and Penelope rose with her. She wanted to go on walking through the woods, catching glimpses of sea as she went, but she was not surprised when Nika said, leaning back and closing her eyes, 'I'll stay here and wait for you. It's so lovely.'

'Nothing,' she thought, as the three of them disappeared up a steep slope and between the trees, 'could ever be lovelier than this. However far I go, whatever else I see, nothing could ever be quite like this again.' She lit another cigarette, thinking how strange it was to see the English packet lying at the foot of these pillars, carefully buried the match. She had not been alone for a long time. One spent most of one's time being available to other people, fulfilling a role. Now she felt free; free of Spencer, free of the children, free even of the child inside her body, who was no larger than – what? an apple? What could she do with this unaccustomed freedom except offer it up to this unknown goddess of the woods, the underworld, and the moon, this lost goddess who loved solitude and built her temple in inaccessible high places? And yet Penelope was free, and suffered because of it. She too had lost the habit of uncommitted thinking, having flowed among her husband and children for so long, like a stream. They were the banks which had regulated her direction; now away from them she was lost, the stream diverted into unfamiliar banks, sweeping over undefined ground, among pebbles, seeking a new course among rocks, declivities, down sloping ground to where? The sea, tidal and anonymous, or to a stagnant pool? Availability and freedom, could one never choose between them?

'I want to know God,' thought Nika passionately, leaning her cheek along the rough ridges of the nearest column, looking up it into the great sky that seemed to spring up and wheel away from its broken top. 'But which one?'

Here in Greece was a sense of many gods; their presences haunted even the labelled neatness of their temples. And here, in this shrine to Aphaea, was a sense of yet another: a different shy, yet mocking, utterly pagan goddess. Pagan, yet committed to the larger wheel of the seasons, of the laws that governed nature, and in this mindless obedience free to find peace within an infinitely mysterious world of unknown, yet logical, cause and effect.

The sky and the sea, the sea and the sky. Strange, the longer she looked at them, the more their blueness seemed to surround her, wash over her, penetrate her. Her body had expanded like a bubble to contain this blueness, blown to rainbow tautness and set adrift on the light airs. She seemed to be somewhere else, wearing blue like a garment. She found herself speaking aloud, and yet with absolute certainty she knew that her words broke on another air, in another place. She spoke of islands. We were all islands, floating or anchored, in whatever gulf. Mind and body upheld on the wise tides, learning when to ebb as they did. Keep hold of your island and be safe. Balance and harmony. Freedom and responsibility. Ebb and flow.

'I think she's asleep.'

Their voices broke in on her from a long way off. It was an effort to open her eyes, to realize that she sat, a burnt-out cigarette in her fingers, leaning against a column and wearing a green dress, not a blue. Three faces looked at her, and gradually they took form and outline through the haze; everything re-formed; the woods, the sea, the hard ground on which she sat.

'Nika, we can go down by car, if you like. There's one waiting in the road below. And there's a man selling pots, quite nice ones; they make them locally.'

Nika picked up the cigarette packet, and went down to join them. She felt both elated and tired, and listened in silence to Douglas's talk of Zeus and the wonderful view, bought a graceful clay pot from the stall below in the road. She had not realized that the road was so near, for she had been away, it seemed, in infinite distances.

As they drove down to the port, passing various members of their party jogging astride dusty donkeys, Penelope asked whether she would like to bathe before they left, if there was time.

'I don't think so. It would be nice, but a rush. Let's have a glass of wine instead. How about you?'

Penelope nodded. The long climb had tired her, and, although she would have been refreshed by a bathe, like Nika she could not be bothered to change.

'I shall miss all this when we get home,' she said, as they sat once more in the *taverna*. Mrs Barlow and her son had gone off to the beach with the others, and the cries of the bathers echoed faintly back.

'You can buy Greek wine in London, surely?'

'Not like this,' said Penelope, missing the teasing note in Nika's voice. 'And I didn't quite mean just that.'

'I know.' Nika wondered whether she could tell her about the temple, but she found she had no wish to explain, or to share the experience. She wanted to think about it alone. Instead she said idly, 'Pye was right about inner harmony. He was talking about it one evening. How wise he is.'

Penelope, too, had been thinking of Pye. She responded at once, warmly, 'You know, Spencer said such an odd thing to me the first time they met. He said Pye had a head like a questing Zeus. Perhaps that's why he doesn't need to come to Greece to acquire wisdom!'

'Spencer can be very perceptive. How he would love it here!' Nika raised her glass. 'Penelope, I'm grateful to you. I can't say any more than that. Let's drink to something.'

'Oh! Well, what better than this glorious sun, and –' She stopped.

'The old gods.' Nika finished for her, although she knew Penelope had no intention of saying any such thing.

They sat on, comfortably, until it was time to leave.

## 19

THE change from the quiet tumbled woods of Aegina to the crowded, grubby, shouting confusion of Piraeus three hours later was cataclysmic. The *Helena's* passengers were borne away from the port in two coachloads, up through the dusty streets of the great sprawling outskirts of Athens. Dazed by the clamour, for they had been at sea for so long, it seemed, serene among islands, watching dolphins at play in the wake of the ship, walking among dead bones of ancient cities, conversant with tombs and myths: used to all these things, they could not at first understand that it was to these Greeks walking the streets, to this town itself, so much alive, that the past belonged. Not to them, the intruders. Here, in this humming modern city, lived the true inheritors of all those ruins; the glories of Periclean Athens were theirs. And these Greeks had not essentially changed over the centuries, despite the fact that they had been conquered by the Turks: vivacious, persistent, earthy, they thrust their reality into the dazed faces that stared out at them from behind the glass windows of the coaches.

The round tour was in progress. Hadrian's Arch, the Temple of Zeus, the Tower of the Winds, the Pnyx. . . . Later, released from the coach, wandering obediently round the Museum, Nika said miserably, 'I *feel* like a tourist. I hate this. Let's go.' She looked numbly at the red walls and the columns, the masks from Mycenae, the frozen groups of beasts and gods, seeing them all through a blur of distaste and fatigue.

Penelope took her arm, relieved. It was certainly too much for her, and they made their way out. Professor Deacon noticed their expressions and came over with a grimace to match their own.

'I know how you're feeling,' he said. 'It's all too much. There's nothing like Athens to cut you down to size, puncture all those romantic dreams you've been having these last weeks. Here you are –' He led them outside and gestured over the large square with its tram-lines, its modern shops, its advertisements. 'Here's your true Greece. And your true Greek. Utterly realistic, isn't it? Like Paris, like London.' Nika made to protest and he grinned down at her. 'All right. Add clarity, perspective. It's as true of twentieth-century Greece as it was of the so-called golden age.'

'It isn't easy,' Penelope murmured, 'especially when one never gets a chance to meet a Greek!'

'I can arrange that,' he said unexpectedly. 'Shall we skip dinner on board tonight and dine here, in Athens? I should be delighted to introduce you both to two very old friends of mine. We'll choose a real Greek dinner for you to remember.'

At once Nika lost her gloom. She had been feeling naggingly unwell ever since they had landed, but put it down now to her fatigue and boredom. They accepted with all the more pleasure, since the invitation had come as a complete surprise. Professor Deacon was called by a small group of the other passengers, and hurriedly made arrangements to meet them at six-thirty on the terrace of the King George Hotel. Some time later, sitting drinking a glass of wine at an open-air café, they watched the coaches drive past, back to Piraeus. The sight freed them and they began to wander about Athens on their own, at last making their way to the foot of the Acropolis, where the old and the new seemed to be jumbled up together, as if a minor earthquake had just happened. Fallen pillars, old newspapers, back gardens and wooden shacks. As night fell, the big gate closed, and they stared up at the Parthenon as the floodlighting was switched on. Seen like this, all the detritus of the lower slopes of the hill hidden, it shimmered, was fragile, and as the city all around them burst out into pin-pricks of light, it took on a *Son et Lumière* quality, so that they expected music from its pillared shell, a declamatory voice.

'We should have gone back to the boat and changed,' said Penelope, vexed. 'I feel filthy.'

'Never mind,' said Nika. 'Let's find the hotel. We can wash there, I expect.'

The hotel was not difficult to find, and they were able to wash off most of the dust, and settle down with drinks on the terrace before the professor arrived to fetch them.

He came, peering through the other people, looking more like a scholarly crane than ever.

'It isn't that I don't enjoy these trips,' he said apologetically, 'but when we get to Athens I like to take some time off. One gets into the habit of showing off, it's a lecturer's disease.'

'What will you have?' asked Penelope, as a waiter came up to them.

'A light beer, I think. Thank you.'

He drank thirstily. 'So many words,' he said. 'I wonder sometimes if they stay in anyone else's mind but my own.' He looked thoughtfully into his glass and went on, 'I think you'll like Dr Stephanides and his wife: purely Greek, and yet European. He was at Oxford with me. I thought you'd prefer to dine in the old city, so I've arranged to meet them at one of our favourite *tavernas*.'

They sat, drinking, and watching the people filling the streets. Nearly every table outside the cafés was taken, lights glowed and sparkled everywhere. Then they set off, slowly strolling, leaving the crowds, along streets that grew narrower, steeper, the atmosphere curiously rural, a chill wind somewhat scented, blowing down from the surrounding mountains. Then they were there, and on the terrace of the *taverna*, a wide, protected place with vine leaves patterning the white walls, two figures rose to welcome them.

At first sight Dr Stephanides was not prepossessing. His eyes, sunk deeply into a face that appeared as brown and plump as the breast of a well-roasted fowl, were round and black. His hair, curly and thick, was pale grey. By his side his wife appeared almost emaciated, her pale skin translucent in the light. Heavy coils of dark hair gave her a top-heavy look and made her neck, which was long and thin, stalk-like.

They sat down and the doctor ordered ouzo. He bubbled with warmth towards Professor Deacon, treating him with the slightly bullying love of an intimate. His wife leaned towards Penelope, her widely set, light, flat eyes looking at her with kindness.

They began to talk about the trip, the doctor teasing his friend about Classical scholars who thumbed free rides in return for a little erudite conversation, and when Nika protested that the professor worked very hard indeed, and that without him half the expeditions would lose their point, he laughed delightedly.

'There's no doubt about it, Frank, you're a success. What a life you lead! Now if only some enterprising company would send me to England. I could talk my head off about – say, Bath and Canterbury and Oxford, and yes, Glastonbury, and put forward yet another theory about Stonehenge.' He turned to Nika, asked, 'But what remains of all this information? Where have you been – Crete, Patras, Mykonos? Yes, of course, and round about all the islands. What do you know about them?'

Nika admitted that they were all a lovely jumble in her mind: piled white houses, the gleam of sun on a dolphin's back, the bougainvillea at the monastery on Patras, bathing on white beaches, the blue and purple of the sea, the smell of thyme, and oh, the climbing woods . . .

'But you could have all these things without Frank!' he exclaimed triumphantly. 'But it's interesting, here's someone with a purely visual memory,' he said, turning to the others. 'Greece to her is a kaleidoscope. And she is right, that's the way to hold on to her. And the Greek himself, Mrs Manley, how does he seem to you?'

Before Nika could reply, Penelope found herself saying, 'He is alive.'

The doctor turned to face her. He was so fluid in his movements, so dynamic, that for a moment he reminded her of

Stefan. His little eyes snapped. She had the feeling that he had taken in, in that one moment, all there was to be known about her. 'But you and Mrs Stephanides are the first Greeks we have really met. It's so good of you to ask us to dinner.' Her smile included Professor Deacon.

'Our pleasure!' the doctor exclaimed, with a gesture. 'So now we will eat. Leave it to me, eh?'

He and the professor squabbled amiably over the food. At last it was decided: more ouzo first, to drink with the black olive and tomato salad, dressed with herbs and oil; then some sort of roe beaten into a paste, then lamb cutlets, and *retzina* to drink with them. Then cherries, *halva*, a delicious crumbly cheese, coffee.

Throughout the meal the conversation flowed freely. Dr Stephanides had been in England a great deal, had lived in France, then, just before the war, had returned to settle in Athens. He refused to speak of the war and its aftermath. He wanted, he said, to buy a house on Poros.

'You like islands?' asked Nika eagerly.

'I love them,' he replied simply. 'I am not romantic about them, but I like them, especially if I can look across to the mainland. One is therefore cut off and yet not cut off, an enviable state.' He looked at Penelope curiously. 'Do you know, Mrs Hinton, your name is so familiar to me. Was your husband James Hinton, by any chance, the painter? I have one of his pictures.'

'Yes, he was.' In spite of herself, the surprise made her hand tremble and she at once stopped eating and clasped her fingers together in her lap. 'There's an exhibition of his work coming on in London this week.'

'And you are missing it.'

'Yes, I am missing it. The opening, anyway.'

He nodded, as if this was perfectly natural.

'A pity he never came to Greece. He would have liked it here.'

Professor Deacon looked up from his conversation with the doctor's wife; he had been making her laugh. 'That's a compliment, indeed, Mrs Hinton. The people George likes would always like Greece, of course!'

'Jamie would have adored Greece,' said Penelope. 'In fact, some of his abstracts have a strong feeling of the country – I've only just realized it. I wonder now why we never came.'

The doctor threw his arms wide. 'It's a waste of time to ask things like that. You never came, there were doubtless other things to do. That is life. That must be accepted.'

Their eyes met, and she nodded. 'Yes,' she said, 'that must be accepted.'

'But really so,' the doctor added, so softly that the others did not hear. They were excitedly discussing the coincidence of Nika's name. She must go to the little temple, the professor was saying, and offer something up, as the Athenians used to do: not as a sacrifice, but more as a symbolic action. Offering the gods things one had finished with – ones' toys on growing up, for instance, or the tools of a trade before retiring.

'The fact that he was a comparatively young man when he died, that must also be accepted,' the doctor was saying, his eyes on Penelope's face. 'From the fact that he spent life on the wing, as creative artists should, I imagine he was lucky to have left so much behind him. I should say, knowing his work, that he – how can I put it? – he was never shot down by a sense of frustration, of an awareness of his limitations, which is another kind of death.' He watched her bent head. Still she said nothing. His voice rushed on softly, earnestly. 'He missed what one might almost call the male menopause. The time when men of about forty-five or fifty start wondering whether they have come to the end of something and despairing that they are too old to start again. Do you know, when I was in my thirties I dreamed of being a great surgeon? When I realized that I had no aptitude I had a breakdown, a bad one. That was when we were living in Paris. It lasted two years.' He shrugged. 'It was a waste of time. We all have to adjust or go under.'

'Why are you saying this to me?' asked Penelope in the strained little voice Pye would have recognized.

'Because, my dear, your problem is in your face. Because I know that some problems are not to be solved and it is an impertinence to try. Because you are in a state of tension.' He bent over a cigarette and his face was illuminated by the flare of the match; a tender, ugly, compassionate face. He tossed the match away and added, 'And because sometimes a woman is foolish not to take a lover.'

He turned away from her as she stiffened, and immediately joined in the talk which centred round his wife, who was now full of animation. She was inviting them all to dinner the following evening.

'Shall we be back from Delphi in time?' asked Nika.

Nika's words broke Penelope's mood. At once she said, anxiously, 'You shouldn't think of going to Delphi, Nika. Remember what –'

'Not go to Delphi!' the professor interrupted in astonishment. 'You might as well not have come to Greece at all!'

'No, indeed,' said the doctor soberly. 'Delphi seems to stretch back to the beginnings of the world.'

'You say that? What! Do I detect the beginnings of a sentimental Hellenist?' The professor was obviously delighted to tease his friend.

'Ah, no.' The doctor lifted his hand. 'You know me better than that. I hope I am a citizen of – well, I must say it – the world. Why we have always got on so well,' he explained to the others, 'is that Frank is not a sentimental Hellenist either, prating of the glories of the golden age – fifth-century Athens and its supreme architect, Pericles. Pericles!' He winked, raised his glass. 'Now there was a realist! But his was an idealistic realism, like your Churchill's. He loved war, and yet he also caused the Parthenon to be built.'

'It's odd, isn't it?' said Professor Deacon, drawn at last, 'how so often only the offshoots of great men's ambitions endure? Napoleon left the Civil Code after all that fever and conquest and tonight the shell of the Parthenon is floodlit. So much for Periclean Athens!' He shrugged. 'But I won't have you comparing Pericles with Churchill, George, it's too facile. If anything, Pericles was a Hitler. I know it looks as if Sparta was the counterpart of Nazi Germany, with its military régime. In effect, if you'll only remember Thucydides, it was Athens who was the bully. He was on the spot, and when he says it was only theoretically a democracy, and in reality it was the rule of the first man we must believe him. And that first man was Pericles. The Athenians were the *Herrenvolk*: only they enjoyed a high standard of living.' He held up his hand in his turn to stem the protest that was already tumbling from the doctor's scandalized lips. He was not to be deflected, and Penelope caught more than a hint of the power with which he would lecture – but really lecture, and with passion – to his students. This ancient history, which meant so little to her, but which he invested with so much fire and topicality, kindled him so that he lost his deprecatory manner and became – for him – almost aggressive. 'But what was all this luxury and culture founded on?' He looked round the table and slapped his hand down so hard that the wine danced in the glasses. 'Slavery! That wasn't unusual, of course. All the great empires were founded on it – Persia, Egypt, Byzantium. But it makes nonsense of the idealistic democratic pose when you realize that every victory, every gold and marble statue to the gods, every temple, the Parthenon itself, was bought with other people's sweat, other people's money and tears and blood. Think of the subject states, bullied into paying tribute. Think of the savage treatment of Aegina, the subjugation of Thasos, the sack of Melos. Then think of Poland and Czechoslovakia in our own times – even nearer, remember the Hungarians, with Russia taking over Germany's role of the constant oppressor.' He threw up his hands. 'The history of the world of the future is written here in Greece,' he finished quietly. 'But we never learn, even from a land consumed to the bone with centuries of folly and fury.'

There was silence. Then Dr Stephanides said quietly, 'Dear Frank, the gods avenged Melos. Athens fell. Hitler fell. Tyrants in the end are subject to Nemesis. Don't forget that in your lectures.'

At last Nika ventured, 'But if Pericles was such a tyrant, why did Greek tragedy flower so in that period? I thought the plays of Euripides and Aristophanes were satires on the political system – or am I wrong?'

Dr Stephanides beamed at her. He refilled her glass, and beckoned for coffee.

'Yes, what about it, Frank?' he said. 'If Pericles was such a Hitler, what about the astonishing amount of free speech which gave you the plays, ensured the literature of the time – and incidentally, dear friend, ensures your livelihood!'

There was general laughter, in which the professor joined. He looked both stimulated and relaxed, and Penelope suspected that the two of them must have had many such an argument in the past. Now he raised a quizzical eyebrow.

'You ask that, George, a Greek, with personal knowledge of the Athenian political genius? I grant you Aristophanes made marvellous fun of Cleon in *The Knights*. Cleon was the Göring of the age, I should say. But Aristophanes suffered for it.' He leaned back in his chair and threw a cherry into his mouth. 'What a man! A fifth-century Chesterton. All that warmth and humour and love of the old order.'

'Well,' put in Mrs Stephanides, 'if Aristophanes was a Chesterton, I'd say that Euripides was the Shaw of the period.' She turned to Nika, who sat next to her, and was startled by the look of pain on her face. For a moment she thought it was something she had said, then she noticed that Nika's hands were gripping the table hard, and she was biting her lip to stop a small sound of protest.

'Poor child!' she exclaimed. 'What is it? Perhaps the dinner was too rich . . . Come . . .'

'Leave her,' said her husband. He sprang out of his chair and walked round to Nika, put his hand on her forehead. 'How long have you been pregnant, young lady?' he asked sternly.

Through white lips Nika said, 'About two and a half months, a little more. . . . I'll be all right. Please don't –' She bit her knuckles as the agonizing pain started again. At once the doctor turned her chair easily in his small, powerful hands, picked her up and carried her down the steps to his car. Penelope and his wife ran to open the door. He settled Nika on the front seat; she had started to shiver. Then he ran back, clicked his fingers for the bill, paid, and putting his hand on Professor Deacon's shoulder, led him to the car. 'This is appalling for a celibate, Frank, I know. But this is one of your party who won't be seeing Delphi tomorrow. Leave this to me. The girl can't go back to the ship – she must stay with us tonight.'

'I must stay, too, Doctor. Is that possible?' asked Penelope.

'We can make room,' said Mrs Stephanides calmly. 'But I think it would be better if you went back with the professor. We can take care of your friend, don't worry.'

'But she is my responsibility. I must look after her.'

The doctor flicked a look at her. 'Yes,' he said dryly, 'so she is, and you shall look after her if you wish. Now, please, we must get home fast.'

They drove for less than ten minutes, and stopped in front of a large house half-way up a hill.

'Now, if you will sit here with Frank and drink a glass of brandy with him, Mrs Hinton, my wife and I will take your friend upstairs.'

The calmness and authority of the little fat man dominated them. Nika was supported out of the room, not caring what they did with her, so long as she could lie down and make no decisions. Penelope sat numbly in a chair, whilst Professor Deacon poured brandy for them both. He seemed at home in this house.

'I'm so terribly sorry about this,' she said at last. 'Nika only told me about it a day or two ago, at Delos.'

Unexpected the professor laughed. 'What an appropriate place to break the news. But poor child, what will happen now?'

'She'll have to go to hospital, I suppose. Don't worry, Professor. I will arrange it. We shall have to fly home, if necessary.'

It was so long since she had taken charge of anything apart

from her own life – and even in that she had been supported by Sybil and Pye – that she felt unexpectedly strong.

Professor Deacon looked relieved. 'Thank God George is a doctor,' he said, 'and a good one. But fancy thinking she could slog up to Delphi in that condition.' He looked so profoundly shocked that she was sorry for him.

'We shall both be sorry to miss it,' she said. She gave him an unexpected, crooked little smile. 'But that is life. We must accept it.'

He looked at her quizzically, and drained his glass.

'She wanted to go and offer Athene something tomorrow,' he said. They sat in silence, both absorbed in their own thoughts, until the door opened and Mrs Stephanides came in. She looked paler than ever as she came straight over to Penelope and put an arm round her.

'It has all been very quick,' she said. 'I'm afraid your friend hast lost her baby. Still, she is young. She is strong, she can have more. She will be perfectly all right now. George has given her a sedative.'

'Oh, God, I'm sorry,' said the professor weakly. He got up. 'I must get a taxi to Piraeus. I've tipped a boatman to wait for us until midnight. He'll row us across to the ship. Are you coming, Mrs Hinton?'

Penelope hesitated.

Mrs Stephanides said, 'You are welcome to stay. I can make up a bed for you.'

'Then if you don't mind, I will.'

'I'll telephone you tomorrow. If you change your mind about coming with us on the trip, we can arrange a place to pick you up. That is, if you feel you can leave her.' The professor stood awkwardly in the doorway.

'No. It's good of you – and belatedly, let me thank you for a lovely evening, although that sounds stupid now.' She held out her hand, shook his warmly. 'I'd rather stay with Nika, she may need me.'

## 20

LEWIS waved good-bye to his father and watched the train jerk slowly, with much steam and fuss, out of the little station. Then he ran to the station-master's office, to have a word with him. Mr Hobyn had always fascinated him, partly because of the odd sound of his name, and partly because he had a silver plate screwed inside his skull.

'Where is it then, Mr Hobyn?' he would ask, as a small boy.

'It's here, back here. Give me your fingers and feel it then.'

The touch was horrible. Under the hair and flesh something more solid than bone even, and the skin on Mr Hobyn's scalp wouldn't move about like other people's. 'Tight it is, see,' the station-master would say, with pride. 'Tight as a drum, boy! That's my ticket from the big war – the real big war your dada never knew about.'

But at ten years old Lewis could only look at the shiny cap, not ask to touch. Mr Hobyn turned as he came in. Greyer, more shrunken than in the old days, his silver plate ached now with the coming of rain.

'You off back to Mrs Matthews now?' he asked.

Lewis shook his head. 'I'm going to Glantamar,' he said. 'I've got my bike. It won't take long.'

Mr Hobyn pushed his cap back and gave the boy a long look.

'Are you expected, then?' he asked. 'Queer old body, Miss Cullen. Like all the shrimp-paste lot, and yet it's taken her a different way, if you get what I mean. Keeps herself to herself.'

Lewis swung his leg idly, kicking the scratched wood of the desk. He could hardly avoid knowing about them, since the shrimp-paste lot, as they were invariably called by the village people, owned most of the land in the valley. Because they had only lived in the Hall for twenty years and were Lancashire, not Welsh, had made their money from a doubtful compound of many different fish ground down, coloured pink and squashed into squat glass containers, the jokes about them were many and various. The activities of the shrimp-paste lot never failed to inspire the kind of oblique wit the Welsh delighted in. They would have been resented if they had tried to take part in the village life, and as they made no effort to do so, not even attending church or supporting the Women's Institute or the Sports Club, they were even more resented. The village bore them a nameless grudge, and at the same time kept a sharp eye on them, exaggerating their eccentricities, which were no more extreme than those of the villagers themselves. Naturally enough, encamped as the Romans had once been, in alien territory, they were driven in on themselves and their kind for social relaxation, so that all the village saw of them – except those who worked up at the Hall and who retailed the latest news of their enormities – were their fast cars, horse-boxes, and the sound of their sharp laughing voices blown back on the wind. To poach on shrimp-paste land was a point of honour in the season.

So now Lewis said, 'I know,' turning his head away like his father. 'Glyn told me.' To avoid further questions, for this decision, or whim really, had only just come to him, and he scarcely knew why, he ducked his head and made for the door. ' 'Bye, then, Mr Hobyn,' he said, and ran away down the platform, veering to avoid a boy pushing a clattering trolley loaded with livestock hampers.

He knew that Aunt Sybil expected him back for tea, but he pushed the thought aside and jumped on his bicycle, turning it up the village street, heading for the two big hills and the valley beyond. As he rode, a feeling of freedom made him want to whistle, and the wind blew the noise back in his face. He free-wheeled down the next slope and the little grey school came into sight. Abruptly he braked, jumped off and leant his bicycle against the hedge, then vaulted over the low wall. In a moment he was peering in through the windows.

He could not believe what he saw. No desks, no blackboard. Only a dusty, empty room, the black stove still there which had roared away in the winter, and by which he had so often fought to sit. The school had an abandoned, not just a closed-for-holidays air. Then he remembered that his friend Glyn had told him about this, too. The new school they had started building just before he left was finished, and this was going to be used as a parish hall for the time being, as last winter's gales had blown the corrugated iron roof off the old one.

Glyn's father had a new petrol-pump outside his pub, too, and council houses were growing up, raw and red, on the scarred meadow where they had once played cricket and football. He pulled himself away from the window, and walked round the building into the playground. The tree they used to shelter under, and tie the girls to, in their rough break-time play, was in full leaf, and under it the concrete had cracked even more, where a big root had forced its way up through the ground. He kicked it, keeping his head down. Over the road, among the embryonic houses, the chimneys of the new school rose against the trees.

He climbed the wall again and got on his bicycle. This time he pedalled slowly and heavily up the hill to the lane at the top that would spiral down the long mile to Glantamar. He stood on his pedals, not knowing why he felt so leaden, and a timber-lorry passed in low gear, the driver shouting to him to keep to the side of the road if he didn't want to be playing a harp by supper-time. It was a green lorry, and at once he thought of the big green van passing the windows of the school on his last morning. That was a year ago. Last summer. Cofio. But he didn't want to remember.

The bridge over the one-track railway, a humped one that made him bounce on the seat, jerked a small laugh out of him: his father would be nearly in Oxoter by now. He would change trains, and catch the fast one to London. The sweep past the farm where five children lived, all as fair as albinos, all small,

all round. The biggest boy had once pushed him into a snow-drift. On again, and past the Humphreys' farm, where the cows were waiting now to be milked, lowing behind field gates across the lane from the buildings. On his return the lane would be spattered with mud and splashed with dung.

He put on speed. He didn't want to see anyone, answer any questions, be exclaimed over or kissed with kindness: he only wanted to get to Glantamar. He wasn't afraid of Miss Cullen, whatever she was like, even if she was one of the shrimp-paste lot. At last here was the wooden gate that swung open on to his home meadows. It was heavy to manage, but he closed it behind him and pushed his bicycle through. Then he stopped. Where was the semicircular wooden bridge over which he had so often heard Lesley's horse pound, hollowly, like Billygoat Gruff? Instead, there was a flat concrete slab, raised about a foot from the bank. He left his bicycle and jumped up and down on the bridge to test it. His face grew sulky with disappointment; the old bridge had swayed when he jumped. Here he had played racing sticks with his father, dropping them in on one side and watching the current eddy them out under the bridge and through the other. There was a blurred photograph at home showing him kneeling there, his head in its woollen cap stuck through the two long bending rails.

'It's not fair,' he said aloud. Again he jumped. It was no good, there was no bounce, no thud and satisfying creak of timbers. It was more like the asphalt playground of his horrible London school; automatically he closed his nostrils against the remembered smell of the lavatories. For a moment it seemed as if the bridge covered the whole river, creeping over the living water with its stifling grey skin. Panic-stricken, he flung himself down on the bank, reaching for some dry twigs that lay in the long grasses. Then, with a ritual precision, he broke them into three different lengths and dropped them into the stream. At once the current caught them, had whisked them away under the bridge and out of sight almost before he could run to the other side to see which had won. He stared after them, enraged. There was a fair-sized boulder embedded in the bank, and he started to haul at it savagely, pulling it loose until he was able to kick it into the water with a loud and startling splash. 'You – you bastard!' he muttered. 'Go on, float that away!'

The swear word, which he had learned his last term, made him feel only half better. Its meaning escaped him, and there was no one to shock, except himself. Or so he thought. As he straightened up he saw a woman standing on the opposite bank: she had evidently been watching him for some time.

'Tell me,' she said now, in a clear, amused voice. 'Why are the young so destructive?'

Lewis felt his whole body turn hot with shock. He had been so sunk in his rage, in his river, his bridge, his aloneness, that when he raised his head he wore an unconscious look of anger, the haughtiness of ownership.

'Oh, so this young one would like to order me off my own land! Who are you?'

He looked up then into a face he had never seen before, but one that was all the same familiar. The woman's high-set, odd-coloured eyes shone piercingly from a wedge-shaped face as tanned and weathered as a labourer's. Astonishment and recognition blazed at him for a long moment, then she blinked and the blaze was dimmed.

Forgetting about the bridge, he said at once, with his father's engaging charm, but a directness of his own, 'You have eyes like Hereward the Wake. He's one of my heroes. He had one brown eye and one blue one. I didn't think real people did.' He made no attempt to approach her or to explain himself, and they looked each other over warily, like animals newly introduced.

'Well, I'm real enough, and so are you. And real people have names. What's yours?'

'Lewis Manley. We used to live here.'

'Yes, so you did. And in a way you still do. Come along. You're a fine big lad, Lewis.'

Lewis turned at once to fetch his bicycle. It pleased him to be called a fine big lad and he forgave her for the rest of her face, which was disappointing. He had a brief impression of a good jutting nose and a wrinkled mouth with a mole near enough to distort the shape of the lower lip. A couple of wiry hairs sprouted strongly from this mole. All the same, as he turned to follow Miss Cullen's strong, broad figure – for who else could she be? – once again he felt that uneasy pull of recognition. She was so familiar as to be part of himself; she belonged. He hurried, pushing the bicycle along the uneven track that led over the meadow, pursued by the irrational idea that this was unreal and that he would wake to find himself in bed in London, imagining it all with his eyes tightly closed.

She had turned to watch him as he drew level, swinging a poacher's bag from her large brown hands. She looked like some kind of gnome, he thought, with that earth-coloured jacket and skirt. The only bright things about her were her eyes.

She said now, in her straightforward, clear voice, 'Hereward was always a favourite of mine, too. Why do you like him? Because he dressed up and crept about the enemy camp?'

'Partly,' said Lewis doubtfully. 'But really because no one knows what happened to him. He just disappeared.'

'Do you want to do that?'

'Oh no. I don't think so. At least –'

She laughed. 'It wouldn't be any use disappearing before you'd done something for people to remember you by, would it? People wouldn't care then.'

'Yes, they would. My family would.'

'But they wouldn't put you in history-books.'

He considered this, but before he could reply she said briskly, 'I expect you've guessed who I am. Prunella Cullen.'

He nodded. There seemed nothing to say to this, but privately he condemned the name.

'Do you know Beauty?' he asked. 'She's – she was – my pony.'

'I've seen her over at Mrs Matthews'. In fact, she's going to lend her to me to pull a little tub trap I've found.'

'The one in the old stables?'

'That's the one. I'm trying to paint it up a bit, then I can drive to market.'

'I don't know whether Beauty will like pulling a trap,' said Lewis. 'She's very lazy and takes a bit of managing. Are you good with horses?'

Even as he asked he remembered that she had some vague connection with the Hall people. She was bound to be good with horses, for they thought of little else. He said glumly, without waiting for her to reply, 'I think she's too old, really. She just used to let me ride her.'

'Then why didn't you ride her over?'

Lewis frowned. 'Aunt Sybil doesn't like me to go out on the road with her. I'm out of practice, you see.'

They had arrived at the big iron gates that led to the garden of the house. He hesitated, half afraid to go in. To cover his sudden brief fear, he said with a touch of impudence, 'Wouldn't the – your relations at the Hall let you have a young pony for the trap?'

She looked down on him, her eyes glinting with amusement.

'The shrimp-paste lot, you mean? They're not really my relations. Let's say I'm a distant cousin. And they wouldn't give me anything, young man, let alone a horse. They like horses.' Seeing the question in his eyes, she added, 'They only let me live here because it's out of the way, and I'm a sort of unpaid caretaker. Everyone thinks the house is haunted, you see.'

He stopped. Stories the boys in the village had told him darted, half-digested, through his head. Haunted. That meant ghosts. He looked round at the garden he remembered. The beech copse, where the snowdrops were; the walnut tree which never bore any fruit; the round lawn in front of the house; the drive. But it was all overgrown. It was a wilderness; the grass waved high as a hayfield, the flower-beds with which his mother had struggled were choked with weeds. In one year. What would it look like in a hundred years? Already it seemed that the house had sagged. In his imagination it had been long and low and white, its windows shining. Now the windows were dirty; it looked smaller, shrunk into itself, uncared for, terribly old. Like Beauty, it had been turned out to grass.

Something moved in the tangle of undergrowth, burdock and buttercup heads shook like water in the wake of a ship. Only this approached. It made a loud noise, then sprang. Lewis shrieked, clutching his bicycle. Miss Cullen turned to him, on her shoulder was a creamy-coated cat, its eyes as blue as the one that showed in the side of the face she now turned to him.

'Don't be afraid, Lewis. This is one of my Siamese cats. She's called Louella. Her mate's in the little hollow under the yew tree. It's their favourite place. I'm afraid they always jump up.'

He gave a sickly smile. 'It's all right, I know about these kind of cats. My mother's friend has one. It's called Mishti-San.' Then her words penetrated. The hollow under the yew tree. Laying down his bicycle, he asked whether he might go there. She nodded, said, 'I'll put the kettle on for tea,' and went towards the house, bearing the cat, sitting upright, on her shoulder.

At once Lewis dived through the rough grass until he came to the towering yew hedge. For a moment he wondered whether he had forgotten the little hidden entrance, then his instinct showed him the way and he dropped down on hands and knees and crawled through a rough scratchy gap. Either it was smaller, or he was much bigger, for it was quite a squeeze.

Once inside, he was able to stand up in the close gloom. It was his secret place, like a cave, the earth brown, damp, the roof and walls of dark yew branches and green leaves. It was almost as big as a room. He could sleep here if he wanted, and no one would ever find him.

'Mr Pog's house,' he whispered, and made his mystic sign of protection. The triangle of fingers and thumb. Suddenly he longed for Mr Pog, now thrust down deep into a drawer in the flat in London. Dear Mr Pog, with his crooked eyes and his moth-eaten white coat. He regretted not bringing him, for he felt they kept each other safe.

A movement on the opposite side of the hollow place made

his hands suddenly clammy. Two eyes the colour of rubies glowed at him with the still alertness of a wild animal; he had seen this look on a tiger's face at the Zoo. There was a sharp smell of cat. This then was the cat Miss Cullen had mentioned, Louella's mate. Even this hidden place was invaded and spoilt. All at once he stamped, started to bark like a dog, growling low in his throat. The two eyes stayed where they were, sharper, bigger, menacing. Lewis began to be afraid – suppose after all it was something *other* than a cat, crouching, waiting, ready to spring? But it was a cat, he had become used to the dim light and was able to pick out its shape. He groped around for a stone to throw; anything to dislodge the intruder. But there was only damp earth. He jumped towards it, letting out an ear-splitting shout. At once the eyes vanished, and something fled past him through the entrance, yowling in fear and rage.

Lewis waited a moment, hugging himself, before he followed, crawling out into the uncertain sunlight, feeling he had won a victory.

Miss Cullen had just come to the front door to call him.

'I always eat in the kitchen,' she said. 'I keep most of the other rooms locked. It's cosy in there in the winter. I've got a fire today as it looks like rain.'

The kitchen seemed quite different. There was a new kind of fire, a stove, with an oven set in it. The stone flags were now covered with red linoleum, with coconut rugs. Two old brown armchairs were drawn up by the fire. An Aladdin lamp stood ready to be lighted. The scrubbed wooden table was still in the same place and the tea was set straight on to it. Two steaming mugs waited for them. There was an odd-shaped brown loaf, butter, jam in a pot and fruit-cake.

'It's my own jam,' said Miss Cullen. 'I live off the land as much as possible. And I bake my own bread. The baker is slowly poisoning the whole village with his white rubbish. Mrs Williams baked the cake. You've come on a lucky day.'

'She used to work for us, too,' said Lewis, remembering the many times he and she had sat talking at the table there whilst he ate his supper. 'Do you see Dai? I liked Dai.'

'I see them all,' said Miss Cullen, with an odd smile. 'Mrs Williams misses you all, she doesn't really approve of me. But she likes to bake, especially when her oven's drawing well. Do you want to go and see her?'

'I don't know,' said Lewis.

At the moment he was hungry, and Miss Cullen cut him slice after slice of her home-made bread. He had never tasted anything so good.

'I wish my mother made bread like this,' he said. 'It's super.'

'And I wish she'd come with you today,' Miss Cullen replied. 'Where is she?'

'She's in Greece. She's gone with that friend of hers who has the cat like yours. Aunt Sybil's looking after it as well as us. They'll be home at the end of the week.'

Miss Cullen frowned. 'And is she quite well?'

'Of course.' Lewis looked at her in surprise. 'She's always well. She's sent us lots of postcards. She's seen hundreds of dolphins.'

'That's splendid.'

They finished tea in silence and Lewis said, 'May I go up to the attics?'

'Do you want me to come with you?'

He hesitated. 'You can if you like, but I know the way.'

She took the hint and started to clear away while he sped out of the kitchen, along the passage and into the hall. There he stopped. It smelt unused, although the front door was usually left ajar, he had noticed. He put his hands in his pockets, began to whistle. Then he stopped. The stones he had put in his shorts pockets weren't there. He had forgotten them when he put on a clean pair that morning. This bothered him, for he liked something to rattle while he walked about. Looking about the hall, he noticed a small table near the foot of the stairs and on it were some candles, a lamp and box of matches. Quickly he pocketed the matches, shaking and jingling them as he went upstairs.

In the attics, at least, nothing had changed. In the first one dust and the neat folded bats still hung from the beams, like dolls' discarded umbrellas, the usual corpses of flies against the window-sills, cobwebs and flaking plaster. But there was a smell of apples and he went through into the next attic. This was where the shell-house had been and he glanced sharply to see that it was in its own accustomed place. Under the dusty glass of the case the cardboard king and queen still sat on their mussel-shell thrones, the canopy above them studded with small pink smooth shells, long spiralled pearly ones. Some of the courtiers had fallen over, there was mice dirt in the house itself. Carefully he reached in and put them upright, leaning them against the sides of the case. Then he shut the door tightly. He was feeling hotter and hotter each moment and wiped the sweat from his forehead as he looked about him. Apples had evidently been stored up here among layers of folded newspaper; a silly place to put them, he noted, it was far too hot, and in winter it was freezingly cold. He rustled through the newspapers in the hope of finding one or two left over from last year. At last he pulled out two, both shrivelled, one bad. Biting into the better one with distaste, he continued his exploration. Domed leather trunks, old suitcases, basketwork containers, a roll of dusty carpet, some broken chairs, a pile of old, curling illustrated magazines.

He hesitated before going along the little passage and up the last three steps into the further attics. His fingers closed clammily around the box of matches. They gave him a feeling of safety. The dry floor creaked, and the silence was broken by a sound that wound its way right up through the house, reaching out to him. Someone was playing the piano, and it wanted tuning. Someone was singing, and even from this distance he could tell the voice was sweet and compelling. He could not hear the words, and for some reason the disembodied song filled him with unease. What was he doing up here, all alone? What was he looking for? The third and fourth attics led out of one another, then, up two steps, the sealed-off one, with the black, blocked window. All at once he felt he was moving in a remembered dream. People were looking for him, he seemed to hear their footsteps coming stealthily up the wooden stairs, very light, a patter almost. They were pattering quietly round in the first two attics, he could hear the rustle of paper. They were doing what he had been doing. The piano was still playing downstairs, and his hair seemed to move on his scalp. Without volition, stepping as stealthily as his pursuers, he went through the third and fourth attics. He must hide, but where? Then he was looking straight across the last attic at the two steps to the fifth. There should be a wall there. But there was no wall. It had been torn away, and beyond, open to him, was the fifth, the one he always thought of as his own, his secret, unknown even to him. It looked dark.

At once he was filled with the same kind of rage that had possessed him when he saw the new bridge, the ruined garden, the cat in Mr Pog's house. Who had torn down the wall? Where could he hide now? He darted across and peered round the lath and plaster partition. There was nothing there; the floor gaped with rotten beams; whatever had been there was gone. He brought out the box of matches and lighted one, holding it up in a trembling hand. The attic was empty. Peering down through the floorboards he lighted another match, held it high, then let it drop. As he looked, he saw a faint light on the floor where the match had landed. It increased, there must be straw there. Of course, it extended over the old stables, next to the kitchen. He'd never realized that before. While he watched, fascinated, the flames below began to strengthen, smoke rose in his face. There was a crackle as more straw caught. He was held, his fear forgotten, absorbed in the lovely leaping fire.

He ran back to the attic with the newspapers and grabbed an armful. At once something reached out and fastened on to his hand. Snatching it away, he saw two long scratches, with blood welling up. He gave a loud cry, and at once the singing stopped. As one of the Siamese cats ran out from under the newspapers Miss Cullen called up the stairs; and her voice was followed by her footsteps, clumping in her heavy brogues.

She looked at his white face as she came into the attic, at the newspapers which he had dropped on to the floor, then looked sharply round, sniffing. Grabbing him by the hand, she ran with him along the passage, the smell of burning increasing. It was quite fierce now, and as they looked through the torn-down wall of the fifth attic they saw a rising glow. Leaving him, she at once went across and peered down between the floorboards.

'Give them to me,' she said harshly. Without a word he handed over the matches. 'Now come,' she said.

He followed her down the steep wooden stairs that led directly into the kitchen, carefully testing each one, for it was dark in this well. Thrusting open the door with her shoulder, she took a large iron key that hung on a nail by the back door and went to the stable door close by. As she turned the key and opened the heavy door, smoke and flames drove out at her hungrily.

She thrust the yard broom into his hands.

'Beat it out with this,' she said. 'I'll get a pail of water.'

They worked in silence, and at last the fire sputtered, and was out.

'At least the beams haven't caught,' she said, 'and the trap's only blistered. I was going to have to paint it anyway.'

She looked at him for a long moment, then raked over the straw and doused it with another bucket of water.

'You'd better come with me,' she said.

They walked in silence, quickly, she taking strides like a man; over the overgrown garden, past the yew hedge and into the field that stretched up the hill to Betsy's Lane.

'Where are we going?' said Lewis, thinking this was some unspoken, unspecified punishment. 'I don't like Betsy's Lane.'

'You'll see,' she said shortly.

The lane was dark under the trees. It led, as he knew, to a haunted pool where a long time ago a girl had drowned herself. Was Miss Cullen going to drop him in there for trying to set fire to her house? Had he meant to? He didn't know. And not knowing, he still could not say he was sorry. Once he looked back; the house was still there, it glowed in the dusk, one window lighted, the window that had been the nursery.

Gasping, for he was getting puffed, he said, 'Why is there a light in the nursery window?'

Miss Cullen looked back briefly. He could not see her face;

there was not much light in between the trees, for they had crossed the haunted lane and were climbing up, holding on to sappy young beeches and elder bushes that sprang back as they passed.

'It's my bedroom now,' she said. 'I have my piano there.'

'Are we going up to the fairy hill?'

'That's right.'

They struggled on. Once his ankle turned in his light sandal, but he fought down an exclamation of pain and went on doggedly, following as closely as he could that dun-coloured figure which seemed to be part of the trees themselves, part of the shadows cast by the bushes, part of the hill itself. He had never been so far up the fairy hill, even for blackberries. His mother had always said it was too much of a climb. He could tell her he'd been up it now, though.

At that moment they broke into the open. The shrubs and small trees finished suddenly, leaving, above them, a smooth, cropped slope, topped by a circle of pine trees. These were the ones he had always looked at from his window.

'Follow me,' said Miss Cullen. He could not tell from her voice whether she was angry or not, but he did as he was told. 'Now,' she said, 'there are lots of dry branches up here. You help me to gather them.'

He looked at her in amazement. Glyn's words came back to him. 'That Miss Cullen's a queer one all right.' But again he did as he was told; if she wanted him to gather firewood at this time of night, he would. Then perhaps he could go home. He longed suddenly to leave Glantamar behind, to go back to Aunt Sybil's big warm house, with electric light everywhere, and her loud laughing ordinary voice that echoed in every room. Sally would be in bed by this time, she would miss him. He felt unaccountably sorry for himself; he was cold.

'Now,' said Miss Cullen, 'put all your branches and twigs here, with mine.' They stood looking at the pile; it was quite a sizeable one.

'How are we going to carry them all down?' he asked, in a small voice.

All at once she laughed, and took the box of matches from her pocket. 'We're not,' she said, 'we're going to light a fire up here.'

He gaped at her. 'Up here? Why?'

She handed him the matches. 'Because this is the place to light a fire,' she said, 'up on a hill, not in a house. You're a big lad now. You light it and we'll watch it burn.'

As he put the first match to the thin twigs and dry brushwood he realized that this was the second time she had called him a big lad. Perhaps he was big. As the flames sprang up, with the careful second match, he began to feel big. As they grew he felt bigger still, a giant. But he had never really thought of himself as big; inside he was as small as Mr Pog. Until now. He snatched a branch from the roaring pyramid and waved it in the air, then thrust it into Miss Cullen's hands. He took another for himself and together they swung the hissing, flaming torches and watched the small sparks fly off into the deep settled blue of the night sky. The sharp smell of resin exhilarated them and all at once he began to feel free, to sing, and he leaped up in the air. He shouted, and his voice echoed among the hills.

'I'm here, King Pendragon, look at my fire!'

Miss Cullen was singing too, singing and laughing at the same time, holding her glowing branch up against the silent dark of the pines. Far below the light from the nursery window glowed steadily, a small, reassuring, watchful eye.

As the fire dwindled, he ran to get more branches, and fed it.

'Do you think they can see it from the village? It's like a beacon!' he shouted, as it flared up once more, the branches liquid and hissing with boiling resin.

'Someone's seen it,' said Miss Cullen, sinking down on the grass. 'Look, there are headlights coming across the field from the bridge. Yes, you've made your mark on the valley, Lewis.'

'Shall we let it go out, then?'

'Just as you like. It's your fire.'

He considered. The bonfire had collapsed, smouldered down to red, glowing in the surrounding grass. An owl hooted, a bat flew above them like a mysterious night swallow. He kicked at the brittle transparencies of twigs, and a light rain began to fall.

'It's safe to leave now,' he said. 'The rain will put it out.'

They watched the rain hiss and dance on the dying fire. Almost regretfully he said, 'We've burned the grass.'

'Grass will grow again,' said Miss Cullen. 'A house won't.'

He did not reply, indeed he scarcely heard, for he had seen the headlights now. They were almost at the entrance of the drive.

'We'd better go down,' said Miss Cullen. 'I wonder who's calling on me?'

They plunged down the hill, Miss Cullen in the lead, calling back to Lewis where to step, to watch the branches, and not to slip. By the time they had jumped down on to the hard surface of Betsy's Lane the rain was quite heavy, and the grass shone silver and slippery in the watery moon that now rose above the hill behind them. All at once Miss Cullen asked who King Pendragon was.

Lewis hesitated. Then he said offhandedly, 'Oh, someone who lives up there. Have you seen fairies on the hill? People say there used to be some.' He spoke as if he did not greatly care.

'I've never seen them,' said Miss Cullen, 'but I know an old woman who did. But that was a long time ago.' She began to sing the song he had heard in the attics.

'*Come if you dare, the trumpets sound . . .*'

'I like that,' said Lewis. 'You have a nice voice.'

As they approached the hedge that divided the garden from the field, she finished the verse and he joined in the final repeat of the words, '*And pity mankind that will perish for gold.*'

'So have you,' she replied.

'I'm going to choir school in September,' he was saying, when a voice he knew well hailed them from the front door.

'Is that you, Miss Cullen?'

Aunt Sybil's jeep stood in the drive, its headlights blazing on to the front door. She had evidently been inside the house, for now she stood, looking about her from the porch in a distracted way, calling into the dusk with the suspicion of a quaver in her voice. He realized with a shock that she was frightened. But what on earth was there to be frightened about?

'I'm here, Aunt Sybil, we've been up on the hill. Did you see our bonfire?'

Miss Cullen followed him into the glare of the lights.

'Won't you come in, Mrs Matthews?' she said, as if it were perfectly normal to come crashing through the spinney in the dark – wet, dirty, and in the wake of a small drenched boy, to find a distraught neighbour pinioned to her door by the yellow blaze of car-lights. 'We saw your lights from the hill, and wondered whose they were.'

Lewis could see that Aunt Sybil was trying to control herself. She was angry as well as frightened.

'I won't stay, thank you. I've come to fetch Lewis. He didn't tell me he was coming over here. Luckily, when he didn't turn up for tea I telephoned the station and Mr Hobyn said that this is where he'd probably be.'

'I'm sorry, Aunt Sybil. I didn't know it was so late.' All Lewis's exhilaration had evaporated; the pin had been put in his balloon. But Miss Cullen rescued him, ushering Aunt Sybil through the unlighted hall and groping with her to the kitchen.

'I'm afraid they've cut the telephone off, Mrs Matthews. But I don't usually need it, so I haven't bothered about it. Now do let me make you a cup of tea, you look upset.'

Lewis noticed that Aunt Sybil had subsided, as if mesmerized, into one of the brown armchairs, but with scarcely concealed distaste. She was evidently not certain whom to blame most: Miss Cullen for not having a telephone or Lewis for not telling her where he was going. Gallantly he tried to draw the blame on himself by saying that after he had seen his father off he had found himself cycling in the Glantamar direction and had sort of landed up here. But Aunt Sybil was not appeased; the injured look she gave him turned to horror as she took in his grimy scratched hands, his smudged face, wet hair and torn jersey. All these things were revealed as the Aladdin lamp was teased into full light.

'No, no, we won't have tea, thank you, Miss Cullen. We must get back, it's nearly eight. And Lewis could certainly do with a bath.'

Lewis looked miserably from one to the other. Miss Cullen was evidently slightly amused, for she had gathered from Mrs Matthews's tone that she could obviously do with a bath herself. She had made no apology, offered no explanation, and to Lewis's enormous relief seemingly had no intention of telling his aunt about the fire in the attics, which he now remembered with shame. He felt an urge of affection. He didn't mind her living here, he could hand the house over to her and forget about it.

'There's another thing,' said Aunt Sybil. 'I must telephone your father, Lewis. He'll be home by now, I expect. The fact is –' She turned a plump, distraught face to Miss Cullen, who stood by the fire, gravely regarding her. 'The fact is –' she repeated, and looked helplessly at Lewis.

'Perhaps Lewis's mother is not well enough to travel home just yet, is that it?' said Miss Cullen. 'Don't worry, Lewis, she will be quite all right in a week or two.'

'But I only had the telegram this afternoon!' Aunt Sybil exclaimed. 'How can you know?'

Miss Cullen shrugged. 'Perhaps living in a house someone else has lived in for so long – and loved so much – brings one very close. But never mind that now. I imagine the children will stay on with you, Mrs Matthews. I do hope you'll let Lewis come and see me again.'

'But what's the matter with Mam?' asked Lewis, in agitation.

'Oh, I expect the foreign food upset her,' said Aunt Sybil, brisk again now that the news had come out so easily. 'You can't trust the food abroad. Would you like to stay on with me, Lewis? You'll miss school, of course.' As he nodded, she seemed suddenly to have lost all sense of grudge; her moods changed rapidly. Now she rose and said they must be going.

At the front door Lewis said, 'Thank you for the tea and everything. Look, I'll come over and help you do up the trap.'

They found the bicycle and loaded it into the jeep and went bumping off down the drive. Behind them the house dissolved into darkness, but Lewis held Miss Cullen's smiling face and her odd-coloured eyes in his mind until they reached the far gate and he jumped down to open it. As he fastened it behind them and climbed in once more he asked her about the bridge.

'The old one was swept away in the floods last winter,' she said. 'This is much safer. They've deepened the river-bed, too. and stocked it with trout. Did you see any?'

He shook his head. He was beginning to feel tired. As they drove past the Humphreys' farm he saw, in the light of the head-lamps, the trail of mud and the liquid sheen of cow-dung. He had been right. Some things never changed, and cows were one of them.

'What an extraordinary woman,' said Aunt Sybil. 'You'd think she'd be lonely in that great house all by herself. And with no telephone.'

'She doesn't mind,' Lewis replied, with the assurance of one whose intimate friend was under discussion. 'She likes it there. I suppose Sally will be asleep,' he added regretfully. Already he was making up a story to tell her. No one had ever had such a marvellous fire, no one had ever dared to light one right up on the top of the fairy hill. He would explain, of course, that you had to wait until you were big; that hillsides were the places for a real bonfire. It wasn't any good otherwise.

## 21

WHEN PENELOPE's letter arrived, following closely on Sybil's agitated telephone call, Spencer's reaction was one of relief. The thought of a third child, the expense and upheaval it would cause, made him shudder, and if Nika was in no danger, being well looked after, as Penelope had emphasized, it was all a great piece of luck. All the same, sitting alone in the empty flat, he felt curiously disoriented.

The visit to Wales had not been altogether a success. He had been able to pick up some very useful orders, and old Mr Brunton had been pathetically glad to see him. He had even hinted that his job could be made available to him again, if he wanted it. Looking at the drooping young man who had taken his place, and who obviously knew nothing about books and cared even less, Spencer could see why. But he could never again, he knew positively, return to that kind of life. The excitement of London, the stimulating, maddening personality of Stefan, was absolutely necessary to him; it was a relief to be sure of that at least. However much they disagreed, argued, even rowed, he would stick it there, build up something he believed in. For the first time in his life he had jumped into a boat that was going somewhere and he liked the feeling.

The visit to Lesley had been flattening, too. He had arrived just after Jory, whom he had almost forgotten. Indeed he had scarcely spoken to him that last evening at Glantamar, then having been aware merely of Lesley's mood, which had wound itself inextricably with the music he had played. The remembrance of that night had often returned, fragmentarily, in dreams; something lost, something elusive, not to be rationalized.

Seeing Jory again, he felt a return of his initial dislike, and wondered how Lesley could stand him. Then, watching them talk together, he had slowly realized that in this cottage, among these people, she had very little choice; she had sunk into the kind of life that suited her and had settled for the second best.

He did not for a moment doubt that Jory was second best.

'Come and see me tomorrow, Spencer,' Lesley had said. 'Jory'll be gone by then,' and he had returned the following afternoon, reluctantly. It had been difficult getting away from the children; he had had to pretend he was going to Oxoter on business, borrowing one of Sybil's cars to drive out to the cottage. Lesley had not been violent or abusive, she accused him of nothing. Instead, they sat like strangers, drinking tea and making conversation. He was bored and again left early.

'What's the matter with me?' he asked himself, alone now in London. 'Of course one shouldn't ever go back, it's madness to try.' These affairs he was so often tempted to start seemed pointless, everything was after all a variation on the same theme; a tempting face, a good body, the promise of immediate intellectual communication, then the excitement of the pursuit, the boredom of success. None of these women had that glimpse of something new he had once caught in Nika, a quality he had not needed to graft on to her; stillness and repose, a tender, undemanding touch. For once, with her, he had not needed to play all the parts himself – hero, heroine, prompter. His neurotic self-obsession had temporarily melted under her reciprocal, simple passion. He was no longer on guard against a feared intrusion of his privacy.

He wandered through the flat, into their bedroom, into the children's. In that room he stopped, for Nika's presence seemed more potent here than anywhere else. Here she had spent hours, it seemed to him, reading to them, playing with them: once he had caught a look of passionate tenderness and absorbed joy on her face as she watched them asleep.

He walked quickly back into the kitchen to make some sort of scratch meal; the memory was still painful, as if he had caught her with some lover. He had felt repudiated then, and even now, with her letters from Greece in his pocket – eager letters, saying she missed him – he still resented the kind of wholeness she possessed; an ability to love, not only him, but his children too. It was then he remembered the only bitter remark Lesley had made to him, thrown to him over her shoulder as he left the cottage on that last afternoon. As with all instantly recognizable, unpalatable truths, he had deliberately forgotten it, but now, as the baked beans bubbled fiercely in the saucepan and his milk boiled over, he remembered her precise words.

'The trouble with you, Spencer,' she had said, 'is that like all egoists your deepest feelings are reserved for yourself.'

Even if it were true, he thought now, he couldn't change, could he? That was how he was made, and knowing it didn't make any difference. He had to live with himself first, and coping with himself and his reactions had always taken up the greater part of his energies.

Scraping the unappetizing mess out of the saucepan he told himself savagely that even if he was a selfish bastard that was the way he was, and people could accept him as such or leave him alone.

He felt in his pocket for his pipe, unable after all to face the baked beans, which had congealed into a sort of coppery blancmange. He'd make do with bread and cheese and coffee. Then he remembered that there was no bread, he had forgotten to buy any. He pulled out his pipe and his fingers came into contact with the last letter he had received from Nika. She had posted it from Athens, probably the same day as she had her miscarriage. He read it through again; there was no hint of any illness – why on earth hadn't she told him about the child? The tone of the letter was loving and gay, and yet all the time she had been keeping this secret from him. Why? Was she afraid of him? Had she feared he would stop her going? Had she intended all along to get rid of the child? This almost seemed an act of unfaithfulness, and he longed to be able to accuse her, face to face.

The telephone bell rang through the silence, and at once he was cheered. It was Rumpelow, asking whether he was going to the opening of the exhibition the next day, and, if so, could he go with him?

'Of course,' Spencer said. 'Didn't you have an invitation?'

'Well, yes, but I shall need a friend there, if you understand me.'

Spencer laughed. 'Let's have a drink first, then. I'll meet you at six. Have you heard from Penelope, by the way?'

'Not for several days. Why?'

'She'll be staying a bit longer in Athens. Nika has had a miscarriage and they're flying home together when she's better.'

'Good God!' Pye sounded horrified. 'Is Nika all right? When are you leaving?'

Spencer said uncomprehendingly, 'Leaving? What do you mean?'

Pye's voice was full of astonishment as he replied.

'Why, aren't you flying out to her?'

'Whatever for? She's in good hands. They're staying with some Greek doctor and his wife, friends of one of the professors. Penelope's there.'

'My dear man! It isn't Penelope she wants. It's you.'

Spencer stared stupidly at the telephone. The thought had not even occurred to him and he felt in no mood to argue now. Briefly he said, hedging, 'I'll talk about it tomorrow. I've got something on the stove now. See you at six at the Three Bells.'


When Spencer and Pye, together with Bonny and Stefan, arrived at the Bergdorf Galleries the following evening, the opening already had a smell of success about it.

At least three important art critics were peering between a forest of women at the pictures dwarfed by hair-dos and sweeping hats; one was even making notes. Julius Bergdorf, tall, elegant and alert, fulfilled his dual role of host and art connoisseur with charm and shrewdness. He joked with the few people who knew about pictures, talking the kind of off-the-cuff nonsense they wanted to hear, the private language of those in the know. With the decorative women they had brought with them he bent with straight-faced seriousness to swop current art clichés. A few young painters were there, sneering and silent by turn, preferring the abstracts to the early portraits and the landscapes. Julius Bergdorf had invited as well several rich dilettantes whom he was encouraging to form their own collections, columnists from the more virulent as well as the polite dailies, and art critics from both left- and right-wing weeklies. There was a smattering of representatives from the larger art galleries in London and the provinces, and of course, many of Jamie's own contemporaries.

The room seemed overcrowded to Pye as he entered. The heated buzz of talk, the smoke, the clinking of glasses, swept out and engulfed them, and he turned to pick up a catalogue. There was an introduction by Jason Temple, a name familiar even to him as a foremost painter and one who had refused the dubious accolade of R.A. and was now rumoured to be the next director of a large national gallery.

Julius Bergdorf greeted them courteously, glancing with interest at Bonny, who had already attracted the attention of several people. She glowed like a jewel in its voluptuous box of dark velvet, her bronze-streaked hair daringly set off by a Hogarthian velvet floppy cap in a curious shade of tangerine. Almost at once she was met by a young journalist eager for copy.

'Half a dozen are sold already,' Bergdorf now whispered to Spencer. 'I think Hinton's on his way back. What a pity he died so young – well, comparatively young. Philip is convinced he was on the verge of a new period, he's writing about him this Sunday.'

He waved his cigarette in acknowledgement at a tall, hatchet-faced woman wearing what looked like a Girl Guide hat done up in a tricorn shape. She was sitting intently upon a shooting stick, planted firmly in front of a large and dashing painting of a French waterfront. 'Lady Bosworth,' he murmured, and went over. Pye watched, amused, then saw that after a short discussion Bergdorf took a small red sticker from his pocket and fixed it to the picture. Another one gone. Spencer had been caught up in conversation with a small group, so he wandered off slowly, threading his way through the crowd, most of whom now had turned their backs on the pictures and were enjoying themselves, trying to find a clue to Jamie, wanting to see the portrait of Penelope at the window.

He glimpsed it at the far end of the room; there she was, half turned from him and the mounting noise, looking into the quietness of the beach outside her private window. A group of men and women stood near-by, half hiding it, arguing about a mural depicting a gang of workers, which hung near-by. He caught snatches of phrases which meant nothing to him, 'tonal truth', 'superficial pictorial mechanics', 'solid form-sustaining surfaces' . . . all he saw, with horror, was that a small red sticker was on the lower left-hand corner of Penelope's portrait. At once he turned, trying to find Bergdorf, for this one could not be sold, unless he was the buyer. But he was trapped by a man's solid back, a square, argumentative, immovable back. Beside this back was a girl whose profile sharply brought Penelope before him. But as he looked closer the resemblance faded.

'I don't think my father thought of anything apart from his painting,' she was saying. 'Of course, he was never a painter in the – the socially aware sense. He never had any axe to grind. He wasn't in key with the flux of the times, the chaos –'

'You'd say then that he sidestepped serious social issues? He was uncommitted in that sense?'

Pye stopped trying to edge past, and listened unashamedly. He guessed that this girl was Sue, the solid man with her her husband. Talking to them with a professional interviewer's manner, both eager and subservient, was a spry ginger-haired man with a face like a ferret. He was taking notes, cryptically. At once Pye knew that Jamie's daughter was enjoying sharing her father's fame, glad that her mother wasn't there to take any of this tardy, though brief, limelight away from her. Instantly he felt fiercely protective towards Penelope, glad, although for different reasons, that she was not here to suffer the glittering thrusts of talk, the mouths opening and shutting, the quick, clever judgments of these people, which nibbled away effort and vision. He found himself in sympathy with Jamie Hinton, who had preferred to paint what he saw through his own eyes, and not to portray a state of flux in which he felt he had no part. This obstinate, private vision was entirely in keeping with the man's marriage. He had protected himself and his work as intently and jealously as he had his wife. A strange man. Pye moved on, seeing a gap. A strange, but not a chaotic man, Jamie Hinton's landscapes breathed calm, his groups of men and women working, in factories, in fields, on the quaysides, all had a common quality of rhythmic absorption in the job at hand. Here, although today the idea would be unfashionable, was the dignity and desirability of manual labour. Jamie had evidently believed in men and not machines. How ironic, therefore, that a machine should kill him!

He found Julius Bergdorf talking to Stefan. The latter eagerly turned to him and said, 'You know Bergdorf? Bergdorf, this is Pye Rumpelow, a partner in the firm. We've been discussing the possibility of a book on Hinton, Pye. Obviously this is the time to cash in if we could get it out quickly. Plenty of full-colour illustrations, and so on. A good job at a good price. Introduction by Jason Temple, and perhaps a short biography by Penelope Hinton. Do you think she'd do it?'

Pye stood very still, watching the two men. Julius Bergdorf, in his turn, watched him from behind a screen of cigarette smoke, obviously wondering why Stefan should ask him this question. Before he could reply, Bergdorf said smoothly, 'Such a pity Penelope couldn't be here. But she was utterly devoted to Jamie, of course, it would have been too painful. They adored each other. And yet – those abstracts give an impression of impatience, of insecurity. Odd, isn't it? Maybe after all he had begun to feel claustrophobic – too much understanding, and so on. . . .'

'I'm not sure whether she's ready to do such a thing yet,' said Pye slowly, not liking the hinted criticism behind the other man's words. 'She's having a difficult time at the moment in Greece. What I wanted to ask you, Bergdorf, was whether you've really sold that picture of her at the far end, and who to.'

They turned and looked, and Pye had to describe it in detail, for there were evidently one or two others of Penelope he had not yet seen, small ones. These he privately decided to buy, anyway. Bergdorf said at last, 'Oh, that one. That's not for sale. Penelope has lent it. I only put the star on it to prevent anyone else buying it. It's good, isn't it? There's a nice feeling about it, almost lyrical. Penelope's a remarkable woman, although some people thought she was rather a mouse. There's far more to her than one actually suspects.'

He was obviously trying to draw Pye out, intensely curious as to his relations with her, and as Stefan went on urging Pye to persuade Penelope to write a biography, saying it would be the start of a new series of art books, Bergdorf's eyes were steady on Pye's face. At that moment a woman thinning into eagle alertness pounced. She waved a long amber cigarette-holder so close to Bergdorf's face that he winced and instinctively stepped back.

'You'll notice that my portrait isn't here, Julie,' she said, her hard blue eyes staring straight into his, for she was as tall. 'Why not? I'm the only other woman Jamie ever painted.'

'Darling Moira!' Bergdorf's voice at once switched in key to an arch wheedling. 'We simply couldn't locate it. Ask Spencer Manley. I think it's somewhere in America. Such a pity. Didn't you come just before his abstract period?'

Stefan turned and winked at Pye and they edged away.

'They're worse than authors, aren't they?' he said. 'That's Moira Ericsson. Bonny knows her. Dabbles a bit in painting herself, writes terribly soulful poetry, a sort of female Lawrence.' As they moved off in search of Spencer they heard her say in her intense, intimate voice, 'But Julie, she fed on him. No life of her own at all.'

Pye stopped, would have turned back, but Stefan had his

257

hand on his elbow and steered him across to Spencer, who was pinioned in a corner showing signs of distress and being talked at by a small dark girl who, by her long, flat eyes, could have been either Jewish or Indian. Her cold Kensington voice had evidently been punishing him for some time. As they came up a flicker of relief enlivened him, and with a murmured excuse he left her and joined them.

'God protect me from the enthusiastic amateur whose mummy lets her study art,' he said. 'Let's go and eat somewhere. Where's Bonny?'

Bonny was at last winkled away from a circle of hypnotized young men whose various incarnations she was detailing, and they left with amused backward glances at Julius Bergdorf, now looking desperately round for succour, lost in cigarette smoke blown from Moira Ericsson's mobile lips.

Once outside, Bonny shook herself like a sleek dog from a river and breathed deeply.

'Let's go to Mario's,' she said. 'I thought I should suffocate in there. But let's walk and be absolutely silent. I've talked so much I feel exhausted.'

They went along in silence, glad of the respite, Bonny and Stefan going ahead, Spencer quietly treading beside Pye, who once or twice glanced at him as if to speak, then changed his mind. It was not until they had settled into a corner table at Mario's and ordered their meal that Bonny looked at each of them in turn.

'Well?' she asked.

Stefan asked. 'Bonny, you're impossible. What were you telling those wretched young men, anyway? They were goggling. Apart from looking marvellous, as you do, of course.' He was a little jealous, but enjoyably so, like a connoisseur whose prize piece has been admired, handled with respect and replaced on its accustomed shelf.

She widened her eyes at him. 'I was merely talking about the Persians. One of those young men was too Persian in his manner for it to be a coincidence, and he told me he often dreamed about Persia .  . but never mind. Did you see that dreadful Ericsson woman, claws out, feathers flailing, livid because her portrait wasn't there? She's convinced that Jamie's wife had destroyed it out of spite. Actually, of course, Jamie Hinton destroyed it himself.'

'How do you know?' asked Pye.

'An American friend of mine wanted to buy it some years ago. I was staying with him and he adored women with long necks – the predatory type, you know; he was longing to be destroyed, poor man. He saw this portrait, or rather a photograph of it Moira had used as a frontispiece to one of her dreadful books. He telephoned Jamie Hinton, and was told it no longer existed. Apparently Jamie said he wished he'd never painted it. He said he thought Moira was a destructive woman and the portrait made him uneasy. He was very cross at its being photographed.'

'You don't think he had a conscience about it?' asked Spencer.

'No, why should he? I didn't ever meet him, but I'm sure – from just looking at his pictures, quite apart from knowing Penelope slightly – that he was wrapped up in his wife to an unusual degree. Without her I doubt whether he would have painted as well.'

Pye looked at her with warmth and relief.

'I wonder why he painted her at all,' he murmured. Bonny looked at him oddly.

'She's a difficult woman to refuse. Also, if you think a bit, isn't a marriage like the Hintons' a constant temptation to certain types of people? Moira dedicated one of her books of poems to him. Oh, no name, just a cryptic line or two about painting and poetry being twin roses on a single branch. Sickening.'

'Perhaps,' said Stefan, with a suppressed grin, 'this Ericsson woman would write his biography if Penelope refuses.'

'If you ever suggest such a thing,' said Pye quietly, 'I shall withdraw every penny I've put into the Press.'

They stopped eating at his words, and looked at him in astonishment. Never before had Pye appeared to them other than good-naturedly shrewd. All the same, none of them doubted this ultimatum, and Stefan went pale with anger at a show of power that could dwarf him and his ambitions. Then Spencer said unexpectedly, 'I think Pye's right, although it sounds a bit rough. There are some things one can't do, Stefan.'

'On the contrary, in publishing that's going to pay and grow, one must be prepared to do anything. That is, until we're established.'

'This is one thing you won't do, though, darling,' said Bonny decidedly. 'It isn't worth it, anyway. Moira Ericsson isn't a big enough name to carry the book, and emphasis should be on a man's work and not on what would be misconceived as his diversions.' She patted his hand. 'Anyway, there's nothing to suggest a mystery, so let's take it that there isn't one.' She turned to Pye. 'Do you think there's a chance that Penelope might write it – or would it be too painful?'

Pye's face had relaxed. He did not regret his words, but knew that they stemmed from a creeping hatred and distrust of the people they had just left rather than from a wish to attack Stefan. But Penelope should never be hurt, never be dragged back into the suffering from which she was only just now emerging, if he could help it. No publishing empire should be built on her pain.

'The fact that Hinton destroyed the picture himself is evidence enough that he thought nothing of it,' he said now, briskly. 'Obviously if Penelope doesn't feel able to write about their life together, one of their mutual friends can do a broad outline. But of course she would have to vet it. If you like, I'll ask her when she comes back.'

'Won't she be back at the end of the week?' asked Bonny, covering up Stefan's long, offended silence, and looking towards Spencer to help her out. Spencer at once explained about Nika, and told them that Penelope was staying on in Athens to look after her.

'Good heavens!' explained Bonny. 'Poor child! Aren't you going out to her? She must be feeling awful in that strange place, however kind the people are. It's such a depressing illness.'

Stefan raised his eyes and nodded. 'Take a week off and go, Spencer,' he said. 'I can manage. You could correct some proofs on the plane if you want to. And there's a firm in Athens I wanted to contact. You could see them at the same time, and we could call it expenses.'

Spencer looked at Pye, who had completely recovered his good humour, and who now smilingly shrugged.

'You could also send Penelope back,' he said. 'Tell her I'll meet the plane.'

Spencer glanced round at them all, pleasurably trapped. Now that the suggestion had come up again, spontaneously, he had to admit that it had its possibilities. The fare had made it seem impossible, but if it could be worked on expenses, why not? He thought of the empty flat, the cold London streets. Then he began to think about Nika, not her self-sufficiency which had checked him so often, but her bewildered face, alone, perhaps afraid; the long red hair containing a soft warmth he altogether lacked, perhaps needed. Wasn't it the negative and the positive that created a magnetic field, that pulsing field of energy he had thought they could never cross, the necessary tension of opposites that created the emotion people called love as opposed to companionship, friendship?

He had once thought that the act of marriage was a kind of alchemy that would change him and give him everlasting joy and fulfilment, but marriage was the start of a new set of conditions, needing special efforts of a kind he had found almost impossible to make. Instead, his marriage had been two people living together within the social barrier, not beyond it. A locked battle or a deadly drift to mutual boredom. The mystique had got lost somewhere in between the two.

'Go on,' urged Bonny. 'It's your turn to be strong, Spencer. She needs you, but she won't ask you to go to her. When did you last have a holiday together?'

'About five years ago. It rained.' Unwilling to give in, he looked at Pye ironically.

'Why don't you go, Pye? It may be your moment of truth.'

Pye shook his head. For a moment his face had a sculptured quality, hard and quiet. 'My moment of truth will be when I meet Penelope off the plane. This is your challenge, Spencer. There are times when an unspoken need must be met. Hang the expense. Go to her. You can't go through life like a closed fist. Lay your hand open now. That's your challenge, as I see it.'


In Athens the hot April sunshine made the city white and sparkling. Life hummed. Penelope walked through the streets as if she had been here all her life; strangely, she did not feel alone, or even a foreigner, for she had somewhere to go and something to do. She had to find the King George Hotel and book a double room for Spencer for a week, buy presents for the Stephanides, book her own ticket at the Hellenikon and cable Pye as to her time of arrival in London. She had decided to fly back in two days' time; by then Dr Stephanides had told her that Nika would be able to get up and go about slowly. They had still not been able to go to Delphi, she realized, as a bus passed her, bound for the Delphi road. But Delphi had existed for a thousand years or more, and there would be time enough to come back. One could not greedily rifle a treasure-chest.

Her errands finished, she went to drink coffee at a small table in a café near the King George Hotel, and experienced once more the surprise and pleasure Spencer's cable had given her; saw once more the look on Nika's face: a fleeting look of hope and anxiety mixed. For physically Nika was well enough, all things considered; it was her mental state that worried Penelope. She had seemed withdrawn and resigned, cried easily. When Mrs Stephanides had said comfortingly, thinking it was the loss of the child, 'You will have more children, you are young,' she had given her a strange smile, shaking her head. Then she had said, once, to Penelope, as she moved about her room, tidying it, 'It proves that nothing can be created out of

262

chaos.' But when Penelope had turned to reply, Nika had rolled her head into the pillow and pretended to be asleep.

Someone came to her table and she looked up to see Dr Stephanides looking down at her.

'May I?' he said, indicating the other chair.

She nodded, wondering what had brought him into the middle of Athens at this time of day. He ordered two more coffees and they sat, drinking and watching the crowds.

'I'm on my way home from the hospital,' he said. 'Have you finished your various errands? If so, I can drive you back.'

'Yes, I've booked a room for Nika's husband, and a ticket for myself. Do you know, Dr Stephanides, it will be like leaving a place I feel – somehow – intimate with? You've both been so kind, I don't know how –'

He raised a hand. 'Please. It has been a privilege to know you. You will come back, I'm sure, and when you do, well, you know you have friends in Athens.' He was silent, turning the cup in his small, capable doctor's hands. 'You look very much better, Mrs Hinton, as if somehow Greece had solved something for you. Or perhaps that is too easy. Let us say, as if you have seen another facet of the truth, for the truth we have to live with – to me, anyway – is like a cut diamond, the light catches it from so many angles.'

'You remind me of someone I know when you speak like that,' said Penelope.

He raised his eyebrows courteously, but said nothing. After a while he asked whether she had heard any news of the exhibition. Had she bought any English newspapers?

'No, I haven't, not yet. But I had a cable from the director of the little art gallery. He seemed to think the whole thing was a success; quite a few of my husband's pictures have been sold. One is going to the Tate. I only heard this morning.'

'I'm glad. Your husband deserves to be recognized.' He looked absently at the passing people and said quietly, 'Now perhaps you will be able to live for yourself.'

She shrugged and smiled quietly, 'For who else, then?'

'Ah, that is your affair. But to be alive is to give, for other people come into one's life constantly. You have given freely to your young friend Nika, who is not too happy, I think. But she will mend, and your responsibility there is over now her husband is coming. I shall be most curious to meet him. Mrs Hinton, I must say something to you before you go.'

She looked at him questioningly, then said, 'You told me the other evening something I shall not forget, Dr Stephanides. You spoke of acceptance.'

'Well, now I shall speak of something else. You have taken a great step forward, but you are in danger of leaving your heart behind.'

She frowned, raised her eyebrows.

'You know what I mean. You have laid your heart like a wreath on a mound of earth, and I think you should realize it is no tribute to the living to make so sure that they are dead.'

'The living?' She thought of Pye at once.

'I mean your husband. What do we know of death? I am a docto, yet I have never seen a surgeon cut out the soul and isolate it. Our business is with the living body; dead, we are done with it. Then it is a matter for the priests; a little later, the worms. And yet who knows whether the greater mystery does not come after all our ministrations? After all, the dead may be like the winter earth, which is cold and bare enough, and yet the spring gives it the lie. You know the many stories and myths of Greece? About the underworld, for instance – Persephone spending six months below and six above? She was not condemned to the underworld for ever, so why should you be? Also, why should your husband be? We know nothing of life after death, Mrs Hinton, and the scientists have proved nothing either way. The Egyptians believed that the soul escaped at death in the form of a small cloud, vanishing into a new life. Here in Greece our heroes are not dead, they are all about us. Now I know this is all very unscientific, and, you may think, in bad taste, and that as a doctor I've no right to what you may regard as fancies, but you can accept it or reject it. I accept. And this acceptance cuts free a dead man's weight.

The living must learn to let go, free the dead wherever they are; the living have their life to attend to, and it is a game that must be played to the end.'

Penelope seemed to be sunk into a long silence, as if she were a tree with the wind merely blowing through her branches. Then she raised her head and said, 'The Spanish have a heartless proverb: "The dead to their graves and the living to their dinner." I suppose it's practical enough.'

The doctor got up, his hands laid flat on the table-top. 'I quarrel with the finality of the word "graves". But the principle is sensible enough. Come along, we'll be late for lunch.' He regarded her quizzically. 'I'm sorry. But there's something about you that makes me want to preach.'

As they got into his car Penelope said, 'You always seem to haul things to the surface of my mind – things I've deliberately stuffed a long way down. You make the oddest things float up, and they look quite different in the light of day.'

'All I would ask of you,' he said, as he manœuvred the little car through the traffic of the square, 'is to be a little happy, a little less earnest, loosen the rein with which you ride your conscience. And that is positively all.'

The noise lessened behind them as they drove through the narrowing streets of the city, up the hillside where the house lay honey-coloured under the sun, the mountains sharp in the distance. Somewhere out there lay Delphi, to which some day she would come.

'Oh dear,' she said. 'Everyone is so wise. Everyone knows the answers, except me. All I can say is that I'll try.'

The doctor stopped the car, and the engine throbbed into silence.

'That's the wisest word I know,' he said. 'Good. And I think we're just in time for lunch.'

## Also available in ABACUS paperback:

### FICTION

| | | |
|---|---|---|
| FOREIGN EXCHANGE | Ed. Julian Evans | £3.50 ☐ |
| THE HOUSE ON THE EMBANKMENT | Yuri Trifonov | £2.50 ☐ |
| BILGEWATER | Jane Gardam | £2.50 ☐ |
| THE SEIZURE OF POWER | Czeslaw Milosz | £2.75 ☐ |
| THE ISSA VALLEY | Czeslaw Milosz | £3.25 ☐ |
| IN COLD BLOOD | Truman Capote | £2.95 ☐ |
| THE WAPSHOT SCANDAL | John Cheever | £2.50 ☐ |
| THE LAST TESTAMENT OF OSCAR WILDE | Peter Ackroyd | £2.50 ☐ |

### NON-FICTION

| | | |
|---|---|---|
| BEYOND THE CHAINS OF ILLUSION | Erich Fromm | £2.50 ☐ |
| IRISH JOURNAL | Heinrich Boll | £1.95 ☐ |
| THE AGE OF CAPITAL | E. J. Hobsbawn | £3.95 ☐ |
| THE AGE OF REVOLUTION | E. J. Hobsbawn | £3.95 ☐ |
| THE PRIMAL SCREAM | Arthur Janov | £3.95 ☐ |
| BLACK AND WHITE | Shiva Naipaul | £2.95 ☐ |
| MRS. HARRIS | Diana Trilling | £2.95 ☐ |

All Abacus books are available at your local bookshop or newsagent, or can be ordered direct from the publisher. Just tick the titles you want and fill in the form below.

Name _____

Address _____

Write to Abacus Books, Cash Sales Department, P.O. Box 11, Falmouth, Cornwall TR10 9EN

Please enclose cheque or postal order to the value of the cover price plus:

UK: 55p for the first book plus 22p for the second book and 14p for each additional book ordered to a maximum charge of £1.75.

OVERSEAS: £1.00 for the first book plus 25p per copy for each additional book.

BFPO & EIRE: 55p for the first book, 22p for the second book plus 14p per copy for the next 7 books, thereafter 8p per book.

Abacus Books reserve the right to show new retail prices on covers which may differ from those previously advertised in the text or elsewhere, and to increase postal rates in accordance with the PO.